I0717187

# BROKEN

USA TODAY BESTSELLING AUTHOR

# J.L. WEIL

# ALSO BY J. L. WEIL

## ELITE OF ELMWOOD ACADEMY
(New Adult Dark High School Romance)
*Turmoil*
*Disorder*
*Revenge*
*Rival*
*Unchained*
*Broken*

## DIVISA HUNTRESS
(New Adult Paranormal Romance)
*Crown of Darkness*
*Inferno of Darkness*
*Eternity of Darkness*

## DRAGON DESCENDANTS SERIES
(Upper Teen Reverse Harem Fantasy)
*Stealing Tranquility*
*Absorbing Poison*

Taming Fire<br>
Thawing Frost

## THE DIVISA SERIES

(Full series completed – Teen Paranormal Romance)<br>
Losing Emma: A Divisa novella<br>
Saving Angel<br>
Hunting Angel<br>
Breaking Emma: A Divisa novella<br>
Chasing Angel<br>
Loving Angel<br>
Redeeming Angel

## LUMINESCENCE TRILOGY

(Full series completed – Teen Paranormal Romance)<br>
Luminescence<br>
Amethyst Tears<br>
Moondust<br>
Darkmist – A Luminescence novella

## RAVEN SERIES

(Full series completed – Teen Paranormal Romance)<br>
White Raven<br>
Black Crow<br>
Soul Symmetry

## BEAUTY NEVER DIES CHRONICLES

(Teen Dystopian Romance)<br>
Slumber<br>
Entangled<br>
Forsaken

## NINE TAILS SERIES

(Teen Paranormal Romance)

*First Shift*
*Storm Shift*
*Flame Shift*
*Time Shift*
*Void Shift*
*Spirit Shift*
*Tide Shift*
*Wind Shift*
*Celestial Shift*

## HAVENWOOD FALLS HIGH
(Teen Paranormal Romance)
*Falling Deep*
*Ascending Darkness*

## SINGLE NOVELS
*Starbound*
(Teen Paranormal Romance)
*Casting Dreams*
(New Adult Paranormal Romance)
*Ancient Tides*
(New Adult Paranormal Romance)

For an updated list of my books, please visit my website:
www.jlweil.com

Join my VIP email list and I'll personally send you an email reminder as soon as my next book is out! Click here to sign up: www.jlweil.com

## HOMECOMING GAME FRESHMAN YEAR

My brother and his friends thought they were gods on and off the football field. Maybe it was because I'd known them my whole life that I didn't share the same opinion as nearly everyone else at Elmwood Academy. Or maybe they really were worthy of being put on a pedestal, and I just didn't want to see them as who they truly were.

To me, Brock Taylor, Fynn Dupree, Micah Bradford, and my brother, Grayson Edwards were massive pains in my ass. Having the four of them constantly around meant I was always under careful watch.

Guys never approached me for fear of having the Elite's cold stare on them. Girls were only my friend so they could hang out with the Elite. No one cared about me. Only what they could gain from me.

I wanted high school to be different, but I wasn't off to a good start. Despite making the cheerleading team, the only reason the four of them were okay with me wearing spanks and a short skirt that showed my ass was so they could continue to monitor me seeing as we were on the same field.

Fucking ridiculous.

Tonight, I didn't give a shit what my brother and his friends said. Mads and I were letting loose. We were going to get shitfaced, dance with whomever we wanted, and have the best homecoming night ever.

They weren't going to ruin our fun or tell us no.

Maddy Clarke, aka Mads, was my best friend. She was also my cousin. Our group was close, and we didn't easily let outsiders in, mostly because we had four overbearing, growling football jocks looming around us at all times.

It made meeting new people, particularly guys, impossible.

From the football field sidelines, I glanced up at the crowd, searching for Mads. She was neither a fan of football nor cheerleading, but my cousin never missed a game. When my eyes met her bored gray ones, I smiled and flipped her off.

The frown gracing her lips flicked up into a twisted smirk she tried to cover up and failed.

I laughed, getting in position for our next cheer.

It was the bottom of the fourth quarter, approaching the two-minute marker. Our rival, the Renegades, missed a pass on their third down and were getting ready to punt the ball back to us. The players hustled to switch positions, our special teams getting into place and the perfect time to hype up the crowd.

My feet touched the ground after coming out of a single-partner flyer, Brady's hands lingering on my waist when I heard "Nice ass, Edwards." Carter Patterson grinned at me, his helmet dangling from his fingers as he jogged onto the field. "It's almost like you aren't wearing anything," he hollered.

The last word barely left Carter's smug mouth, and he hit the ground, my brother standing over him. "What the fuck did you say to my sister?" Grayson growled. Our boys were still working on the whole teamwork aspect of football. Like you weren't supposed to tackle your guys.

The whistle blew from the sidelines, and a white flag fell onto the green. Carter shoved off the grass, jumping to his feet. "It was a joke, man. You know what a joke is?"

Carter was an idiot. He might be the Elite's teammate, but he also knew saying anything to me, hell just looking at me, would get him knocked on his ass and off the field. He was lucky my brother hadn't knocked him out.

Grayson got into his face, my brother's helmet hitting Carter's forehead. "Only when the joke doesn't involve my sister's name. Got it?"

This whole thing happened only a few feet in front of me and close enough to catch what they were saying. Carter gritted his teeth, the playfulness gone from his features. "Jesus, Gray. We're on the same team."

Carter wasn't a bad-looking guy. He was cute with his sandy hair, blue eyes, and body built like a running back, fitting since that was his position, but despite his cuteness, he didn't hold a fucking flame to Fynn Dupree. At least not in my eyes.

I didn't need to see behind the helmet to know my brother sported a nasty scowl. "That doesn't mean shit to me."

"You're supposed to be hitting the other guys, not ours, Edwards," Carter fired back.

"Get your asses off the field, or you're both on the bench for the rest of the game!" Coach yelled at them from the sidelines, two seconds away from losing his shit.

Heat seeped into my cheeks, and I prayed Grayson wouldn't further embarrass me.

Grayson stared Carter down for a long second before walking off, and I exhaled. He really needed to chill on the overprotective brother act.

I glanced at the scoreboard as the game continued. We were

trailing by three points. All night, we'd gone back and forth with the Renegades, play after play, constantly trading places for the lead.

The two-minute whistle blew.

We needed a field goal to tie the game, which would send us into overtime. Not ideal. Or a touchdown for the fucking win. I was betting our boys would secure the W.

Inch by inch, our team drove the ball down the field. Our quarterback, Brock Taylor, put the ball into number twenty-two's chest, and Carter's fingers came up, securing it as he darted to the left, curving down the outside of the field. He made it seven yards before being tackled by the opposing team.

Chewing on the inside of my cheek, I clapped my pom-poms together, doing my best to stay cheerful. It was my fucking job after all.

The clock continued to wind down with under thirty seconds to go. Brock called out his next play without a huddle, rushing the guys into position. He yelled the countdown, catching the snap flawlessly as he backed up a few steps. Brock's sharp eyes quickly read the field, looking for his man, dodging not one but two tackles as he waited for a receiver to get open.

Finally, Brock's arm pulled back, and the ball snapped out of his fingers, spiraling down the field. As I held my breath, my eyes followed the ball straight into Micah's ready hands. He caught the ball at the corner of the endzone, securing it to his chest as he dragged his feet behind him, making sure he stayed inbounds. The second the referee's hands flew up, giving the touchdown signal, I jumped up and down, shaking my blue and black pom-poms in the air and screaming along with the deafening crowd.

Elmwood Academy just secured another victory under its belt.

No one was surprised, not with the addition of the Elite to the team this year.

And now we could all relax. Let loose.

The homecoming dance was Saturday night, but that didn't mean we weren't celebrating our victory. As customary, one of the football players threw a party. Tonight, it was my brother, and everyone was hyped. Grayson's bashes were legendary.

Our parents were out of town conveniently. They normally never missed an opportunity to see Grayson play. They were supportive like that. One of them was always in attendance, so it was weird they weren't here tonight, but all the better since I planned to get drunk.

Grayson made me wait outside the locker room with Mads after the game. Since our older brother, Sawyer, passed away, Grayson took his brotherly duties a bit too far. We all dealt with grief in our own way. Grayson became more protective, and I pretended everything was fine. I could fake happiness like I was born to be a Broadway star, but I wasn't sure I was fooling anyone except myself.

He came out freshly showered, his dark hair damp, and not smelling like a mixture of sweat and earth. He smelled good but not as nice as Fynn Dupree beside him.

Did I have a crush on Fynn since the moment I realized boys weren't icky?

Yes.

But Fynn was clueless, or if he did know, he did a damn spectacular job pretending ignorance. Boys were so brainless when it came to girls, except my brother and his friends seemed to know what they were doing, considering they were always surrounded by a sea of sluts.

One thing for certain, I was done waiting for Fynn to get a clue and see me as someone other than his best friend's sister. Tonight, Fynn would really see.

For months, I'd been talking myself into getting Fynn's attention and making my feelings known, but I never seemed to have the gumption to do or say anything. If losing Sawyer taught me anything, it was time was too short to prolong the things you wanted in life. I didn't care how drunk I had to get. Tonight, I would make my move.

First, a bit of liquid courage.

Our house was packed with bodies, and I wasn't even sure if half of them went to the Academy. Elmwood Public High School was known to crash our get-togethers. They came for the free booze, party favors, and the fights.

Micah jumped up onto our table, a Solo cup in his hand. "I better not see a single person without a drink tonight. If you don't have a cup in your hand, why the fuck are you even here?"

The crowd went wild, a sea of red plastic cups surging into the air, liquid spilling over the brim on half of them.

"He's such a dumbass," Mads said, handing me a shot. What she really meant was why the fuck does she find Micah so hot? That was a question I never had an answer to. Micah was adorable in a flirty, boyish way, but he wasn't my type. My cousin, on the other hand, had a serious crush on the Elite playboy.

I took the tiny glass filled with an amber liquid and clinked the rim against hers before tossing it back. The liquor went down smooth, a warm burn coating my throat and the taste of cinnamon lingering on my tongue.

Micah came up behind Mads and draped an arm around her. "You better pour us a shot. There's no way we're not toasting to me being a fucking badass on and off the field."

Brock, Fynn, and Grayson moved in, flanking my cousin and me. Mads rolled her eyes but lined up six shot glasses on the counter, tipping the liquor bottle over each one. "Micah's not giving the toast this time."

The guys snickered. Hell, even Micah chuckled. "Whatever, fuckers. Just raise your glasses. We're going to have a blast this year."

I couldn't argue with that.

Brock's lips curled in a wry smirk. "We're going to run this school."

"Hear, hear," my brother cheered, flashing a rare grin.

The six of us clicked our glasses together and knocked back our shots. I wiped a drop of liquor from the corner of my lip, my eyes connecting with Fynn's. Mads noticed and bumped my shoulder lightly with hers. "Careful, Kenna."

"Bitch," I playfully muttered under my breath.

Mads knew I planned to make it very clear how I felt about Fynn. Now I just needed the courage. If I kept waiting for Fynn to cross the line, I had a feeling I'd be pining after my brother's best friend for life and missing out on all the really good shit love had to offer.

Like sex.

Mads and I were down one drink each before she took my hand. "Let's dance, bitch!" she shrieked, pulling me toward the makeshift dance area in our family room. Some of the football players had moved the furniture out of the way, creating more open space for people to move, not that furniture stopped anyone. If they weren't dancing around tables, they were freaking grooving on top of them.

We wedged ourselves into the center of the room under the chandelier, its lights shining down on us. Mads interlaced our fingers as we began to dance, bringing them over our heads. "We're going to have the best time tomorrow."

Homecoming. Our first one. We were going as a group with the guys, neither of us with official dates. My brother nixed that shit immediately. He could be so annoying. "Fuck yes, we are," I agreed, thinking about the dress I spent hours shopping for with the thought of Fynn seeing me in it. That's what I was really looking forward to.

"Ladies." Micah grinned, sliding up to us with two drinks in hand. "You were looking a little thirsty."

I rolled my eyes but took the drink. I was parched as fuck and slammed down half the contents without breathing.

"And you're looking like a douchebag," Mads said, scrunching her nose. This was her way of flirting with the playboy.

Micah laughed, enjoying the game Mads and he continually played. "Cute, Mads. Payback is you must dance with me." Before she could squirm away, Micah snaked his arm around her waist, moving in and stealing my girl, but I didn't mind.

Despite herself, Mads giggled, but she gave up fighting after a moment, swaying her hips and rotating her body.

Dancing alone never bothered me. I enjoyed dancing with or without a partner.

But I wasn't alone for long.

Tossing back the rest of my drink, I fell into the music, spinning around, and finding Fynn watching me. Our eyes locked, and I realized this was my opportunity. I couldn't let it pass. Without missing a beat of the song, I swayed my way to where he stood at the edge of the clustered dancers.

"Look at us, we're nearly dancing."

Fynn had all the moves on the football field, but get the guy on the dance floor, and he froze.

He lifted a brow.

"Try moving your hips," I teased, shifting intentionally closer to him.

"You want to dance, Kenna?" His lips tilted into a frown, but it was the intensity in his eyes that made my heart go erratic.

Something about Fynn's green eyes flustered and turned me on at the same time. I couldn't seem to control my body when he looked at me like he was now. My fingers glided up his chest, slowly running over his shoulders. Fynn's eyes darkened, and I bit the inside of my cheek to keep from smirking.

With the alcohol coursing through my system, I was feeling bolder and hella sexy. He didn't step away or remove my fingers when they wound to the back of his corded neck, toying with his dark curls. I took that as encouragement.

My hips bumped side to side in a slow rhythm as I moved in, brushing our bodies together. I felt him, felt *it*, his arousal.

*Holy shit. He's hard.*

A rush of warmth stole over my skin. I was already hot from dancing and drinking, but this was a different form of heat. This started low and spread.

Fynn's eyes flashed to mine, his fingers grabbing my hips but neither pushing me away nor pulling me nearer. He just kept me suspended. "What are you doing?" he growled, the shots of fireball heavy on his breath.

I didn't bat an eye and forced my gaze to stay on his instead of shying away like I wanted to. "What do you think I'm doing?" I intended my response to sound coy and sexy. It came out as neither, making me wish I had another drink.

"Stirring up trouble," he replied, his breath warm on my lips. He was so close, staring at me with eyes hot enough to melt me from the inside.

"Would that be such a bad thing?" I lifted on my tiptoes. Even with my height of five-seven, I still had to crane my neck up to look at him. One of the tallest boys in our school, Fynn could have been a stellar basketball player if he had any interest.

His head shifted to the right a fraction, my lips grazing his incredible cheekbone instead of his lips. "Kenna, don't." The fingers holding my hips pressed a bit firmer into my flesh, confusing me.

Heat flared on my cheeks and the back of my neck. Did he have any idea how much fucking courage it took me to make a move? His denial stung. Embarrassment flooded my system, and with it came anger. "Why not? Are you going to stand here and tell me you don't want me?" I dared. I'd damn well felt the full proof of his desire, but I also knew dicks got hard practically over anything. If a guy's pants rubbed the right way. If a girl bent over in a pair of tight jeans. When they woke up first thing in the morning. Basically, high-school boys walked around with a bulge in their pants ninety-nine percent of the time.

His expression hardened. "You know why."

My fingers toying with the curls at the nape of his neck halted, and my eyes narrowed, fighting back the tears that suddenly wanted to fall. If he was so hellbent on us only being friends, why was he still holding me? I couldn't decide if he was trying to convince me or himself. "I thought you were different."

Fynn's fingers went to my wrists and unwound my arms from around his neck. "It doesn't change that you're Grayson's sister. We don't mess around with family."

The Elite and their stupid rules. "Your rules are fucking stupid," I retorted with sarcasm, echoing my thoughts and pretending my voice hadn't hitched.

"Kenna." The way my name left his lips twisted something inside me, and I hated how much I wanted him to kiss me, to say screw the rules, to say I was more important. The resigned look in his eyes told me everything I didn't want to see. Fynn wouldn't give me what I wanted. Not tonight.

Not ever.

Tears pricked at the back of my eyes. I had to leave. I had to get away from him. I needed another damn drink and a bathroom to cry in.

Ripping my wrists out from under his grasp, I spun around, leaving Fynn where I'd found him. I broke through the crowd, my misty eyes lifting and connecting with my brother's glowering ones. Grayson scowled at me as I passed by, but I only shook my head, letting him know I didn't want to fucking talk.

In the kitchen, I reached for the first drink I saw, throwing back the concoction like it was grape Kool-Aid. Hell, there probably were traces of it, but the mixture was mostly booze. Vodka, I thought. Not that it mattered. As long as it did its job of dulling the ache and making me forget.

I was so over Fynn's good-guy best-friend bullshit. He made me feel foolish, and I hated that more than the embarrassment. Smudging the tears clouding my vision, I turned and leaned against the counter.

Fine.

Fynn didn't want me.

I'd find someone who did.

My eyes swept the room and collided with a pair of twinkling blue eyes. Not with humor or fun. No, his eyes brimmed with trouble, and in my current state of pissed-off rejection stinging through me, I wanted trouble.

I wanted the ache inside my chest to vanish.

And the liquor wasn't helping. Not yet.

Holding Carter's gaze, I made my way to him, weaving through the crowd of bodies swaying, grinding, and moving to the music. "Get me a drink?" I asked when I reached him. I held my hands out in front of me, drawing his gaze downward. His eyes lingered on my chest just like I planned. "My hands are empty," I said.

"A crime," Carter replied, the side of his lip lifting. His eyes remained on my pushed-up boobs for another moment before rising. "You know the rules. No one can go without a drink."

"Exactly why I need your help." I pouted.

He glanced over my head for a few seconds, chewing on the corner of his lip as if to decide if it was a good idea—if *I* was a good idea. He must have decided he didn't care because he grinned at me. "Purple or green?"

I smiled in return. Truthfully, it didn't matter to me what color or flavor the drink was as long as he kept my cup topped off, which he did.

Considering I was already well past tipsy, it didn't take long for me to slide into drunk. I lost track of the drinks, but that wasn't all I lost track of. Hours of the party went by, or at least I thought they did. A huge chunk of the night was nothing but a gaping hole in my memory. I'd never been blackout drunk before. I'd also never been rejected either. Guess this night was full of firsts.

Leave it to my brother to throw a memorable party. It just wasn't memorable in the way I dreamed. What was supposed to be the best night of my life turned into the fucking worst.

"Which one is your room?" Carter whispered into my ear as I stumbled up the stairs beside him, one of the last things I remembered. After that, it was only snippets of memories, but they felt like I was watching a movie inside my head rather than living the moments. A nightmare might be more of an accurate description.

Rough hands. Hard kisses. Sharp pain. The mattress bounced. The room spun. The endless hell continued.

I was trapped inside my head—in my body. Unable to get out. Unable to scream. Unable to move.

And yet, I wasn't sure any of it was real.

My eyes closed and didn't open again until late morning.

Groggy, I tried to peel open my eyes. My head felt wrong. It was more than a headache. A heaviness weighed me down as if I couldn't detach my head from the pillow. When I did manage to open my eyes and keep them open, I was relieved to see I was in my bed except...I was naked.

And I was alone.

A whoosh of relief tore through me.

I rolled over on the bed, my body fucking sore in places it shouldn't be. One place particularly. I winced at the painful flare of tenderness between my legs. Horror clenched my heart, squeezing it. My eyes landed on something discarded on my floor, not far from the dress I'd been wearing last night. A small square foil wrapper—a condom wrapper.

And it was opened.

## 1

## KENNA

### PRESENT DAY

**M**y eyes flew open. *I can't breathe. Holy shit. I can't breathe.* My heart pulsed erratically in my chest, the sound of it thundering in my ears. I wasn't a stranger to panic attacks, and I found ways of managing them over the years, but fuck me if they didn't still suck. Especially the ones that woke me out of a dead sleep.

Every time, it was like my heart forgot how to pump correctly and started skipping beats. My lungs struggled to take in air and release it. I clenched my fingers and closed my eyes to focus on my breathing. Thousands and thousands of dollars invested in therapy sessions taught me to control my breath. So, I counted the inhales and exhales, thinking only about the air moving in and out of my lips.

One. Two. Three. Four. Five.

Over and over again until my heart leveled out.

"Fuck." I stared at the ceiling of my dorm room. My fingers shoved strands of dark hair out of my face.

The dreams rarely happened anymore, but when they did, they took me right back to the worst night of my existence. The only thing that made the dreams bearable was the *other* memory I had of Carter.

When the nightmares sprung on me, I remembered the night that chased the cold in my veins, filling them with the fire of revenge.

There were moments in our lives that shaped us—defined who we were. I refused to let those foggy moments with Carter that formed in my dreams determine who I was and who I would be.

He'd already taken so much from me, and it had taken years for me to get to a point where dating was something I wanted. How fucking weird was it that partying was okay, and the taste of alcohol no longer sent me into a ball in the corner? Yet being one-on-one with the opposite sex caused my skin to break out in hives. The red, splotchy rash never happened when I was the Elite. Go figure.

They always did make me feel safe.

I'd gotten my justice, and now the asshole was rotting in jail for the time being.

Some people would think I'd find peace now and would be able to move on with my life.

They were wrong.

I was still a million shades of fucked up. The difference between the months after it happened and now was I embraced the shadowy parts of my soul. I didn't try to banish the darkness lingering within me. It was a part of me just like the coffee color of my eyes or the beauty mark high on my cheek. I accepted the flaws, but that didn't mean I still didn't battle with demons.

It had been a long time since I thought about *that* night. What no one knew was the reason why I flirted with Carter. No one but Fynn, that was.

It had been Fynn's attention I wanted. And Fynn who turned me down.

And still to this day, I hadn't told anyone how I tried to kiss him or how he pushed me away. Neither had he, for if Fynn mentioned it to Brock, Micah, or Grayson, for that matter, I would have heard about it.

Not that it mattered because all anyone talked about the days after were the pictures of me Carter took. I never made it to the homecoming dance Saturday, but come Monday, Carter made sure I was the talk of the school.

*Fuck Carter Patterson.*

That bastard had taken so much of my life from me in a single night. I stopped letting my fear and anxiety control me. The anger lingered. It helped he was behind bars, but the day would come when he would be set free, and I would have to deal with the fact he was out in the world.

After the attack, Brock made the entire school believe we were an item. The problem with fake dating, especially at a young age or when I was so damn lost and vulnerable, was lines got blurry. They never did for Brock. Those smudges in the definition of our relationship at school versus at home were made by me. Trying to use Brock to make me forget how utterly messed up I felt inside hadn't been fair, yet still, I clung to him then, and the hope he'd love me as more than a sister.

He never did.

But he did fall in love with my actual sister.

A little fucked up considering she and I were part of a set. Triplets. I asked myself the same questions a million times. What was it about Josie he fell in love with? What was it he saw in her but didn't see in me? Why didn't anyone love me?

Josie and I were both damaged, just in different ways.

It was no surprise Brock fell hard for a girl whose life was the opposite of neat and tidy. He would be attracted to complicated and messy. That was who he was.

Full disclosure, I wanted Brock to be Fynn. I'd been substituting my feelings back then. I never blamed anyone for what happened the night with Carter. No one but myself.

The boys didn't see it that way.

Brock and I were only ever friends. Every moment between us was staged and fake as the tits of half the girls at Elmwood Academy.

It wasn't fake when I got annoyed at all the girls who would hang around Brock. It was annoying, but it was equally as irritating when they did the same thing to my brother, Micah, and Fynn.

I'd been jealous of the attention Brock gave Josie because I was no longer the center of attention. It hadn't been that I was in love with Brock or had any delusions of us really being a couple. I was used to being the center of the Elite. I was the one the four of them protected. I didn't like sharing. Not even with my sister.

At least at first.

I found ways of dealing with the turmoil swirling inside me. Not all of them were healthy, but as long as they helped me cope, I didn't give a shit.

Realizing I'd been staring at the ceiling for too long, I was about to roll out of bed when a small knock sounded on my door. I turned my head in the direction as the handle turned and the door cracked open.

Josie poked her head in, her worried brown eyes finding mine. "You okay? I thought I heard something."

That was my sister's polite way of saying she heard me cry out in my sleep. My college room was next to hers, and the walls were thin. Too fucking thin considering she shared the room with Brock. It took one night in the room for me to realize I either had to move out or find a solution to the lack of soundproofing. So, I got not just a fan I ran at night but also an air purifier, both of which stayed on high whenever I needed a moment of peace. Not an easy feat to find when you roomed in a rowhouse with five other people. The library, the coffee house, and the common rooms on campus were fine when I didn't mind a bit of background noise, but I had moments when I didn't want to see another soul.

I forced a half smile on my lips for her benefit, not mine. "Yeah. I'm good."

Josie padded into the room wearing just one of Brock's T-shirts, the hem hitting the top of her thighs. Her signature pink hair was tousled, and the messy second-day curls framed her face. It might be vain to say she was beautiful seeing as we shared a damn similar face, but she was. We had the same slim nose, the same color eyes, and the same full, pouty lips. It was the structure of our faces that differed slightly. Her cheekbones were a tad higher and her chin a fraction rounder. "Are you still going to the shop today?" she asked, sitting on the edge of my bed.

I nodded, pushing myself upright on the mattress. "Tonight. You haven't said anything, right?"

"Believe it or not, I do know how to keep my mouth shut. If you're worried about anyone ruining our plan, it should be Ains. I love that girl, but she can't control her tongue."

"And your best friend would just have to go and fall in love with our brother. Do you think Grayson has any idea?"

"Only one way to find out."

We smirked at each other. Ganging up on Grayson had become a newfound favorite sisterly pastime. It was so much more fun for the two of us. "FaceTime?" I proposed.

"Absolutely," she agreed. "We'll give him another hour of sleep. Are you sure you should be going by yourself?"

"Well, can't ask the pregnant friend to come. And Mads is busy tonight. She has a group session with her marketing classmates. And if you come with, Brock will either demand to chaperone or he will ask too many damn questions. It makes the most sense to go alone. Fewer problems, and I don't have a boyfriend to answer to."

"I don't answer to Brock," Josie said.

My brow lifted, the corner of my mouth tugging up. "It's cute how you delude yourself."

She tackled me, tossing her body onto the bed as she wrapped her arms around me. I squealed, not expecting her to attack me.

"What are you doing?" I grumbled despite my smile and tried not to laugh.

She settled beside me, sharing my pillow while keeping her arms secured around me. "Everyone needs a hug sometimes. Just embrace it. Don't fight the love."

"God, you're weird." Affection laced my tone as I turned to face her. It had been three years since I found out Josie was my sister. Each year, we grew closer. I imagined the progression of our relationship was sort of what it was like gaining a stepsister. There were incidences in our past that bound us together, making us tighter than we might have been otherwise.

"But you're happy I came home," Josie said, beaming at me.

I rolled my eyes. "That's because I'm screwed up."

"Who isn't, dear sister?" she joked. I knew what she was doing, distracting me, and I was grateful. It worked.

"Please tell me I'm not dreaming," someone with a deep, husky voice said in awe from across the room.

Josie's head and mine whipped toward the door to see Micah leaning against the frame, staring at us with a lopsided grin. His sunny blond hair was messy in a way that looked intentional despite him just rolling out of bed. "Don't you have a girlfriend to gawk at?" Josie pointed out, flipping onto her back.

With twinkling light-blue eyes, Micah gazed at us, the stupid grin on his lips widening. "You can't deny a man one of his most thought about fantasies. Twins in bed. I just need a moment to soak it in."

My nose scrunched. "We're not twins. We're triplets," I reminded him, a deliberate reminder Josie and I had a brother who wouldn't think twice about kicking his friend's ass.

Micah shook his head, an expression of disappointment descending on his features. "Okay, you're ruining the illusion. I don't want to think about your brother."

Josie grabbed one of my furry white decorative pillows and hurled it across the room. "Get the fuck out of here before *my* boyfriend finds you ogling and having some sort of twisted fantasy about his girl."

Micah chuckled, catching the flying ball of fluff. "He knows. It's no secret. Fuck, where's my phone? Don't move," he ordered, pretending as if he was going back to his room to retrieve it.

Narrowing my eyes, I glared at him. Micah's flirtatious antics were part of him and something I'd grown accustomed to. "If you even think about it, you'll find yourself single so fast."

He sighed, tossing the pillow back at us. "It's a good thing I love her."

"God knows what she sees in you," I mumbled, making Josie laugh.

Micah sauntered on down the hall, leaving Josie and me alone in my room. Her head twisted toward me. "How did he ever become friends with our brother?"

"Good question. Rogues attract each or some shit the same way douchebags do."

She pinched my side, causing me to squirm away from her. "Get up," she ordered. "I made coffee." Josie always made coffee.

And I loved her for it. "How would any of us survive college without you?"

"I love you too," she whispered, giving me a quick hug before rolling out of bed and leaving me alone once again.

I stayed in bed for another minute before shuffling into the bathroom in no hurry to start the day. On Fridays, I didn't have any classes, which meant sleeping in late, staying in my pajamas until it was time to go out, and eating crap food all day. My perfect way to kick-start the weekend.

My day went pretty much as planned. The goal wasn't to do anything out of the ordinary and trigger one of the guy's radars. Luckily, we only had two to deal with until later tonight, and by then, I'd be gone.

Having a lunatic hellbent on seeking revenge for his sister's death made our lives complicated. It hadn't mattered that his sister took her own life, not to Sterling. In his eyes, we were all at fault. Micah might have been the one who hurt her broken heart, but the rest of us were guilty of protecting and siding with Micah.

Since the night we'd learned the bastard hadn't died in the fire that left my cousin scarred, my friends and I had been doing our own search into Sterling's whereabouts. The guys would rather we sit back, safely tucked at home, than get involved, but fuck that shit. I was not going to sit on my ass while some fucker stalked me or my friends. We were done waiting around for him to make his next move. *We* were going to make the next move.

And the first step happened tonight. A few nights ago, I'd overheard Brock talking with my brother about this guy in Fairway Lake who worked at a tattoo shop. This guy apparently had a side gig, but the only way to get information from him was by booking a tattoo with him, which was exactly what I did. My appointment was tonight.

Whatever information he had on Sterling, I wanted to know. It was more than being prepared. Killing him was an option, but seeing as I didn't want to go to jail, my other choice was to put this prick behind bars.

The Elite wouldn't tell us shit, not when it came to danger that could potentially get us hurt. It didn't matter how many times the guys promised no more secrets. There were always more secrets. And just as many excuses.

Securing my hair back into a high ponytail, I fluffed out the loose curls in the back and readjusted the ones framing my face. I tucked my phone into the back pocket of my jeans and grabbed my keys and wallet before heading outside.

For May, the air was warm, and a gentle breeze carried traces of the impending summer. Just enough to tease me. I loved summer. The heat of the sun. The star-strewn night skies. Sunbathing in bikinis by the pool. Most of all, I looked forward to our trip to Fynn's beach house in Oceanbay, an annual trip we started after graduating from high school.

I got behind the wheel of my Jeep and turned on the engine, triggering the pink ambient lighting to cast a soft glow onto the floorboards. The tattoo shop, Blue Magic, was in the town of Fairway Lake, about forty-five minutes from my college.

I queued up my playlist and nestled into the leather seat for a cruise. Night driving didn't bother me. I found it relaxing, particularly when the roads were sparse as they were tonight. Perhaps it stemmed from growing up with two brothers who raced. Nothing could compete with the open road, the evening breeze blowing through my hair, the stars shimmering over my head, the gentle vibrations of the engine, and the music turned up loud. I loved it.

Almost as much as I loved some of my other nighttime activities.

I had my bag of tools in the back seat. You never knew when inspiration might strike, but my vice for graffiti wasn't a hobby or an artistic war. It was an expression of sorts, and it had meaning, usually to call someone out on their bullshit. I didn't know what I would label it. I just knew how it made me feel, the rush it gave me, the control and power I needed in my life.

Passing under the highway bridge, I admired the designs of true artists, not like what I did, but it was part of the dynamic of art. There was no right or wrong level of skill. Everyone had their own interpretation of what was beautiful. The ability to express your heart in a variety of mediums.

Tattoos were art.

And I could hardly believe I was about to get my first one tonight.

I'd wanted a tat for a long time and had thought hard about what design I wanted permanently inked onto my skin. The boys all had multiple tattoos, including the compass with a dagger as the needle they all shared. The dagger pointed in a different direction for each of them. Brock was north—the way home. Grayson was west—the movement for the four. Micah was south—passionate and energic. Fynn was east—the reason.

I wanted something as meaningful to me, a reminder of what I'd overcome, of who I was today. Something to showcase both my lightness and my darkness, because I definitely wasn't the good girl everyone wanted or thought me to be.

The clock on my dash read almost nine o'clock when I killed the engine in front of Blue Magic. The shop sat in the downtown part of Fairway Lake. All the roads were brick, the stores were old and charming, and most of them were houses converted into shops. Each one was unique with two stories. Blue Magic was on the upper level of a redbrick house with black shutters. It had a set of stairs attached outside leading to the shop's entrance.

Making sure I had everything I needed, phone, keys, and debit card, I locked my car and started up the iron stairs. The railings were a little rickety as I climbed, but my mind dwelled on other things.

I hadn't been nervous before, but a flutter of apprehension bounced in my gut. My nerves had nothing to do with meeting Riley or the information I wanted. It was the damn tattoo that had my stomach suddenly going into knots.

I was a badass who had a fear of needles.

My hand paused on the door handle.

*Fucking hell.*

*I'm doing this. I have to do this.*

With a deep breath, I flung the door open, a little annoying bell chiming my arrival. My senses were hit with the scent of jasmine on a rainy night, floral and earthy. As I stepped into the small lobby, a stick of incense burned next to the receptionist, a guy in his mid-twenties. He glanced up from the tablet in his hands, greeting me with a friendly smile. The lip ring curved with his mouth. It wasn't his only piercing. His nose had two hoops, his eyebrow had a stud, and both ears sported numerous piercings. A three-day stubble covered his chin and lower jawline. And what a fucking jawline it was.

My first thought was *holy shit is he hot.*

I got sucked into the depths of his gray-blue eyes, utterly capti-vated. A thin smudge of black eyeliner outlined his eyes making them pop. He was gorgeous in a bad-boy way that made me want to commit crimes.

*For crying out loud. Get a hold of yourself, Kenna.*

"Do you have an appointment?" he asked.

*Dear god.* His voice was like honey, gliding smooth and deeply over my ears.

Swallowing, I struggled to find my voice but managed to reply,

"With Riley." I hadn't physically talked to Riley. We communicated through the shop's app when I booked my *appointment*. He made it clear what the cost of services was. I had to admit the tattoo shop was a great cover for Riley's side business. Or maybe it was the tattoo shop that was the side hustle, not the other way around. Regardless, I didn't give two shits how Riley operated as long as I left here with something useful.

I imagined Riley to be this brawny, bald guy in his mid-thirties with a full-ass beard like a Viking, covered in ink. It wouldn't have mattered what he looked like, just that he had a light hand when marking me up. The Elite had gotten enough tattoos over the years for me to understand the process.

The hot guy behind the glass-encased desk full of body jewelry twisted his head toward the hallway. "She's finishing up with her previous appointment. Should only be a few minutes."

*She? Riley was female. Interesting.* "Oh, good," I replied with a timid smile. "I'm still figuring out what I want to get. And where," I added with a nervous laugh.

He watched me, angling his head to the side as he reclined back into his chair. "A virgin?"

No, thanks to Carter, but that wasn't what he meant.

I nodded, whipping my palms over my jeans-covered thighs. "That obvious?"

"You have the look about you," the guy admitted, flashing me a pair of dimples that made my knees weak. "Here, why don't you take a look through one of these? Maybe it will help you narrow down a style you like. Riley can take it from there. She's really good. One of the best."

"Thanks," I said, taking the big, thick flash book. I sat in one of the waiting chairs and began to thumb through the pages, scanning the designs, doing my best not to be so damn aware of the guy behind the counter.

It had been a while since I felt anything for a guy, let alone interested enough to wonder what his lips tasted like. Being assaulted really messed up your ability to date and trust. I'd never been with a guy. I didn't count the night Carter took my virginity.

I tried dating. Was still trying, but the last few years, I'd focused on my family, friends, and myself.

At some point, I needed to get back out there.

Why not try tonight?

Picking up the book, I set it open-faced on top of the counter, drawing sexy's eyes up to me. "Hi," I said with a smile, searching deep for the confidence guys found irresistible.

"Did you make a decision?" he inquired, returning my grin.

I leaned against the counter. "Not quite. I was hoping you would have a suggestion. I need an expert's opinion."

His lips curved to one side, setting aside the tablet to fully give me his attention. "I might have a lot of tats, but I'm no expert. Piercing is my thing."

"You're a piercer?" I asked, genuinely interested and completely forgetting the reason I was here.

"Thinking about putting another hole in your body?" he asked playfully, and for a second, I contemplated doing just that if it got me more time with him.

I licked my lips, liking the way his eyes were drawn to my mouth. "As tempting as the offer is, I better stick to just one needle tonight."

"Fair enough. Okay, let me see." His fingers came to his chin as his eyes ran over me, sizing me up.

"Not too big," I clarified. "Small. I want to test the waters first."

"Dainty it is." He turned the book around sideways. "I think I have just the one." Flipping through the pages, he stopped at one covered in different flowers and pointed to one. "The lotus."

It was pretty. "What does it mean?" I asked.

"Rising from a dark place," he informed, meeting my gaze.

Surprise flickered over my features. "How did you know?"

He shrugged. "We all have our damage."

My lips twitched. "So, you're saying we're all fucked up."

His brows lifted. "Aren't we?"

I grinned as a woman with long, wavy silverish-blond hair came around the corner. She wore a black corset bodysuit and a pair of curvy jeans. Both of her arms were sleeved, the tattoos climbing up her shoulders and trailing behind her back in one cohesive piece. She was a knockout as my brother would so eloquently state.

Her bold cherry-red lips greeted me warmly. "You must be Kenna. I'm Riley. I've got about five more minutes if you don't mind hanging out until then."

"Sure, I'm in no rush," I assured, offering her a smile. It was hard for my head to wrap around this being the Riley who had a connection with Sterling. She seemed so nice and normal. Two things Sterling wasn't.

She moved around the desk and grabbed something from one of the drawers. "Good, Nico will take care of the paperwork."

Nico picked up the iPad, swiveling in his chair toward Riley. "She's narrowing down her options. I think we figured out what; now we just need a where."

"Thanks, Nico," Riley said with a wink and sauntered back down the hall.

Sexy's name was Nico. How did I get him to ask me out?

*Focus, Kenna. You're not here for a hookup.*

True, but it wasn't every day I ran into someone as attractive or tempting as Nico. I couldn't really let the opportunity slip by. After my tattoo, I'd discreetly slip him my number, assuming he was still here. *And* I didn't make an idiot of myself and pass out during the ink.

This shit better be worth it. I'll be pissed if I go through all the trouble of permanently marking up my body for useless information. Blue Magic would so be getting some colorful new artwork on their building if I got screwed over. Not even a cute guy would be enough to deter my vengeful heart.

2

—

FYNN

**B**uzzzzzz.

The needle rapidly pierced my skin, infusing the ink into my knuckles. I sat on the chair, my head resting on the back, watching Riley do her thing. I was here for one purpose, and it wasn't the tattoo. That was an added perk or, in Riley's case, the cost of her help.

She was an interesting character, both tough and feminine. It worked for her.

Perched on a rolling stool, her head bent over my hand, she carefully traced each line. Most of the work she'd done tonight had been freehand.

She was on the last finger, my index, but if Riley had a location as she claimed, I'd gladly tattoo my entire body. Well, the parts of skin I had left.

With Ainsley due at the end of summer, the pressure to end things with Sterling weighed heavily on us all. Grayson more so. There was nothing we wouldn't do to protect this baby, not just the four of us. It was eight now, and as much as Brock, Micah, Grayson, and I wanted to keep the girls out of this, they were involved.

We all were.

Knowing the girls in our lives wouldn't sit on the sidelines made keeping them safe ten times harder. I swore, one of them was always finding a way into trouble, but a huge part of the fault fell on us. It was what the four of us did, the threats we posed, and the mess we left behind that created the problems.

I don't think any of us could have imagined what we started in high school would have reached the level it was now. More than once, I'd thought about destroying our little digital black book. It fell on my shoulders to keep what we had safeguarded and secured, to make sure no one could break into our digital book.

With a disposable cloth, Riley wiped at the fresh ink on my index finger, examining her work. The tattoo gun buzzed as she touched up a few spots, thickening the lines. Riley's crew did more than ink and piercings. I'd used her services in the past, collecting information on people not so morally.

She sat back on her stool, the tattoo pen still in her gloved grasp. "What do you think?"

I glanced at my hand, studying the fresh tattoos gracing the bottom of my fingers just below the knuckles. The four aces. "That your line work is killer, especially with such intricate designs on small spaces."

She set aside the tattoo pen. "The fingers are tricky, but it suits you. I'll clean it up and wrap it for you. Then we can get to why you're here."

I angled my head left and right, cracking my neck and working out the kinks of sitting in the same position for an hour. "Do you have what I asked for?"

Riley's blue eyes sparkled as she attended to my fingers. "Have I ever disappointed you?"

My lips remained in a straight line. "Not yet."

"I'll grab the info for you." She finished wrapping each of my four fingers and walked out of the back room.

I swung my legs over the side of the chair, pulling my phone out to check my messages. I had one from Brock, but otherwise, it looked like a quiet night. For most people, a quiet night would be a reprieve, an escape. Not in my world. The longer the calm stretched without a taunting text from Sterling, the edgier it made me. I wasn't alone. We were all feeling the bout of calm before the storm hit. It was not knowing when the thunder would strike that unnerved us.

Sending a quick text to Grayson, letting him know I was about done, I stuffed my phone back into my pocket as Riley came back and sat on her stool. She had a phone, most likely a burner in her hand. "He was spotted at the Tanglewood Tower two nights ago. His parents own the building."

Of course, they did. I'd already looked at his parents' holdings, but I must have missed something. Unheard of, but there was a first for everything. "You're sure?"

"Have a look for yourself. The building is owned by Sky Management, a subsidized company of his father's. It took some digging, but we were able to catch him on the security camera. He's there."

A breath whooshed out of my lungs. *I got you, bastard.* "Do you know for how long?"

"A few days, maybe more. My guess is he won't be sticking around for long. If he's as smart as you say, he'll be on the move again soon."

This wasn't information we'd sit on. Grayson and I were heading straight to KU from here. We'd be on campus in less than an hour and discuss our next move, but I imagined tomorrow night the four of us would be making a trip to Tanglewood Tower. "Can you AirDrop what you have to me?"

"Already did," Riley said, dropping the phone onto the worktable beside her. "If you lose or delete the files, they're gone. We don't back shit up."

"Not a problem. I do."

Riley grinned. "If you need anything else..."

I straightened to my full height, eager to talk to Grayson. "At this rate, we're going to be tattooing over tattoos."

Riley followed, getting to her feet to walk me to the lobby. "Nothing wrong with a coverup piece."

Nico was chatting it up with some girl leaning over the counter. I didn't spare her a second glance until I heard her laugh. My fucking head snapped up so fast I startled Riley beside me. She stiffened, reaching behind her back where I'd noticed she kept a blade.

The girl laughed again. It was a sound I would know in my damn sleep. It had been tormenting my dreams since I was fucking ten. Probably earlier. I'd woken up with my first stiffy because of this girl. It was easy to say she left an imprint, and years later, I was still trying to erase the stain splotched onto my heart.

My eyes ran over her body to make sure my ears weren't playing tricks on me. Her perky ass was unmistakable, especially in those tight jeans, the ones that screamed squeeze me. Curls fell from her ponytail, cascading over the sweater slipping off one shoulder.

For a few seconds, I stared at her back, torn between thumping my head against the wall and throwing her over my shoulder. I settled for something in between for the time being, but I might change my mind.

"Kenna?" I growled, my lip curling.

A dark head turned my way, the ponytail flying with the move-ment. Her features instantly changed when her eyes landed on me. I could nearly hear the silent *oh fuck* cursing through her head. "Fynn." My name tumbled tartly out of her mouth, a scowl replacing the smile. She folded her arms and faced me. "I'd like to say I'm surprised to see you, but I'm not."

She shouldn't be here. "Well, I'm sure as fuck surprised to see you. Why are you here?" I stepped closer, my jaw hardening.

Her eyes gave me an obvious look. "To get a tattoo."

This was a mistake. She had no idea the game she played or how dangerous the players were. "No," I stated.

She blinked. "What do you mean, no?"

Nico and Riley stared at us with curious eyes, but I ignored them.

My only concern was getting Kenna out of there. "Just like it sounds. No. You're not getting a tattoo." I firmed my voice.

"Like tonight? Or like ever? Because honestly, neither option is going to fly with me. You don't get to decide what I do with my body," she snapped.

"The hell I don't." My dark gaze lifted, turning to Riley. "She's leaving."

Riley looked between Kenna and me, assessing the situation. Her hands fell to her sides. "I can see that. Normally, I would ask you to unhand my customers, but I'm guessing she's yours?"

I nodded. "Yeah. Since you already gave me what I asked for, she no longer has any need of your services."

Kenna was in front of me now, glaring up at me with flares of fire in the center of her eyes. "The fuck I don't."

Riley's lips curved in appreciation as if she approved of Kenna's spunk and her will to rile me up. "She's not going to make this easy for you."

"She never does," I huffed, preparing for things to get heated. Or for Kenna to get heated. I tended to be the one who stayed lethally calm. Kenna was all expression.

Riley fully smiled. "I like her." Her attention shifted to Kenna. "If you ever want that tattoo when your boyfriend's not around, call me."

"He's not my boyfriend," Kenna hissed between clenched teeth.

My arm slipped under her elbow, getting a firm grip because I wholly expected her to make this difficult. "I am tonight, brat."

Tugging her arm, she spat, "Don't call me that."

I yanked her to me, her head snapping up to give me a familiar death glare. "Would you rather I called you doll or baby?" I asked, lifting a brow.

"Fynn," she growled, but she stopped fighting, the heat from her body seeping into mine, making me all too fucking aware of her.

My intention was to make her docile, not seduce, but those damn eyes flickered with a different flame, and my blood warmed.

I cursed.

Nico stood, eyes pinching together as if he couldn't decide whether to get involved. Riley shook her head, and from the down-turn of Nico's mouth, he didn't like her call but obeyed.

"Move," I ordered Kenna.

The minx didn't budge.

I was about to lose my patience and take a deliberate step back so her body wasn't flush against mine. Not that it helped. The damage was done. "Kenna, don't make me haul your ass out of here."

She glared at me for another long moment before spinning around with a huff. I released her arm, allowing her to storm out through the door. I caught up to her at the base of the stairs before she could run off to her car.

"Not so fast. We need to talk." I grabbed her arm.

This time, she jerked it out from under my fingers before I could secure her. "Fynn, touch me again, and I'll deck you."

She was being serious, yet my lips couldn't help but twitch despite my anger with her. "Answer the question, and I'll let you hit me."

Her fists clenched at her side, a low growl of frustration vibrating from her. "You ruin everything. That guy was so going to ask me out."

I blinked, the muscles in my jaw tensing at the mention of another guy. "Nico?"

"Yes, Nico," she reiterated with more sarcasm.

"You came here for a date?" I clarified, trying to wrap my head around Kenna's thought process. I rarely ever did understand this girl.

Aggravation had her rolling her eyes. "No, you jerk. The date was an added bonus."

"You know better than to mix business with pleasure," I warned, my own annoyance growing at the thought of her and the piercer going out together.

A snort breezed through her nostrils. "Does that rule only apply to us? Fuck this. And fuck you. Isn't breaking the rules everything the Elite stands for?"

She had me there, but I wasn't about to admit it. "We can argue about how reckless you're behaving on the way home." I glanced around the dark lot and the streets crossing, getting the sense we weren't alone. *Where the fuck is Grayson?* "We need to get out of here," I said, dropping my voice.

This time when I reached for her, she didn't pull away, sensing the sudden change in my demeanor. My newly tattooed hand slipped to the small of her back, keeping her tucked at my side.

Too close for comfort, a rock skipped over the road as if someone had kicked it, but as my gaze darted through the darkness, I couldn't see anyone.

"Did you hear that?" Kenna whispered.

A car pulled in just then, headlights beaming over us in the middle of the small parking lot. Grayson stepped out looking like he was about to murder his sister. His chilling frown turned on me.

"Look who I found lurking around Blue Magic," I greeted.

Grayson stared hard at Kenna, his dark eyes narrowing. "Kenna, what the fuck?"

Her gaze faltered, and she inched closer to me as if I would shield her from Grayson's wrath. "You came with my brother?" she hurled at me accusingly like it was the worst decision I could make.

I chuckled.

"Kenna, explain yourself," Grayson demanded.

She sighed, and I felt her chest fall against me. "Calm down, don't blow a gasket. It's not a crime for a girl to get a tattoo. You guys are flipping out over nothing. You're acting like I walked into the middle of a gang war unarmed and helpless."

Grayson and I shared a glance. *She damn well might have done just that.*

"Not funny. Get in the damn car. We're taking you home," Grayson ordered, looking every inch the pissed-off brother.

Kenna's chin lifted. "I have my own wheels, but thanks, bro."

"Keys?" he held out his hand, waiting impatiently.

"No." Kenna remained firm.

Grayson had been driving my Infiniti, running errands while I met with Riley. My car idled as they argued. "I won't ask again. And you know I really don't need them to drive your car, but the other way will cost you though. I figured I'd save you the money."

"Asshole," she muttered, fishing out her keys and dropping them into his palm. "I'm not riding with you." To prove her point, she stomped to the passenger side of my Infiniti and got in.

"Good luck," Grayson muttered, scanning the lot for Kenna's Jeep.

"Thanks," I replied sourly, folding my long legs into the driver's seat.

Kenna sulked half the way to KU, giving me too much time to stew in my anger, because if I didn't hold on to the fire licking inside me, I would be thinking about things that were off-limits.

It was nearly impossible for my dick to not get hard when she was around. Her smell alone drove me insane with need, a primal desire to claim her. Cramped alone with not just her but the damn scent of her was pure torture, but I'd been fighting this urge for the better part of my life.

At first, it was because she was my best friend's sister. That excuse worked years ago but not anymore. Not to me.

Then it was her trauma. I wanted to give her space and wait until she was ready.

I was still waiting.

Rolling my window all the way down to let in the spring's night air, I glanced at the sky, a crescent of moonlight shone off to the side, following us along the road.

Kenna turned to me. "Are you hot?"

"Something like that," I grumbled, leaning a hand out of the window, the other guiding the steering wheel.

"Nice tats," she said as I flexed my fingers. "What were you really doing there?"

Using the controls on the steering wheel, I turned up the music, indicating I didn't want to talk. Well, not true. I did want to talk to her just not about why I'd been at Blue Magic. Anything but that.

Kenna hit the volume down again. "You're being ridiculous. And don't even give me any of that sexist bullshit about you being a guy. You'll only piss me off more."

By the time I got to KU, the dull throbbing at my temples would be a raging headache at this rate. "You don't think I'm angry?"

She gave a one-shoulder shrug. "I honestly don't give a shit."

"Kenna," I rumbled.

She tossed a hand in the air. "Oh, don't Kenna me. Are you going to tell me what you found out? We both know that neither of us went there for a tattoo."

"No," I stated flatly, my eyes straight ahead on the road. I couldn't look at her, look into her fiery eyes. It wasn't because I would give in and tell her what I'd learned tonight about Sterling. It was because I might jerk the car off the road and devour her saucy mouth.

Tugging on her seat belt, she twisted her body toward me, her legs tucking up on the seat. "If you say *no* one more time, I'll do more than scream. I'll jump out of this car," she threatened. Kenna's intimidation tactics were as unpredictable as she was.

I didn't hesitate. I loved testing Kenna just as she thrived on pushing my boundaries. "No."

She shrieked. Not a full-on scream but high enough to get her point across.

I laughed, shaking my head.

God, she fucking amused me nearly as much as she drove me mad.

Her hand flew over the seat, whacking me in the arm. The car jerked slightly from the impact, and I scowled at Kenna, all traces of my humor dissipating as I corrected the car back onto the road. "Are you trying to kill us?"

"If that's the only way I get you to tell me anything."

"You're such a brat."

She changed maneuvers, her expression turning serious. "Fynn, this isn't me looking for trouble despite what you guys think. This is me protecting my friends. This is us letting the asshole know he won't break us. I need to find him as much as you do."

My fingers tightened on the steering wheel. I glanced at her before my eyes returned to the road in front of me. "Your brother's going to be livid."

"Story of Grayson's life. If my brother isn't angry about something, I'd be worried."

I fell silent, contemplating how much I could tell her. She was genuinely concerned, and I didn't always agree with Brock's decision to keep the girls on a need-to-know basis. I didn't like leaving them blind. "We know where he has been staying for at least the last week," I finally revealed.

Kenna perked up, sitting straighter in the leather seat. "Where?"

I narrowed my eyes. "I'm not stupid. If I told you where he was, you and your troublesome pack would do something reckless like show up at his house."

"Isn't that what you're planning to do?" she challenged, hitting the mark on the head.

I sighed, turning in to KU's campus. I was done arguing with the little brat, and damn, if I didn't need some space—some distance.

Kenna didn't wait for me to open her door but bolted out of the car and straight inside the house. Grayson sauntered over as I closed my door behind me. "How did that go?" he asked, a sadistic smirk ghosting his lips. His eyes glanced to the front door Kenna had disappeared into.

Leaning against the side of my car, I exhaled and rubbed at the back of my neck. "Your sister is relentless."

"It runs in our DNA."

"No shit."

Grayson shoved the phone in his hands into his back pocket,

dropping his overnight bag onto the ground. "Brock and Micah are on their way out. I texted them. Figured it might be better for us to talk outside than try to find a quiet spot inside without one of the girls listening."

"Good call," I agreed. "They're getting too good at this crap, and we have no one to blame but ourselves."

Grayson leaned on the car beside me, both of us facing the rowhouse, worrying about the four girls inside who made our lives hell and yet better somehow. They made us better. Or want to be better. "It feels like the harder we try to keep them out of this part of our lives, the deeper they push their way in."

"Maybe we stop trying," I suggested.

"You can't be serious," he responded, just as I figured he would.

I shrugged. "Are you saying that you weren't a little bit impressed Kenna showed up tonight?"

He was. We both were. I was still wracking my brain over how she obtained the information.

"She's going to get herself killed. I can't take any chances. Not with Ainsley," Grayson said.

Grayson had more to lose than all of us now with Ainsley having his baby. I could understand his qualms about looping the girls in.

Before we could discuss it further, Micah and Brock exited the front door, coming toward us. Once we were together, I flicked my gaze to the house, checking the windows for any peering eyes. "He's staying at the Tanglewood Tower. Riley gave me footage of him leaving and entering the building." I relayed what I learned, keeping my voice low.

"Can you get a unit number?" Micah asked from where he stood under a tree on the curb.

I nodded, already planning on doing that when I got inside with my laptop. "Yeah. I'll at least narrow it down, weed out the units that are occupied, and cross-reference the residence against his family friends, but my guess is he's holed up in one of the empty units. I say we start with those."

"Tomorrow night then," Brock deadpanned.

We all nodded.

Tomorrow it was.

And this time we would be one step ahead of the bastard. He wouldn't know we were coming.

# 3

## KENNA

I was supposed to be planning Ainsley's baby shower, an event Mads, Josie, and I were hosting this summer after we got back from Fynn's beach house. What was I doing instead?

Plotting how I'd get the address to Sterling's place and what message I planned to leave the bastard tonight.

I wanted to do more than leave a taunting note but also knew when not to push my luck. I didn't want to do anything that would have him running again, but I also wanted him to know we were getting close.

He deserved a bit of torment after the shit he put us through.

Since I was short on time, I decided to stick with what I did best, something comfortable. The guys hadn't come out and said anything, but they were up to their own shenanigans. We all felt it.

"What do you think they're planning on doing?" Mads asked.

Kenna, Mads, Ainsley's preggers ass, and I were huddled upstairs on my bed. Mads stuck her spoon inside the pint of Ben & Jerry's Chubby Hubby. Ainsley had the other spoon.

The guys were outside doing the same shit we were inside, minus the ice cream. They might have taken a case of beer out with them on the front stoop.

Josie and I chose booze over ice cream. She passed a can of zero-carbs vodka to me. "Burn the building with him in it," she suggested.

Ainsley shook her head, leaning her back against a mountain of pillows as she tried to get comfortable, and licked her spoon. "They wouldn't. Not with so many other people involved."

Mads held out the container for Ainsley, her legs crossed in a pretzel. "Perhaps not, but they would like to."

"Wouldn't we all," I mumbled, taking another swig before handing the can back to Josie. "He should have died in that warehouse."

Josie pinned me with a wtf look.

"What? You know we're all thinking it," I replied.

"She has a point," Ainsley said, a hand lying protectively over the bump that really popped a week or so ago.

Cute didn't begin to describe Ainsley as pregnant. She carried my little niece, and I couldn't freaking wait to meet her, to hold the little bundle of joy in my arms. "Thank you," I said, glad to have someone on my side.

"So how are we finding out where he's staying?" Josie asked, circling back to the problem at hand.

We all looked at Mads.

She had her spoon deep inside the ice cream pint and looked up to see us staring. "Me? Why me?"

"Because we all know Micah can't keep his mouth shut about shit. He'd be the one to spill the deets," I said.

Mads's chest deflated. "I can't even argue with that."

"So, you'll see what you can find out?" Ainsley asked, looking hopeful. How the hell was she going to deny the pregnant girl?

"Yeah," Mads reluctantly agreed, swallowing a scoop of the fudge-covered pretzel ice cream.

"I could always go through Brock's phone when he's showering," Josie offered.

I shook my head. "It needs to be before tonight."

"Is there a deadline we're unaware of?" Ainsley asked, taking the pint Mads offered her.

Josie turned her suspicious eyes on me. "Kenna, what are you up to?"

Sometimes being a triplet sucked. We didn't even have the bond most did from growing up together, and yet she found ways to read me. Sometimes better than Grayson. "I'm still working out the kinks."

Mads's gaze narrowed. "There are kinks?"

I rolled off the bed, moving to the window. "Not really," I said over my shoulder, glancing down at the front yard. I caught a glimpse of the guys' shadows below.

Josie shifted on the bed, her feet dangling over the side as she turned toward me. "You're going there."

Leaning against the glass, I leveled them a look. "We all agreed to stop sitting around and waiting for the guys to take out the big bad wolf."

I expected an argument from one of them. Instead, I got a partner. "I'm going with you," Josie stated, unblinkingly.

My snort came out short. "And risk Brock's wrath? No fucking thank you." Of all the guys outside of my brother, Brock was the one I knew the best. It had been hard for me when I first came home seeing him with my sister and not with me. It was jealousy but not because he was in love with Josie. For years, I'd been the center of these four guys' life, and despite my relationship with Brock being fake, we'd still been close because of it.

I knew better than to wake the quiet beast.

Josie crossed her arms, her chin firming in a defiant movement I used too many times. "Well, we're not letting you go alone."

My expression remained unchanged. "I'm the only one who doesn't have a boyfriend breathing down her neck. It makes sense that it's me."

Mads shook her head, a frown on her lips. "I don't understand why you must go at all. Why can't we take a breath and come up with a solid plan that doesn't involve you going rogue?"

"I need to do this." I had to do something. Sitting around drove me crazy. I was tired of always having to look over my shoulder, wondering if someone was watching me, waiting for me.

They felt it too.

"If we figure out where we both will go," Josie stated, holding my gaze. She was as stubborn as I was.

"Fine," I conceded. "But if Brock finds out you came with me, I'm abandoning you. I don't need him on my ass about putting you in danger."

Her lips twisted in a familiar smirk, and it was like looking in a mirror. "Then we just make sure we don't get caught."

* * *

A few hours later, a soft knock rapped on my bedroom door. I dropped my phone on the bed, bored with the endless scrolling I'd done for the last hour. I was dying for a distraction. "Come in," I said loud enough for the person on the other side of the door to hear.

Mads came in, her eyes finding me in the center of the bed, surrounded by a cloud of blankets. I sat up. "Did you get it?" I asked, eagerness unmistakable in my voice.

She dropped a little white slip onto the bed. I glanced down and picked it up, unfolding the square. It was an address.

I quickly looked up, my heart beating faster in my chest. "How did you get it?"

Mads flopped onto my bed, her arms bracing behind her. "I sucked his dick and told him if he wanted to cum I needed to know where Sterling was."

Scrunching my nose, I said, "I'm sorry I asked, but damn, I didn't know you had it in you. Impressive."

"You have your skills. I have mine," she said with a wink, her lips curving.

I scrambled out from under the blanket cloud, scooting to the edge of the bed. "Where are they now?"

Her eyes lost their sparkle. "Getting ready for poker night at the football house."

Going to my closet, I threw open the door. "Perfect."

"Don't get yourself killed, kidnapped, or caught." I didn't have to see her face to know my cousin was scowling.

I tossed a glance over my shoulder. "Josie's coming with me. She's the levelheaded one."

She wrapped her arms around herself. "That's what scares me. They're going to lose their ever-loving fucking minds when they find out."

"I know. I can't wait."

Mads shook her head. "You have seriously crossed wires in your brain."

"Love you too."

Collecting my supplies, I filled the black duffel with my favorite cans of spray paint. We waited until the guys had been gone for twenty minutes before leaving the house, and like two thieves in the night, Josie and I got into my Jeep. She put the address into my GPS as I drove the car toward the campus exit. It was nearly midnight when we pulled up to Tanglewood Tower, a luxury apartment complex. This place definitely had security and probably cameras.

Neither would deter me.

The complex wasn't far from where our parents lived, just a few miles from the Academy. I made sure to park a block over from the building and tossed a mask into Josie's lap when I turned the car off. "Put this on."

She unfolded the mask, staring at it. "Really? The Powerpuff Girls?"

I grinned. "Fitting, huh?"

"And you claim I'm the dork," she retorted, regarding me with unamused eyes.

Pulling my lip in, I bit back a grin. "Just put it on."

She did as I asked, tugging on the knitted mask I picked up online months ago for occasions such as this. I didn't bother to suppress my laugh. She fucking looked too damn cute when her head twisted toward me.

Her brown eyes blinked where Blossom's would be. "I'm glad one of us is having a good time." She pulled down the visor mirror and examined her reflection. "Why Blossom?"

"Pink hair obviously." Blossom's hair was red in the cartoon, but her clothes were pink, which made me think of Josie and her signature pink hair. I'd been a fan of the show when I was younger and in awe of the cute girls kicking ass. Poor Mads, I forced her to spend countless hours role-playing parts of the show, pretending I was Bubbles. Back then, I'd been bubbly and sweet.

Mads always picked Buttercup. Oh, how times had changed.

Josie rolled her eyes. "Which one did you pick?"

I pulled out my knitted face cover and held it up. "Buttercup."

"Wearing that doesn't make you a badass."

Buttercup was known to be the tough, hotheaded one of the group. She was my cartoon doppelgänger. "For tonight it does." I pulled the hood over my head, shielding my hair. All that was visible were my eyes. "You ready?"

Blossom nodded and my lips tugged. It hadn't been intentional, but the duo masks relieved some of the tension and adrenaline that had built inside me on the drive over. It was amazing what a laugh could do, regardless of how short or unexpected.

After I tossed my bag over my shoulder, we hiked through the connecting yard from the street behind the building, avoiding the motion sensor Josie pointed to as we approached. I nodded, letting her know I saw it. We moved through the parking lot, using the cars to hunch and duck behind.

"Do you think one of these cars is his?" I whispered in case anyone lingered outside for a late-night smoke or was coming home from a shift.

"Probably. I doubt he's walking everywhere." Sarcasm was Josie's default. I liked that about her.

I shoved her shoulder lightly. "My guess is the Viper or the Tesla."

"We're not slashing the tires on every car in the parking lot," she hissed, reading my train of thought.

We inched toward the side of the building. "Am I that predictable?"

"I just know how your corrupt mind works."

"If that's true, then a part of you must be corrupt as well."

"No thanks to you," she mumbled.

"This kind of feels like that time we went after Carter," I said, smiling fondly under my mask.

"Yeah, it does," she agreed.

It was a memory neither of us would forget—the beginning of our bond as not just sisters but of two people who shared similar trauma. Not identical, but we both knew what it was like to be tormented by Carter Patterson.

And now Sterling.

Canvassing the perimeter of the building, we took note of the cameras. There were two entrances in and out, the main one at the front of the building and another less grand entrance at the back. Both had a security camera. The parking lot we snuck through bordered two sides of the building. A nicely landscaped courtyard with benches and a winding pathway leading to a small lake with a gazebo greeted the patrons out the back exit.

Peering around the corner, I surveyed the front doors. They were double glass etched with the name of the complex covered by a portico. The tiny camera in the corner angled down, picking up residents and visitors before they went in. A keypad sat to the right of the doors, which were undoubtedly locked, preventing us from strolling in unannounced.

The idea Sterling was inside, lounging worry-free in one of those units, sparked my anger. What he'd put my cousin through was something I could never forgive him for, regardless of how much he begged.

"Where are we doing this?" Josie asked beside me, her voice slightly muffled by the mask.

I chewed on my lip, studying the camera to make sure I wasn't wrong about how far its scope reached. "Somewhere front and center. Somewhere he can't miss. I want it to be the first thing he sees when he walks out."

"The door?" she suggested, following behind me as I moved toward the front but staying far enough away not to trigger the camera.

I'd considered it, but it didn't seem bold enough. "What about right here." I stopped and looked down at my shoes.

We stood a few feet from the covered portico. Josie's eyes glanced down. "The brick sidewalk? I like it."

Unzipping my bag, I pulled out a few cans of paint, tossing one to Josie. "Make it big and splashy, li'l sis."

She caught it midair. "Twelve minutes doesn't make you older. Besides, you know what they say about the middle child?"

I shook the can, distributing the liquids together. The little ball inside rattled, a sound that was like music to my ears. I loved the way paint smelled. It was like sniffing permanent markers at school or gasoline while filling up your car. "Why do you think I need to be the center of attention?" I retorted.

Josie popped the top off her can. "You can have the spotlight. I'm starting to appreciate my mask."

"Keep it. Brock might like it. He can be the villain." He didn't need to pretend for that role. He was the damn leader of villains. Or perhaps a corrupt vigilante.

Her nose moved under the mask. "Maybe I'll make him wear the mask."

I snorted, dropping my bag to the grass bordering the sidewalk. "Say no more. You're going to ruin my adrenaline high." Testing my spray on the grass, I glanced over at Josie before we began.

"Don't get too close to the covered section of the entrance," I warned her.

She saluted me with her can. "Got it, boss."

We got to work, spraying the letters across the two-person-wide sidewalk, the words spanning the entire width. I added a few finishing details as Josie completed her part, the hissing of her can filling the night. No one came or left the building, and if the camera did pick us up, anyone monitoring the feed had to be taking a snooze. We finished uninterrupted.

Taking a step back, Josie and I admired our handiwork. Written in black and pink letters was a message that wouldn't make sense to anyone except those with secrets.

**PEEK-A-BOO. I SEE YOU.**

Grinning under my mask, I put the cap back on my spray can. "We're fucking geniuses."

Josie dropped her paint into my bag. "I'm not sure I'd go that far."

Gathering our stuff, careful not to leave anything incriminating behind, I stepped into view and flipped off the camera before we left. Sterling probably had a direct feed to the security. Perhaps he was watching right now, jerking off.

Giggling, we turned and ran, not stopping until we got to my car.

"Josie," someone with a familiar deep voice growled.

I whipped around so fast I felt sick and dizzy from the movement. Josie mirrored me a second later.

*Oh shit.*

Four extremely murderous guys stared at us.

## 4

## FYNN

"Fuck." The curse breezed through Josie's lips, a mere wisp of a sound. She ripped the mask off her face.

Grayson groaned, seeing both his sisters caught red-handed doing precisely what they shouldn't be doing. "Seriously," Grayson hissed.

Josie's eyes hadn't left Brock's. I wasn't sure she saw anyone else. "What are you doing here?"

Brock's nostrils flared. "Nuh-uh, Firefly. I'm asking the questions. Why are *you here* instead of where I left you."

I stood beside Micah, my eyes flicking to Kenna.

Kenna stepped slightly in front of Josie as if to protect her from Brock, which was insane. Brock would rather cut off his own arm than hurt his girl, but I could see how he might be scary to other people. This was Kenna. She knew Brock. Her narrowed gaze pinned Brock. "Lay off, Taylor. If you're going to growl at anyone, it should be me. This was my idea. Josie was just being a good sister, like always."

"I'll deal with you later," Brock said, dismissing Kenna.

"Ooooh," she mocked, holding up her hands in pretend fear.

"Kenna," Josie warned firmly, her shoulders going rigid. "I don't need you to defend me."

"Usually, the king does that for you," she snapped, glaring directly at Brock.

He hated the term king. All through high school, the title had been thrown around. Nothing pissed him off more. In his eyes, he wasn't perched on a pedestal above the rest of us. He didn't wear a crown. Kenna knew how to push his buttons. "And I will continue to do so, but the two of you make my job nearly fucking impossible."

Josie angled her head to the side. "Why are you here?"

Brock's expression darkened. "For the same reason you are, I imagined."

"You spray-painted the building too?" Kenna said without blinking.

My lips twitched despite being furious with her. Micah chuckled beside me. If there was one thing you could count on, it was Micah being amused by the antics of these two girls. The crazier shit they did, the more entertained he was. As long as it wasn't Mads. Where his girlfriend was concerned, it was the only time our retired playboy was serious.

Grayson shoved a hand through his hair, feet shifting over the ground in restlessness. "You didn't?"

Kenna gritted her teeth. "Look for yourselves if you don't believe me."

"I do believe you; that's the fucking problem," he said, his tone dripping in anger. "Do you have any idea what could have happened? What if he came out and saw you? What if he was armed?"

Kenna caught her brother's stare and held it. "He didn't. I don't see the point in wondering about all the horrible shit that could have gone wrong."

"You don't think, and that's the goddamn problem," Brock replied in a sort of condescending voice that would get under Kenna's skin.

"Fuck you, Taylor. I'm not your girl to order about." Kenna tossed the mask clutched in her hand at Brock before spinning around and storming off.

"Kenna!" Josie called after her, but Kenna didn't acknowledge her and had no intention of coming back.

My eyes stayed on Kenna's back, the darkness swooping in around her.

Brock reached for Josie's arm, his hand clamping around it. "Josie, let her go."

Josie faced Brock, her eyes sizzling with heat. She opened her mouth, but I quickly cut her off.

"I got her," I told Brock. "Just go. I'll bring Kenna home once she's cooled off."

"Fynn?" Josie called as I was about to take off after her sister.

My eyes found hers, and I forced my lips into a placid smile. "It's okay, JJ. I'll keep her safe."

"Good luck," Grayson muttered, pushing off the back end of Kenna's Jeep.

"You want me to stay?" Micah offered, a mixture of humor and sympathy in his light-blue eyes.

I shook my head. "Nah, go home to your girl. I can handle Kenna."

"You might be the only one. Or the only one stupid enough to try. I can't figure out which," he retorted.

"Neither can I," I muttered.

Scooping the mask off the ground, I took off in the general direction Kenna disappeared off to. It didn't take me long to find the girl pacing under a mature willow tree. The thin dangling branches brushed against her face and arms, and she knocked them out of the way again and again.

Her head snapped up as I approached. Ire still glowed in her eyes. "How did you find me?"

My gaze fastened to hers as I walked right up to her. "I'll always find you."

Her gaze flicked to my lips for a second. "Comforting," she replied dryly.

I chuckled. "Old habits are hard to break." *And because I cared. Too damn much.*

"God, he's such a self-righteous prick," she scoffed. It was Brock she was upset with. If it wasn't him, then it was her brother. Micah and I seemed to get a pass. Most of the time, but not always.

Kenna and I had our fair share of disagreements over the years. She was so fucking stubborn and had been even before the Carter shit. That was one thing about her that hadn't changed.

I didn't know how I'd feel seeing Kenna again after two years, but when she strolled into the party, confronting Josie and Brock, it felt like I'd been sucker punched in the gut, the air knocked the hell out of my lungs.

I remembered I couldn't stop staring at her.

It was ironic or just fucked up that Brock and I fell for two girls who couldn't resemble each other more physically yet couldn't be more different. I'd be lying if I said I hadn't entertained the idea of Josie and me together when she had showed up. I had. How could I not? She was so much like Kenna; it was almost like getting her back.

But it became very clear early on that Brock claimed her. He'd never shown any true interest in a girl before Josie. I couldn't interfere with that. Not to mention, it didn't take me long to separate the two once I got to know Josie.

She was definitely not Kenna.

Then Kenna came home.

And three years later, I still hadn't made a move.

*What the fuck is wrong with me?*

*What am I waiting for?*

*A damn sign to fall from the sky?*

Not likely.

The only sign I'd been given was the cold shoulder from Kenna. A huge reason why I'd kept my distance. She had moved on.

Perhaps it was time I did the same.

Except...I couldn't.

Just as I couldn't stop from touching her.

Tugging on a piece of her long, dark hair, I cocked a single brow. "What am I?"

Kenna looked like a goddess under the moonlight. "A slightly less prick."

Her hair fell through my fingers. "You know how dangerous what you did was." I tried to reason with her. "Brock can't help but worry. It's what he does."

Her frown grew a bit deeper at my nearness. "That and order everyone about."

"True, but someone has to take the leadership role."

Kenna sat on the curb, her fingers covering her thumbs as she cracked her knuckles. "Tell me how what we did was any less risky than what the four of you had planned? Or were you just tracking us?"

"That's part of why he's so pissed off." I sat down beside her. "Sterling wasn't in the building. He's probably already moved on." I didn't mention the note he left behind for us to find. "And now I'm going to have to keep closer tabs on you."

Her eyes narrowed. "Try it and see what happens."

She was close. A little too close, her thighs pressed against mine. "Why do you have to balk at everything we do or say?"

"I just can't help myself." A wicked smirk flashed on her lips, but it didn't last long. "He wasn't there?" Her tone dropped.

I shook my head.

"I guess that means all Josie's and my work was for nothing. I fucking give up." She let out a long, aggravated exhale.

Slowly and deliberately, I leaned close to her. "Liar," I whispered, my breath caressing the sensitive spot on her ear I knew drove her crazy.

A tiny shiver went through her body and sent a spike of smug satisfaction in me. I hadn't wanted to push Kenna until she was ready, but seeing that she was affected by me, I couldn't stop toying with her and torturing myself. I enjoyed knowing she wanted me. Enjoyed it too fucking much.

The anger was gone from her eyes, but in its place was an emotion as dangerous. Perhaps more so.

The problem with playing with the fire was the sparks often went up in flames. If I wasn't careful, these little feelings I enticed would blow up in my face. I might be the one who got burned. I might be the one who leaped without thinking. I might be the one who ruined everything. Kenna wasn't just some girl.

For all the tough act she put on, I knew the truth. She had a fragile heart afraid to love—afraid to get close to anyone.

I'd been patient.

But my patience was running thin.

I reached out, and my fingers traced the edge of her cheek. Her skin was so damn soft. "I have a proposition."

Her eyes fluttered, affected by my touch. "I'm listening."

"Since you're so hellbent on interjecting yourself into getting Sterling, I need your help."

Suspicion wrinkled along her forehead. "Help? You never ask for my help."

I had to stop touching her. I needed something to do with my hands, so I leaned back on them, my fingers sinking into the grass behind me. "Times change. Besides, I can't trust an outsider with this. It must be someone who can play the role flawlessly without raising any doubts. We need to blend in."

The willow tree canopied over our heads, but through the weeping branches, streaks of moonlight passed through. It hit the side of her face. "Play a role? What are you up to, gorgeous?"

I stared at her for a minute, my chest expanding a full breath. She'd thrown around the endearment casually for years, but only when we were alone, never around our friends. Despite how nonchalantly it left her mouth, my pulse jumped. "I haven't said anything to anyone yet. This stays between you and me for now."

She grinned like a temptress about to lure her prey. "Fynn going rogue. What the hell has the world come to?"

My skin heated. I didn't know a man alive who would be able to resist that look. "The Westons are hosting an annual event for one of their corporations," I explained, filling her in on what I only learned an hour ago.

Her thoughts went right to the point. "You think Sterling might be there?"

"Yeah, I do. And I also managed to get two invitations," I said, the corner of my lips curling as a light of understanding sparkled in her eyes.

Twisting her body more toward me, she let her knees rest against mine. "You're going."

The trace of excitement in her voice should have worried me. It did, but I also understood. "That's where you come in. I need a date."

Her gaze narrowed. "Since when does Fynn Dupree need a pity date?"

I scoffed. "That's not what this is. I can't trust just anyone, not with this. An outsider will ask too many questions, particularly when we have to use fake names. The tickets I scored are for a couple who won't be attending, but we will in their stead. I don't want to involve anyone else because Sterling is unpredictable. I don't want anyone else's blood on my hands." *And I can protect you,* I silently added. I wouldn't protect a stranger the same way I would Kenna. With my fucking life.

The fifty questions weren't over yet. "Why haven't you said anything to the guys?" she asked.

A frown pulled at my brows. "I haven't had the chance."

She bumped my shoulder. "I don't buy that."

"I plan on it."

"And?" she prompted.

"And I'm avoiding the discussion where we figure out who goes to the party. It only makes sense that it's me, but knowing them, they will argue. In the end, I'd still be the one to go. I have less to lose. I don't have a girl waiting for me."

"We have something in common," she said quietly.

I nodded. "Which is why it makes perfect sense for it to be us."

"I agree. Thanks for including me, Fynn. I mean it," she added, watching the change of expression on my face. "I can't tell you how hard it is for me to sit around and wait for something to happen. These last few months since the Demon's Park incident have been torture."

Demon's Park was a memory I longed to forget, as did the rest of us, particularly Grayson and Ainsley. That night could have gone wrong in a million different ways, but a girl died, and as horrible as it was, despite the toxicity she brought into our lives, we were all relieved it hadn't been one of our girls.

A late-spring wind swept down the street, shaking the willow branches surrounding us. "There will be rules."

She didn't like that. A wisp of moonlight highlighted the soft dusting of freckles on the bridge of her scrunched nose. "Way to go and ruin my excitement."

I shook my head. "What am I going to do with you?"

Her brow cocked, irritation shifting to devilish teasing. "Do you really want me to answer that? Or was it a rhetorical question?"

"Kenna," I rumbled. "We should go before I do something I can't take back."

She stood up, dusting off her ass. "Live without regrets, Dupree."

I got to my feet, my gaze falling to her smirking lips. "Get in the car. I'll even let you drive."

"Fuck yes, you will. It's my car, asshole." A scowl formed along her face.

I bit back a chuckle. "You never did tell me if you'll come."

"As if I'd miss the chance to cause some fireworks," she said.

I took that as a yes.

* * *

During my weekends at KU, Grayson and I slept on the couches. Well, that was before Grayson hooked up with Ainsley. Now my lonely ass slept out here alone. I didn't mind. The truth was I liked being alone. I liked solitude. I liked quiet. It gave me time to do what I did best, other than football.

With my laptop open, I opened the camera feed, combing through the video files from today. When I came across the clip of Kenna in her Buttercup mask flipping off the camera, I chuckled. It shouldn't have been funny, seeing how close she'd been to Sterling, that he could have been inside the building watching her. Or in the parking lot waiting.

The idea of either raised my blood pressure.

I took a sip of my beverage, a little nightcap. Bourbon on the rocks. I could always count on Josie having a bottle stashed somewhere in this house.

The ice sloshed in the glass as I set it back on the table, continuing my search through the camera roll. Twenty minutes might have gone by, maybe more, and I was about to close my laptop for the night when someone came out of the double glass doors, a hat pulled down low, shielding most of his face. The quality of the video was fuzzy and complete shit, but it was *him*. Sterling. I'd bet my car on it. And any lingering doubts were erased the second he turned over his shoulder and peered directly into the camera, a cocky, smug smirk curling at the corner of his mouth. The expression came across as if to say *I see you.*

"Asshole." I leaned closer to the paused screen. "I got you." But no victory swirled within me, not when I felt with certainty he was toying with us. Or with me specifically, as I was the techie of the group. He would know it was me behind the computer.

I stared at the screen, my fingers clenching. I didn't care what it took. I would get this bastard.

My phone buzzed on the coffee table, jerking my focus off my laptop. I bent forward and picked it up, seeing a message from my little sister, Avery. At nine, she just started to become a handful.

With her teenage years approaching, I didn't know if I was glad to be out of the house or fearful I wasn't there to protect her.

**Hey, bro. You up?**

**Yeah. I could ask you the same. Why are you up this late?** I texted back, the three little typing dots appearing on my screen seconds later.

**Couldn't sleep.**

**Did something happen?** My mind went to all sorts of scenarios from a bully at school to a fight with her best friend. But the worst idea was that whatever bothered Avery could have anything to do with public enemy number one.

So far, he had only fucked with us, not our families, but the torment was escalating, and I wouldn't put it past Sterling to go so low as to involve the *other* girl in my life I cared about.

The longest twenty seconds dragged by as I waited for Avery's response. **Put the guns away. I'm fine.**

Lying on the couch, I stretched out with my phone in hand and exhaled. I read her text again, and this time, I smiled. When she referred to guns, she was talking about my biceps. **How's school?**

**Didn't you hear? I dropped out.**

**Funny.**

We went back and forth for another ten minutes, texting about nothing in particular, just catching up. Closing my laptop, I took my phone to the couch and stretched out, my feet hanging over the side. I closed my eyes.

When my phone buzzed again, I figured it was Avery.

I was wrong.

**Well played. You're finally learning the game. My last pupil ended with a smash.**

My fingers crushed the phone. From upstairs, one of the guys swore. It sounded like Micah, and I assumed we all got the same message.

5

## KENNA

After my late night, I spent most of the day in bed, bingeing episodes of *True Crime*. The house was quiet when I emerged from my room hours later looking for something to eat. My stomach couldn't be silenced anymore, and the persistent rumbling interfered with my ability to lounge my Sunday away.

It didn't really matter. The curtains were drawn in my room, keeping the sunlight out, so I had no idea what time it was when I wandered out into the hallway. Opening the fridge, I stared at the contents. An empty carton of milk because some asshole in this house didn't know how to throw it away. Leftover white containers of Chinese someone ordered. Bottles of beer. Coffee creamer because coffee was the one thing this house never ran out of. And a bunch of random condiments. We basically had shit to eat.

I glanced at the microwave to check the time, contemplating if I wanted to order delivery. Just past six. Everyone else was probably out on dates, having dinner, and here I was alone, about to eat a half bag of Cheetos left open on the counter.

Flinging open the freezer, I grabbed a pint of ice cream. There were worse things to have for dinner. I fished out a clean spoon from the dishwasher yet to be unloaded and hopped up on the counter to eat my pathetic dinner alone.

"Hey."

I screamed, and the spoon halfway to my mouth clattered to the floor.

Frowning, I found the culprit of my surprise, and my shoulders relaxed. "Damn it, Fynn. You almost got a spoon tossed at your head."

He grinned, and I forgot where I was. Hell, I forgot my name. "It would have been worth it. The look on your face was priceless."

I glanced down at my half-eaten pint and then at the spoon so far from where I sat. "I thought I was alone."

He was shirtless.

*Why is he shirtless?*

I bit my bottom lip, and my gaze, of its own damn accord, ran over his body from his shoulders to pecs to his flat-ass stomach, rippling with muscle, to lower yet, where the small patch of dark hair disappeared behind the waistband of his shorts. His chest donned a collection of tattoos trailing up over his right shoulder, the other side of his arm completely untouched by ink. For now.

*God, why does he look so good?*

I had to hand it to his parents for creating such a flawless specimen of a male. He had his mother's sparkling green eyes that changed the slightest in shades depending on his mood or the clothing he wore. They were the purest in color against the deep gold of his skin. He got the best features from his mixed heritage.

When my gaze returned to his face, Fynn's eyes searched mine.

I should be embarrassed I'd been caught devouring him with my eyes. A heat did move into my body, but it wasn't caused by modesty or bashfulness.

Since starting college, I made a promise to myself I'd start dating. Or at least try. And to my credit, I had gone on a few dates, but none of the guys worked out. I couldn't decipher if it was me that was the problem or if it was the men. I had an excuse for everyone.

Not my type.

Too tall.

Not tall enough.

Weird laugh.

Doesn't laugh enough.

Gave me the ick.

And so on.

It got to the point where I stopped trying.

Yet here I was drooling over a shirtless Fynn Dupree, thinking how I'd like to do more than date him.

Having spicy thoughts about him was a big deal to me because no one, not a single other guy I'd encountered over the last two years, made me have an impure thought about them.

"I just finished my run," Fynn explained his sudden appearance.

A thin sheen of sweat covered his skin, and I thought about licking his abs instead of what was in my hand. I wondered what he tasted like. Then my mind wondered what the combination of his body and my ice cream would be like. Sweet and salty.

*What the hell had he said?*

*Something about a run?*

"Are you leaving tonight?" I asked, trying to act normal when I felt anything but.

He nodded, leaning his hip against the counter I sat atop. "As soon as Grayson and Ainsley get back." His finger dipped into my pint, scooping a glop of ice cream and bringing it to his mouth. I watched him suck it off. "Ice cream kind of night, huh? I was craving a sundae."

The pint in my hand was melting. "I bet you were," I muttered, swallowing. "I'd offer to share, but someone made me lose my spoon."

"Here," he said, shifting his body closer to me. "I think I can help with that." He took another glop of my chocolate peanut butter ice cream with his finger, but this time, he held it up in front of my mouth.

My lips parted automatically, not thinking about what I was

doing, sucking ice cream off his fucking finger, or how damn intimate the simple act would be. I figured it out a second later when my tongue lapped against his skin, my lips gliding along the length of his finger. But it was too late then.

I made the dumb mistake of looking into his eyes while I finished licking the last of it off him. My tongue darted out, swiping over my lips to catch any extra drops of ice cream. I got my sweet and salty, the taste of him lingering on my tongue.

This was not what I planned for my evening, but the temptation of Fynn in front of me might be too much to resist. We were alone. And my curiosity had been piqued. What would it be like to kiss someone who I had feelings for?

I'd kissed a few guys but nothing special, nothing I wanted to repeat, and nothing that had me craving more. Yet something told me pressing my lips to Fynn's would be a different experience entirely.

Perhaps it was past time I found out. Could I put myself out there again for him to possibly shut me down?

I wasn't sure.

My eyes stayed on his as his hands went to my thighs. He brushed the inside of my leg with the pad of his thumb a moment before he parted my legs enough for him to settle between them.

My breath hitched at the contact of his body so close to mine. I'd never felt anything like I did right now. It scared me slightly, but under the fear, intrigue pressed forward. "What are you doing?"

His mouth hovered a mere inch from mine, and his lips curved, drawing my gaze. Regardless of my question, I wanted his mouth on me, but he lowered between my legs. Warmth cascaded through me, and my breath quickened. Countless times I'd imagined Fynn in a compromising position as he was now. It could only end in one way.

Right?

Wrong.

He didn't lick the inside of my thigh as I hoped. He didn't press his hand into my throbbing center.

I'd wondered so many times how my body would respond. For

once, I didn't want to shrink away or have my stomach pitch. Neither happened with Fynn.

The prick held up my spoon from the floor with a naughty smirk. "You dropped this."

*Asshole.*

If the ice cream wasn't a shake by now, it would be from the heat emitting from me. Fynn churned me up inside, and I didn't know if I should toss the pint aside and sink my fingers into his hair or kick him to the ground. "Why do I need that when I have your fingers?" I retaliated, leaning forward purposely, aware that my loose V-neck would let him know I wasn't wearing a bra.

His eyes shifted right where I wanted them. He wasn't the only one who could play dirty. "Careful, Kenna," he warned, but it held little grit when his eyes were undressing me. "Neither of us is fifteen anymore."

"You're the one between my legs."

With deliberate slow movements, he stood to his full height. "Am I crowding you?"

*Yes!*

"Maybe you should take a shower and cool off," I suggested, angling my head to the side."

His lips twitched. "Are you going to join me?"

My eyes flew to his, and I could tell what had come out of his mouth had been spontaneous, a thoughtless flirt. He had probably said something similar to a dozen girls before. But this was me. Neither of us had crossed the line in many years.

*What is going on?*

*What changed?*

Why was Fynn staring at me as if he wanted to lay me down on the counter, rip my clothes off, and make me scream as if no one was home?

*Shit. No one is home.*

Panic made my heart race, a gut reaction I wanted so much to overcome. For once, I didn't want the near thought of being alone with a guy to send me spiraling. This was Fynn. He would never hurt me.

"What the fuck, Fynn. We're not hooking up just because we're the last wolves left in the pack." I shoved at his chest, forgetting I still held the pint in my hands. The pliable carton smashed against his hard muscles, ice cream oozing over the sides and dripping down his abs.

My gaze flicked down, and damn it, my first thought wasn't *oh fuck*. No. It was *should I lick it up?*

"Kenna," he growled, lacking any scary oomph that was usually present when he said my name. His green eyes were bright when I met them again. "You're going to pay for that."

I didn't have time to evade or scramble out of the way. Fynn's arms came around me, and the dickhead tugged me to the edge of the counter, wrapping me in a bear hug as he smeared chocolate and peanut butter all over my fucking shirt.

"Fynn!" I shrieked, pushing at his shoulders, but it was useless. He was too damn strong, so I gave up, relaxing.

It worked.

He wanted me to squirm and wiggle. When I didn't, Fynn pulled back.

I stared at him, eyeing the smear of chocolate all over his chest. Then I laughed. We looked so ridiculous, and it had been a while since anything ridiculous happened.

And just like that, the sudden tension between us broke.

Jumping off the counter, I took a few steps away from him, creating much-needed space. "Fynn, you'll pay for that. It might not be today or tomorrow, but watch your back. Revenge is my specialty."

He twirled the spoon between his fingers. "Good thing I'm leaving in an hour."

"You're cleaning up this mess while I shower. *Alone*," I added, overemphasizing.

"Lock the door, Kenna." The seriousness in his tone made me shudder.

I gave him one long, suffering look, a million pros and cons of why I shouldn't stroll back and jump into his arms running through my head. Clueless as to what was happening between Fynn and me, I shook my head. "Am I keeping out potential enemies or you?"

Face stoic, he replied, "Both."

* * *

Shopping was a pastime I once lived for. The mall had been like a second home. Then something happened and sucked out all the joy. Not just from shopping but everything in my world as if someone had come in and erased all the color, leaving my life in black-and-white. It took me some time to paint the colors back in, but when I did, I found the things I once loved weren't what I was passionate about anymore. I was different, and with the change, so were my interests.

Now shopping was a chore, but it had to be done.

"Why do you need a dress?" Mads asked as we stepped over the threshold of what had once been my favorite store.

I roped Mads into coming with me to look for something to wear for my upcoming undercover op with Fynn.

Hesitation swirled in my gut. Had Fynn mentioned the party to the guys? If so, had Micah kept it from Mads?

Unlike the guys, I didn't want to hide or keep secrets from my friends. We had a pact. Were there certain parts of my life I kept to myself? Of course, but if it could affect or involve those I cared about, I believed they deserved honesty and truth.

Too bad I couldn't always be honest with myself.

Taking a sip of my boba, I glanced around the store, searching for the section of evening wear. "Fynn asked me to attend a gala with him next weekend. Hence the need for a dress. And shoes," I added.

"A gala? Are his parents hosting a charity event?" she asked, confused. Our families were close. If the Duprees were having a party, she would have heard about it.

Chewing on the inside of my cheek, I replied, "No, it's not his parents hosting. It's the Westons."

Mads's face blanched for a few seconds, but my cousin quickly regained her composure, taking a long swig of her brown sugar milk tea. "Why are Fynn and you attending an event *his* parents are throwing?" She kept her voice lowered, but I could tell she hated the idea.

I lifted my brow. "Think about it."

"Kenna," she rumbled. "I don't like this, even if Fynn's going to be there."

"What could happen at a fancy party surrounded by some of the wealthiest people in the country?" I reasoned.

She shot me a pointed look.

"It's not the same," I argued, reading into her expression. With just a knowing glare, she referred to the night I was drugged by Carter Patterson. It had been at a party full of people, and yet he managed to slip Rohypnol into my cup and lead me upstairs to my room without anyone questioning him. "Besides, as you said, Fynn will be with me. He won't let anything happen. Not to me."

We weaved between the freestanding racks, moving toward the back of the store, while also freely perusing the displays. "True. But if he thinks Sterling really will be in attendance, you don't think Sterling will also be waiting for you? Or one of us?"

"Probably," I admitted. The bastard wasn't dumb.

Mads ran her finger over the sleeve of a cream sweater. "And if he's there, what do you and Fynn plan to do? Attack him in front of everyone? In front of his parents?"

"We're not letting him get away." My voice got a bit louder, drawing a few glances from the salesclerks. Ignoring them, I lowered my voice. "This might be our only chance to catch him, and in front of witnesses has to work in our favor."

Mads didn't appear convinced. "I hope so."

With the matter settled, I turned to her. "Now use your magic and find me the perfect dress."

She frowned, not focusing on the clothes. "I need a smoke."

"Stop," I groaned. "Drink your boba. Chew some gum."

After a dramatic eye roll, she smiled. "Bitch."

For the next hour, Mads and I pulled dresses off the racks and handed them to the nice sales lady looking to make a fat commission off us. She stored them in a dressing room for me to try on once we'd finished combing through the selection.

Mads sat on a cushioned bench, sipping the last of her drink, while I walked into the dressing room and shimmied into the first dress. "What's up with you and Fynn?" she asked, her voice carrying over the door.

I met my eyes in the mirror, a stricken look of panic staring back at me as I recalled the other night in the kitchen. "Nothing. Why?" I replied, leveling my tone as I wiggled the dress up over my hips. No way could she know about the ice cream. I could hardly believe Fynn nearly kissed me. He might have if I hadn't started to get so nervous.

"I don't know. I'm picking up some tension between you. Did you guys have a fight?"

Stepping out of the door, I turned around for her to zip me up. "I fight with everyone. Fynn's no different."

She set her cup on the ground and stood up, working the zipper closed. "Well, that's true. So, you still don't have a massive crush on him?"

I glanced over my shoulder, a knowing smirk pulling at my lips. "I never said that."

"You do," she retorted, taking a step back.

"What's not to like about Fynn Dupree? Not that it matters." I gave a one-shoulder shrug. "We're friends."

Her lips pursed. "Uh-huh. I'm going to let that very huge lie pass for now."

Turning around, I faced her, the fabric of the gown twirling at my ankles. "I need a dress, Mads. Not a boyfriend." Frustrated, I walked back into the dressing room to change into another gown because the champagne dress was not it. The plunging neckline in the front was flattering, but it had too many ruffles on the bottom, too flowy. I wanted a killer dress, nothing sweet or soft.

"When was your last date?" Mads asked, unfazed by the door separating us.

I chewed on my inner lip. "Why does that matter?"

"Because I'm your best friend. I should know what's going on in your life."

"Nothing's going on," I insisted, wondering how the hell we got on the topic of dating. "You know basically everything because there's nothing to tell."

"Micah wants to set you up on a blind date," she blurted.

I whipped the door open so fast it slammed into the wall. "No." I held the deep-red satin dress to my chest.

"He's nice. Really nice," she added as if the extra *really* would make him more appealing. It didn't. "A football player, of course, but I think you'd like him if you—"

"No," I stated firmly, making it clear this discussion was over. My features softened after a moment. "I'm not ready."

She put her hands on my shoulders and spun me around, adjusting the back of the dress and lacing up the corset. "I'm not pressuring you. I'm the last person who would, but you won't know if you're ready unless you try."

Perhaps she was right. I hadn't properly dated since I came home —hadn't wanted to. I didn't know how to date. I'd never had a real boyfriend, and the one time I'd had sex, it had been against my will.

Mads had good intentions. She worried about me. Wanted me to be happy. And I wanted all those things too, but right now, I couldn't dedicate the time and energy needed in figuring out myself, what I liked, what I wanted in a relationship. Not until I felt safe.

*You might never feel safe*, a little voice in my head not so kindly reminded me.

Perhaps not. Perhaps even after Sterling was dealt with, the lingering fears inside me would remain.

Perhaps I needed to schedule a session with my therapist. It had been a while since she and I talked.

"I'm scared," I admitted, being vulnerable with one of the few people I could.

"That's normal."

Twisting left and right, I studied my reflection in the mirror before grinning at Mads. "Holy fuck. Who knew my body could curve like this?" The deep-red strapless dress had a square bodice that dipped low on my chest, tying in a crisscross pattern in the back and leaving the section from my shoulders to right above my ass exposed. As stunning as the back was, my favorite part of the dress was its sexy simplicity and the obscenely high slit on the side exposing most of my right leg. Daring. Bold. And seductive. It was perfect.

Mads gave a little squeal, so unlike her. "This is the one."

"You sure?" I asked, glancing down at the silky material hugging my body.

Her expression grew serious. "I mean, as long as a tit doesn't pop out. Just don't dance, and you'll be fine. To be safe, try not to move." She couldn't quash her smirk any longer.

"A tit falling out is an iconic moment. Who wouldn't live for those five seconds of fame?" I teased.

"I can see this is important to you," she replied dryly. "But what I'm trying to figure out is if it's Sterling you're impressing or Fynn," she said, still hung up on the idea something remained between Fynn and me.

Before this weekend, I would have said no despite the sparks that danced along my skin whenever I was near him. But now uncertainty made me wonder if Fynn wasn't just messing with me. I didn't understand him.

Brushing at a few wrinkles on the dress, I replied, "Neither. Can't I just want to look good?"

"You don't need to try, Kenna. You damn well know you always look amazing."

"True, but there's nothing like a fucking sexy dress to amp up the confidence levels, and I need to walk into the party like I own the bitch." I felt like the leading lady in a James Bond movie.

"Mission accomplished."

I went to go back into the dressing room, but I caught a glimpse of Mads looking at herself in the full-length mirror. I saw the change in her expression. Minor, but it was there if you knew her as well as I did. She didn't often get tripped up by the scar running down her cheek, especially since it had lightened some, but even with makeup, you could still make out the mark in the right lighting.

Her gray eyes turned stormy.

Coming up behind her, I wrapped my arms around her waist, dropping my chin onto her shoulders as I met her gaze in our reflection. "You're beautiful, Mads. He didn't break you. He never will."

She put a hand over mine and squeezed, drawing in a breath. "I know. I'm alive. We all are, and that's what matters. Promise you'll be careful. I couldn't handle it if anything happened to you—" Her mouth quickly shut as if she stopped herself from saying more.

*Again.* The unspoken word which had been on the tip of her tongue.

"You know why this is important to me, but I promise." I hadn't been able to fight back the first time. Carter took away not just my choice but also my will to fight.

Never again.

This time, I would kick, scream, scratch, and claw until the very end.

This time, I would get revenge and justice for my cousin. She deserved to feel safe.

We all did.

Especially with a baby coming soon into our lives. I was going to be an aunt, and I swore before this baby took its first breath she wouldn't have to worry about anything other than having her diaper changed and her next feeding.

Sterling wouldn't be a problem.

## 6

## FYNN

Micah went into the kitchen and opened the fridge before plopping down on the empty chair, legs kicking out on the coffee table scattered with my shit.

"Do we have anything on Professor Whitman?" he asked, opening the energy drink. The last thing Micah needed was more caffeine.

"Why?" I asked, my eyes locked on the laptop screen.

"Because I'm going to destroy his career," he said casually. We could have been discussing football or the weather as easily.

I lifted a brow. "Any particular reason, or are you just feeling end-of-semester boredom?" Which Micah was prone to. Whenever things got too quiet, he got antsy and stirred up trouble.

His light-blue eyes flashed. "The bastard's sleeping with students. He hit on Mads."

I needed no other details. Despite having a shit ton on my plate, I couldn't turn him down. Between getting ready for the gala tonight, keeping up with my studies, football practice, and monitoring the feed where Sterling might or might not be still staying, I was fucking stretched thin. "Consider his career as a professor finished."

"Thanks, Fynn. I know it's the last thing you need."

Even if I didn't find any dirt on the professor, the internet could be a powerful tool, especially in wrecking people's reputations. All it took was planting a seed of doubt, and social media would do the rest. "It's what we do."

A minute of silence passed with guzzling his energy drink and me on my laptop. "Do you ever think about how long we will do what we do?" he asked, surprising me. Micah didn't get deep often, but I could tell by his expression he wasn't being flippant.

I scrolled through the video feed, speeding it up. "In some capacity, probably forever. We'll have families eventually. Some of us much sooner, and our net of protection will grow and continue to grow as we get older." Pausing the recording, I met Micah's gaze. "What would you do if some guy hurt your little girl?"

He didn't hesitate. "I'd kill him."

His answer mimicked mine. "Or you'd find a way to destroy him."

"As long as I got to put my hands on him." Micah shook his head. "Can you imagine me a father? Having a little girl?"

It was Grayson about to become a dad that had Micah contemplating a future past his college years. The playboy as a father probably scared the shit out of him.

The idea of little replicated Micahs running around scared the shit out of me too. But it also, made me smile.

Picking up the TV remote, he clicked it on and scrolled until he found the football game. "Shouldn't you be getting ready?"

My eyes flicked to the corner of my laptop, checking the time. "Yeah."

"We should be going with you," he stated stonily.

"I was only able to score one pair without it drawing attention." I'd had this discussion with the guys earlier, and like I predicted, I was the best candidate.

"The four of us show up with dates, we're making a goddamn statement."

"Exactly what we don't want," I reminded. "Not to mention, do you really want Mads with you?" There's no way in hell Grayson would let Ainsley step foot anywhere near the gala. Even with the sliver of a chance Sterling might be there."

He winced. "Who gives a fuck about the rest of the pompous assholes. We need to corner him, make him feel boxed in."

"Which is why you, Brock, and Grayson will be covering the exits. Did you guys figure out what to do with the girls?"

"For once, we don't have a problem. They're busy. Can you believe that?"

My lips twitched. I wondered if Micah considered them being busy a ploy. They never sat around and let us handle things. Without a doubt in my mind, they were up to something. "How fucking dare they have a life outside of us."

"Exactly," Micah said, slamming his Monster down on the table, splattering shit on my stuff. He grinned, flashing the dimples that got him in more trouble than I could keep track of.

"I'm going to kill you," I deadpanned.

A sparkle lit the center of his eyes. "Not a chance in hell. On or off the football field, I'll take you down."

"Stop the shit talking," Brock said, coming down the stairs.

Micah put his arms behind his head, leaning back and grinning like a fool at me.

"Is everything set?" Brock directed at me, his aqua eyes sharp and already into game mode. Brock got this look about him when shit got serious. It was the same on the football field. Laser-focused.

I nodded, closing my laptop and setting it aside far from Micah's reach. "You downloaded the app I sent you?"

Brock confirmed with a nod.

"It will give you access to the front gate as well as the security cameras around the country club," I explained. "You should be able to get in and out without leaving a trace."

"Good. If anything goes wrong..." His voice trailed off with an air of doom.

"I got this. And as I promised Grayson, I will make sure Kenna is safe," I assured him. This was a risk but one we had to take.

Brock gave a short nod. "Then I guess we're set. With any luck, we'll catch the bastard."

* * *

While I adjusted my bow tie, the clatter of heels coming downstairs drew my gaze. We were already late, but rushing Kenna would only make us later, so I left her alone to do her thing, but if she had been another five more minutes, I would have carted her down the damn stairs.

A whoosh of air left me. "Finally," I muttered under my breath. Only Kenna and I remained in the house. Micah, Grayson, and Brock had left ten minutes ago. Josie and Ainsley went to the movies about an hour ago to see some film they'd been gushing about for weeks. And Mads was at another group study for a big upcoming end-of-term project she needed to complete.

This was our last weekend on campus before summer break, and more than anything, we all wanted to put this feud with Sterling behind us and enjoy a summer free of drama, and why tonight was so important.

Kenna's legs came into view, deep-red fabric twining in and around her thighs as she descended the stairs. Only a few times in my life had I ever been left speechless. Kenna in this dress went on the list.

"Shit," I mouthed. *I'm in so much trouble.*

When my eyes stopped ravaging her from head to toe, I noticed something was different about her. "What did you do to your hair?"

She touched the ends of the short bob with one hand, the other holding the front of her very low-cut dress. Gone were her long locks. The color was darker too, a midnight black. Her red lips curved. "Do you like it?"

I swallowed. I liked it too much. She looked like an enchantress about to reign hell upon the world. "I'm not sure."

She gave a careless shrug. "Well, don't worry. It's a wig. I thought since we're going to the gala under false names, I should look the part."

"And this is how you think Amelia Hauser looks?"

"Nothing wrong with a little creative liberty." She turned around, showing me her back. Like all of her back. The dress covered none of it. "Can you lace me up? I can't do it on my own, and everyone is gone."

I stared at the thin crisscross strings.

When I didn't do anything, she glanced over her shoulder. "Just pull the ends and tie a bow. It's not rocket science, gorgeous."

That wasn't the problem. Touching her was, but if we were going to get through the night as a loving couple, then I'd better get used to my hands on her.

Grabbing the dangling strings with my fingers, I looped a knot, tightening it.

"Not too tight," she complained. "I need to breathe."

"Then you should have bought a dress you can breathe in," I grumbled through my teeth.

"You know nothing about women's fashion."

The side of my hand brushed against her lower back. Kenna gave a sharp inhale that went straight to my dick. I tied the bow with slow deliberate movements, my fingers a whisper over her skin.

She shivered.

This had gotten far too intimate. As late as we were, I shouldn't be entertaining thoughts like pressing Kenna against the nearest wall with her palms splayed on the painted drywall. I shouldn't be thinking about pressing the hard length growing inside my pants against her ass or spreading her legs with my knee. I shouldn't be wondering what her skin tasted like. I already knew how damn soft it was.

I cleared my throat and forced myself to step away from the vixen. "We should go. Are you ready?" I asked gruffly.

Her lips curved at the corners. "You have no idea how ready."

I groaned. She was fucking killing me.

She pushed the slit across to the other side and revealed a leg strap high up on her thigh, a knife nuzzled against her skin.

"Kenna," I growled. "What the fuck is that?"

Her finger grazed over the sheath. "Protection. A girl never leaves home without it."

I should rip it off and toss it onto the counter, but I didn't. "Get in the car before you hurt yourself. And leave the blade," I ordered.

"The only way this knife is coming off my body is if you physically remove it. Are you going to take it, gorgeous?" she challenged.

Kenna knew I rarely backed down from a dare. "Don't tempt me."

With a smug smile, she brushed past me and said, "I thought so."

Already my night started off with a bang. I couldn't wait to see what the rest of the hours would bring with Kenna by my side.

Outside, we were greeted by the cool May evening. It had just enough of a bite to need a jacket or a sweater, neither of which Kenna brought with her. As we walked to the town car waiting for us, I glanced sidelong at her. "Do you want my jacket?" I offered.

"No, I'm okay," she assured, her face lifting to the sky. More than a few stars were visible tonight. "It feels nice."

If I saw one goose bump on her, I was going to tie her into my coat.

The driver opened the door for us, nodding in greeting. "Good evening, sir."

"Thank you, Oliver." Oliver had been my family's driver for over a decade. Discreet was his middle name. I didn't have to worry about what he might see or hear. The man would turn a blind eye. His loyalties lay with my family regardless of the situation, and that was important in an employee. I could trust him, which said a lot. There were very few people in this world I could trust.

Oliver had the partition between us closed off, leaving me alone with Kenna, and we settled into the back of the car. The side of her dress slipped off one leg, unveiling far too much skin. Another inch and I'd have been able to see the color of her underwear or if she wore any at all.

*Christ, why am I thinking about her fucking underwear?*

Now was not the time. I needed my head clear and focused, not filled with Kenna's expensive perfume that smelled of a moonlit garden.

I pressed my fingers into my knees and glanced out the tinted windows. Not that I could see anything. It was so dark. As we pulled onto the highway, the view became nothing but a blur of lights and trees.

Kenna fumbled with the invitation in her hand, opening and closing the envelope flap.

"It's okay if you're nervous," I said, glancing at her beside me.

"This is excited energy you're sensing."

"You ever consider being a spy instead of...what's your major again?" I asked, unable to remember since she'd changed it so many times.

I got the smile I'd been looking for and trying to pull from her for the last ten minutes. It didn't usually take me this long, and as tough as she wanted to appear, some of that energy bouncing in her was nerves. "Every night. I'd be a banging spy."

"I'm going to assume you're joking."

Her smile wasn't reassuring, especially when I could all too clearly picture Kenna sneaking out in the middle of the night like Catwoman.

I scowled in the dimly lit car.

Kenna took out the invitation and snorted. "Forrest and Colleen Weston cordially invite you to their annual charity gala," she read in her best hoity-toity rich girl voice. Join us at the Royal Marian Golf Club for this black-tie event supporting *Sadie's Dream*." Kenna dropped the invitation into her lap. "I used to love it when my parents threw fancy parties. Now, I just want to trash them."

I understood part of her resentment. The idea of a charity was to give back, do good, and bring awareness, but half of the people who attended these events cared little for their cause. "We're not here to ruin their night," I clarified before she got any ideas.

"I know," she said, wrinkling her nose. "But perhaps a message left in the bathroom wouldn't hurt."

"Kenna," I said sternly.

"Fynn," she retorted, mimicking my tone.

I let out an exhausted groan. "Perhaps now would be the best time to go over the rules."

"Don't bother. I won't hear a word you say." She turned away from me to look out the window, basically snubbing her nose at my upcoming rules.

"Too bad. I'll have Oliver take you home right now if you can't agree to a few cautionary measures."

Crossing her arms, the minx glared at me, impatience snapping in her gaze. "Fine, go. Be a dick, but I'm peeing alone."

"First, don't do anything stupid." I ticked off one finger.

Her fingers lifted, toying with the dangling strands of her earrings. "Could you be broader? That's practically like telling me not to breathe."

Another finger went up. "Second, other than peeing, I need to always have eyes on you. That means you don't wander from my side."

"Yes, Daddy."

Why did she have to make that sound so dirty? "Third, and the most important point, you do whatever I say."

She batted her thick lashes at me and purred, "Whatever you say?"

*God, save me.*

Kenna licked her bold red lips, and my eyes glued to her mouth.

I dragged my gaze from her and the deliberate seduction of her lips. "This isn't the time to be cute, brat. I'm serious."

"And that's your problem. You're too serious. Lighten up, Fynn. This is a party. We're supposed to like each other, remember." Her finger trailed up the buttons on my shirt. She twisted slightly, a wicked grin on her face as she lifted her other hand, undoing the top button. "There, don't you feel better? More relaxed?"

I shifted in my seat, the bulge in my boxers waking up after just settling down, and I had Kenna to blame. "No," I grumbled, frowning.

She laughed as if she knew precisely what she did to me.

We arrived at the gala, and I couldn't be happier for some fresh air and a moment to breathe air not laced with Kenna's scent. It would only be a very short reprieve, but I'd take it.

Oliver opened my door, and I stepped out of the car under the porte cochere, moving around to the other side. I offered Kenna my hand. Her twinkling brown eyes glanced at my hand before they lifted to meet my gaze. She placed her slim fingers into mine as she stood, her silky dress flowing to her feet.

Slipping my palm to the small of her back, I whispered in her ear, "Have I told you how damn sexy you look?"

She radiated sophistication with an air of mystery. She turned heads exactly as she intended.

A rare blush stole over her cheeks. "I didn't think you liked my dress."

I stopped the words that almost came out of my mouth. My first thought had been how I'd like her more out of the dress, but I quickly changed course and said, "As if anything you wear could look bad on you." A safer option.

Our strides were in sync as we strolled down the rolled-out carpet. "Such a way with words."

"Remember, for tonight, you're not Kenna," I whispered for her ears only.

"Whatever you say, Sebastian dear," she replied, already slipping into her role.

My lips twitched.

The Royal Marian Golf Club sprawled over two hundred acres of lush greens. Standing three stories high, the pale-yellow main house was a stunning focal point of the country club. Tall, bright windows glowed warming and welcoming from all floors. A black runner had been laid out from the drop-off to the front double doors.

Greeted by the staff, I handed the attendant my invitation.

"Good evening, Mr. and Mrs. Hauser. Welcome to Royal Marian Golf Club." He directed us to the event room after checking our invitation.

The country club and events like these weren't my forte, and I usually avoided them at all costs, but I'd been to my fair share and could blend in with the upper crust despite my disdain for most of them.

I frowned as we walked into the room, and I forced my lips into a neutral position, relaxing my pinched brows. As I glanced around the room, I leaned close to Kenna and murmured, "Don't forget the rules, brat."

Her fingers tightened on my arm. "You should have made me sign a contract or an NDA."

"You don't think I can fake one?" I escorted her around clusters of pretentious partygoers with fat wallets ready to write a check for a good cause so they could cleanse their conscious or make them feel better about themselves.

"You're the worst," she said, a small, amused smile tugging at her lips.

Most of the attendees were my parents' age, which was expected considering Sterling's parents were the hosts. I'd scanned the guest list to make sure we wouldn't run into someone who might recognize us. Only a few names stood out as acquaintances of my parents, but none were close enough to have me worried. "Champagne or wine?" I asked, spotting a server coming our way with a tray of flutes.

"Both."

I grabbed one of each and offered her a glass. "We can share."

She took the bubbly. "Afraid I'll get drunk and not be able to handle myself?"

My lips twitched. "The thought crossed my mind."

Touching the rim of the glass to her mouth, Kenna took a sip. "Then you should also know I don't get drunk, not at parties."

My first initial sweep of the room came up flat. I hadn't expected Sterling to be standing openly in the room, but I'd hoped it would be that simple. "I do. I kind of wish you would get plastered. I'm more worried about what you'll do sober."

With our drinks in hand, we wandered the room, keeping busy. Politicians, heirs to hotels, famous actresses, rich housewives, oil tycoons, and plastic surgeons filled the event. More money mingled in this single room than in a bank vault. The dirt I could collect on these people. It was tempting, so tempting, but my focus was only on Sterling.

He was all that mattered tonight.

When I came up with the idea to have Kenna by my side, I hadn't factored in how much of a distraction she would be. Or how much my mind worried and wandered to her safety. It was a constant thought in the back of my head.

She laughed. "Loosen up, *Sebastian*." She emphasized my alias for the night, reminding me we were playing a part. "We're here for a good cause, remember?"

Kenna keeping *me* on task? Who would have thought? I didn't like how good and convincingly she portrayed her role.

The country club had done a beautiful job setting up the event. Mood lighting spotted the walls in an ombre of deep pink to royal blue, the hanging chandeliers reflecting the colors and sparkling. Potted wisteria trees dangled tendrils of creamy flowers here and there and perfumed the air. Black linen tablecloths covered the tables, vases of fresh-cut flowers at the center of each table with white linen chairs scattered around the room. At the head of the space sprawled a stage housing a podium and a movie-theater-sized projection screen, the name of the charity splashed across it. On the far side of the room past the tables was a dance floor, a live band to the side of it already strumming this evening's warm-up set. They kept it low and peaceful allowing the crowd to mingle. The whole ensemble gave off a garden fantasy vibe on an upscale level, of course.

"Over there, by the stage..." I indicated to the older couple. "Those our are hosts, Forrest and Colleen."

She eyed them critically. "They definitely don't look like grieving parents who lost a son, missing or dead."

"No, they surely don't," I agreed, doing my best to keep the frown of disdain from my expression.

"Did you want to meander our way over and have a little friendly chat with our gracious hosts?" She wiggled her brows.

"Kenna," I warned. "Rule number one."

"Right, don't do anything stupid."

"It's best if we avoid them. We wouldn't want to trigger any memories of the warehouse fire." Due to their son's involvement in the fire, they more than likely knew about Mads's part and the accusation she slandered on their precious heir. For influential people like the Westons, kidnapping and assault weren't labels you'd want attached to your son's name and therefore attached to yours. The whole thing had been quietly swept under the rug just as their daughter's suicide had been years ago. Not a single newspaper or website reported on the incident at the warehouse.

The Westons had a business to protect. It wasn't just a business but a family legacy Sterling was supposed to take over. Kind of hard to do when he was living in hiding.

"Fine." She sighed regrettably, her lips falling into a disappointed frown. "Have you seen any sign of him?"

"No, not yet."

"Well, we can't just stand here scowling at everyone. We should find our table before the presentation begins," she suggested.

I'd really wanted this to be a quick venture, in and out, but it didn't seem as if the night would go in that direction. I wanted to rush Kenna out of here. I couldn't help but feel as if we were caught in the enemy's lair, and Sterling waited on the sidelines ready to trap us in a cage.

"We're skipping dinner tonight."

With a polite smile, she said, "You owe me dinner then later. A fancy dinner. No damn McDonald's."

If Sterling wasn't working the floor alongside his parents, then he was lurking somewhere in this building. It was a lot of square footage to cover, but while the rest of the partygoers wined and dined, Kenna and I would be doing a little recon. "Anywhere you want. You pick the time and the place."

As people started to take their seats, Kenna and I slipped out of the room. The staff at the entrance to the hall didn't give us a second glance. We headed toward the doors where we had entered, but as we approached a hallway, I glanced over my shoulder to peek at the two event greeters. They were shooting the shit among themselves, paying us no attention. I grabbed Kenna's arm and yanked her down the corridor.

"Hey—"

I put my finger to her lips, silencing her protest.

Her eyes narrowed, saying all the things she wanted to verbally throw at me. "Next time you want to toss me around, give me a heads-up," she grumbled quietly, keeping her voice low.

"Take your shoes off," I ordered. "Your heels make too much noise on these floors."

She lifted one foot, slipping off a shoe. "Is there anything else you need me to remove?" The other one came next as she balanced on one leg.

I dug into the pocket of my black trousers and pulled out the earpiece, fitting it inside my ear. Pressing the little switch, I steered Kenna down the vacant hallway, her heels hooked into her fingers. "Status?" I said, the earbud picking up my voice for Brock to hear.

"Nothing yet," he replied a few seconds later. "Just a few smokers and staff on break."

"If you see anything—"

"You'll be the first to know." He swore before I could finish. "I'm assuming it's been a dead end for you too?"

I raked a hand through my hair. "Yeah, not a trace yet."

"Is that Brock?" Kenna interrupted, rising on her toes as she leaned in close to me. "Tell him to suck a nut."

Brock chuckled in my ear. "Good luck, man."

The connection went dead, and I pulled the earbud out, dropping it back into my pocket.

Kenna pouted, yet it wasn't sincere. "Rude. How come I didn't get one of those?" she demanded, referring to my earpiece.

I regarded her. "For the sole reason you would abuse the privilege. Now focus."

"On what? He isn't here," Ms. Pessimist snapped.

"Maybe not. But we are not leaving until we've searched every room. Even the locked ones."

"Sounds exhilarating," she said dully.

"I'll let you pick the lock."

Her lips twitched. "Finally, something I can get behind."

The main floor had another event room as well as the pro shop, locker rooms, and a lounge. The Normandy room wasn't being used tonight and was completely dark as Kenna and I stuck our heads in. A set of stairs sat just outside the hall. We had to check the other side of the first floor, but we could do that on our way down once we finished upstairs.

I'd studied the layout of the club earlier in the week and had a copy of the floor plan on my phone for reference. The second level had a bar and outdoor patio, and the top hosted the main restaurant, but none of them were open tonight and were off-limits to guests, making the upper levels like a ghost town.

We rounded the top of the stairs, walking to the first set of doors leading into the bar. Only a few security lights were on in the otherwise dark room. Kenna moved behind the bar, picking up a bottle and holding it up with a grin.

I shook my head. "You don't need liquor."

She pouted again.

A light flashed down the hallway, and I whirled in the direction of the open door behind us.

*Shit!*

I automatically reached for Kenna's hand. "Someone's coming," I whisper-hissed. My eyes darted left and right, looking for somewhere to hide. Behind the bar was our only option, but it provided little coverage. We'd be spotted with a single swoop of the security guard's flashlight. Keys jingled in time with the guard's footsteps. I had no choice but to come up with a valid reason for us to be in a restricted part of the club. My fingers intertwined with Kenna's, and I yanked her against me, catching her waist with my other hand.

Her eyes went wide as she looked up at me, palms flattening on my chest. "What are you doing?"

The pad of my thumb ran over the inside of her wrist was meant to assure her everything would be okay. Her pulse leaped under my touch. "Improvising. Unless you want to get kicked out." I didn't give her a chance to protest. Lifting my other hand, I cupped the side of her face, watching her eyes darken.

This definitely wasn't how I pictured our first kiss, but fuck it. I had few other options. "I'm going to kiss you," I whispered. It was her choice. I would never force her to do anything. "Okay?"

When she only stared at me, neither arguing, panicking, or pulling away, I took that as encouragement, but I needed her to say it. I needed to hear it.

The light shone right outside the door, growing brighter. "Kenna, tell me—"

"Yes," she said breathily, lifting on her toes, her eyes never leaving mine.

A little gasp tumbled from her lips right before I took possession of them. Her mouth was so fucking soft. A million times I'd thought about kissing those pouty lips of hers, but nothing prepared me for having them pressed to mine. She stayed still, a little rigid in my arms, and that wouldn't do. I ran my tongue along the crease of her lips, tasting her. I wanted to slip in and let her discover the taste of me, but now wasn't the time for any of that despite the wants.

Kissing Kenna would change everything because this wasn't part of the gig. Everything I felt was very real, including the instant lust that slammed into me.

Greedily, I wanted to do more than commit the taste and feel of her to memory. I wanted to make her mine.

7

———

KENNA

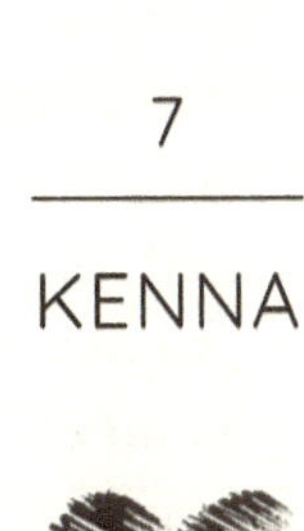

**A** million times I'd thought about kissing Fynn. What it would be like to have him pressed against me, to take me into his arms, to wrap himself up in the passion created by a single kiss. I always envisioned our first kiss would be intense, feverish, a bit desperate, and hungry. Years of suppressed need releasing and crashing together in a tangle of wild passion.

Fynn kissed me with such careful restraint I almost wondered if he didn't feel what I did. Perhaps it was all an act, a cover to keep us from being caught snooping around.

But then his tongue traced over my mouth a second time, and I realized he was holding back. He was giving me the opportunity to change my mind. To put an end to the kiss whenever I chose.

The problem was I didn't want to stop kissing. Ever.

I wanted more.

More of Fynn.

More of the tingling warmth he created.

More of his kiss.

I faintly saw a flash of light behind my closed eyes, but any thoughts of who entered weren't in existence, not when every part of my brain brimmed with Fynn.

Parting my lips, I invited him to take the kiss deeper, begging him to. And as if the message wasn't clear enough, I pressed farther into the hard planes of his body, my fingers traveling up his chest and over his wide shoulders to wind around his neck. Fynn didn't disappoint. His tongue dove into my mouth, brushing up against mine for the first full taste of him and coaxing me to play, teasing and tormenting. I was game.

My core tightened, and I whimpered against his mouth, my fingers tangling into the ends of his hair.

Someone cleared their throat. Neither of us pulled away. In fact, I was annoyed by the interruption. I didn't want to stop. The glorious heat swirling within me was a feeling I'd never felt before.

There was more.

I could sense it.

And I wanted to explore it with Fynn.

The clearing of a throat sounded again, louder and more forceful.

Fynn's hand moved from the side of my hip to the small of my back and began to trace up my exposed skin. He left behind little sparks of excitement. I shuddered in his arms.

He ended the kiss slowly, like a man who didn't want to quit, and I moaned at the loss of his lips, the warmth of them, but he kept me close, his arm around my waist and not letting go.

"You can't be in here," the club security guard said, shining his flashlight onto our faces unnecessarily. It was dim in the room but not wholly dark enough to need the extra light.

My cheeks blazed but not because we'd been caught. I buried my face into the side of Fynn's neck, inhaling his scent. My lips brushed just under his ear, and his pulse quickened, causing a heady bloom of pleasure to fan in my chest.

I wanted to find all of Fynn's sensitive spots. I wanted to know what drove him crazy. What pushed him over the edge. What made me groan. What made his eyes darken with lust.

And more importantly, I longed for him to discover those very same things about me because I didn't have the first clue what I liked or didn't like.

Not true.

Thanks to Fynn, I now knew I very much loved kissing him.

And I couldn't wait to do it again.

In fact, I was having a very hard time keeping my lips off him. And my fingers.

This was new territory for me.

Why, of all the places in the world, did we have to be here?

Then again, perhaps I should thank the guard. If he hadn't shown up, I might still be only dreaming about kissing Fynn Dupree, instead of actually having kissed him.

"Sorry, we were looking for a moment away from the crowd," Fynn explained, squinting against the light blinding us. His body stiffened against mine, and I could tell he didn't like having the momentary disadvantage.

"This section is closed to guests," the guard replied, moving farther into the room, the light from his flashlight bouncing with his footsteps. "Only the first floor is open tonight."

Fynn lifted his hand, blocking the flash.

"Fynn? Is that you?" the guard asked, finally lowering his light so we could get a look at his face. Something in his tone changed.

*Fuck.*

The security guy was no older than we were, and a cord of familiarity struck me as I stared at his face. Fynn must have sensed it too. I thought maybe we had gone to the Academy together, but I couldn't recall the guard's name for the life of me.

Fynn gave an annoyed sigh.

"Sorry, man. I didn't know you were here." The security guard started to back out of the room, a smirk on his face. "Just pretend like I was never here." His gaze shifted to me, the grin slipping a fraction.

He had recognized Fynn immediately but not me at first. With a second glance though, he realized who Fynn had been kissing.

"I can't let you leave," Fynn said coldly, unfolding the arm secured around me.

*What?* My head whirled to Fynn as he stepped toward the guard.

I blinked and Fynn's fist went flying, crashing into the guard's face. The poor idiot's eyes rolled back in his head, and then he fell, his body thudding to the ground.

My mouth fell open. "What the hell, Fynn? Why did you hit him?"

His jaw was still clenched. "He saw you."

I rolled my eyes. "That isn't reason enough to knock the guy out cold."

Fynn pulled his glare from the unmoving form. "It is to me. Come on, we need to return to the party."

"You think?" I replied sarcastically. "What about him?"

"He'll be fine," Fynn said, unfazed. "By the time he comes to, we'll be gone hopefully. He won't say anything regardless."

Without giving me a second to protest, Fynn took my hand and dragged me around the body and out of the room. We never made it to the third floor. "You don't think we should continue our search while he's out?" I asked as we trotted down the stairs to the main level.

"My gut is telling me it's a waste. He would want to be close to the party, close to his sister. He might not want to show his face, but he would still want to honor her."

Fynn was probably right. At least one of us was thinking clearly.

After a kiss like that, I needed a moment to get my emotions and more importantly, my body under control. There was this humming still moving through me. If I continued to stay in Fynn's presence with him hovering and so close, I'd do something reckless like shove him into an empty room and take full advantage of him, completely forgetting the real reason we were here.

It wasn't to get laid.

"I need to pee," I said when we walked back into the hall. "And yes, I can manage alone." Dessert had been served. Most of the guests had finished and were sipping on coffee, the chatter of the evening continuing.

After I slipped my shoes back on, Fynn guided me to the bathrooms, beside the bar. "You got two minutes before I come to get you."

"*I'll* find you when *I'm* done," I insisted. Fynn might try to strongarm me, but we'd known each other too long for that shit to fly with me.

His scowl deepened, and I could tell he wanted to argue. I didn't give him the chance and spun on my heels, heading to the ladies' room. Once inside, I closed myself into a stall until the two women freshening up their hair and makeup finished and left, leaving me alone.

Flushing the toilet, I strolled to the sinks, dropping my wristlet onto the counter. My hands came to rest on either side of the sink as I stared at my reflection. I looked quite the sight. My lipstick was faded and worn off by Fynn's kiss. I brushed a finger over my lip, my mind wandering back to the feel of Fynn's mouth on mine.

I wasn't supposed to be lingering over Fynn's lips or his taste or the scent of him, but damn if he hadn't affected all my senses at once.

Frustrated on multiple accounts, I ripped off the wig, tossing it on top of my wristlet with a sigh.

*Where is this asshole? Why hasn't he shown up yet?*

I didn't want all the effort that went into this night to go unrewarded. Sterling was here. I felt it in my bones, but he was cunning enough not to show his face. This was a charity in honor of his sister, a cause for suicide prevention. He wouldn't miss it. That I was certain of.

Pissed off, I needed to do something.

Digging around in my purse, I shoved the contents around until I found what I searched for—a tube of lipstick. It wasn't spray paint. I had to improvise, but it would still get my point across.

I'd been joking earlier with Fynn about writing on the bathroom mirror with lipstick, or perhaps subconsciously, I planned to do it all along.

I quickly flipped the lock to the bathroom entrance so I wouldn't be interrupted by anyone, including Fynn. Uncapping the tube as I lifted on my tiptoes, I leaned over the sink, and began to spell out a warning. This might be the ladies' bathroom, but I had a sneaky suspicion Sterling would still see or hear about what I left behind. No one liked to whisper more than rich housewives.

If he wouldn't show his face, the least I could do was leave him a note. He would do the same.

Perhaps he already had, and we'd been looking for the wrong thing. Perhaps we should be searching for clues instead of a person.

Something along the lines of do you see the monster staring back at you? I see you for who you are. It needed a little work, but I liked where my mind was going. Chewing on my lower lip, I started to write it out.

After writing two words, I cocked my head to the side and admired my handiwork. My lips curved, a smile forming on them.

"I was hoping we would get a moment alone."

I jumped, nearly falling into the damn sink. After steadying myself, my eyes flew up, looking off to the side of the mirror at the sound of his voice.

Sterling.

*How the fuck?*

*I locked the door. Hadn't I?*

Yes, I distinctly remembered flipping the lock. I wasn't a careless vandalizer. Then how had he gotten inside the bathroom? Unless there was a secret entrance, he'd already been inside the ladies' room, or had he followed me inside? I didn't remember hearing the door open when I'd been inside the stall, but it was the only thing that made sense.

Fear spiked in my blood, icing the rush I'd felt just seconds ago. "So, you are here. I was beginning to wonder if you were too scared to show your face."

"Kenna." He laughed, my name sounding sharp on his tongue. "I knew you wouldn't disappoint, but I must admit I was surprised he brought you. Ballsy." He shifted, giving me full access to his face.

I gasped, immediately regretting the reaction. The left side of his lower jaw and neck, perhaps farther on his body, was covered with scars. They were minor burns, not nearly as horrible as some victims suffered, and from a distance might not be visible at all, but up close, there was no denying he'd endured his own demons from that night almost two years ago. It was crazy to think that this fall would be two years since the warehouse fire, since he tormented my cousin, leaving her with a scar of her own.

Sterling's amber eyes darkened. Displeasure showed in the furrowing of his brows. I got the feeling he was disappointed in my response to the scars. "An unsightly reminder of our past."

He mistook my surprise for disgust, but it wasn't revulsion I felt.

Gathering my composure, I wanted to turn around and face him, but I also didn't want to take my gaze off him for a single moment. Pretending I hadn't heard his comment about his disfigurement, I responded to his previous remark. It seemed a safer less hostile conversation where fewer emotions of hatred might be involved. The last thing I wanted to do was enrage Sterling. "Fynn's balls are quite large," I replied.

His lips curved. "I'll take your word for it." His attention flicked off me to my unfinished message. "I've appreciated your means of communication. A little outdated, but I like the touch of femineity."

My fingers clutched the lipstick tube. "Yeah, well, I find your means of communication weak and pitiful. You hide behind your phone."

His head angled, regarding me. "And you hide behind your hoodies in the dark of night. How are we so different?"

"For starters, I don't want to kill anyone." I spun then, a quick, whirling movement. "Except for you, that is."

He stood between me and the door, my only means of escape. "I knew I'd like you. I've been thinking perhaps you and I should join forces. Imagine what we could do together?"

All I could think was to keep him talking. "And why is that?"

His lips twisted to one side. "Other than we both enjoy tormenting people with words, I think we have a lot in common. With me, you would be the star that shines. You wouldn't have to compete with anyone else. You wouldn't have to take orders from someone who thinks they know what's best for you."

"Tempting, but I can only deal with one psycho in a relationship, and that position is currently being filled by me."

He took a cagey step closer. "You believe someone like Fynn complements you?"

"That's not what I said. Why would you think that?" I snarled.

The black tux he wore was tailored to his form, moving with him as he adjusted the cuff at his wrist. "He enjoys watching you, almost as much as I do."

I banked the shudder that tapped up my spine. "Creepy."

"The two of you look awfully close tonight. Or is that part of the gig? I like the wig, by the way. Nice touch."

He'd been watching us. It was expected. He liked to watch, to pretend he had eyes everywhere. Spying had always been his thing. Even in college, prior to learning of his vendetta against Micah, I remembered the video setup in the frat house and how he had cameras in various girls' dorms, including ours.

Vile burned the back of my throat, but I refused to show him the terror he craved. He wasn't the first monster I'd faced, and as difficult as it was to keep the fear at bay, I would rather go down fighting than ever show fright to an asshole like him.

My fingers slipped to the inside of my thigh, brushing over the strap holding my knife. "Fynn and I have always been close."

He chuckled. "You know what I mean, Kenna. *Close*. As in his tongue down your throat. Not exactly the ideal place for an ass grab, is it? I'm sure half our guests tonight would be appalled by your behavior."

"But not you," I pointed out, my ass pressed firmly against the sink.

"I mean, for the price of these tickets, a show isn't that unreasonable."

Was he threatening to show a video feed? It was a kiss. He didn't really believe I would care if anyone saw me lip-locked with Fynn. I'd been exposed for way worse. "I think we've come to the oh shit part of the show." I grabbed the end of my blade, yanked it out of its holster, and pointed it toward Sterling.

He grinned, backing up a step or two. "I love a plot twist."

"Unlock the door," I demanded, keeping the blade steady in my hand and aimed at Sterling.

Excitement radiated in his amber eyes. "Do you really think I came here to hurt you?"

I moved a step forward. "It doesn't fucking matter to me. Unlock the door, or I cut you."

"Normally this is where I would call someone's bluff, but I actually believe you would enjoy hurting me."

He was right. I would. "Smart." I angled the knife closer to his chest for a bit more encouragement because impatience swam in my blood. I wanted to get away from him so I could breathe again without the pain in my chest.

Never taking his eyes off mine, he backed to the door. With slow movements, he lifted his hand, blindly searching for the lock above the knob.

*Click.*

The lock flipped open.

He stayed in front of the door, the cocky grin firm on his lips. He found amusement in our situation, enjoyment even. "By the time you find him, I'll be gone."

I moved off to the side, giving Sterling room to strut away from the door. "I guess we'll find out. Get inside one of the stalls."

Every order I barked entertained him more, but he shifted toward the second bathroom. Perhaps he really didn't have any intention of harming me because I think we both knew he couldn't get a better opportunity to do so than now.

*What is his agenda?*

*What is he up to?*

I should be rushing out the door, racing toward freedom. "Why have you waited so long? Why now?" I asked, peppering him with questions that had plagued my mind.

He gave me an awkward shrug. "Have you seen this face?"

I shook my head, strands of my tied-up hair breaking free. "I'm not buying it."

"Smart girl."

I opened the door, wedging my leg in the hole, and used my foot to prop it wide enough for me to slip out while keeping my hands free. My eyes never wavered from Sterling's. Not even when the bastard winked. "I'll be seeing you soon, Kenna darling."

Shooting him a snarky grin, I retorted in the same wily pitch, "I hope sooner than you think."

His lips twitched. "Say hi to the boys for me."

*Bastard.*

There was no lock on the outside of the door to my great disappointment. I didn't want to leave him and risk the chance he'd escape, but I also had to find Fynn.

I didn't have to look long or far. Fynn's gaze connected with mine at the end of the hall, a scowl marring his lips. As I rushed toward him, he noticed something was wrong and started toward me, his long legs carrying him more than halfway to me. "What happened?" he asked before I could utter a word.

"Sterling." I breathed through slightly parted lips. "He's here."

His muscles tensed. "Are you okay?" Fynn's gaze ran over my face before moving over my body to check for himself. I'd completely forgotten about the knife still clutched in my grip until Fynn took it from me.

Exhaling, I nodded. "He's in the bathroom."

Fynn surged past me, heading to the ladies' room. He didn't

think twice about bursting inside. I didn't follow him inside but stayed in the hallway chewing on my thumbnail waiting for him to return.

From the racket from the other side of the door, I could guess Fynn kicked each stall door in, searching for Sterling.

Before Fynn came bursting back out of the bathroom, the pit in my gut told me Sterling was already gone. Fynn wouldn't find him in there.

The pit turned into a sinking rock when I saw Fynn's face. Nothing about his expression looked friendly. His green eyes were cold chips of ice, ready to freeze a man.

"He's gone," I muttered, a chill skirting down my spine.

Fynn nodded. "What did he say to you?"

I should have stabbed him. Regret weighed heavy on my shoulders. "He said he wouldn't hurt me."

Fynn snorted.

The room was suddenly colder than it had been before I went into the bathroom. I rubbed my hands over my arms. "And he asked me to join his team."

He cast me a dark look. "What the fuck does that mean? Join him? In what, destroying us?" he growled.

I blinked. "I don't know. I didn't stick around to ask what his nefarious master plan was and what my role would be."

"This isn't a joke, Kenna." Fynn snatched my arm, and then we were moving briskly through the hall. He inserted his earpiece, calling Brock again. "Be ready," he said quietly. "The bastard's on the move and probably looking for an escape." With a click of his finger, he ended the call.

We were drawing a few wary glances, but I was past caring. "What the hell's the plan if we catch him?"

"I haven't thought that far ahead. And it's not our problem. You and I are leaving."

I yanked my arm, fed up with being hauled around by him. "Fynn. What the hell? We're so close. Why would we leave now and let him slip through our fingers? You can leave, but I'm not going anywhere."

He whirled on me. "Do I need to remind you of rule number three?"

"Fuck your rules. I'll find him myself." I was angry. He'd been right in front of me. I should have brought my stun gun instead of a knife. The bastard would be writhing on the bathroom floor.

"Don't make a scene, brat," Fynn hissed through gritted teeth and a false smile.

I grinned. "You should know me better than that. I love being the center of attention. Negative attention? Even better."

He let out a growl of frustration. "Kenna, for once, can you not make everything difficult?"

"No. Can we go kick his ass now?" He made me want to pull my damn hair out.

"Thirsty for violence, brat? Who knew you could be so murderous."

The sigh expelling from my lips was long and brimming with exasperation. "Fynn."

He threw up his hands. "Fine, have it your way."

I relaxed, and that was my mistake. One moment. That was all it took for Fynn to dip down and haul my ass over his shoulder as if I weighed nothing. A slew of reactions ran through my head, but none of them would get Fynn to release me. I wanted to fight him with teeth, claws, fists, whatever I had at my disposal, but I blew out a hot, angry breath. With my ass in the air and my head hanging down his back, he walked us out of the party and into the hallway.

I ignored the mutterings and whisperings. They only fueled my rage.

He didn't put me down until we were outside. Oliver was there with the black town car waiting for us. He didn't blink twice at seeing Fynn carrying me out of the club, and he wisely kept his face neutral as I smacked my date in the chest. Oliver just stood with the door open, waiting for us to get in.

"You'll pay for that later," I promised Fynn, my voice pledging sweet revenge when he least expected it.

Fynn gave me one of his unreadable looks, nothing about his posture or demeanor changing. "Get in the car. Oliver will take you home."

"Do you honestly believe I'll stay home?" The second the threat left my lips, regret was instant. I groaned. Why hadn't I kept that information to myself? There was no way Fynn was letting me leave alone now. I figuratively shot myself in the foot.

Fynn cursed under his breath, crowding me closer to the car with his body. He trapped me between him and the open door with no chance of escape. The only way to go was in. I considered going through the car and out the other side, but the jerk was right behind me as I climbed into the back seat.

Fynn leaned into the car, the spicy scent of him surrounding me. "Scoot unless you want to sit on my lap."

I bared my teeth. "Right now, I don't even want to be in the same car with you."

His hands went to shimmy under my legs, but I scrambled to the other side of the seat before he could touch me. As soon as the door shut, the car took off through the circular driveway of the country club. I sat back in the seat, giving Fynn the silent treatment, and glared out the dark window.

Ten minutes went by without a word. If he didn't say something, I was going to throw myself out of the car. I wanted a fight. He knew I wanted to argue, to yell at him. Sometimes having him know me so well drove me batshit crazy.

Shedding his jacket and tie, he undid the first few buttons of his shirt. "Should we talk about what happened?" His tone softened, losing some of its rough edges.

I tried to keep hold of my anger. "I thought we said all there was on the matter. *You* gave up. *You* bailed ship. *You* let him get away."

Fynn's gaze was on me as he rolled up his sleeves. "I protected you. Besides, I wasn't talking about Sterling. I meant what happened upstairs."

The kiss.

He wanted to discuss our kiss.

I'd been so fixated on Sterling that I'd pushed what happened between Fynn and me to the back of my mind, but now that he mentioned it again...

I peeked at his lips. *Why did you do that? Don't look at his mouth. Don't even think about his lips.*

Fuck him for being so damn hot.

And fuck me for being so damn weak.

I forced my gaze to his eyes, fixing him with a narrowed glare. "Nothing happened. Nothing ever happens between us, Fynn."

"Do you want something to happen?" His voice lowered, and I hated that my body responded to him.

"You know I did once. But we grew up. We're friends now. And I got over my crush." The words felt raw and wrong as they left my mouth.

Lies. It was all lies.

But I wasn't sure if I was lying to him or myself.

8

———

FYNN

enna was wrong.

But I could wait.

I wasn't as patient as Brock, but I also wasn't a hothead like Grayson. I fell somewhere in between.

I wouldn't push her. Not yet, but tonight I'd gotten an answer to a question that had lingered in the back of my mind for six years.

She tasted far sweeter than I imagined and a hell of a lot more tempting.

And she'd kissed me back. Not just a simple kiss for show. She lost herself, and damn, if I didn't want to reach across the seat, drag her into my lap, and show her what else I could do with my lips.

Her every response heightened the exploration and discovery of what could be.

Kenna was complicated. If I pushed too much too fast, I risked the chance of spooking her. When it came to relationships, she didn't easily trust or let people in. She had to be the one to drive this thing between us, or at least I had to make her think she was.

The car stopped in front of the rowhouse, and Kenna's hand flew to the handle, but before she got out of the car, she turned to me and said, "Oh, he has scars on his face from the fire. I'm not sure how helpful that is, but it's more than we knew about him this morning."

I filed away the information to share with the guys when they returned.

Thanking Oliver, I sent him home and got out after Kenna, watching her stomp off inside the house. I stayed on the front porch, sitting on the steps. A rare calmness settled over campus, the only sound coming from a fly buzzing around the outside light as it continually flew into the sconce.

Defeat and fury coursed through my blood as I waited but not for my friends to return with news they hadn't seen Sterling. When I hadn't heard a word from Brock, Micah, or Grayson, I figured as much. No. I waited for the text I knew was to come.

Sterling didn't disappoint.

My gaze lifted to the sky, and I counted the number of stars I could see. It distracted me and kept my mind away from thoughts I didn't want to have, kind of like counting sheep to fall asleep. By the time I reached forty-seven stars, my phone buzzed in my back pocket.

I leaned to the side, to see what smartass torment Sterling had waiting for us. He no longer hid behind an alias as he had with Kate. There was no need to with the four of us.

My phone screen lit up, a message from an unknown number waiting to be read.

**Haven't you heard, nice guys finish last, but don't worry, I'll make sure Kenna finishes first. Multiple times.**

An unbridled storm of rage rippled inside me, threatening to destroy anything in my path. The urge to slam my fist into shit didn't happen often, but it hit inside me with an overwhelming impulse. It was either my phone or the banister. My body twisted slightly as my fist went into the wooden beam. The porch shook at the impact, the wood groaning from the force of my hit.

I didn't give a shit about my knuckles or the cuts bleeding. The only thing I cared about was destroying this asshole before he hurt someone else. Threatening hit a nerve, especially the implication behind his text. I was furious at him, but I was also angry with myself. Because of me, he'd been able to get close to Kenna. He'd been alone with her.

I couldn't forgive myself for putting her in danger. I knew better.

It wouldn't happen again.

* * *

Finals were this week, and then I'd be packing up to head home for the summer. The first month would be at my beach house with the crew, something we habitually started after high school, and as much as I was looking forward to getting away, my mind wouldn't be able to fully decompress, which was the whole point of the trip, to unwind after months of studying, grueling football practices, and the stress of being an Elite.

I had family responsibilities this summer. My parents were giving me a month with my friends before I was expected to fulfill those duties. I'd given myself a personal goal to find and deal with Sterling before the semester ended.

I fucking hated not meeting my goals. It looked like this operation to destroy the bastard would bleed into my summer, and after the month at the beach house, if Sterling still lurked in the shadows, I'd have to find a way to keep Kenna safe. It would be harder when the eight of us went our separate ways. The dynamics were changing. We were getting older. With a baby on the way, Grayson and Ainsley were looking for a place together. Despite how large the Edwards's household was, adding a baby would take over the house. They might be small, but it was amazing how quickly an infant could throw chaos into a home.

I had a younger sister and remembered very clearly the day my parents brought her home, but for me, it had been a happy chaos having Avery in our lives. I hadn't even minded being woken up by her loud but tiny cries.

Kenna and Josie tried to convince Ainsley and Grayson to stay once their baby was born, but by then, we'd all be starting our junior year in college.

Ainsley and Grayson weren't the only ones looking to move out of their parents' places. Josie would be spending most of the summer at Brock's house. And Mads and Micah were also talking about moving in together. It was the natural progression of life. Of relationships.

Things were evolving.

This summer would be our last together like this. Unburdened from responsibility. Carefree. A crew.

I wanted it to be the best summer of our lives. One we always remembered and not because of Sterling. I had to do something. I had to draw him out. I had to end this feud.

Walking from the library, I stopped and grabbed a protein shake before heading toward the east side of campus to the house Grayson and I shared.

The University of Dalton wasn't as large as the KU campus. A private and prestigious establishment, the college acceptance rate was half of KU's. It boasted wealth and history the second you passed under the large, bricked archway with its carved details and trailing ivy. Trees as old as the campus shaded the grounds and surrounded the old buildings beautifully maintained and preserved. There was nothing ancient about the education at Dalton. The standards for its students were high. Unlike KU, where parties were a major, most of Dalton's enrollees took their education seriously.

My mind never shut off or stopped working, and from having an overactive brain, insomnia plagued my nights. I just didn't seem to require as much sleep as the rest of my friends and was always the last one to go to bed and the first one up, annoyingly so.

I should be studying for my final tomorrow, but I had my laptop open, the smoothie long gone as I weeded through forums, looking for something useful, a sure way to trap Sterling.

Grayson wandered into the kitchen, his dark hair wet from a recent shower. He opened the fridge and took out a bottle of water. "You're quiet tonight."

For him to notice was telling. Grayson and I were comfortable in our silence together. Our house on campus wasn't like the others' rowhouse where noise and commotion were a constant norm but expected when six people were living together.

At Dalton, it was just Grayson and me. We were also two of the chillest members of our group, men of few words, which was why we roomed together so well. Days could go by without either one of us saying a thing. The silence in our house was like a third person living with us. Always there.

"I'm always quiet," I replied, grinning, but the grin didn't fool him.

"We'll get him," Grayson vowed, knowing what occupied my thoughts tonight. It was on all our minds.

"I know," I sighed, leaning back in my chair and stretching my neck out left and right. I'd been staring at this screen for too many hours. "I wanted him dealt with before we left school." My worry-free, leisurely summer didn't look like it would happen.

Grayson slumped into the chair across from me. "We all did." Grayson tended to spend more weekends at KU with Ainsley lately since the incident at Demon's. It was hard for him to leave her each week, and it made me wonder if he would return to Dalton in the fall.

He had some big decisions to make this summer, and by the end of it, his life would change.

He would be the father of a little girl.

I was both excited and worried for my best friend. I imagined he felt the same but tenfold. Navigating his new life would take effort and sacrifice, but Ainsley and he had a strong group of friends who would do whatever it took to make sure this baby was happy and healthy.

Their little girl hadn't even been born yet and she was spoiled as shit.

We hadn't talked about the last text we received, and I honestly was sick of discussing Sterling. When I wasn't concentrating on classes or football, my thoughts were cursed with the psychotic prick, worrying about what he might do next.

"I'm so over this fucker," I said, rubbing at the back of my neck.

There was no downtime for anything else. Another reason I'd been so looking forward to the summer. We could have conversations that didn't involve stalking, death, revenge, resentment, and scheming.

Grayson uncapped his water and took a drink. "He didn't say anything to Kenna?"

Shaking my head, I frowned across the table. "I should have put a mic on her." The regret was evident in my tone.

"You can't blame yourself, Fynn. Kenna's as unpredictable as Sterling. We should be grateful she didn't try to take him down herself."

"I have this bad feeling," I admitted. "Maybe it's because we went so long without a shred of proof he was alive, and now that he is, the tension is back. But it feels different this time."

His brows inched together in deep thought as he considered my reservations. "I get it. He'd been so singularly focused on Micah before and hurting him."

My expression remained stony. "Kenna said he has scars on his face from the fire. Someone like Sterling's going to see that as our fault. He will hold us accountable for the pain he suffered."

The hand clenched around his water was white around the knuckles. "Good. Nothing he suffered will come close to paying for what he did to Mads."

That we could both agree on. "There's something he said to Kenna that's bothering me."

Grayson's inquisitive brow lifted.

Hardness entered my voice. "He asked her to join him, or something along those lines. That they would make a great team."

He stared at me with narrowed eyes. "You're concerned he might shift his attention to my sister."

I nodded, picking up a pen off the table and twining it between my fingers. "Perhaps." Or something worse. "If he knows about her past..." I couldn't help but think of his last text and the implication behind it.

Grayson frowned. "He could really hurt her."

He wasn't talking about just physically. It was the deep scars in Kenna's past that had nearly healed but not completely. They were the kind of wounds that could be easily reopened with the right triggers, and none of us wanted Kenna to go back to the dark place that took her two years to crawl out of.

I applied pressure to the pen sandwiched between my fingers, listening to the plastic crack. "We won't let that happen."

I'd learned it was easy to make promises. Easy to think you're stronger and smarter than your opponent. Easy to let cockiness overrule levelheadedness. I was guilty of all.

I wanted to believe this time would be different—that we had the upper hand—that we would prevail. I didn't believe this had anything to do with good versus evil. It was more like the lesser of two evils. Or perhaps it was greater.

"But I do know that killing yourself all night on your laptop is going to burn you out," he added. "Get some sleep tonight. And more than just an hour or two."

Grayson meant well. "I can sleep when we get to the beach."

"Uh-huh," he mumbled, disbelievingly. I couldn't blame him. I was incapable of slowing down. There was no on-and-off switch, but damn, if I didn't wish I had one some nights.

Tonight particularly.

Grayson stood, taking his bottle of water. "I better not see you slumped over the table when I wake up."

I made a gruff, inaudible response, my attention already back on my laptop.

His footsteps traveled to the back of the hallway, his door clicking shut, and a few moments later, the silence returned. Our rented house was only three bedrooms; the third was unoccupied per our request and used as an office that also doubled as a spare bedroom for when we had guests.

He was right. I should go to bed, and I would in shortly after I checked a few things.

## 9

# KENNA

As I left my last class for the semester, I broke free from the art building and took my first step into summer vacation. I swore the air felt cleaner in my lungs, or was it that my chest was lighter?

The reprieve from the pressures of school would be short, but I'd freaking take it.

Unlike my friends, I didn't have a clear path of what career I wanted for the rest of my life. It seemed like such a daunting decision to make at twenty. Not to mention a fucking commitment. Neither of which I was ready to make.

My friends were so confident in their choices, and I felt like I was floating through college, taking the necessary required classes with no real objective. Being here for the *experience* wouldn't cut it during my last two years of school.

I needed to figure my shit out.

Exactly what I planned to do this summer, but first I had thirty days of sun, sand, and endless margaritas on the beach. I looked forward to doing nothing but lying around and binge-watching movies with my friends. Bonfires at night with the guys roasting marshmallows. Cookouts on the deck. And the best part? No Sterling. No one knew we were leaving. We made sure to keep it between us and our parents.

I wanted thirty carefree days before I got serious about my future. Once I returned home, my parents would hit me with the questions I'd been skillfully dodging since college started. They were only concerned and mostly supportive, but because they cared so much, they also worried.

Of course, I *should* be pondering my future. As much as I liked scheming and serving justice, I thought about doing something in law enforcement, but I didn't like rules as much as Grayson did. Or blood for that matter. It didn't seem like a good fit.

Maybe a private investigator. I could start my own business.

Still, I didn't know if that was me.

But the art major I currently had on my file at KU couldn't be more far off on the spectrum than being a PI. I was clueless.

I had other things on my mind.

Since my encounter with Sterling, I couldn't stop thinking about something he said. It gave me this idea, and I had been mulling it over, trying to work out details and convince myself it was a horrible idea.

And it probably was, but sometimes the worst ideas turned out to be the best-laid plans. Or so I hoped.

Regardless, the goal was to have the details ironed out by the time I left the beach house. While everyone else read books, took naps on the beach, or played volleyball, I'd use those downtime minutes to plot.

Mads met me at the fountain where our Thursday classes intersected. She grinned at me as I approached, a ray of sunlight beating at her back. Her long honey hair fell loose over her shoulders, pieces framing her heart-shaped face. "We're free, bitch," she said, looping her arm through mine as we continued to walk through campus. We only had a few blocks to get to our house.

Our footsteps matched. "I never want to see another math problem again."

She laughed. "Well, you have a few months at most."

I groaned, rubbing at the bridge of my nose. "I can guarantee that I will never need to know logarithms again."

Her gray eyes sparkled. "God, let's hope not."

"Are you packing up and leaving this afternoon?"

Mads nodded. "Yeah. You?"

A guy speed-walked past us, eager to get out of here as much as I was. "Please. My bags are already packed. I'm dropping them off at home and will be headed to the beach first thing in the morning. Mom and Dad made us swear to a family dinner before we leave."

"Are Aunt Liana and Uncle Chandler still planning to spend a few weeks in Europe?" my cousin asked.

My parents had been saying for years how they wanted to tour through Europe once we were older, and this summer, my dad surprised my mom on their anniversary. "Yeah. They'll be gone for six weeks. Part business and part pleasure."

"We need to plan a trip somewhere. It's been forever since we went on a proper vacation together," she said, and I couldn't agree more.

"Spring break next year?" I suggested.

Her lips curved. "I wished we would have done something before the baby comes."

I lightly bumped my shoulder against hers. "What do you think we're doing for the next four weeks?"

"True. I so need this."

"I think we all do," I agreed. "Nothing beats an Elite summer."

"Nothing does, does it? Are you riding down with Grayson?" she asked, assuming my brother and I would drive up together like we usually did.

A breeze blew through the trees, carrying a whiff of something sweet in the air. "He wants me to, but I'm going to drive myself. I need the solace. Just me, the open road, the top down on the convertible, and the music cranked."

Mads tucked her hair behind her ears. "I'm not going to lie. I'm a little envious. Micah has the worst taste in music."

I chuckled. "But he does have a fantastic voice." I'd heard him belt out some of the best rock 'n' roll like he was born to sing. Out of the four guys, Micah was the only one who could hold a tune.

"If you don't mind listening to "Joker" on repeat," she said dully.

I rolled my eyes. "That would be his favorite song."

When we got to the house, I went straight to my room and collected my bags. Since we renewed our lease for the next term, we didn't have to pack up all our belongings. I only had one bag to grab the clothes I wanted to take home with me, and the rest of the stuff I was leaving here. Still, the fridge had to be emptied and the trash had to be taken out, both of which I thought Brock and Micah had dealt with.

As much as I loved school, I was anxious for summer. I loved all seasons, but there was something about summer that spoke to my soul. Maybe it was the hot days and long, warm, star-strewn nights, but from June to October, I was in my element.

As I took one last wistful look at my college room, a sense of sentiment ribboned through me. This room had been my haven for the last year. "See you in the fall," I murmured, shutting the door behind me.

* * *

The drive home had been uneventful except for the moment when my brother raced past me doing well over the speed limit. He was such an asshole. Unlike Grayson and Sawyer, our older brother who died, I didn't share their love for reckless speeds.

I thought they were insane. And after what happened to Sawyer, my heart sunk a little each time Grayson entered a race. If our mother found out he'd followed in Sawyer's footsteps, she probably would sell all the cars. I thought about telling her once or twice, but I never seemed to be able to betray my brother.

A notion I blamed on our triplet bond.

But nothing beat the drive to Oceanbay.

The trip was a little over three hours, and the majority of the ride hugged the coast, making it one of the most scenic routes on the East Coast. I couldn't have asked for a better day to travel. The sun was high in the cloudless sky, beaming down on me through the opened convertible. I had traded in my Jeep for something a little more fun to zip around in while at the beach, and the wind blew through my hair, sending it flying around my head in a messy halo. The big shades protected my eyes from not just the sun's rays but the windblown strands of hair.

Taylor Swift's newest album distracted me from getting caught up in the thoughts I wanted a break from. I sipped on my iced coffee, singing and enjoying this feeling of happiness that for me came in spurts. Depression was a beast. It didn't care about how much money you had, how big your house was, or how many friends were at your side. It didn't give a shit about the expensive clothes you wore or how fabulous your life might seem, or if you were currently happy. When it snuck up on me, nothing else mattered. It sucked me in, digging its claws in, and at that moment, depression felt as if it would never let go.

I hadn't felt the clutches of depression in years, and I wouldn't let it creep in this summer. Whenever I sensed even an inkling of those shadows looming was when I broke out the spray cans. At first, it had been for revenge, a way to get back at all the people who I thought were my friends. If trauma and tragedy taught me one thing, it was that people's true colors were exposed during trying times.

Reaching the beach house, I pulled into the driveway. I had barely put the convertible in Park, and Josie was already swinging my door open, a stupid grin on her lips. "Finally," she said dramatically. "We can start drinking. You're the last one here." The driveway was packed with four other cars.

Unfastening my seat belt at the same time I killed the car's engine, I turned in my seat to hop out. "I'm surprised you waited."

Her feet were bare, and she wore cutoff shorts and a bikini top. Her smile turned wicked. "Who said I did?"

Micah came out behind her, giving me a quick hug before reaching into the back seat and grabbing my two duffel bags. "The shots are poured and waiting."

"Ainsley's having grape juice," Josie added, bounding up the porch steps in front of us.

In the distance, the rolling ocean waves crashed into the sandy beach in a harmonic lullaby. I couldn't wait to fall asleep on the deck, listening to the water ebb and flow. Between the hammock, the lounge chairs, and the outdoor sectional couch, the beach house was in no shortage of sleeping spots.

"I need to pee first, and I swear you better not have already picked rooms," I warned as Josie held open the door.

She held up her hand. "I plead the fifth."

Micah flashed his devilish dimples and winked at me as he slung my bags over his broad shoulders. "Don't worry, KK. We made sure to stick you in the room next to Fynn."

"You better sleep with one eye open, Bradford," I warned. "I'm going to spray-paint all that glorious hair."

Micah chuckled, loving the banter. "Is that what's in one of these bags?"

The Duprees spared no expense when it came to their second home. They had a few houses, but the one in Oceanbay was my favorite.

The three-story white home had multiple porches. Each of the five bedrooms had its own outdoor space, and the huge deck out back overlooked the beach and ocean below. Not a room in the house had a bad view. There was a private walkway to the sandy shores and a pier for fishing, jumping, boating, or whatever crazy stunt Micah thought up on the spur of the moment.

They even had a stereo system installed so music could be heard from any part of the house, inside and out. As we drew closer to the front door, Post Malone crooned through the screen, greeting us.

This was the perfect escape.

Micah dropped my bags just inside the entryway, and I followed the voices to the kitchen at the back of the house. The interior was airy and coastal, instantly instilling a calmness that sent me into vacation mode.

Over the music, the chatter of my friends grew louder. They were huddled around the island, laughing and talking all at once. "Hey, fuckers, thanks for waiting for me!" I raised my voice, smiling.

The room erupted into cheers, and I freaking loved it.

"Okay, everyone grab a shot," Mads ordered, her eyes twinkling at me from across the counter.

I wiggled my way in between Fynn and Grayson as Josie sidled up to Brock while Micah wrapped his arms around Mads. Fynn handed me a tiny glass filled to the brim with a bright orange liquid.

Our fingers brushed, and the tingles I should be used to crackled from his hand to mine. My eyes lifted to his, and the glint there was one I recognized. As usual, Fynn confused me. I gave him a what-do-think-you-are-doing glare, which made his lips twitch.

Brock held up his shot, breaking the contact between Fynn and me. Brock's gaze panned to each of us, and he grinned. "Let's do this shit right. Here's to a summer that we'll never forget."

"And not because someone's trying to kill us," Micah added, lifting his shot.

Mads rolled her eyes beside her boyfriend as we followed suit, raising our glasses before knocking them back. The shot definitely had Amaretto, OJ, and something else. It was tasty and dangerous. The sweet ones always were. At least it wasn't bourbon, Josie's personal favorite.

"One more and then we hit the beach," I said, slamming my glass onto the counter.

Two shots didn't end the liquor consumption. The guys had fully stocked the drink fridge and busted out the beers and White Claws.

It was the first night, and we were going to let loose. Tomorrow be damned. All that mattered was now and having the best damn night.

We weren't the only partygoers tonight on the beach. It seemed as if everyone else along the strand had the same idea. Micah, being the social creature that he was, of course, invited every soul he encountered to hang out. A party wasn't a party to our resident retired playboy if there wasn't at least a houseful of people. Or in this case, a beach crowded with offshores, what the locals called those who showed up only for the summer, like us.

The evening grew nippy, but the fire the guys started as the sun dipped below the horizon burned brightly as we circled around. I pulled in my legs underneath me, grateful I'd tossed on a lightweight sweater. The heat from the fire wasn't enough to chase away the late-May chill. It wasn't officially summer, but those sweltering days weren't far off. I could smell traces of sunscreen in the air.

We talked about everything and nothing, avoiding the heavier shit. For one night, it was nice not to think about Sterling Weston. It helped to have other people around who knew nothing about the psycho prick.

Fynn got up to get another drink. My eyes followed him, appreciating the way his ass looked in shorts. As he unearthed a beer from the cooler, he got sidetracked by Mason Blackwell who lived two houses down.

The night wound down, and people started to stumble their way home giggling. Grayson and Ainsley were the first of our group to head inside. Josie and Brock followed next, but I wasn't anywhere near tired.

Needing a breather from the smoke and heat, I strolled toward the water's edge, letting the cool sand squish between my toes. Was there anything more beautiful and serene than the ocean at night? The moon's reflection rippled with the gentle flow of waves.

I picked a spot just close enough to avoid the tide and sat down, inhaling the salty air. The gently rolling waves overcame the chatter from around the bonfire, leaving me with my thoughts and the endless ocean stretched out before me. As I stared out into the horizon where the night blended with the dark waters, it was almost impossible to tell where one began and the other ended. It made me feel as if I was the only girl in the world.

What a lonely thought.

I spread my toes out in the cool sand as I brought my knees up, resting my chin on top and wrapping my arms around my legs. My mind, slightly buzzing from alcohol, wandered. *Would I always be solo in life? Would I ever have what my friends have found?*

Love.

*Did I want love?*

I believed humans had a natural desire to want to be loved by another—to find their one person in the world. Making friends or connecting with people wasn't my problem. It was the closeness where I struggled. The spark you're supposed to feel when you meet someone you're attracted to. The tingles you get when they accidentally brush against you. The heat flushing through your body when the spark ignites into a flame—true desire.

I lacked all of the above. Except with Fynn, but Fynn was comfortable.

I could fake a lot of emotions.

But desire wasn't one of them.

A few minutes had gone by when I sensed someone joining me. Glancing over my shoulder, I expected Micah or Grayson, but it was neither; it was a face I didn't recognize.

A newcomer.

Fresh meat. Just what I needed.

I took in the mysterious newcomer's dark hair and midnight-blue eyes. Well, it was hard to tell their true color with just the firelight. He grinned, and I realized I'd been staring.

"You're Kenna, right?" he asked, his gaze never leaving mine.

Curious, I lifted a brow, feeling slightly at a disadvantage that he knew who I was when I knew nothing about him. Other than he liked to drink beer. A half-drunk bottle dangled between his fingers. "I am, and you are?" I asked.

Humor spread over his expression as he sat down on the sand beside me. "Lucky enough to find a seat next to the prettiest girl here."

"Really? The prettiest?" I dropped right into my old habit of flirting. The dance of glances, mincing of words, and coy smiles. I excelled at it, enjoyed it even, probably because I never took it seriously—never took the guys seriously either.

For the last two years, I'd searched to find someone who I desired to move past first base with. It took me this long to kiss someone, but anything further was where I ran into problems. I pulled away, shrinking inside while playing bashful. I was tired of feeling broken inside and was ready to fucking feel.

"Might even be the prettiest in Oceanbay," he added, flashing a single dimple.

A flatterer. Most boys in their early twenties were. They all had the same thing on their mind. A quick tumble. Very few were interested in something long-term. I'd watched the Elite long enough to know the game. "Only Oceanbay, huh? You're going to have to do better than that. I'm vain as hell."

He chuckled, and I liked the sound, but I had no real interest in *getting to know* him, not in the way his glittering eyes suggested. "Noah Wilde, quarterback for the Ravens," he informed proudly.

An easy smile slid over my lips. "Ah, a fellow football jock. Makes sense."

Leaning back on his hands, he stretched out his legs, getting far too comfortable. "What makes sense?"

I toyed with the end of my hair. "The confidence. The cheesy pickup lines. The smirk."

He lifted a brow. "Cheesy?"

"You know you use that line on every girl you meet," I retorted.

His gaze swept over me, and a chill that had nothing to do with the wind chased down my spine. "Would you believe I'm not the kind of guy who meets a lot of girls?"

"No," I replied honestly, softening the response with a forced smile.

"How about I get you another drink and I can convince you just the kind of guy I am," he offered.

It was the wrong thing to say. At least to me.

My heart skipped in instant dread. When it came to parties, I had many rules, but number one was don't have a drink I didn't get myself. There were exceptions. Four of them. Brock. Grayson. Micah. And Fynn. They were the only guys I'd ever trust to get me a drink.

The color in my face paled, but I hoped the darkness concealed the sudden change of my skin. I swallowed, forcing my voice to remain light and playful. "I think I can figure it out without the drink. Jocks are all the same." Another group of people got up from around the fire to leave, passing by where Noah and I sat. "Besides, I'm done drinking for the night."

"It's still early, and I just sat down," he pushed lightly, and a wisp of anger licked inside me.

A shadow fell over us, and I glanced up, seeing Fynn scowling at the guy next to me. "You're in my spot." Fynn's gaze flickered to me and then back to the guy, a silent exchange that implied it wasn't just the spot that was Fynn's.

Noah looked up at him. "Sorry, I didn't realize—"

"Yes, you did," Fynn interrupted before Noah could finish.

Whoa. The intensity went up several notches.

Noah stiffened, all playfulness erasing from his features. "I'm not looking to start trouble."

Harshness clouded Fynn's eyes. "Good, if you leave, we won't have a problem."

Noah turned to me, regret shining on his features. "I'll see you around, Kenna," he said, shoving to his feet.

Fynn took a step up to Noah, holding his gaze with a hard glare that made me hold my breath. "No, you won't."

Noah only nodded and left.

Shoving to my feet, I rounded on Fynn the second Noah was out of earshot, turning my back to the bonfire. "What the hell, Fynn!" I hissed. "I could have handled that on my own."

The hardness in Fynn's features lightened as he stared at me. "I couldn't."

My brows pulled in a straight line of confusion. "What does that mean?"

The muscle along his jaw flexed. "It means that I don't want to see another guy with his hands on you."

What was happening? Had I stepped into an alternate universe? I didn't understand what had gotten into Fynn. "You're taking this big-brother act too far. You do realize I already have one of those."

Fynn tucked a piece of stray hair that kept flying in my eyes behind my ear. His touch was warm, and I wanted to lean into his hand. "I don't want to be your big brother." He exhaled loudly.

My breath hitched. "What do you want to be?" I asked, but I had a hunch despite my mind rejecting the idea.

"You know, Kenna. You've always known."

My stomach flipped in a series of a dozen cartwheels. He couldn't possibly be serious. Years. Fucking years had gone by, and he'd never so much as made a single move on me except for the night of the gala. "I can't do this right now."

He cupped the side of my cheek. "Handle this, brat."

Before I could collect my thoughts and give Fynn a proper tongue lashing, the jerk kissed me.

He kissed me.

And my mind went fucking blank.

# KENNA

Fynn caught me off guard again, but this time, I was quick to respond, my body coming alive under the pressure of his lips. He didn't grind hard against my mouth, yet the weight of his kiss wasn't feather soft either. It fell somewhere in the middle.

Sighing into his mouth, I lifted onto my toes, wrapping my arms around his neck. This was only the second time our lips had ever met, but I loved the shape and feel of them. The way they coaxed and moved against mine, skillfully so. It was clear Fynn had experience. I knew he'd been with other girls. Hell, he was surrounded by the opposite sex at any given moment. I was used to it, seeing girls throw themselves at the Elite. It was annoying when it was my brother. That I didn't understand. But Fynn, I got the appeal.

Who wouldn't be attracted to over six feet of muscle, flat-ass abs, and shoulders I wanted to sink my nails and teeth in? Fynn Dupree was the damn ideal specimen of a male.

And the asshole smelled so damn good.

His scent alone had hormones I thought were dead buzzing alive.

As his fingers moved to the small of my back, my spine tingled. He urged me closer, our bodies pressing together, and I shivered.

I wanted his tongue inside me, to reacquaint myself with the taste of him. I wanted to continue the exploration. There was so much I'd never experienced, and there was no one I trusted more than Fynn with not just my body but opening myself up and being vulnerable with another human.

I was the one who demanded more, a concept until this second that had been completely foreign to me.

I wanted.

Not just more of Fynn's lips.

I wanted his hands to touch me.

I wanted to feel the length of his hard body pressed into mine.

I wanted my fingers on his skin.

*Holy shit, I want him.*

Turned out, I wasn't utterly broken after all. I just needed the right guy.

In the five years since Carter drugged and raped me, my heart had only pounded for one guy.

Fynn.

Of course, it would be him. If anyone could show me the good side of sex, it would be Fynn. If anyone could wipe the ugly memories of intimacy and replace them with glowing promises, it was Fynn.

Once the idea popped into my head, like everything in my life, I jumped before thinking it through. I believed Fynn cared about me. And he didn't seem to have a problem kissing me. He said he was done waiting, so in my mind, this was a win-win situation.

Fynn and I were friends. I trusted him wholeheartedly.

Tracing a finger down the side of his face, I gazed into his eyes. "Sleep with me." The words tumbled out in a whisper.

Fynn blinked, desire clearing from his green eyes that looked brighter in moonlight. "What?"

Color stole into my cheeks, but the darkness concealed my uncertainty. I'd already thrown it out there, and I wouldn't back down now.

Opening my eyes, I looked directly into his and said, "I want you to sleep with me."

The hands at the small of my back fell away, dropping to his side. "Back up. I tell you I have feelings for you, and you think I just want to have sex with you? That's not what I meant."

My eyes rolled. "I want you to teach me," I stated matter-of-factly.

"About sex?" he clarified, staring deeply at me and appearing a little confused about how we had gotten from point A to point B.

I didn't expect him to understand my thought process. Few could. Me included. I closed my eyes for a second as what I'd just propositioned settled in my mind. "Yes. I want you to teach me everything there is about sex," I reiterated so the idea would sink in.

"Kenna, hold up, I—"

I pressed my finger to his lips silencing him. "Just hear me out. Don't say no, not yet." This might not make sense to anyone else, but the act of sex was the one hurdle I had yet to tackle. I'd done a lot of work in therapy and found ways to deal with regaining my power. I loved who I'd become and loved how stronger I felt, but the one part of my life lacking was intimacy.

I wanted to do this with someone who cared about me. Someone who would be patient. Someone who wouldn't hurt me. It might take me months or years to get to that level of trust with someone, and kissing Fynn made me realize I didn't want to wait.

Not anymore.

There was no one else but Fynn who met all those qualifications and who I was attracted to physically.

I wasn't ready for a relationship, not like what Fynn was waiting for. It was the one downfall. He could get hurt.

But then I reminded myself. This was Fynn. He was never serious about girls. This would work. I just had to assure him I wouldn't fall in love with him.

It seemed unlikely to me. The Kenna who had a mad crush on

Fynn when she'd been fifteen wasn't the same Kenna who stood before him now.

With a deep inhale, I figured the worst that could happen was he could turn me down. It would be awkward for a few days, but things would go back to normal, and we'd laugh about it later.

But if he said yes...

I didn't want to think how that might affect our friendship.

"This isn't about you. Well, it's a little about you, but mostly it's about me. I need your help. I know it's insane and unconventional, but nothing about my life has been normal. For once, I want to feel close to someone. I want to know what I like and don't like. Most girls experiment. They hook up with guys to find their sexuality, but I'm not like other girls. It has to be with someone I feel comfortable with, and there's no one I trust more than you."

Fynn raked a hand through his wavy hair. "I get what you're asking. It's just I've never treated sex as a transaction or lesson."

My smile brightened, trying to convince him this was a good thing. "Perfect. It's a first for both of us."

"That's not quite how I meant it," Fynn grumbled, still looking unsettled by the idea.

The more I tried to convince him, the surer I became. "If you're worried about it being weird, don't. I promise we'll still be friends. I promise I won't fall in love with you. You and I will always be friends, gorgeous." I tried to downplay his seriousness with the playful nickname reserved only for when no one else was around. "How can we not? We've been through too much shit."

Fynn's frown deepened. "You might be okay with it, but I'm not sure I will be."

"Why? You have sex with random girls all the time," I pointed out. "How's this any different?" I was really trying to sell this. For reasons I couldn't explain, this was something I had to do. And it had to be Fynn.

He glanced off into the dark waters, mulling over my proposition before turning those shrouded eyes back to mine. "It just is, Kenna. You know it is. I don't have a relationship with them."

"I'm not asking for a relationship. Just sex."

"You've made that point clear, but what if I am?"

This was an unexpected kink and not a sexual one. Fynn had been single as long as I had and I hadn't considered he wanted something more than hookups. "You want a relationship? Are you seeing someone? Is that why—?"

"No." He quickly cut me off. "I'm not dating anyone."

I shifted my feet in the sand, my mind racing. "Is it me?"

"Not for the reasons you think," he instantly replied.

"What's that supposed to mean? You kissed me. Twice now. I thought that meant you found me attractive. Am I wrong?" And this was why I needed Fynn. Was I way off the mark? I might be naive when it came to sex, but I damn well knew when a guy wanted me. Fynn definitely had that look in his eyes. He said he had feelings for me. I hadn't read him wrong.

I was pretty sure.

But the longer Fynn stared at me, the more self-conscious he made me feel.

Fynn stepped closer to me as a breeze blew in off the ocean, ruffling the curls falling over his forehead. "No, I want you. Desire isn't the problem."

I gnawed on my lip, unable to see the problem. "Then say yes. Say you'll be my teacher."

## FYNN

*ucking hell.*

I groaned at her choice of words. Why did it sound so damn sexual in her voice? Kenna could be a skilled flirt when she wanted to be, and up until tonight, I hadn't been sure of her inexperience. I'd guessed, but seeing as I wasn't with her twenty-four-seven and we did attend different schools, she could have very well been with other guys.

Knowing she hadn't raised the protective alpha within me. The beast wanted to toss her over my shoulder and haul her ass upstairs into my bedroom, lock the door, and begin her *first lesson.*

*Am I actually considering this scandalous proposition?*

If Grayson found out, he'd kick my ass. Hell, I'd give him permission to kick my ass. The others would as well.

But how could I say no to her when she looked at me like that? Pleading eyes. Pouty, full lips. An excitement and hopefulness beamed in her expression, and I didn't want to be the one to extinguish it.

I snuck a quick glance over to the bonfire and house, making sure no one had wandered down or was at risk of picking up pieces of our conversation. My focus returned to the girl in front of me, eagerly waiting for a response. I should tell her I needed to think on it, but I wouldn't because my answer would be the same. "You want to do this right now? As in tonight?" I asked, my lips still buzzing from when I kissed her. My body wouldn't object to going farther. Shit, I was ready to get down and dirty in the sand with Kenna, but I didn't think that was precisely what she had in mind.

She sucked her bottom lip between her teeth again, a habit she did when contemplative. "It doesn't have to be this second. I don't know when, but maybe not with so many people around. We could start with basic stuff. I want to do this, but I also don't want to rush it."

I tugged on a piece of her hair. "I haven't agreed to anything, brat."

Fuck me if that wasn't disappointment flashing over her face. "Fynn, I need to do this. I need to prove to myself that I'm not broken."

A frown built along my brow, not liking how upset she looked. "Why would you think that?"

She started strolling down the beach unable to stand still. Her restlessness bounced off her. "I don't know. Maybe because I haven't dated anyone. Ever. I'm fucked up. I don't need you to pretend otherwise."

I followed suit, keeping my pace with hers as I gave her a sidelong glance. "We're all a little fucked up one way or another."

A snort breezed through her nose. "I know that's supposed to make me feel better. It doesn't."

"If I agree to this, what do I get in return?"

She grinned as I hoped she would, easing some of her tension. "Spoken like an Elite."

I lifted a brow. "It's an Elite you want, isn't it?"

Stepping a few paces in front of me, Kenna turned, walking backward so she could face me. "Not just any Elite, Fynn. I want you."

For two, maybe three, more steps, I studied her. The reasonable part of my brain was being swayed. Halting in the sand, I reached for her hand and tugged her closer to me before dropping my forehead to hers. "You're fucking killing me, brat," I groaned.

She could see my resistance slipping from me. "Would having sex with me be such a horrible way to die?"

I chuckled, and the vibrations rubbed against her pebbled nipples poking through her shirt. "I can't decide if it would be torturous or damn heavenly," I said, lifting my head to look down at her.

A smirk twitched at the corners of her mouth. "I like either option."

"Kenna." My eyes searched hers with such heat and depth. I sighed. "Fuck it. I'll agree to your proposition under one condition."

Her eyes brightened, a sense of victory beaming over her too damn pretty features. She was used to getting her way, and tonight had been no different. "Name it," she happily said.

"Seven days. That's how long you have. When everyone else leaves, you stay here with me for another week. In that time, you're mine. And then when we go home, we can do weekends or date nights. Anything else you need."

Her gaze strayed to my lips. "Okay, I can agree to that. And...?" she prompted, her eyes flicking upward to mine, knowing there was more.

"And when this is over, if what you want is to go back to being friends, we do just that," I said simply.

"No one can know. That includes my brother," she said, adding a stipulation I wasn't comfortable with.

I narrowed my eyes. "I don't keep secrets from them."

"I know." She sighed.

"But unless one of them straight out asks me, I won't say anything," I conceded, my fingers sliding to her waist.

"Then we have a deal." Taking a step back, she held out her hand.

I ignored her gesture to shake hands, my eyes lingering on her lips. "The only way to seal this deal is with a kiss."

Her palms flattened on my chest as she stared up at me. "Seems fitting, considering."

I grabbed her chin, tipping her face back. "I won't kiss you again after tonight until you ask."

"Okay," she replied softly, her tongue darting over her bottom lip.

The throbbing heat I'd come to anticipate unfurled within me in waves the second I took possession of her mouth. My pulse quickened at the sweet taste of her lip gloss. She didn't need me to coax her lips apart. They parted of their own volition, allowing me full advantage as I slipped my tongue inside. Hers met mine halfway, brushing, teasing, and dancing. The student was a quick study.

A low growl sounded at the back of my throat as I changed the angle of the kiss and deepened it. My fingers wove into her hair, cupping the back of her head. I had only meant this to be a short kiss, a prelude to what was to come, but I didn't want to let her go. I had to have more.

I also didn't want to push too hard, too fast, but...I wouldn't know how far was too far unless I tested the waters.

Tugging her closer against me, I let her breasts crush into my chest as her heart beat wildly against mine. Kenna and I always had this unspoken connection, but shit, this explosive need made me want to spend hours exploring every fucking inch of her.

Her hand stroked the side of my cheek, the stubble scratching the inside of her palm in such a way that made me want to lean into her touch. I'd never been with a girl I wanted to be vulnerable with. I was always the one in control, the one demanding, the one making the rules.

I kept an arm secured around her, the other falling from her hair to caress down her arm. The thin sweater she wore exposed her shoulder, but it was also in my way. I wanted it gone.

What I needed to do was find the strength to pull away. Now was not the time. We weren't alone, and as sexy as making out under the moonlight on the beach sounded, my experience was sand just shouldn't end up in certain places.

Before I lost all control completely, hauled her to the ground on top of me, and said fuck the sand, I broke off the kiss, but I didn't release her from my arms. I needed her close for another minute while my body calmed down, which in hindsight didn't work. As long as Kenna was anywhere near me, my body responded to her.

I was a glutton for punishment because I couldn't make my arms release her.

Not yet.

"See, you're a quick study," I rasped. My hands stayed at her hips to keep her steady until she regained her composure. "You okay?" I asked when she didn't say anything. Kenna wasn't the silent type.

"How the fuck do you do that?" she asked, genuine curiosity shining in her expression.

"Elaborate."

"Kiss like that?" she clarified.

I grinned. "Lesson number one. No one kisses like I do. If you think the next guy will be able to make you feel what I just did, you'll constantly be disappointed."

Kenna pushed lightly at my chest, but I didn't budge. "Arrogant prick," she replied.

Taking her hand, I started leading her back toward the house. It was late, and I needed to bank the fire before going to bed. "Just keeping it real."

Her fingers squeezed mine. "We'll see at the end of the month who's begging who."

"Challenge accepted, brat." I said cockily, caught up in the moment with her. It wasn't until I was alone in my room, the sun only mere hours away from rising, that I got hit with the full impact of the deal I'd struck with Kenna.

*What the fuck did I agree to?*

Literally a week of pure fucking blissful torture. How the hell would I handle the end of our time together?

I was lying to myself if I thought I could do all I planned to do with this girl and then suddenly stop. Friends? I hadn't even properly touched her yet, and I fucking knew there was no way in hell I could return to being Kenna's "friend."

How would Grayson feel about me teaching his sister about sex? I doubted he would pat me on the back and thank me.

*Fucking hell.*

As if I didn't already have enough to deal with.

* * *

The next day, I woke up with the same thought I had right before drifting off to sleep. *God, what have I gotten myself into?*

I couldn't hurt her again. When those brown eyes held mine, I saw the courage it took her to ask this of me.

Being her teacher?

Fuck, I should have said no.

This was going to backfire on me, I was certain, but I couldn't say no. How could I? I'd never been able to deny Kenna anything except the one night when it should have been me instead of Carter. I wouldn't have done what he did, but if I had kissed her instead of pushing her away that night, he wouldn't have had the opportunity to do what he did.

A part of me felt as if I owed Kenna. This was a way to make amends with myself and alleviate the guilt that still ate at me like a fucking parasite I couldn't get rid of. It was also a punishment. I needed to be penalized, to be tortured, to suffer for all the pain and horror Kenna went through. I should have been the one to save her. I should have been the one to save her from all the tears. I should have been the one to make her happy instead of drowning in eternal sorrow.

And then after all she'd been through, Kenna had to crawl out of the hole alone without any of her friends by her side.

It was the biggest regret of my life. I shouldn't have left her alone. Not at the party. And not after.

So, yeah, I said yes. My own feelings and needs be damned.

If Kenna wanted a teacher and wanted to explore her sexuality, I'd be the fucking best teacher. Very thorough.

And when she didn't need or want me anymore...

I'd deal with the pain, the heartache. It was what I deserved.

How did I end up entangled in a web of sex with Kenna?

*Because you're weak where she is concerned.*

True.

A week with the girl of my dreams. Sounded like a fantasy, and yet I had a feeling it would be the longest seven days of my life.

Of course, there was one small hitch. My father.

He wouldn't be happy to learn I'd be postponing my internship at his company for another week. It hadn't been easy for him to give me this month off to begin with, but I didn't see what the point of the internship was. I had no interest in taking over his business. Real estate was not my thing. Football was. The plan had always been for me to play professionally, and I was on track to make that a reality. My name was already being tossed around by scouts, and a few teams were expressing interest in me after college. It wasn't a matter of if for my professional football career but a matter of when.

My father would get over his disappointment. I was certain.

But Kenna, I saw what this meant to her. I couldn't say no.

And if I was being honest, the prospect of having her to myself... I grew hard just thinking about it. All the things my body desired to show her.

I'd be her first in many ways.

That itself fucking turned me on.

She might not realize it, but Kenna was mine. Always had been. She just needed time to find herself, to feel comfortable in her skin. She needed a guiding hand. She needed me.

The thought of being the one to see Kenna explore her body, learn what she liked and what she didn't, and watch her come unraveled nearly had me cumming in my fucking shorts.

I told her I was on her timetable, and I meant it, but after the seven days were up, I had no intention of letting Kenna go. I wouldn't let her run from me.

Tasting her lips alone hadn't been nearly enough, and a week with her would be like a tease. It wouldn't be enough. Not after tasting her. Hearing her sighs of pleasure. Seeing her eyes darken with lust. Being deep inside her, surrounded by her wet warmth.

I had strong willpower, but fuck me, this would test my restraint beyond any challenge I'd faced.

For Kenna, I'd make it unforgettable.

She wasn't broken as she believed.

She was perfect.

And I'd do everything in my power to make her see how desirable, sensual, loving, and natural she was.

I had my second cup of coffee to my lips when a voice bellowed through the house.

"Someone's at the door!"

It was Micah. I hadn't even seen him yet since I woke up. Hell, the only person I'd seen was Brock when we grunted at each other on the way to the kitchen for our first dose of caffeine.

Dragging my ass off the kitchen stool, I ran a hand through my hair. "Yeah. Yeah," I mumbled, moving through the hall. I hadn't drunk that much last night, but holy crap was my body feeling the repercussions this morning. When I got to the door, a man in a postal uniform stood on the other side. He had a package in his hand. I opened the door, stepping out onto the porch.

"Fynn Dupree?" he inquired.

"That's me," I grumbled, squinting against the awfully cheery sun.

"Sign here," he instructed, holding out a tablet for me to electronically sign with my finger.

I scribbled something on the screen and took the package he offered me.

"Have a good day," he said, taking off down the porch steps to his parked truck.

"You too, man," I retorted after him, my attention already shifting to the box in my hands.

With a narrowed gaze, I examined the wrapped parcel. The return address was blank, instantly raising a red flag. In my experience, mystery packages were never a good thing. It crossed my mind to toss it in the trash, but seeing it addressed to me struck a chord of curiosity.

The package wasn't large but about the size of a tissue box. Sitting down on the porch steps, I ripped the tape off the seam and opened the flaps. Inside, nestled in bubble wrap, lay a can of pink spray paint.

Dread sunk into my gut. For anyone else, receiving a random spray can might be weird and probably considered junk or useless. Not in this group. Any of us would see this and instantly think of Kenna.

Had she bought supplies and had them shipped to the beach house? It was a rational explanation, and if she had, Kenna and I were going to have a talk about her not vandalizing my neighbors.

I reached in and unearthed the bottle of paint, the little metal ball rolling around in the can. It had a black bow tied around the cap. Odd. What kind of place put ribbons on something as trivial as paint?

This seemed more like a gift than a purchase, and that feeling in my gut grew bigger.

A note fell out of the box, landing near my feet. Picking up the slip of paper, I unfolded it, my eyes scanning the words.

**_For our little rebel, in case she's out of lipstick. May the best man win._**

What the fuck did that mean?

It was suddenly very clear who the package was from and why there had been no return address. Sterling. By sending me this message, he conveyed two things. First, he was letting me know he knew where we were, and my secluded getaway suddenly made me feel like we were sitting ducks. Second was that he had an interest in Kenna, the scariest realization. Something happened the night of the gala that caused him to divert his focus to Kenna, just enough to put her on his radar.

But what?

And why?

His mark had always been Micah, and I figured he would continue to be Sterling's main goal. The rest of us were standing in Sterling's way. We were the collateral damage he had to get rid of before he got to the prize.

I read the note again.

Why would he send this to me for Kenna? Why send a gift to Kenna at all?

**May the best man win.**

This line in particular worried me. Was he suggesting that he and I were in a competition for Kenna?

Over my fucking dead body.

I'd kill him with my bare hands before I let him anywhere near her. The night at the gala was the last time he would ever be alone with her. If I had to stay glued to her side, so fucking be it.

Kenna might not appreciate it, but for the next few weeks, I at least had a valid reason.

Anger climbed up my spine, and I crumpled the paper up in my hands, ready to set fire to the world. Or at the very least to Sterling's arrogant note.

I wanted him to be man enough to face me.

*Soon*, I promised. *Very soon.*

## 12

KENNA

My phone said it was eleven forty-three in the morning when the ding of the doorbell sounded. I groaned into my pillow, deciding if I should get up or go back to bed. I *should* get my ass up and be a productive member of society, but this was vacation, and if I wanted to stay under the covers all day, so be it.

The problem was I could hear people moving about now I'd been pulled out of sleep. I had a vague memory of Josie popping her head and mumbling something about going to get muffins with Ainsley, but then again, I could have dreamed it. Regardless, I wanted a fucking muffin now. Preferably a lemon blueberry muffin with a strong cup of coffee.

I left the window open last night, and the lull of the waves beating against the shore drifted into the room. Yawning, I rolled over and nearly poked my eye on a thorn. A single pink rose lay on the pillow next to mine, the long green stem covered in pointy thorns. Had someone been in my room last night?

Obviously. How else did a rose appear on my pillow?

A smile curved my lips. It was too early for smiles this big, but the thought of Fynn sneaking into my room and giving me a rose was so over the top I wondered if it was Josie or Mads instead. Not that Fynn couldn't be romantic, but flowers weren't his style. The gesture, regardless of the motives, was sweet. Another thing Fynn wasn't, not on normal guy levels. If we were rating the Elite's nice-guy status, Fynn would be at the top with my brother or Brock at the bottom.

I trailed a finger over one of the velvety petals. A scarce hint of a floral aroma lingered in the air under the salty scent of ocean water. It was a lovely thing to wake up to—the sun shining high, a warm wind drifting through the window, the bed cozy underneath me, and the room perfumed by a single rose.

I was suddenly ready to toss on my bikini, lie out by the pool, and scroll through my phone for hours. Vacation mode had arrived.

Leaving the rose on my pillow, I padded into the bathroom to wash my face, brush my teeth, and empty my bladder. The essentials. It took me more time to decide which bathing suit I wanted to wear, but I settled on a classic black two-piece with cutout details. I planned to spend the day working on my tan, maybe catching up on a few podcasts.

Being in Oceanbay made me feel different, lighter as if I'd left all my problems in Elmwood. I hadn't realized how much I needed this.

As I slipped on my flip-flops, a pair of shades, and a coverup, I glanced back at the rose, and the memory of last night trespassed into my thoughts. The rational part of my mind wanted to blame alcohol for my irrational request. Sometimes saying the first thing that popped into your head wasn't the best way to approach an idea. But damn, if my brain on booze didn't know how to filter things out or simmer on a thought.

Yet, as I stared at the rose, I didn't regret my bargain with Fynn. No. Just the opposite.

I was excited.

And those stirring butterflies fluttering inside my belly told me I'd made the right choice.

Might it be a bit awkward this morning seeing him?

Probably.

But it wouldn't last. We were too comfortable with each other to let something like this drive a wedge between us. I hoped it would do the opposite—bring us closer. Not I'm-trying-to-trap-him-into-a-relationship close. I had no expectations other than Fynn teaching me that sex didn't have to produce panic attacks—that I could be intimate with someone and not freak out or shove them away.

It was more about overcoming trauma than teaching me, but since I'd never willingly done anything past kissing, it was both. For the first time, I wasn't feeling dread at the thought of someone touching me.

Careful to avoid the thorns, I picked up the rose to put into some water and carried it downstairs. Micah was in the kitchen when I walked in, an opened bottle of champagne and orange juice on the counter in front of him.

His light-blue eyes lifted to me. "Mimosa?" Micah offered, the slim glass in his hand half gone. From the sparkle in his eyes, I doubted it was his first one.

I went to the cupboard under the sink and grabbed a thin vase Fynn's mother kept there. She had a few of different sizes stashed. "I hate making decisions so early in the morning," I replied, wavering between booze and coffee. I should have both.

"Dude, it's noon," he proclaimed, reaching for an empty flute.

"Exactly. Mimosa." I grinned.

Micah flashed me his dimples. The former playboy had a grin that made girls' hearts break. It was lethal when he unleashed all that charm. Hell, I wasn't even immune, but there'd never been anything but friendship between Micah and me. My cousin had been in love with him almost as long as I'd been hung up on Fynn.

"You scared me for a second," he said.

I took the vase and moved to the sink. "Nothing like chasing away a nagging hangover with more liquor."

He reached for a glass and the champagne bottle to make me a drink. "The best cure is to stay drunk."

Filling the vase with water, I stuck the rose in, setting it down on the center of the island. "Spoken like a guy with a problem."

"Bottoms up." He handed me my drink and reached for his.

My lips twitched as I touched the rim of my glass to his. Micah amused me. Always had. Without him, the Elite would be such a freaking bummer to hang out with. "Where's everybody?" I asked, taking my first sip. Just how I liked it, heavy on the champagne. The house was noticeably quiet for having eight people staying in it.

All the windows in the kitchen were open, including the multiple sliding glass panels that invited the outside in. I kept my shades on. I needed protection from my hangover.

"Mads is at the pool. Ainsley and Josie went into town," he said, filling me in on the girls' whereabouts, but he left out one important detail. The one I was really fishing for.

"And Fynn?" I prompted, trying to sound nonchalant. It wasn't that odd for me to ask where he was. Everyone knew besides my brother I was the closest to Fynn.

"Outside, I think. Someone was at the door."

I drank another healthy gulp of my mimosa. I probably should have started with water or coffee, my body telling me I was dehydrated. "So, the doorbell hadn't been in my dreams," I mumbled more to myself.

Micah lifted a brow. "Not dreaming, KK."

"Thanks for the breakfast," I said, lifting my glass to go hunt down Fynn. I wanted to get any awkwardness out of the way so we could both enjoy the rest of our time with our friends.

"We'll be having daiquiris for lunch." Micah winked before I turned my back on him to stroll into the hallway.

I laughed over my shoulder. "At this rate, I'll be plastered before dinner."

"That's the plan. I fucking love the beach."

Rolling my eyes behind the shades, I took my drink with me to the front of the house in search of Fynn. I found him sitting on the front porch steps, glaring inside an open box like he wanted to run it over with his car.

"I thought I heard the doorbell," I said as the screen door swung shut behind me.

Fynn's head turned in my direction as his hands closed the flaps on the box, obstructing my view inside. "Just the postman with a delivery."

Okay, his sudden weirdness to hide whatever he'd been glaring at enticed my suspicious nature. "Anything interesting?" I asked, plopping down beside him.

"No. Not really," he retorted, but his scowl said otherwise.

Super unconvincing, but I knew Fynn, and I could read his moods. He would remain close-lipped about the package for now. I would just take a sneak peek later when he was preoccupied. "You look like you can use this more than me." I held out my half-drunk mimosa.

Fynn eyed the glass. "Micah?"

I nodded, slipping the sunglasses up on my head and immediately regretting it. I winced at the sun. "Yup. The only breakfast he knows how to make."

"God bless him," Fynn replied, knocking back the rest of the contents in one swoop.

"Looks like I need a refill."

"I'm sure he is offering bottomless mimosas all day."

"Only until lunch," I informed. "Then we're switching to daiquiris."

He shook his head, a ghost of a smile on his lips. "We're going to run out of liquor before the end of the week."

"I bet we don't make it two days. Oh, by the way, flowers aren't necessary. I don't need you to romance me. It wasn't part of our deal. Sweet, but not required."

He frowned, confusion shifting into his eyes. "Flowers? What are you talking about?"

"The rose. On my pillow." Even as the word left my mouth, I

realized I got it wrong. It wasn't Fynn who gave me the rose.

"You hate flowers," he said, setting the glass aside on the porch.

True. I did. If I was going to get a gift, I didn't want it to die in a week. Not to mention, I was expected to care for it. I didn't possess a green thumb. No flower lived longer than a few days in my care. "It was probably Josie or Mads," I rationalized. "Forget I said anything."

Something in Fynn's eyes made me doubt it was either my sister or cousin. His jaw was rigid, and a fire burned in his eyes. I noticed it when I first came outside, but Fynn had an adept skill of hiding his emotions. "What color was the rose?"

Glancing out in the distance, I could see part of the ocean between two houses off to the right. "I don't see why that matters."

"Kenna," he stated firmly. "Just tell me what color it was."

I gazed sidelong at him. "Fynn, what's going on? What was in the package? Why are you so on edge?"

Before he got the chance to respond, a truck pulled up in front of the driveway. Fynn and I both watched the driver hop out of the front seat, carrying a white bundle in his arms. He eyed Fynn warily. "Is there a Kenna Edwards here?" he asked, his gaze shifting under Fynn's hard stare.

"That's me," I piped up before Fynn could step in and scare the driver off. Fynn was sporting his I'm-going-to-kick-some-ass scowl. It might not be directed at the poor delivery guy, but he would suffer the consequences seeing as he was the one who got stuck with the delivery.

"These are for you." He stretched out the bundle for me to take.

Standing, I took the parcel and judged by the weight and feel of it what was wrapped inside.

Flowers.

Tendrils of unease spouted inside my stomach. "Thanks," I mumbled. My eyes stayed fixed on the package as I sat back down, and I didn't notice the delivery guy leave. As I peeled back the white paper, my heart drummed against my chest at the sight of the pink roses. I didn't have to count them to know how many were inside.

Eleven.

The twelfth had been on my pillow this morning and sat in a vase of water currently.

A little card dangled from one of the stems. With dread in my heart, I twisted it around and read the note scribbled on it.

*One rose is never enough.*

No signature.

But he didn't need one. I had my guess of who they were from. Nothing was certain, but from the darkening of Fynn's features, his guess ran parallel to mine.

"I've never had a stalker romance me before," I said in a pathetic attempt to lighten the dark mood that descended over our heads. Fynn's expression alone told me how furious he was.

"Kenna," Fynn growled. "This isn't cute or funny."

I shrugged in a sad attempt to lighten the heaviness. I didn't want Sterling to ruin our short reprieve at the beach. "What can I do if someone wants to send me flowers?"

"Fuck that," Fynn said, hurling the empty flute glass into the driveway. It shattered on impact. "We both know it's more than that. This isn't a gesture of goodwill."

He was in a fucking mood today, and I was close to following him. "Should we toss them on the ground and stomp on them? Do you want to take them out back and burn them? Or we could pluck each petal and let the ocean carry them away."

The vein along his corded neck pulsed. "This is serious."

I snorted. "You've made that point."

"Then I'm wondering why you aren't—"

"Freaking out?" I interrupted, completing his complaint. "Isn't that what he wants?" I shrugged. "I'm not in the business of giving assholes what they want."

Fynn's stormy eyes held mine. "No, you're not."

* * *

Fynn took the roses, and I gladly gave them over if it would make him less like a grumpy prick. I had no idea what he did with them. Didn't ask. Didn't give a shit.

The two mimosas I drank did little to squash the bitterness lingering in me. It had nothing to do with the mixture of OJ and champagne. Like Fynn, I was pissed, but I also refused to let Sterling and his taunts ruin my vacation.

Josie and Ainsley came back with a box of pastries, and my stomach rejoiced at having something to soak up the alcohol, which then, of course, allowed for more consumption. I could probably blame Sterling for the desire to be drunk all day. Not the kind where I wouldn't be able to walk without falling into the pool but that happy buzz of fun and giddiness. It helped conceal the true emotions from my face.

We were all hanging around the pool, the speakers bumping a playlist Micah put together consisting of songs from multiple genres. His musical taste covered a wide spectrum, but none of us were complaining. They were summer jams.

Stretched out on a chaise lounge with a beach towel underneath me and my skin warmed by the sun, I might have dozed off for a bit, but the splash of cold water hitting me from head to toe startled me awake.

Through my designer Chloé sunglasses, I bolted upright in the chair, glaring at the pool. Next to me, Mads squealed, also a victim of the cannonball. Wading in the pool, Fynn and Brock chuckled.

I didn't need to do a head count to know who was behind my rude awakening. "What the hell, Micah!" It was always Micah. If he wasn't splashing in some fashion, he was tossing us in the pool, and knowing him, that would be next on his list.

Micah came out of the water like a fucking cologne model, throwing his head back, closed eyes lifted to the sky as he slicked back his golden hair.

Snorting, I looked at my cousin. "Your boyfriend's so immature."

"Hmm." She pressed her lips together, agreeing, but at the same time eyeing him appreciatingly. I couldn't fault her for it. He was nice to look at, and the bastard knew it, which took away some of his natural sexiness. "But he's amazing in bed."

I wrinkled my nose. "Just not in the pool. And definitely not in the hot tub. Take that energy to the ocean if you need to get laid in water."

Mads laughed, a husky, throaty sound. "I need a cigarette now."

My cousin might not love her bad habit, but she was good at not smoking around Ainsley. "How's it going? Are you still trying to quit?"

She nodded. "I've made it my goal for the summer."

"Do any of those gums or patches help?"

"A little. Distractions are better for me." She took her bottom lip between her teeth, and I followed her eyes.

I groaned. "Oh, for the love of God, go get distracted for all our sakes."

She laughed again.

"You've been dating for over two years. Isn't the honeymoon stage over?" Although the question came out cynical, it masked my general curiosity.

Mads's lips curled. "Not when your boyfriend looks like that."

"Jesus, you're as bad as Josie. She and Brock still can't stop groping each other every second they get. It makes me sick." As if on cue, Brock pulled Josie into his arms as she walked into the pool, immediately sealing his lips to hers.

Yes, my stupid heart sighed. They were like watching a live-action romance movie, and despite everything that happened to me, I was a sucker for romance, just not when I was the starring actress. Those were more like horror film scenes.

"You're just jealous," she said playfully.

I couldn't argue with her logic, regardless that she meant no harm. A part of me was very much jealous. "Hard not to be when everyone around you is in love."

"You'll find your person."

My eyes automatically went to Fynn leaning on the edge of the pool. As if he sensed my attention, his gaze clashed with mine.

Mads glanced over, peering at me through her rose-tinted sunglasses, a trace of humor tugging at her mouth. "Or perhaps you've already found him."

She couldn't see, but I rolled my eyes. "Shut up."

"I'll be back." She winked, moving to the edge of the pool. A moment later, she jumped in, landing not far from where Micah drifted in the water, and I got splattered a second time.

I wiped droplets of water from my sunglasses. "She's going to pay for that," I mumbled.

An hour went by, my tan was coming along fabulously, and I was down two strawberry daiquiris. It was safe to say I felt good. Taking a break from the sun, I sat under the umbrella, munching on a bowl of chips and dip Ainsley brought out. I mindlessly scrolled through my socials and was in the middle of watching a funny cat video when I got a text.

Switching apps, I opened the message, noticing the unknown number. My stomach turned, and for the first time today, the alcohol no longer sat sweetly inside me but soured, threatening to come up.

Only one reason an anonymous number texted me.

Sterling.

Reading his message, any shred of hope I'd been wrong about the roses being from him was smashed.

**Everything beautiful comes with pain. Roses have thorns, like you.**

*Fuck.*

Was he giving me a compliment? I read the slightly ominous poem again. In a roundabout way, I think he implied I was beautiful.

I didn't know how I should feel about receiving a compliment, no matter how backward it was.

You would think after the past few years and seeing what my friends went through, I would have been prepared for this moment.

I wasn't.

The bastard found us.

More importantly, Sterling had been in my room.

He could have always hired someone to do his dirty work, but I had a hunch he was done with puppets. He was back to finish the job himself. I don't know why he targeted me, but he wanted me for something—to use me, I was sure.

For what purpose?

To hurt the Elite?

To lure them?

To destroy them?

For most girls in my position, their first thought would be to run to the Elite, and honestly, it was a smart move. I'd seen what the four of them could do, the lives they could destroy, and it was fucking impressive. The difference was I'd watched and learned from the best. Why have someone else do what you can do yourself?

I liked to handle my shit.

Perhaps Sterling's message and gift were a test to see how I would react. Maybe I should give him a test of his own. The idea made me smile.

I sat under the umbrella, my face neutral despite the quaking anger heating my belly as the first tingles of revenge stirred, and I thought about how I would use this to my advantage.

If Sterling believed I was one of those girls who would cower under a novice threat, he was sadly mistaken and didn't know shit about me. It would take more than some fucking faceless texts and textbook stalking techniques to break me. The bastard was going to need to try a whole lot harder.

In the meantime, I would give him as good as he dished out. A rose for a rose. But mine wouldn't be pink and beautiful as he said.

A dried black rose on the cusp of death.

*Take that as you want, Sterling. A symbolism of your future when you fuck with me.*

# 13

## KENNA

The next few days were much like the first, but as the week drew to an end, we'd settled into a routine of eating, drinking, laughing, sleeping, swimming, and tanning. Basically, living the life of a bunch of rich kids with no responsibilities. We'd taken Fynn's boat out yesterday, packed a cooler of the essentials, and spent the day riding the waves.

It reminded me of my life before it changed. Before I got dark and messed up. When I'd just been an innocent girl who didn't appreciate everything she had and the beauty in naivety. I liked the world more when I was clueless about the evil lurking, even among the wealthy and influential. No place was safe.

All good things must come to an end.

We could thank Sterling for the sudden dose of reality.

I never said anything to the girls about the roses, and if Fynn told the guys, no one said anything to me. But the flowers were just the first of the *gifts* to arrive.

By the start of week two, another unexpected package arrived addressed to Josie. My sister stared at the empty bottle of bourbon, confused lines creasing across her forehead. Her eyes scanned over the little white note attached. "Like mother, like daughter," she read in a soft voice.

The note didn't refer to our mother, Liana, but to the woman in jail for kidnapping Josie, Angie, the woman who raised her.

Brock jerked the bottle from her hands and hurled it out into the street, shattering the glass on impact.

Fynn and he seemed to have the same reactions about Sterling's *presents*.

Mads received the next gift during our third week. Micah interceded before she had a chance to unwrap it. She had stared at the package, fingers shaking. Seeing my cousin visibly upset made me want to hit Sterling in the head with a baseball bat. Repeatedly. Violence swam in my blood, uncontrollably and molten hot. If someone touched my skin at that moment, they would have been burned.

Ironic since inside the box was a charred teddy bear, ropes tied around its hands and feet. Even if the package hadn't been addressed to Mads, we would have known. It was a nod to the night he tied her up in an abandoned warehouse and the fire that left his body scarred.

Sterling knew what buttons to press and how to rile the guys—how to fire them up.

Toying with the women they loved.

That's what he did. The gifts were always sent to either Josie, Mads, Ainsley, or me.

It was clear a pattern was emerging. Each week, Sterling sent a tormenting present. We were on our final week together at the beach house, and we were all on edge waiting. If I thought Mads's gift was horrible, Ainsley's was downright disgusting. Grayson tore the paper off the box. Ainsley was napping upstairs when it arrived, and none of us questioned his call to keep this from her. She didn't need to see what was inside. The sight of the baby doll with a noose around its neck churned my stomach.

I turned away, only for Fynn to tuck me against his chest, his arms so damn strong and safe. I let the tension pressing on my shoulders go and leaned into him. He rubbed circles over my back as my brother trashed the doll.

Our vacation turned out to be anything but relaxing.

Each delivery took a toll on our group.

The laughter diminished. The sun felt less warm and bright. The crashing of the waves became turbulent. The alcohol tasted bitter. Everything I loved about summer dulled.

Exactly what Sterling wanted—to ruin our time together, and we were letting him succeed.

I walked out of the house, heading down to the water. It messed with my mind how peaceful the world could be when my life spun in turmoil. Water lapped serenely at my feet, washing sand in between my toes as they sunk into the beach.

I couldn't believe how fast the days went by. At the end of the week, the eight of us would be splitting up, spending the rest of our summer separately. Ainsley and Grayson would start looking for an apartment. Josie would be at Brock's most of the time. Mads and Micah would be wrapped up in each other.

And Fynn and I would be here at the beach house for another week...alone.

My nerves started to become more prominent with each passing day. At the start of the summer, it seemed like such a good idea. I'd wanted to go into my junior term of college feeling like a woman—an experienced woman who understood her sexuality, what she liked, what she didn't, and what she desired. Someone who could handle dating for more than a week.

Thanks to Sterling, I'd been too preoccupied to be caught up in the feelings Fynn stirred within me.

I wouldn't let him wreck my week with Fynn. No guy would take anything away from me again.

Despite the warm evening breeze coming in off the ocean, I wrapped my arms around myself. With nothing but the waters panning out in front of me, I could think of no better place to be alone with my thoughts. I loved my family and friends. Loved spending time with them. Unlike Grayson and Josie who could go days without speaking to another person, I enjoyed the company of others. But sometimes...I had to get away to cancel all the buzzing and noise in my head. Sometimes the anger inside became too much, and if I didn't run away, I'd explode, detonate like C4, shaking the ground underneath me and destroying everything in my path.

Destructive behavior my therapist would call it.

The itch to vandalize property with spray paint grew strong within me. I wanted to sneak off down the dark beach with my fun bag of tools and piss off someone other than me.

I'd like to graffiti Sterling's face.

*God, he was such a lunatic.*

I thought I was fucked up.

Chewing on the inside of my cheek, I stared out over the rippling ocean's surface contemplating the best way to sneak out of the house tonight.

My biggest obstacle was the guy watching me from the shadows.

Fynn.

I didn't need to turn around to know he was behind me. There was no real privacy with a psycho killer on the loose. To be fair, Sterling hadn't killed anyone yet, but he had all the makings of a killer. He was, however, a hardcore stalker. That shit was very real.

On numerous nights, I sought the solitude of the beach, but I was never really alone. Fynn always kept an eye on me. Sometimes he would join me, but more often than not, he let me have the isolation I sought.

I couldn't blame him for worrying. It would be such a Sterling maneuver to try to kidnap one of us from the beach the second one of the guys wasn't paying attention. Unfortunately for Sterling and fortunately for me, Fynn was a damn hound dog when it came to protecting me.

It should be sweet.

I felt suffocated.

Not by him, but by my lack of freedom.

I felt confined by the invisible restraints Sterling caused in my life. Now he was back and openly tormenting us. Would I be able to go or do anything alone again?

The mental distress he inflicted wore us all down.

It was only a matter of time before he struck.

But I wanted to strike first.

The guys had to feel the same. I was tired of waiting to be a victim.

Screw that.

Never again.

I angled my body sideways, searching the shadows for Fynn. "You can come out. I know you're there."

"I'm losing my touch," he said from the darkness, his voice deep.

Snorting, I followed his figure until his face was visible from a spot of moonlight. "You're implying you had skills to begin with."

He sat down on the sand beside me. "My expertise goes beyond spying."

I touched my lip, remembering the warmth and softness of his mouth on mine. "I'll keep that in mind."

Specks of somberness flickered in Fynn's eyes. "Are you worried about *him?*"

"A little," I admitted. "I'd be a fool not to."

His gaze angled out to the ocean's horizon as he rested his arms on top of his knees. "I'm not going to let anything happen to you."

He was mistaken. The unease inside me had nothing to do with my safety. It was my friends I worried for. "What if I want something to happen to me."

His head whirled to me. Shadows were in his eyes now. "Don't talk like that."

"Why?"

His thumb pressed into my chin as his index finger hooked underneath. "Because I wouldn't be able to deal with it."

My eyes lifted, colliding with his. Such conflict shone in them. I couldn't tell him what was really on my mind. He might understand, but he wouldn't condone it.

"Kenna," he growled. "I know that look. What are you plotting?"

I had to think of something quickly. Something to distract him from pulling the truth out of me because even I wasn't entirely sure what nefarious plan I was concocting. Not yet. I hadn't ironed out the details let alone the rough draft. I barely had a sketch. Just an idea without any shape or form. But later, when I was in bed, perhaps it would start to have lines. Until then...I closed the fraction of distance separating our bodies, angling my head to the side. "Kiss me, gorgeous. That's what I'm thinking."

Fynn's eyes flicked to my mouth, and I deliberately let my tongue dart out, running it over my bottom lip. A beat of silence passed before he said anything, and in that time, my heart sped up. "Do I need to remind you the week hasn't started yet?"

"Fuck your calendar," I replied, my voice throaty and sexier than I knew it could sound.

"We had a deal," he reminded me, a little less steel in his tone.

I was wearing him down, and better yet, he wasn't trying to pry inside my head. "There's nothing wrong with working ahead," I said.

A single brow lifted. "Is that what we're doing?"

"Just fucking kiss me," I whispered against his lips before brushing mine lightly over his in a teasing, feather-soft kiss.

His fingers came to my hips, and I wasn't sure if he planned to pull me closer or shove me away. I wasn't sure he knew either. A low groan left him, his breath mingling with mine. As his fingers pressed into my hips, the first sting of disappointment ached in my chest, but then he kissed me, and my heart soared.

I felt like I was flying over the ocean, and I sighed into his mouth, my body sinking against him. He was so warm and hard and smelled so fucking good, his scent mixing with the salty ocean air, an intoxicating combination that went right between my legs. It was an ache I'd never felt before, a subtle throb eager to feel more.

I wasn't so naive I didn't know the inner workings of sex. My best friends were having plenty of it and talked way too freely about the details of their sex life. From their cars to the couches, showers, hot tubs, libraries, and probably every room in my house, they were doing it almost everywhere.

But after trying to have any sort of feeling for years, I'd assumed I was broken, that my body didn't work like my friends' bodies. For the first time, I began to believe it wasn't me. It had always been the wrong guy.

Fynn was my person.

His mouth moved over mine with a hunger demanding to be matched, and I did, lifting onto my toes as my hands curved up his neck and into his hair. Tendrils of soft curls weaved between my fingers, my nails digging into his scalp.

I tasted rum and something sweet on his tongue like Coke.

"We should stop. Slow down." He wasn't the only one who needed to be distracted. I did as well, and Fynn was the fucking perfect diversion.

"Uh-huh," I agreed, slipping my tongue inside his mouth. He was right. We needed to stop, and I knew this, but my body didn't give a shit, and neither did my lips. I wanted more. I never wanted more. This was a big deal for me. How could I stop when we were just getting started?

This wasn't part of the plan. I was distracting Fynn not seducing him. The idea almost made me chuckle, and my lips did curve slightly. I didn't know the first thing about seducing anyone.

"Kenna," he growled.

The prick was always growling my name, and normally it aggravated me, but this time, I wanted him to say it again. And again.

I bit his lower lip just hard enough to make him growl a second time, and the sound spread fluttering tingles in my belly, along with the warm glow of female prowess. "I love the way you kiss."

"So do thousands of other girls," he murmured.

Fynn wasn't usually an asshole on purpose. Not to me. To other girls, sure, but rarely to me, and his words stung. More than I wanted to admit. I jerked back, putting space between our faces as I glared at him, the delicious buzz his lips created fizzing out of me. "You're a dick."

Unfazed, he angled his head to the side. "And?"

I stuck out my chin. "If you really wanted to stop, you could have done so more tactfully."

"Not all guys are saints," he replied roughly.

Shoving to my feet, I dusted the sand off my hands. "I don't need a lesson on the number of creeps and jerks in the world. I'm well aware. I didn't ask for your help to be humiliated."

Fynn followed, glaring down at me with a frown marring his lips. "Look, brat, we're doing this on my terms. And don't think I don't know what you did, using a kiss to deflect."

I don't care that he outed me. Fynn had always been smart. "Whatever. It worked."

An ominous look hardened his features. "For now."

* * *

I tossed and turned under the sheets, a restlessness humming inside me. I couldn't decide if I should get a bottle of vodka or grab my cans of spray paint. The solitude at the ocean didn't quiet the energy bouncing within me, and the encounter with Fynn only made me crazier.

If I couldn't leave, I had to find some other way to release the turmoil swimming in my blood. After tonight, I wasn't confident Fynn would let me crawl into his bed, and as much as I longed to sneak out, he would probably be waiting downstairs to catch me in the act.

My thoughts shifted to Fynn and our kiss. It was unbelievable that part of my antsiness stemmed from this unsatisfied feeling I wasn't used to. My body still yearned to be touched by him, my lips to be kissed.

With a frustrated huff, I rolled onto my back, the cool sheet rubbing against my nipples. The friction instantly made them pucker, and my nails dug into the bed. I had to find a way to quiet all this buzzing energy.

Closing my eyes, I dipped my fingers into my shorts, moving lower between my legs. It had been too long since I touched myself. I started to rub, moving my fingers slowly at first over my bud. My body didn't need much coaxing for the pleasure to build. I bit on my lower lip, my hips moving in time with my hand—until my fucking phone buzzed, the screen lighting up the dark room.

I ignored it, continuing to caress and grind to a rhythm that worked for me. Five seconds later, my phone went off again. And again. With a growl, my frustration reached new heights. I was ready to kill whoever was on the other line. My eyes darted over the string of texts from, shocker, an unknown number.

**Hello, Kenna doll.**

**What are you doing under the sheets?**

**If you keep that up, you won't be the only one coming.**

*What the fuck?*

I gawked at my phone, and a moment later, I sat upright in bed. My gaze flew from the screen to the window. I'd been sleeping with it closed and locked since the morning I received the rose on my pillow. As much as I missed the sound of the ocean while I drifted off to sleep and the breeze carrying traces of summer evenings, I valued my privacy and life more.

But this shit was going too far.

I'd often wondered how he and Kate had known details about Ainsley and Grayson only my brother and his girlfriend should have had. Grayson spent hours looking for hidden cameras only to come up empty-handed. So, the question still remained, how the fuck was this bastard seeing me?

I glared harder at my phone, my fingers flying over the letters as I typed out a response. **You like to watch, don't you, perv?**

I didn't expect a response, but then...my phone buzzed. Looked like someone else couldn't sleep tonight. **When the subject is as beautiful as you.**

I snorted in the dark. **Tell me those lines don't actually work on your victims.**

**Do you want to be a victim again?**

Swallowing over the sudden lump in my throat, I stared at the message. *What am I doing? Why am I encouraging conversation with an unreasonable psycho?* I should turn my phone off and go to sleep.

I didn't turn my phone off but set it aside, determined to ignore him.

When the phone didn't light up or buzz again after a minute, I snatched it up, my eyes boring into the screen. He hadn't sent another message. Was he waiting for me to respond?

Fuck it.

I had nothing else to do tonight. Why not have a chat with a lunatic?

**If you want to talk to me, don't hide behind your disposable phones.** I hit send, knowing I shouldn't engage, and yet I couldn't stop myself from replying.

I watched the three little dots on my phone move. **You want to meet in person?**

Was he insane? Okay, yes, he was, but did he think I was insane then? **I'm not stupid.** My phone made the little send sound as my text back went off into the cyber network.

**That's what I like about you. (heart emoji)**

I blinked, my gaze fixating on the little heart. Why did he send a heart? We weren't friendly enough for fucking emojis. In frantic annoyance, I hit the stabby knife emoji like ten times, my finger hovering over send. Backtracking, I sent a text instead. **I don't want you to like me at all.**

**Too late.**

I rolled my eyes. Go figure. I would attract the fucked-up ones. I started to type out a reply, but my phone vibrated, and I jumped, not expecting a call this freaking late, yet I knew who it was. Had he really taken what I said to heart and flipping called me?

Did I want to speak to him?

I continued to stare at the numbers flashing across the screen, the phone buzzing in my hand.

Was I really going to answer his call?

I'd provoked him. Dared him to stop hiding.

With a deep breath, I hit the accept button and waited, saying nothing.

"Hello, Kenna doll," he greeted in his deep, rich voice.

Heat zipped within me. "I'm not your doll," I snapped.

"Not yet, but we have time," he replied lightly.

Clutching the bed sheet, I clung onto it against my chest, feeling exposed. A touch of fear trickled into my veins. "Time for what?"

"To get to know each other." I could hear the smile in his voice. He was amused by me, by our conversation.

I had a different reaction. The more we talked, the more annoyed I became. "Is that why you called me? Why you sent the flowers? To get to know me?"

Through the phone, I swore I heard the gentle roll of waves. Was he on the beach? "You sound surprised."

Despite the tendrils of fear, I carefully got out of bed and tiptoed to the window. "You've been terrorizing my friends for two years. Probably longer."

"My gifts arrived then?" The joy from him made my skin crawl.

"What's the point in this? It's gone on long enough, don't you think?" I asked, my fingers slowly pushing the sheer curtain aside.

"They will suffer for every day I lived in agony." His voice darkened with such rage and bitterness I shivered.

Peering into the twilit beach below, I searched the shadows, only a thin crescent of moonlight to provide any light. "Whose fault is that?" I spat.

He laughed, a chilling sound that grated on my nerves.

I could see nothing outside. "Does that mean you've given up on your vendetta against Micah?" I pressed.

"Do I seem like the type of guy who gives up?"

"Honestly, you seem like a jealous prick. They have the life *you* want."

"They do have something I want. It's been a long time since I wanted anything. Anyone," he added.

I swallowed, a cold sweat breaking out under my armpits. *Don't say it. Don't fucking say it.*

"Care to guess, Kenna doll?"

Wariness circled inside my gut like a hawk stalking its prey. Flopping back down on the rumpled bed, I kept the phone to my ear and gritted my teeth. "Fuck off."

He chuckled. "Say it again."

My mind ran a million miles a minute. "What's wrong with you?"

"I think you understand me more than you are willing to admit. I saw something in your eyes the night of the gala. Something I see in myself, and I knew then." I hated how smooth and calm his voice remained. It made me want to scream.

"Knew what?" I found myself asking despite telling myself not to fall into the trap of being baited. A curse went off in my head as soon as the words left my mouth. I closed my eyes for a second.

"You," Sterling answered.

*Fuck.*

I wasn't shocked.

He'd been alluding to this, and I'd been avoiding hearing him say it. And now that it was out in the open, I felt as if I'd lost this game we'd been playing. It fired my blood. I hated losing.

"What do you want?" I demanded, my gaze narrowing in the shadowy bedroom.

"Isn't it obvious?"

A tightness pressed down on my chest. "No."

"I'm a patient man."

"I'm a stubborn bitch," I retaliated.

His deep chuckle brushed against my ear through the phone, and I wanted to hurl the device across the room. I shivered. I couldn't put the call on speaker for fear of someone hearing Sterling's voice. I'd have a lot of explaining to do then.

"This is why you're perfect for me. A date. You and me. Alone. No bodyguards. No Elite. No tricks. Just us," he said, laying it out on the table.

My response came automatically. "No. Not happening. I'd rather eat glass."

He laughed again, losing a bit of the edge in his voice. I couldn't tell if he was laughing at me or if he was just amused by my spunk. It didn't matter. Regardless, I didn't like it. "Ah, Kenna doll, don't be like that. You might hurt my feelings."

A snort breezed through my nose. "As if you have feelings. That would require you to have a heart, which we both know you don't."

"I haven't had this much fun in years. One date. We can strike a deal."

God, he knew where to poke my interest. I didn't know how because we didn't know each other. Not well enough to understand my likes and dislikes. "If I agree to this *date*, you'll leave my friends alone. No more taunting them, no more games, and this rivalry with Micah is quashed. You're done." I wanted the terms to be clear. Not that I trusted him to keep his word.

"That might take more than a single date," he negotiated.

Hesitation dug a line over my forehead. "One date," I repeated, hardening my tone.

A long pause stretched on the other end, and I began to wonder if I'd lost him. Then he sighed. "We might be able to work something out."

I bit my lip harder. "How can I trust you? How do I know you won't hurt me?"

"We'll meet in a public place," he offered. "Will that satisfy your reservations?"

*NO!* "I need to think about it," I heard myself say.

"Don't keep me waiting."

A soft knock sounded on the door, right before the doorknob turned. "Kenna? Are you awake?" Josie asked quietly into the dark room.

I quickly ended the call, dropping my phone onto the bed and shoving it under the covers. "Yeah. Can't sleep." My heart beat so hard in my chest I swore she would be able to hear it. "Why are you up?"

My sister strode across the floor, coming to sit on the edge of the bed so we weren't whispering across the room. "I got up to pee, and I thought I heard voices. Were you talking to someone?"

Why did I feel like I nearly got caught doing something terrible? I shook my head. "No. I was on my phone scrolling. I'll turn it down."

Her brows drew together. "Weird. I swore I heard your voice."

I hated lying, so it was best to change the subject. "Did you need something, or did you just come to annoy me in the middle of the night?"

Josie snorted. "Definitely annoy you. This is how I know we are sisters."

"It's not telepathy or whatever. I just understand how your warped mind works."

Her lips quipped. "Okay, well, I'll let you try to get some sleep." She stood up but hovered near the bed. "Are you sure you're okay?"

I made my shoulders relax. "Yeah. I'm fine. I swear."

She exhaled. "That's how I know you're lying. None of us are fine."

"At least I'm not running around tagging shit," I pointed out.

"You want to."

I shrugged. "Maybe."

If anyone understood this part of me, it was Josie. She nodded. "Night."

Josie left and I immediately wanted to call her back. I'd wanted to get rid of her, but now that I was alone, I didn't want to be by myself.

Not if Sterling had a way to see me. I couldn't see him, could no longer hear his voice, but it felt as if he was in the room with me.

Tapping my finger on the mattress, I stared into the darkness, my mind playing over my conversation with Sterling. What the fuck had I been thinking engaging with him?

A date?

It had to be a trap.

I'd be an idiot to believe anything he said. The jerk had no good intentions. He wasn't capable of them. If I truly believed he would keep his word and stop the shit, letting the grudge go, I would agree to this stupid date in a heartbeat.

My family and friends meant that much to me.

Honestly, I would sacrifice myself for them.

Essentially, that was what Sterling asked of me.

I flipped on the bedside light, bathing the room in a soft yellow glow and chasing the shadows out of the corners. It did nothing for my pounding heart and the anxiety tightening my chest.

Two minutes passed and I was out of bed, padding toward the door. I peeked into the hallway, looking to see if anyone lingered about. I waited ten seconds before leaving my room and tiptoeing toward Fynn's. I couldn't very well sneak into Mads's or Josie's room. I doubted Brock nor Micah would be thrilled about a third wheel or me kicking them out of their bed.

There was only one bed that wasn't occupied by two people.

Fynn's.

He might not want me in his room tonight, but that's what he was getting. Sleep. All I wanted was to sleep in his bed.

I stared at his closed door with no light streaming from underneath. Should I knock? If I did, he'd have the opportunity to turn me away. Fynn would ask questions. Questions I didn't want to answer. I had no intention of telling him about my conversation with the enemy or my suspicions that Sterling had somehow hacked my phone. From Fynn, I knew crazy things were possible, especially since Sterling and I had been in the same place during the gala. Or when he dropped off the rose. I'd bet my left ass cheek Sterling had done something, installing software that gave him access to my phone and God knew what else.

It was what Fynn would have done.

Hell, I wouldn't put it past Fynn to have already done something similar to Sterling.

Opting to forgo knocking, I turned the doorknob, relieved to find it unlocked. His scent instantly tickled my senses, growing stronger as I pushed open the door, poking my head inside.

"Fynn," I whispered.

14

———

FYNN

"Fynn," Kenna quietly called again.

I'd been awake when the door opened, and I stayed still, hoping if she thought I was asleep she would close the door and go back to her room. As much as I wanted to answer her and invite the brat into my bed, tonight wasn't a good night. Not after the kiss on the beach.

It had left me in a mood.

"Are you awake?" Something in Kenna's whispered voice bothered me. I couldn't tell yet, but it sounded as if she were upset or afraid. Both possibilities sent alarm through me.

The door clicked shut, and I remained frozen, listening. She left. Perhaps I'd been mistaken. Perhaps I misheard the slightest tremor in her tone. I was about to unleash the breath I'd been holding when I felt the mattress on the other side of the bed dip.

*Shit.* I had it wrong.

She hadn't gone away. The little minx climbed into my bed.

I lay there, debating about whether I continued to feign sleep or rolled over and demanded she tell me what she was doing in my bed.

She settled into the pillow next to me, inching close enough I could feel her body heat. The bed was big, and despite me taking slightly more than half the space, her slim frame had plenty of room, yet she curled in close to me.

A soft sigh left her lips.

My back was to her. I didn't turn and face her. I couldn't. Not yet. Not when I'd gotten a whiff of her scent and my body immediately responded. "Kenna, what are you doing?" I asked gruffly.

She didn't answer right away. "I had a nightmare and couldn't fall back asleep."

Her nightmares were no secret to me, but she'd always dealt with them on her own. Kenna rarely asked for help. So, what changed? Something was wrong. "You're lying. Why?"

"Do you ever stop being suspicious of everything?" she huffed.

Flipping over onto my back, I searched out her eyes in the dark. They were wide. "What happened?"

Guilt warmed her cheeks. "Nothing, I just want to sleep. I swear."

The problem was sleep was the last thing on my mind. "You might not want to talk about it, but I'll find out eventually."

She blinked heavily, tucking a hand under the pillow. "I'll be sleeping in here next week anyway. What's a few days early?"

I groaned slightly inside. Why would she remind me?

She meant it as an offhanded comment, but it influenced me, arousing feelings I tried hard to bank. She wasn't making it easy, and I was coming up to the point of not giving a shit about being the good guy.

"Kenna," I warned.

Her eyes held mine as if she just realized something was up with me. We stared at each other, neither of us moving. Hell, we barely breathed.

*Close your eyes. Go to bed.*

*That's all you have to do.*

I couldn't figure out if it was Kenna I internally pleaded with. Or myself.

She sucked in a breath as my hand lifted to brush aside a strand of her hair. It was a simple touch yet produced an electric current traveling through my fingers. Her gaze never left mine as my hand trailed along the column of her neck.

I glanced down to see she was only wearing a white tee that barely covered her ass. Under my gaze, her nipples hardened, poking through the shirt. I could have all the willpower in the world, and it still wouldn't have been enough for me to stop dipping my head and taking her into my mouth. But first...

My eyes flicked back to hers. She was right. What was a few days? There was nothing wrong with starting her lessons early. "I'm going to kiss you but not on your lips. Do you understand?"

She nodded.

"If you want me to stop, you just have to say the word." I prayed she didn't tell me to stop.

I wanted my mouth on her, but I forced myself to go slow, running the pad of my thumb over the peak of her nipple, drawing little circles. A tremor wracked through her. I gazed into her face, watching as her eyes grew darker the longer we stared at each other.

She was fucking beautiful.

Then I dipped my head, flicking my tongue where my fingers had been. A flame exploded in me. I introduced each new movement one at a time, allowing her to really appreciate or tell me if she didn't like something. So far, Kenna proved to be a receptive student.

Through the thin cotton tee, I closed my mouth around her nipple. The friction from the material only heightened the experience.

Mewling, she shoved her fingers into my hair, her chest rising and pressing into my mouth. I clamped my teeth lightly against her, applying slight pressure, not wanting to take things too far but wanting her to know there was more for when she was ready.

So much fucking more.

I shoved the shirt up her torso, exposing her flat belly. She shivered as my hot breath fanned her skin. I kissed her just above the belly button and again higher and higher until I skirted just under her breasts. I pushed the tee hampering my desire to touch her skin up to her neck.

My hand slipped over her belly up to her breast. It was heavy and full. When I swiped my tongue over the sensitive bud, her head sunk further into the pillow as her back bowed slightly off the bed, a moan escaping her lips.

"Fynn..." Her voice trailed off as I took the peak of her breast fully into my mouth.

"Just relax," I whispered roughly, tilting my head slightly so I could see her face. "I won't hurt you. And we're not having sex. I'm just going to show you what else I can do with my mouth."

She nodded.

I sucked and teased her until I felt her give herself up to the pleasure swirling within, and then I dragged my tongue down her belly.

"Lesson two, you need to get used to my touch." I ran a hand up her leg, starting at the ankle, moving to the calf, past the underside of her knee to her thigh. Her eyes stayed locked on mine, never straying. The only thing that changed was the hue of her irises, shifting from a warm brown to a darker shade that nearly matched her pupils.

I pulled off her panties, and my dick throbbed at my first sight of her. She was clean-shaven, and I groaned, drawing on my last crumbs of strength. Every inch of me wanted to slip inside her, but I wouldn't. Not tonight.

But that didn't mean I wouldn't take my fill.

Her knees pressed together. Not tightly but not loosely either. I could sense her hesitation. "Are you okay?"

"Yeah," she said breathily.

I spread her legs open, running my tongue over her center. Her fingers clenched the sheets, a gasp tumbling off her parted lips.

"Fynn." She panted, her fingers moving into my hair as my tongue played. The sound of my name in her sexy needing voice spiked victorious pleasure through me.

She was wet and ready. I slipped a finger inside, and she whimpered, her head turning to the side. God, she was so tight and warm. The sweet torture began as I pulled my finger out and pushed it in again, slowly working her. I let her adjust to the feel of me before adding a second finger, all the while licking her and nipping at the inside of her thighs. When her hips started to move, I groaned against her as one of my hands slid over her hips to squeeze her ass.

My dick was so damn hard, but this wasn't about me or my release. Removing my fingers, I replaced them with my tongue, licking and teasing her core. She moaned, her hips moving faster with more confidence and encouragement. She writhed under my mouth. I alternated between my tongue and fingers, her hips lifting in perfect sync, and seconds later, she came undone in an explosive orgasm.

"Fynn. Oh god. Fynn," she cried, and I'd never heard a sweeter sound.

Her muscles spasmed around my fingers, and my seed spilled into my boxers, soaking through onto the sheets, my cock pulsing.

I drew out her pleasure for as long as I could, and only when her muscles stopped pulsing did I withdraw my fingers. Neither of us moved, our breathing the only sound in the room. I rested my forehead on her flat stomach.

*Holy shit, I want to do that again.* If it had been any other girl than Kenna in my bed, she wouldn't be coming only once tonight.

The fingers in my hair gently moved, running through my dark strands in a caress. We stayed wrapped up in each other for an infinite time, each processing what we'd just done. This was Kenna. And I'd thought about having my mouth on her for years. It was safe to say she didn't fucking disappoint. Already, I thought about and looked forward to the next time.

"Are you okay?" I asked when I settled onto the pillow beside her, a little disappointed to be moving away from her.

She stared at the ceiling for a moment before a feline grin spread over her lips, and she glanced sideways at me. "I don't think I've ever been better in my life."

I chuckled. "I'm that good, huh?"

Long, dark hair spread out in a messy halo on the pillow. Even in the shadows with just a sliver of moonlight streaming into the room, I could see her flushed cheeks and swollen lips. "Christ, I swore I died and went to heaven."

"Just wait," I murmured, brushing a kiss over her cheek. "It gets better."

She adjusted her shirt but forwent slipping her underwear back on. Truthfully, I didn't know where they were. Probably tangled up in the sheets somewhere, but my mind was too busy contemplating how the hell I would sleep knowing her kitty was uncovered.

Her smile turned wicked. "Promise?"

I shook my head. "Temptress, little brat."

"What about you?" she asked with the sleepy eyes of a satisfied cat. "Should I...?"

I caught her wrist as her hand trailed down my chest and tugged her into my arms. Her head resting on my shoulder, she lay a hand over my heart. "Don't worry about me, brat. Go to sleep."

This was mostly about Kenna—for Kenna, but I also tested myself and my restraint.

I gave up any pretense of sleeping tonight. She needed it more than I did. My fingers gently brushed over her hair as her head rested on my chest and her breaths grew long and even.

* * *

Warmth touched my cheeks, rousing me from the little sleep I'd gotten. Beams of sunlight streaked across the bed, and as I blinked back the lingering remnants of a dream, I glanced over fully expecting my bed to be empty.

It wasn't.

A dark curtain of hair spilled over the pillow beside me.

Kenna.

And at that moment, the dream merged with reality. I hadn't been dreaming after all.

We were both turned in toward each other, lying on our sides. I stared at the girl who captured my heart, watching her sleep. What kind of nightmare had she had last night that sent her running to my room?

Being this close to her, I wanted to touch her but didn't dare for fear of waking her up.

Carefully sliding out of bed, I left Kenna asleep. She needed it.

After tugging on a tee and basketball shorts, I silently left the room, closing the door softly behind me. Downstairs, someone had already brewed coffee, and I could have kissed them. I poured myself a cup and sunk down at the table where my laptop sat charging. Was it a bad habit to get online first thing? Probably. But it was the world I grew up in.

Sipping the piping-hot black coffee, I opened my laptop and went through my morning rituals of checking emails, scanning security footage, and reviewing the alerts I had set up on the girls' phones. Every call or text gave me a notification, time and date stamped. I could get the details, but for privacy's sake, I had keywords set up to flag me if anything suspicious came through.

Late last night, Kenna had a string of texts and a phone call right after, ending minutes before she came into my room. My pulse hastened. Dread and anger simultaneously climbed up my chest.

I opened the files, skimming through the texts. My hand curled and tightened around my untouched coffee cup as it grew cold. The nightmare she referred to suddenly formed into a picture.

I moved on to the video file, unsure if I wanted to hear the conversation between them. Slipping on my earbuds, I hovered the pointer over the file icon. Their voices filled my ears, and when the line went dead, I hurled my coffee cup across the kitchen. Glass shattered on impact and dark liquid spattered the walls and floor.

"Fuck. Fuck. Fuck." Dark rage pumped in my veins. It had been a long time since I felt the violent urge to not just hurt someone but kill. I wanted to take Sterling's life, watch him take his last breath.

He had another thing coming if he thought I would let him

move in on my girl. Of all the scenarios, Sterling hitting on Kenna hadn't crossed my mind. God, the thought of her going on a date with him fucked with all my emotions, but primarily, it made me furious.

That cloud of wrath hung over my head the rest of the day. My friends saw the change in my attitude. The hard part was navigating Kenna. I didn't want her to think any part of my anger was directed at her. Last night had been nothing but fucking spectacular, and I had to ensure she knew how special last night was, which meant I couldn't be a dick.

Easier said than done when fire burned in my blood.

She eyed me warily throughout the day. I felt her eyes on me many times.

I didn't deal with the situation in the most delicate manner. Avoiding her seemed like the coward's way, but I was afraid once I opened my mouth I wouldn't be able to control what came out. Why hadn't she told me? What other secrets was she hiding from me? She'd been bluffing, right? No way would she risk her life by meeting him somewhere.

The truth was, Kenna was always the wildcard. I didn't know what she would do, but she had the guts and bravado to meet him, especially if she thought she could trap him.

I had to talk to the guys first before I confronted her.

"Can someone tell me what the fuck is going on?" Kenna demanded from where she stood in the open doorway leading to the back deck.

"Inside," Grayson growled at his sister.

Kenna crossed her arms, her mouth in a thin line. "I'm not leaving until I get an answer. Fynn?" Her brown eyes turned to me.

I cast my gaze down to the glass in my hand, spinning it on the table. "Nothing, we're just having a drink."

"Bullshit," she hissed.

"Damn it, go bug Josie," Grayson spat.

"You aren't the only one with secrets." Kenna spun, hair whirling as she stormed into the house, slamming the doors shut behind her. I'd rather have her pissed at me than hurt by me.

I'd make it up to her later because, eventually, Kenna and I were going to have a sit-down.

"Jesus Christ," Grayson muttered under his breath. "You guys are lucky you don't have sisters. Except for you, Fynn, but at least Avery's still young."

"Are you going to tell us what's been up your butt all day?" Micah got straight to the point. "You've been acting like an asshole. If it were Brock and Grayson, I wouldn't blink twice, but it's you."

"He has a point," Brock said. "Despite being indirectly called an asshole."

We could always count on Micah to call us out. "I know. I've been sitting on this information all day, and it's eating at me."

"What is it?" Grayson asked, his brows furrowed.

"I think it's better if I show you." I pulled out my phone and glanced at the house. From where the four of us sat, we could see through the expansive glass doors lining the kitchen where the girls gathered at the table playing cards.

They were out of earshot. That was what was important.

I hit play.

"That's Kenna," Grayson interrupted at the sound of his sister's voice.

I nodded, letting the recording continue to roll.

"You've got to be fucking kidding me," Micah hissed halfway through. I shared his outrage. Hearing this a second time didn't provoke a lesser reaction from me. If anything, stewing all day only fueled my fury.

"The bastard has balls," Brock said when the recording finished. He'd said this before, and we all agreed Sterling didn't lack guts and fortitude.

Micah's gaze lifted from my phone to me. "How the fuck did you do this?"

Smoke and bits of ash floated up into the sky, the fire filling the air with the scent of burning wood. "Do you really want to know the logistics?"

Micah blinked. "Fuck no."

I lifted my glass to my lips and took a long swig of the drink. "That's what I thought. The real issue here isn't my methods. It's what we are going to do with this info."

Brock shifted in his chair, a hard expression on his features. "Has Kenna said anything to anyone?"

I shook my head. "Not that I know of."

Grayson forked a hand through his hair. "Shit."

"He was fucking flirting with one of our girls. We're going to bury this bastard," Micah seethed.

"For once, I'm going to agree to one of Micah's ideas," Brock said, his eyes cold as he glanced at each of us.

Grayson nodded. "Yeah."

"It's the only way," I said. "The bastard should have died in the fire."

Brock's jaw tightened. "We won't make the same mistake twice."

Plotting murder. We'd done a lot of dark things over the years. Death followed, and not always at our hands, but plotting murder... We were older and had so much more to lose now. Grayson had a baby on the way. Despite how much protection we thought we had, there was always a chance things could go south. I refused to let my friends ruin their lives. We had to be smart about this.

Over beers and moonlight, we schemed and tossed around ideas. Most of Micah's were vetoed. Nothing new.

I would do whatever it took to keep Sterling away from Kenna. She was mine. She'd always been mine. And I wouldn't let him take what was mine.

## 15

## KENNA

It was our last day together at the beach house.

After my night with Fynn, he acted strange the next day— off, and of course, I wondered if it had anything to do with me. I hated the insecurity. Worse was showing any self-doubt. I refused.

He was angry. Like I'm-going-to-rip-someone's-head off angry. So, I gave him space. And the next day, things were better. Fynn seemed less secluded and no longer gave the don't-talk-to-me-if-you-want-to-live vibe.

His attitude change and the secretive bonfire Elite meeting later that night led me to believe they were up to something. Whatever it was, a decision had been made, and Sterling was the target. I didn't need to overhear or spy to know they plotted against him. Our month vacation was up, and we were going back to our lives. Sterling had to be dealt with.

I hadn't heard from Sterling again, which should have been a relief. It wasn't. The longer his silence stretched, the greater my unease because it meant he was up to something. I even stupidly tried to text him from the number he'd called me from. My threats came back undelivered. And when I got the gumption to call the number, I received the "this number is no longer in service" message.

Fucker.

But today I refused to think about the prick. I would hang out with my best friends, enjoy our last day together, and drink way too many mojitos Micah currently was mixing up in the kitchen.

"God, it's sweltering today," I said, sinking into a counter stool as I fanned my face with a book I had no intention of reading.

Micah grinned. "This will cool you right off." He pushed the glass over the marble countertop and winked.

Sweat beaded at the back of my neck, and despite having my hair up in a messy bun, it did little to cool me off. This had to be the hottest day of the summer so far. Shit. I wouldn't be surprised if Oceanbay was having record-breaking temps today. Even the pool offered little relief. I sought the air conditioner after being outside for the last hour. I might be dying, but my tan had never looked so good. "You're a godsend," I gushed, taking the drink with both hands and letting the condensation cool off my fingers.

"That's what Mads says." Micah lifted his glass over his smirk and drank.

"I don't want to discuss the weird shit you and my cousin whisper to each other in bed." The mojito went down cool and smooth, satisfying my thirst as I drank. Minty with a zest of lime.

"Oh, it's definitely not just in the bed. This counter." He made a point to smack the marble with his hand. "The pool. The couch. The beach. The Hummer. The shower," he continued to list off each place his sex-driven brain could recall. He flashed his cocky dimples. "Your room."

I scrunched my nose. "Fuck, Micah. Have mercy on her. She's only one girl with one pussy. And stay the hell out of my room."

Twisting so he faced forward, he leaned over the counter as if he were about to tell me a big secret, his drink cupped between his hands. "That's the thing. It's her. Not me. Apparently, she's hornier when she's ovulating."

I blinked, unable to believe the word ovulating came out of Micah's mouth. "Do you even know what that means?"

He shrugged.

"What means?" Brock asked, coming out from the deck with Josie beside him. My sister blew out a long breath and tipped her head back as a wave of air conditioning hit her. I knew the feeling well.

I swirled the ice in my cup, taking another sip. "Oh, Micah was just sharing his sexual exploits with my cousin."

Brock shook his head, opening the fridge. "I knew better than to ask," he mumbled.

"Would you care to share yours?" I shot back playfully. Little did I know it would come back and shoot me in the foot.

Brock raised a brow at me. "Not unless you're sharing as well."

The room fell silent.

Micah, Brock, and Josie regarded me.

Josie clasped a hand over her mouth, hurrying around the island to stand in front of me. "Holy shit, Kenna. Are you having sex?" She took my drink without asking and downed half of it.

My wits finally returned, and I frowned at her. Partially because she drank my drink. "No. Why would you get that idea?"

Micah's grin widened, his dimples winking, like the devilish rogue he was. "She totally is."

Lips turning downward, I narrowed my eyes at Micah. "Shut up and pour me another mojito."

He complied but with a lopsided smirk that usually got him in trouble. "She's deflecting."

I rolled my eyes.

"Who's deflecting what?" Grayson asked, entering from the patio door Brock and Josie had walked through a few minutes ago.

Fynn brushed passed him, shirtless and glowing like a golden god. The month under the sun had bronzed his already tan skin. His shorts were damp, having been in the pool not long ago. Our eyes met for a brief exchange, and my stupid heart skipped in my chest. *God is he gorgeous.*

Every time I saw him since the night I slept in his bed, I couldn't help but think about what we'd done. What he had done to me. To my body. And it never failed—heat flushed over me from head to toe. I'd been tempted to sneak back into his room night after night since, because the second I laid my head on the pillow, all I thought about was Fynn's mouth on me. I'd never experienced such pleasure. Never knew intimacy could be so freeing. I felt connected to him on a deeper level, and it made me curious about what it would feel like to have him inside me.

"Your sister," Micah answered my brother's question, bringing my wandering thoughts back to the present.

Grayson stayed hovering at the open door, letting all the cold air escape, his eyes glancing back outside as he said, "Which one? I have two, remember."

"Kenna. She's having sex," Micah the shithead replied.

*Damn it.* I thought it had been hot outside. Inside was worse. My cheeks grew warm. "I am not," I insisted, which was in fact the truth. Fynn and I had done nothing but fool around...so far.

But the other night, when I'd snuck into his room, I thought I wanted to do more. And that was huge for me, and no one's business but mine. The rest of them might love to boast about their sex life but I preferred to keep that shit to myself.

Grayson waited for his girlfriend, and Ainsley waddled inside, a hand under her growing belly. Over the last four weeks, I swore her stomach doubled in size, and yet she still rocked a bikini, proud of her baby bump. "Who's having sex?"

I tossed my hands in the air. "Oh my god. This is getting out of hand." It was always a hot mess when we got together. And I might secretly love it when I wasn't the subject.

Fynn offered no help. Saying nothing, he leaned against the table where the spread of snacks was laid out and tossed a piece of fruit into his mouth.

Grayson's features pulled. "She's not having sex."

I crossed my arms and pinned my brother with a look. "What makes you think I'm not?"

He pulled out a chair for Ainsley to sit on. He might be the most annoying triplet sometimes, but turned out he was an exceptional boyfriend. I would like to say I was surprised, but I wasn't. He stood behind Ainsley's chair, hands resting on her shoulders. "Because unless you met someone on the beach, it would mean you're fucking Fynn."

Heads snapped up. The room got pin-dropped quiet. Everyone pondered the idea as if it had merit.

Josie coughed, covering a grin yanking at her lips.

*Fuck.*

When neither Fynn nor I were quick to deny the assumption, things got awkward.

"Oh, shit," Ainsley murmured, surprise lighting her features.

"We're not having sex." *Yet*, I silently added, but the rebuttal came too late. No one believed me, especially because Fynn just sat at the table popping grapes into his mouth as if I wasn't caught in the middle of a shitstorm. "Listen, just because you all are doing it morning, noon, and night, doesn't mean some of us don't have a life outside the bedroom."

"She does spend a lot of time in there," Josie said, talking about me as if I wasn't right in front of her.

Spinning in my chair, I took the refill mojito Micah poured me. "This is ridiculous. The conversation is over."

Mads came moseying from the hallway in her two-piece swimsuit covered by a black sheer top. "What's ridiculous?"

"Oh, good, the whole crew's here," I said sarcastically. "Let's make the announcement so we can stop talking about it. Fynn and I are fucking."

My cousin didn't even blink or falter as she walked around the counter to Micah. "About time."

Micah slipped an arm around her, glancing down at his girl. "Why aren't you surprised?"

She gave a one-shoulder shrug and moved to the table where platters of food were spread out. I'd kill her if she responded with something like *she's been in love with him her whole life.* "Because I'm not clueless."

"So, it's true?" Micah pushed, being the pot stirrer that he was.

I sighed, so over this topic. "Believe what you want. I'm not going to say it again."

"Let's just ask Fynn," Micah suggested.

All eyes turned to him in the room. He continued to toss grapes into his mouth and without hesitation replied, "My lips are sealed."

No one pressed him, and I was more than delighted when the conversation shifted off me and onto someone else. Specifically, Ainsley.

"Oh," Ainsley said at the table as she stretched to reach for a square of cheese.

"What's wrong?" at least five people asked at once.

A breath of silence passed. Josie moved away from Brock, walking to the seat beside her best friend. "Please tell me your water didn't break."

Ainsley shook her head. "No, the baby kicked. I swear she's trying to bust her way out."

An audible exhale left Grayson. I swore my brother's golden face had paled slightly in those few seconds.

"Sounds like Grayson's kid already," I muttered.

Josie grinned, sitting down and resting her hands on Ainsley's belly. "I have to feel."

"Me too," Mads exclaimed, ditching Micah's arms to bounce across the kitchen.

From where I sat a few feet away from Ainsley, I watched her stomach do an alien squirm, and I couldn't decide if I was fascinated or freaked out.

"And that's my cue to get back into the pool," Micah said, taking his drink and heading outside.

"That's so insane," Josie gushed in awe, smiling at Ainsley as the other guys followed Micah, leaving us girls inside the cool kitchen.

"I can't believe there's an actual human in there," Mads commented.

"Me neither. Weird, right?" Ainsley lifted her eyes to me. "Kenna, did you want to feel her move?"

*Did I?*

Silently, I slid off the stool and strolled to where Ainsley sat at the table. Crouching down, I flattened my palm on her protruding belly and waited.

Although I hadn't grown up around a ton of babies, I was beyond excited to be an aunt, but I wasn't going to lie; I found the idea of growing a baby inside a belly strange.

Did I want to be a mom?

I thought I would like to be someday, but I didn't know how good I would be at being responsible for someone else.

Then Ainsley's stomach full-on shifted, distorting its shape as my niece wiggled around inside. My eyes flew up to Ainsley's. "Holy shit," I whispered.

Ainsley grinned. "Pretty wicked. You can talk to her if you want. She can hear you."

I stared at her belly. "That's insane."

Resting her hands on top of the bump, Ainsley's face shone. "She gets excited when Grayson talks."

My nose scrunched. "Normally information like that would make me sick, but how stinking cute."

"Have you picked a name yet?" Mads asked, reaching for a square of cheese.

"Kenna is a fabulous name," I not so subtly suggested.

Ainsley chuckled. "We're narrowing down the list. It's one thing about her we can't agree on."

"Why does that not surprise me," Josie muttered.

Dropping my hand from her belly, I stood up, a smirk twisting at my mouth. "Let me guess, you want something unique like Towel or Bucket."

Ainsley reached for a triangle of pita and dipped it in the hummus. "Not quite, but we're playing around with a few names."

Josie picked up the drink I set on the table, once again helping herself to my mojito. I scowled, about to tell her to get her own damn drink when she said, "You're going to keep her name a secret."

Ainsley stuffed another triangle of pita into her mouth. "I want to see her before I decide."

"Well, no matter what her name is, she is going to be the most spoiled little girl in the world," Mads said.

"Ugh," Ainsley groaned. "You have no idea how much that worries me. With this group, I wouldn't be surprised if she gets a damn private plane for her first birthday."

I lifted my brows. "That isn't a far-off gift idea. We can have her name detailed on the side of the plane. AirKenna."

Ainsley shook her head. "We are not naming her Kenna."

I winked at Ainsley. "So you say. I still have a couple of months to warm you up to the idea."

I loved this crew—my family. They were all I had. And I would do whatever it took to keep them safe.

* * *

The scream woke me up, startling me out of a dead sleep thanks to a day of booze and sun. For a second, I couldn't figure out if the scream had been in my dream or real, but then I heard voices and footsteps. Racing out of bed, I darted across the room, flinging open my door as a flood of light hit me in the face. I blinked and stepped into the hallway, waiting for my eyes to adjust to the brightness. Brock and Micah were both already in the hallway.

"What's going on?" I grumbled. "I thought I heard someone screaming."

"It was Ainsley," my brother said, coming out of his room.

"Is she okay?" Brock asked with instant concern in his voice. Josie popped up behind him, resting a hand on his shoulder, looking like she was sleepwalking. Her eyes were half closed.

My brother raked a hand through his hair. "Yeah, just shaken up."

"What happened to you?" I asked, noticing his disheveled hair, winded breath, and torn shirt. Was that blood on him?

His scowl deepened as if I brought up a painful memory. "I got into a fight."

Worry charged into me. "Are you hurt?"

He shook his head. "No, but the bastard got away."

"Was it Sterling?" Micah inquired, jumping to the same conclusion I had.

My brother blew out a frustrated breath. "I wish, but it might as well have been. It wasn't his face and body, but the order came from him. That's what matters."

A sleepy Mads appeared next to Micah. "What's going on?" she asked with a yawn.

"Everything's okay now," Micah assured, pulling my cousin protectively against him.

Everything wasn't okay.

"Where's Fynn?" I asked, noticing he wasn't in the hallway with the rest of us.

Brock glanced toward the stairs. "Checking the house."

"I'm going to find him," I said, rubbing my eyes. There was no point in pretending any of us were going to get any more sleep tonight. Only a few hours remained before everyone left. Everyone but Fynn and I, that was.

"I'll make some tea," Mads offered, trailing after me as I meandered down the hallway.

We left the guys upstairs. Mads flipped the light switch at the bottom of the landing, the soft glow pouring into the corridor. Still half asleep, Mads traipsed into the kitchen, the small light over the sink flicking on a moment later. I waited until I heard her opening a cabinet before veering off to the side of the house.

No one paid any attention to me. As they shouldn't. Ainsley needed them.

I went into the laundry room, shuffling through my duffel bag until I found what I was looking for. This part of the house was dark, and I didn't bother to turn on any lights or draw attention as I moved. I snuck out the back door, shaking the spray can as I jogged down the steps onto the beach.

This shit had to stop.

My toes sunk into the cold sand as I stomped down to the beach. Behind me, all the other houses on the strand were dormant except ours. The yellow glowing in the windows was like a beacon, guiding me home.

Was it reckless to be out here alone?

Yes.

Did I give a shit?

No.

I was going off pure instinct.

Shaking the can in my hand, I stopped far away from the ocean so the paint wouldn't be washed away, somewhere in the middle between the house and the water. The breeze whipped my hair around my face as I worked, crafting out the letters in black spray paint. The waves lapped smoothly behind me. Nothing else stirred; only the wind, the water, and I moved.

Taking a step back, I glanced at the bold letters written in the sand. It wasn't easy to see at night, not unless you were walking on the beach, but in less than an hour, the sun would be creeping up on the horizon.

ONE DATE.

Satisfied, I trotted back to the house, dropping my spray can under a bush for now until I could retrieve it without suspicion. I didn't want to take the chance of someone spotting me as I entered the house. Fynn's eyes lifted to me as I casually came back into the family room, his brows arching questioningly. He'd noticed my absence even though I'd been gone five minutes or less.

Things seemed to have settled down. I skipped the tea and excused myself, telling everyone I was going back to bed for the few hours that were left. I was relieved Fynn didn't follow me.

I needed to be alone.

Checking the window, I half expected to see a shadow on the beach. There was no one. No sign of life.

I had no intention of climbing into bed. My body was too wired for sleep, so I paced the room, checking the window every few minutes. I had a perfect view of the beach. Twenty minutes later, I shoved aside the curtain for the fiftieth time and stared at the spot I'd tagged. Did I really think Sterling was stupid enough to show up?

He was smart and cocky, which was exactly why I thought he would.

Something irrational like disappointment fell in my chest each time I glanced through the glass. It was a different sort of disappointment than I might have felt if I'd been stood up by a friend or Fynn. This feeling inside me was spurred by revenge.

I was about to let the curtain fall when a flash of heat lightning zipped across the sky, brightening the beach. I saw him. Just a quick glance for as long as the lightning lasted. The flickering flashed in the sky like a caution sign from the heavens.

*Sterling.*

Our eyes locked as I looked out my window.

His lips curled, and a moment later he was swallowed by darkness.

I released the breath I'd been holding, willing the damn lightning to hurl through the night again.

When it finally did, too many seconds later, he was nowhere to be seen, the spot on the beach where he stood empty.

It didn't really matter. He'd gotten the message.

Threatening Ainsley was like threatening me. I would do anything to keep this baby safe. Even go out with the enemy.

## 16

## FYNN

"What are you doing?" I stared down at Kenna as she dug in the sand looking like she was attempting to make a poorly executed sand angel or covering something up. Knowing Kenna, she was up to something.

Her head lifted from where she was on her hands and knees, squinting against the sun's bright rays. "Looking for something. I dropped a ring."

It was a quick excuse. Believable. And yet, I didn't buy it.

"Was it important or expensive?" I asked, crouching down to help look for the supposed lost ring.

She shrugged, sitting back on her legs. "No. I just really liked it."

My fingers combed through the sand, searching for a shiny object. "And you're sure you dropped it here?"

She shoved her dark hair off to one side. "Shit. I don't know." She was upset. Her features had a sadness to them, her lips tugging into a weak frown.

Everyone else had left for the trip back to Elmwood. It hadn't been the start to summer as we planned, and we'd made memories we wouldn't forget. I was just disappointed not all of them were good.

After I finished cleaning the kitchen, I went hunting for Kenna and found her here.

I wondered if she was sad everyone left. Or was it something else that bothered her?

Studying the girl who sometimes could be such a mystery, I shoved my hand deeper into the sand. "You don't have to go through with this week. You can back out at any time. Right now, if you want. I won't pressure you, Kenna. Ever. There's no rush or timetable for these things. No one else's opinion matters."

Her chest inflated. "Thanks, Fynn. I really mean it. And this is precisely why I'm here. With you."

I dusted off the sand on my hands, thinking the search for her ring might be a lost cause. "Are you really here though?" I posed. "You seem preoccupied, but I guess we all are. I'm not sure this is something you should do when you're not in it a hundred percent."

Her lips tipped up. "Are you trying to back out on me, gorgeous? Not getting cold feet, are you?"

The corner of my mouth twitched. "I wouldn't dream of it."

"Then we're good," she said as if the matter was settled and then added in a softer tone, "I still want this. I want you."

I swallowed. "There's no going back."

Kenna sat back in the sand, a frown on her face. "I don't believe in looking back. I'm living in the present. And right now, that's with you."

"There's nothing else going on? Nothing else you want to talk about?" I'd hoped when we were alone she would come to me and open up about Sterling contacting her. It was the second time since the fire he'd done so. Normally he hid behind his texts. Nothing more. Something about Kenna drew him out, allured him.

She was beautiful, but that wasn't what captured Sterling's attention. He thought he and Kenna were similar, a kindred soul perhaps. I didn't believe it. Not for a second. She wasn't anything like the bastard. She had heart.

Wrestling with her bottom lip, Kenna held my gaze. I could see her weighing the pros and cons in her head. "Like what positions I like?"

I shouldn't be amused. The feeble chuckle shouldn't have left my lips, and yet I couldn't stop myself. I shook my head. "That wasn't what I had in mind, but we can talk about that too when the time comes."

A kernel of tension crackled between us at the mention of what was to come. She changed the subject and avoided what really nagged at her. "When will that be?" she asked, a hopeful lightness entering her tone.

If she wanted to dilute the serious mood, I could accommodate her...for now. "Are you eager or afraid, brat?" I tugged on the ends of her ponytail.

"Both. I think," she admitted.

"Good. That's normal."

A sparkle appeared in her eyes. "Are you telling me when you're about to have sex with a girl, you get afraid?"

"Well, no. But that's different." My lips curled fully. "I'm experienced."

"I'm trying not to think about the girls you banged," she groaned.

"It's probably not as many as you think."

"Doubtful." Her gaze drifted over my shoulder to the house, a somber glint shadowing her expression.

What did she see?

What was she thinking?

I glanced over my shoulder, seeing nothing but the beach house. When I looked back at Kenna, she had a soft smile on her lips that didn't reach her eyes.

"Did you want to go to dinner tonight? Get out of the house for a little bit?" I suggested, wondering if a change of scenery would be good for both of us.

Her black hair blew in the wind as she shook her head. "I'd rather stay in. We can cook together. Or order in."

"Okay," I agreed.

She held up her hand, a slim gold band between her fingers. "Found it."

My focus stayed on her face. We both knew she hadn't lost the ring to begin with, but if she wanted to continue the charade, I would be patient. Sterling wasn't the only one who was skillfully patient.

* * *

Hours later, we were in the kitchen, taking inventory of what we had in stock to scrounge something up for dinner. After pulling out ingredients from the fridge and cabinets, we stacked everything on the counter, which Kenna now sat on, her golden legs hanging over the side, distracting me from the task.

"So what's on the menu tonight, chef?" She grinned, happiness shining in her eyes that hadn't been there in days. Weeks maybe.

Her smiles could fuck me up inside.

Neither of us could claim to be a fabulous cook, but I had more experience. "Pasta."

Her hand went to her chest. "God, you know the way to a woman's heart. Carbs."

I rolled my eyes. "You can pick out the wine."

She had on a sundress that left little to the imagination, particularly since she wasn't wearing a bra, and I could see her nipples. How the fuck was I supposed to concentrate on not burning the food when her nipples were literally screaming for my attention?

"Fancy. Do you plan on getting me drunk before taking advantage of me?" The smile she sent me was wicked.

I frowned at her tacky joke. "Kenna, not funny."

"Lighten up, gorgeous. I was just messing with you. I wouldn't be here if I thought there was any chance you would be a guy like that. And for the record, I know you're not despite your history with girls."

With a narrowed gaze, I reached for a knife and cutting board. "Thanks, I think."

"You're welcome," she said cutely.

I started washing and prepping some vegetables and herbs for the sauce. "Can you put on a pot of water to boil? And don't forget to add salt."

"Yes, sir," she saluted before jumping off the counter. The movement had the back of her skirt flipping up slightly, flashing me a side of her ass. She was wearing a black thong, which was basically like wearing nothing.

*Dear god. How am I going to make it through the preparation without flipping up that damn dress?*

*Focus, Fynn, and not on her nipples winking through the thin material.*

I checked out her ass when she bent over to get a pot and fill it with water. My lips curled as she stared at all the little knobs on the stove, trying to figure out how to turn it on, and because I didn't want the beach house to burn down, I did it for her.

"Where did you learn to cook?" she asked, leaning against the counter as she watched me mince garlic and onion.

I shrugged. "Mostly from being away at college."

"A matter of necessity. I see." She reached over the counter and plucked a slice of yellow pepper from the cutting board.

I finished chopping the rest of the vegetables and herbs, set them aside, and pulled out a pot to start working on the sauce. Nothing too extravagant. A doctored-up jar of red sauce because I was still a guy who didn't have a lot of time to cook. Quick, easy, yet tasty. "Watch and learn."

"Oh, I am. Guys who can cook are hot."

My brow arched, and I sautéed the veggies until they were golden and then dumped in the jarred sauce. "Why? Because you can't?"

She grinned. "Exactly." After tying up her hair, she lifted the lid and leaned over the simmering pot. "God, that smells so good."

The kitchen was filled with the aroma of cooked tomatoes, garlic, onions, and spices, and yet, her scent still reached me. My chest inflated. "I've cooked for you before."

"I know, just never one-on-one. It's always been as a group where everyone pitches in."

I stirred the sauce, mixing all the herbs in. "Everyone but you," I pointed out.

She shrugged with a twist of her lips. "Someone has to supervise."

I'd never cooked for a girl. Not like this. As Kenna noted, the only girls I'd cooked for were the ones in our crew.

She dipped her finger into the sauce, scooping up a bit onto her finger before sucking it off.

"Hey, it's not done," I protested, a slight frown tugging at the corners of my mouth.

A glint of mischief flared in her eyes. "Don't you know a chef always tastes the food while preparing?"

My throat dipped as I swallowed. "And? How is it?"

"Hmm. I'm not sure." She plunged the tip of her finger in again, but before she could bring it to her mouth, I caught her wrist.

"The least you could do is share." Lifting her hand, I took her finger inside my mouth, licking the sauce off her skin. Watching her watch me had to be one of the sexiest things I'd experienced.

"And?" she prompted, angling her head. "What does the chef think?"

I leaned forward, and my cheek grazed against hers. The little rough hairs from not shaving for a day scratched slightly over her soft skin as I whispered in her ear, "I might need a second taste."

A shiver ran through her. "My thoughts exactly." She moved closer, her eyes locked on me.

A growing ache spread inside me with each passing second, and I couldn't decide if the glass doors, the countertop, or the table was the best place to start our lesson. I wasn't sure how much longer I could keep my hands off her.

Her cheeks were slightly flushed from the stove's heat or something else. "I want you to kiss me, but I don't want to ask anymore. I want you to kiss me whenever you feel like it."

My brows lifted. "Permission eternally granted?"

She laid her palm on my chest, right over my rapidly beating heart. "I don't know about eternally, but until I get tired of you."

A snort breezed through my nose. "That won't happen."

She lifted a rebellious chin. "Aren't you going to kiss me now?"

I shook my head. "No. Not yet. Not when you asked. The next time I take your lips, it will be on my terms. Is that what you want?"

"Yes."

"Good. Let's eat. You grab the bread, and I'll pour the wine." I left her blinking after me. A small smirk curved on my lips, knowing she damn well expected me to kiss her, that she had wanted me to. Kenna hated not getting her way, and it made teasing her that much sweeter. What she didn't know was our lessons had already begun, and this was a bit of foreplay.

She was still slightly pouting when I returned with two bowls of spaghetti, setting each one on the table, and poured wine into our glasses. She'd lit the tapered candles my mom kept in a drawer, and the soft yellow glow of the flames danced over her face.

I sat in the chair beside her instead of across, needing to be close to her. She reached for her wine and took a sip. A drop clung to her lips, and before her tongue could dart out and lick it up, I brushed it aside with my thumb. I lingered. "For the record, not kissing you kills me."

Her eyes stayed on mine, and her lips softened.

"Don't sulk. You'll ruin your appetite, and for what I have planned later, you're going to need it," I said.

"You swear?"

I nodded. "But if you keep looking at me like that, we'll both go hungry."

"I love cold spaghetti."

"Kenna," I moaned.

She rolled her eyes and purposely stabbed her fork into the bowl, twisting the noodles around it, and stuffed it into her mouth. "Happy?" she asked around a mouthful of food.

Hardly.

Her face changed as she chewed, shifting from sassy to surprise. "Holy shit," she moaned after the first bite. "What are you making tomorrow?"

I chuckled. "Takeout."

She pouted again, but then she ate another forkful of pasta, and her eyes closed in pleasure. "If you cooked like this for me every night, I'd have to take the gym seriously."

"We could work out together," I offered though I knew what she would say.

Her face scrunched. "I'll pass. I've seen your routine, and I'd rather lick a sweaty sock than put myself through that torture."

"A sweaty sock, huh? I can think of something else you can lick." The retort left my mouth thoughtlessly.

She didn't bat an eye. "Will that be part of the lesson?"

The fork stopped halfway to my mouth. "Fuck, I hope so."

Her lips twitched.

Some of the tension had been deflated. But not all of it. My dick made sure to let me know it wasn't happy about being made to wait, but I could enjoy dinner and Kenna's company.

"Now what?" she asked, leaning back in her chair, her bowl of spaghetti wiped clean.

I polished off the last swig of wine. "I'm too damn full to do the dishes tonight. Let's hang out and watch some TV."

"You want to watch TV?" she asked, a bit put off.

A smile lifted the side of my mouth. "We have all night, Kenna. All week actually. Just relax and trust me. I'm not rushing this or rushing you."

"But what if I want to rush you?" Her voice was throaty and sexy as hell.

My pulse sped. "Well, tonight is also a lesson in patience."

She sunk into her chair. "I'm starting to regret asking for your help."

"You won't in a few hours," I vowed cockily.

"Oh, fun. More false promises," she grumbled, somehow looking too damn adorable.

I wanted to shove everything on the table to the floor and take her right there. "Just get your ass upstairs."

"To your room?"

If she didn't leave now, we wouldn't make it to my room, let alone upstairs. "Yeah, my room."

The flare of irritation in her features cooled. "I pick the show."

We wouldn't really be watching TV, so I didn't care what she picked. Carrying our dishes to the sink, I flipped off the kitchen lights and checked the doors to make sure the house was locked up, and we headed down the hallway.

"Should I put on something sexy?" she asked over her shoulder as we climbed the stairs with me trailing behind.

"You're wearing something sexy." I hadn't been able to take my eyes off her ass.

She shot me a faint smile. "Have it your way. I need to use the bathroom first."

I turned on the TV and cleaned up any discarded clothes I'd left lying around until Kenna bounded into the room and climbed into my bed. She made herself comfortable, fluffing the pillows. I got in beside her, opening my arm for her to crawl in, and handed her the remote. She snuggled into my arms, flipping through the shows until she found one.

I groaned, rolling my eyes. "How many times have you seen this movie?"

"Does it matter? It relaxes me."

"Only you would find a cheerleading movie calming."

"It has some football scenes," she defended.

Tucked into me, she settled down, getting engrossed in the movie. She recited half the lines, but I honestly didn't care what was on the screen. My focus was mostly on her.

I traced my fingers along her spine to the small of her back, drawing lazy circles over her skin. The dress had a low back and thin straps that easily slipped off the shoulders. I ran my hand up her arm, pressing a kiss onto her shoulder as a finger hooked under one of the straps. Kissing her again, I slowly guided the thread of material off her shoulder. After each touch of my lips, goose bumps rose over her flesh.

I moved to her throat and up the column of her neck, my mouth opening as I tasted her skin before taking her earlobe between my teeth. My hand moved from her shoulder to the front of her neck, and with a bit of pressure, I turned her head to face me, my lips brushing over hers with a teasing laziness.

I was pleased with the sound of her moan. She hadn't flinched, and the fingers that dove roughly into my hair were full of hastiness. I gave her a little more, sneaking my tongue inside her mouth to toy with hers. She tried to deepen the kiss, but I retreated before starting the torturous process over again.

And when she was completely lost in my kiss, in my touch, in me, I covered her mouth in total ownership.

She was mine.

Slanting my head to the side, I gave in, giving us both what we longed for.

My hands went to her hips, tugging her onto my lap, the movie long forgotten in the background. She settled on top of me, her soft center pressing into my hard, throbbing length. I'd been ready before she got into bed, and now my dick was raring to go.

A groan vibrated deep in my throat as I let Kenna drive the kiss.

I wanted to rip her dress off. Her nipples puckering through the material were driving me mad. I had to taste her. I had to feel the buds peak in my mouth. I had to suck them.

I *had* to slow down the trail of lust coursing through me before it hurdled to the point of no return. That wouldn't do Kenna any good. I didn't want to push her too fast, but fuck, my dick was harder than it had ever been and throbbing to be deep inside her.

"Are you nervous?" I murmured, her breathy pants caressing my mouth.

She shivered, lips parting. "I don't get nervous."

I gauged her, my eyes running over her flushed face. "Liar."

"Fynn," she scolded, sinking farther into my lap, unaware of the pleasure it created.

"This is part of the lesson, brat. I need you to be honest with me."

"Fine," she conceded. "I wasn't nervous until you asked. You were distracting me from thinking at all."

The pad of my thumb brushed over her swollen lips. "Good, if at any time you want me to stop—"

"I don't. Please," she begged. Her cheeks were the sweetest shade of pink.

Was there a man alive who could have said no to her? Who could have denied the beautiful girl in my lap?

I certainly didn't have the strength. I never wanted to please a girl as much as I did her.

If I ever thought there was a shred of a chance I could let her go after a week, it no longer existed. She'd been in my bed one night, and I already never wanted her to leave. I shouldn't have agreed to be her *practice* lover.

The one who would get hurt was me.

## 17

## KENNA

I loved the way Fynn kissed. The soft plumpness of his mouth pressed against mine. I loved the ribbon of thrill twirling inside me as the kiss grew hungry—needy. He had skill, not like the sloppy or bruising clumsiness of other guys.

They hadn't produced the ache in my core Fynn did. Nor the flush of my skin. Or the want of his hands on my body. These were all new feelings as if Fynn had unlocked a hidden door within me. He was the only one with the key.

But I didn't just want him to kiss me. Or touch me.

I wanted him to devour me.

To own me.

I'd never wanted to be possessed by anyone, and instead of losing control, the idea filled me with heady power.

Feeling how much he wanted me added to my desire, heightening it. I'd thought this intimate dance was about me, but really it was about us. His desire was my desire. My wants were his wants. I never realized how much power came with sex, and I wanted to explore and test what I could do with it.

But I had no idea what I was doing.

My fingers wove into his dark curls, and I tightened my hold, pressing my nails into the base of his neck. Underneath me, the hard length of him rested between my legs. He was so fucking hard. And I was fascinated by that part of Fynn.

Lifting my hips slightly, I circled my tongue with his as he kissed me. His hands moved to my ass, fingers squeezing, but then I sunk back down, shifting my hips so my center rubbed on his dick filling his shorts.

He groaned at the friction, causing my stomach to flutter in response, the muscles in my core clenching.

*Holy shit.* That felt... amazing. I wanted to do that again. And again.

So I did, rubbing and grinding against him, the ache building. I reveled in the sensations produced in my body. I could tell Fynn enjoyed it as well. His hands flanked my hips, encouraging me to move.

"What does it feel like?" I asked curiously.

"What feels like? Sex?" His voice was raspy, heavy with desire matching his eyes.

"No." I shook my head, keeping my gaze on his. I *was* curious about that as well, but right now, I had something else on my mind. The green in his eyes was dark. I shifted my gaze downward. "You," I murmured.

A smirk graced his mouth. "If you want to know, you'll have to find out for yourself. My body is yours to do with it as you please. You don't need permission."

I sat back in his lap, putting some space between us, and glanced down at him. I could see the outline of his obvious arousal straining against the fabric of his shorts. Catching my lip between my teeth, I took a breath.

"Do you want me to help you?" he murmured, seeing the hesitation in my face.

I nodded.

His hand covered the top of mine and slowly brought it to his shorts. He didn't force me but let me decide what to do next. My palm pressed over him as my fingers wrapped around his length. His dick was hard and yet not like plastic. There was still something soft about it. Soft wasn't the right word.

After a moment, he released my hand, leaving me free to roam.

I wanted to touch him without any barriers. This time I didn't ask.

My fingers edged the band of his shorts before slipping past them into his boxers. His dick was waiting for me. With tentative fingers, I traced my nails down his shaft, gently rubbing the silky tip.

The features on his face tightened, and his head fell back. "Jesus," he hissed.

I stroked down his velvety skin. It was so smooth.

His hand wrapped over mine through his shorts and began to move, guiding my fingers up and down. "Like this," he instructed.

It took me only a few moments to get the hang of the rhythm, and his hand fell to my thigh, moving my dress up.

"This has to go." He pushed the flowy material higher up toward my hips.

Pressing a kiss to his jawline, I replied, "I'm assuming you can handle that."

Then my dress was gone, discarded somewhere in the room, leaving me in a matching set of lacy undergarments. I hadn't exactly packed a slew of sexy lingerie for the beach. Sex hadn't crossed my mind. It hadn't even been on my radar then.

And yet, here I was with Fynn. Alone. Nearly naked in his bed.

"Your turn." I wanted to see him. All of him.

His shirt was the first to go. I crawled off his lap so he could shed his shorts and boxers. I'd seen guys naked before, but holy smokes, Fynn was impressive. Perhaps too much. A flutter of nerves danced into my belly. How the fuck was *that* going to fit inside me?

"I know what you're thinking," he said, watching me and noticing where my eyes lingered.

Swallowing, I lifted my gaze. "Do you?"

His green eyes were molten hot. "It will fit," he said intently.

I laughed. "This is a conversation I never imagined I'd be having with you."

He lifted on his elbow, staring down at me as he rested the side of his temple against his hand. "Well, while we're talking, do you have any other questions?" he asked as his fingers started to trace down my neck to the middle of my chest.

It was damn hard to concentrate with him touching me. My boobs grew heavy and strained against the lacy material, begging for his hand to move either left or right. I did have a question. "Will it hurt?"

One of his fingers drew lazy circles around my nipple, but there was nothing sluggish about the way my body responded. "I'm going to do everything I can to make sure it doesn't. The key is to relax and trust me. If at any time you feel uncomfortable or pain, tell me. If you want to stop, just say the word. It's important you know that you're the one in control. Not me."

Fynn Dupree was exactly the right guy.

I couldn't believe how much sensation and sensitivity nipples had or that they had a direct line to my vagina. "Okay." The statement came out breathy.

When his hand moved away from my breast, I moaned in protest, but then my bra snapped open. The cool air whispered over my skin, soothing the warmth capturing my body. The reprieve was short-lived as Fynn dipped his head, sucking the little bud into his mouth.

"Your skin is so soft," he murmured, his breath causing my nipple to pucker more.

Lust pooled between my legs, making me antsy for the friction I'd felt from rubbing against him. I turned my body, trying to get closer to him, but I got distracted by his chest and all the rippling muscles and ink covering them. I ran my hand over his pecs. He was gorgeous, his skin a deeper golden color from the last month at the beach.

"Of all your tats, this one is my favorite." My nail traced the lines of the rose petals turning into a tangle of vines and thorns trailing down from his pec to the side of his stomach. The flower represented his sister, and the snarl of thorns was her protection. If anyone dared to touch the rose, they would get pricked.

He had told me before when I asked. I loved the sentiment then and more so now.

There was a second rose I didn't remember being there before. "Who is this one for?" I asked, pressing a kiss over the ink.

His response didn't come immediately. "You," he finally whispered.

My gaze flew upward. "Fynn—"

He kissed me, cutting me off from saying any more, but I didn't even know what I would have said. I already felt too much.

I broke off the kiss, running the pad of my finger over his swollen bottom lip. "There's something else I'm curious about." Instead of telling him, I wanted to show him.

My lips cruised down his flat stomach. More tattoos. More muscles jumping under my touch.

He got the picture when my fingertips skimmed over his sex. "You don't have to do that."

"I want to. I've always wondered what it would taste like."

His breath hitched as my hand found him fully again, closing over the hardness pulsing and dying for attention. "You're killing me, brat."

"Don't die just yet, gorgeous," I said right before my tongue licked the tip.

Fynn's fingers curled into the bed, his eyes fluttering closed as he moaned, "Sweet Jesus."

It tasted saltier than I thought. Not unpleasant, and the sounds coming from him made me want to keep going. I'd never given a guy head before, and I had no idea what I was doing. Letting my tongue run over the top, I used my hand to hold the base of his erection. I moved my hand like Fynn had shown me as I took the tip into my mouth, sucking gently.

From the strain in his muscles, I could tell he fought against making any sudden movements that might alarm me.

My mouth and hand moved in unison, creating a flow alternating between slow and fast. I grew more confident, licking and sucking him. The surprising part was his pleasure turned me on.

"Kenna." He choked, his hands shoving into my hair to pull my head back.

Blinking, I glanced up at him. "Do you want me to stop?"

The grip on my hair lightened, an expression of almost pain crossing his features. "You can't be serious. I would be happy for the rest of my life if you never stopped sucking me off, but if you keep that up, I'm going to come."

An unwitting smile touched my lips. "Why did you stop me then?"

"Is that what you want?" he asked roughly, a spark of hopefulness in his eyes.

My breath spiraled out of my lungs. "I think so. If I do, does that mean we won't have sex?"

"There's always tomorrow night. Or the night after," he reasoned, but they seemed so far off.

"Or later tonight?" I countered.

"Or later tonight," he confirmed, his tone low and strangled.

"In that case..." My mouth descended onto his dick, and I moaned as his hips started to move, a shockwave of pleasure shuddering through me.

* * *

*Buzz. Buzz. Buzz.*

The annoying noise woke me, vibrating close to my head. It took a moment to realize my damn phone was going off. I fumbled around under the pillow until my hand came in contact with it. I didn't want to open my eyes but forced them to do so anyway. The room was dark except for the glow coming off the screen.

As soon as I saw the string of texts, I knew who they would be from. Suddenly awake, I skimmed the messages.

**June 25<sup>th</sup>**

**6 p.m.**

**I'll text you the place the day of.**

**See you soon, Kenna darling.**

I snuck a glance over at Fynn. He was still asleep, blissfully unaware.

Scowling, I glared at my phone. I hated that Sterling interfered and ruined my perfect night. This late, his texts didn't even warrant a response.

Through the window, I saw darkness still blanketed the sky. Night wasn't completely over yet, meaning there was still time to salvage what was left.

Something about Sterling's text left me cold, and Fynn's warm body was there beside me. I wanted *his* warmth. I needed *him* to chase the cold Sterling injected me with.

Fynn slept on his back, an arm tucked under his pillow. It was the perfect spot for me to curl up into. I inched across the small space separating us and rested my head on his shoulder. His breathing didn't waver, and the man didn't stir.

I relaxed into his body, a small sigh leaving my lips at his warmth encompassing me. My hand rested carefully on his bare chest, just above his heart.

We'd both fallen asleep without any clothes. I'd never spent the night naked with a guy before. Looking at Fynn and how the rumpled sheet fell loosely at his waist, I could see the appeal. It wasn't enough to just be sidled up next to him.

I thought about what I'd done last night, a phantom, shameless smirk touching the corners of my mouth. Who was I? The girl I was with Fynn was someone I'd been trying to be since I was fifteen and a victim of rape.

I hated thinking about that time in my life, but somehow Sterling roused those memories and feelings. My mind worked like dominoes, one piece falling into the next. From Sterling to sex to Carter. My brain connected them, going back to when I hadn't had happiness or hope or love.

Carter left me in shambles after that night. Sadness had chipped away at me until I couldn't take it anymore. It was then my parents decided I needed help. When I'd left Elmwood, I spent months trying to fill in the blank spots the drug took from me, and when I couldn't remember, I grew frustrated and angry. That darkness inside me festered and multiplied. I started having outbursts and acting out. I'd gone from one extreme to the other.

But when I'd finally accepted there were some answers I might never uncover, I was able to let pieces of rage go bit by bit. Those embers of fury were sparking within me again.

They scared me.

Yet not enough to bank them.

I would meet Sterling. It hadn't been a question of if but when. Now I just had to figure out a way to trap him.

"Kenna?" Fynn said sleepily, yanking me out of my dark thoughts.

I'd been so close to spiraling and hadn't even been aware. My fingers were curled against his chest. His voice echoed in my head. Just my name. I loved the way he said my name in that husky, half-unaware voice. It made my spine tingle.

Loosening my clenched fingers, I lifted my head to peer at him.

"What's wrong?" he asked, studying my face. I don't know what he saw when he looked at me, but Fynn always seemed to know when I wasn't okay.

I didn't want to talk—not about Sterling or Carter—not when we were in bed like this, so I kissed him. It was a short-term solution because Fynn was like a dog with a bone. He wouldn't forget the shadows he'd seen in my expression or the flames in my eyes. Later, he would ask again.

But it gave me time.

And his lips, his hands, his body offered a means to forget, even if temporarily, and I wanted that more than I needed oxygen to breathe.

My tongue touched his lips, asking him to part them for me. I wanted inside. I wanted his tongue against mine.

He parted them, and everything became a hazy blur of desire.

His kiss was different. Or maybe it was how I kissed him that was different. Regardless, I felt it in every crevice of my body. It was a kiss that claimed my soul.

Branding.

Promising.

Consuming.

Lethal.

Fucking unforgettable.

Every single one of those was a problem. This kiss was a problem.

All the tangled feelings it provoked weren't part of our deal, and yet I couldn't stop them, just as I couldn't pull my lips from his.

The kiss became frantic, spurred by such need inside me I should have been scared. I was, but it wasn't normal fear. This was a different sort of trembling, and it was easily pushed aside by desire.

His fingers trailed over my body, igniting all the nerve endings I possessed. He draped a leg over mine, slipping it between mine so he lay half on top of me, not fully covering me with his body.

The pressure he applied with his thigh against my center made me moan into his mouth. I ground against him, creating friction I was aching for down there.

My fingers forked into his hair, nails digging into his scalp as Fynn growled, "I can't fucking think straight. I need to have you now."

He read my damn mind. I nodded, giving him the okay.

"Are you sure?" he asked, offering me the opportunity to slow down or put the brakes on. Neither of which I had any interest in doing.

He grew harder between my legs. "Yes. God, yes. I'll kill you if you stop." I pressed into him, unsure of myself, of what I should be doing, but the throbbing between my legs was insistent. "Do you have a condom?" I wasn't on birth control. Never had a reason to be.

His head gestured over my shoulder. "In the top drawer."

I rolled slightly on the bed and pulled open the top drawer on the nightstand. The foiled packages were sitting on top. I ripped one off with my teeth and stuffed the rest back inside.

His seductive eyes were fixed on me. "That was hot."

I grinned. "I just roll it on?"

I thought he might laugh at me, but I should have known better. That wasn't Fynn's style. Micah, yes, but not Fynn. "Yeah."

My fingers fumbled with the wrapper, tearing it open. *I could do this. Not a big deal. Just pull it out of the wrapper and slap it on. bada bing, bada boom.*

It was a bit more complicated than that, but once I got it rolling, no problem.

My breath hitched as he fitted the tip of his cock right at my opening, nudging in slightly. This was where I was positive the panic would rear its ugly head, and I did begin to feel the prickles of unease.

*No,* I told myself, rocking my hips against Fynn's tip and pushing him in a tad bit more. I wasn't backing out now. I'd worked too hard to get to this moment. Nothing would spoil it. Surely not my insecurities.

Fuck all those who hurt me.

This was Fynn.

He wasn't like anyone else.

"Are you okay?" he murmured, the muscles on his arms stretching as he held himself over me.

I peered up at him, infatuated by the turbulent dark green of his eyes. "Yes," I assured. "I want this. I want you."

"It might hurt for a second, but I swear I'll make you feel good," he promised.

My entire body hummed, and I didn't know how it could feel anything but wonderful.

I was surprised at how he slid inside me with ease, and there wasn't pain necessarily but a tightness as my body adjusted to him filling me.

"Fuck, you're so tight. Don't move. Not yet." Restraint pulled at his voice, and his muscles coiled with control.

The problem was I very much wanted to move. My hips were screaming at me to roll them, anything to create the relief my center craved. I gave in, lifting my hips to take him in a bit farther, and moaned.

*Fuck me. That felt so damn good.*

Like holy shit.

I had to do it again, but Fynn growled my name.

"Kenna. I told you not to move." From the strain in his voice, I couldn't tell if he was in pain. I didn't understand how he could be when having him deep inside me was literally the closest to heaven I'd ever been.

"Fynn," I whimpered, begging him to understand. I had no choice but to move.

He seemed to comprehend and kissed me right before he started to shift in and out with slow, languid, torturous movements, his dick massaging my inner walls. Little breathy sighs escaped my lips. I didn't realize they were coming from me until Fynn whispered, "I love the noises you make when I do this." He thrust inside me, and my back bowed off the bed, my eyes rolling in the back of my head from the pleasure coursing through me, as I chased the orgasm that was so damn close.

We fell into this synchronized rhythm, my hips rising to meet his. This was sex. This was what it was like to be connected with another human in the most intimate way possible. I pressed my nails into his back, raking them down to his tight ass.

Every time he inched out, this emptiness and loss played with my emotions. Then he filled me again, and I burst inside with inconceivable bliss, my core clamping around him.

His lips were on my neck, sucking, nibbling, kissing. "I'm going to take everything from you."

I would give him everything. He didn't even have to ask or demand.

"More," I rasped. I had to have more.

"Kenna," he moaned, and the lust in his voice sent a thrill whirling inside me. The leash holding him back was close to snapping, and I loved that I was the one driving him to the edge.

He took my hands from around his neck and put them over my head, keeping them pinned to the mattress. His hips moved faster, as he thrust in and out of me, his eyes never leaving mine to make sure I was okay.

I was better than okay.

I was fucking flying.

My eyes fluttered closed, and I curled my fingers around his, clinging to them. I rocked with him, faster and faster, my hips moving up to meet his. I gasped for breath.

Heat stole over my entire body, the pleasure I craved right there, teasing and tormenting me. Fynn's low groan whispered into my ear, and I felt the first pump of his release inside me, and that was all it took. My orgasm rolled through me in waves, pulsing and clamping against Fynn's dick as he emptied himself into the condom.

I rode through the waves that kept coming, my body trembling.

Fynn collapsed on top of me, his weight sinking into me, and instead of feeling trapped, I savored the feel of him pressed against me. I was glad he hadn't pulled out instantly. I wasn't ready for him to leave. Not yet.

*Holy crap. I'd had sex. With Fynn.*

And I loved every second of it. I wasn't broken. Not completely. I still had shades of darkness staining my soul, but this huge part of my life I never thought would fully heal was no longer a gaping wound inside me. Because of Fynn, I felt like a woman for the first time in my life.

Catching my breath, I turned my head to look at the guy beside me, his chest glowing. He was gorgeous. "When can we do it again?"

Fynn chuckled, and his stomach rumbled as he raked a hand through his hair.

I grinned. "Next time, I want to be on top."

# 18

## FYNN

hat guy in their right mind would say no to that?

I was thrilled she wanted a next time. That meant I'd done my job. Maybe too good.

When was the last time I'd been so desperate to have a girl?

Never.

I'd never wanted anyone the way I fucking wanted Kenna. I'd thought a million times what it would feel like to be deep inside her, the pulsing of her orgasm beating against my throbbing dick.

But fuck me.

The first clench of her muscles and I'd been exploding with her.

Goddamn it, if I didn't want her again.

I had the rest of the week. There was no reason to rush. I could pace myself, but then she went and looked up at me with such feline satisfaction, asking when we could do it again.

No point in sleeping tonight.

I didn't let girls stay in my bed. I didn't let them stay the night.

Of course, Kenna was different. She wasn't some random hookup despite this being an arrangement between us. Going to bed beside her and waking up next to her felt...right.

It felt like home.

She was home to me.

Despite her eagerness, Kenna drifted off to sleep shortly after returning from the bathroom. I waited twenty minutes to make sure she was well into a dream before crawling out of bed. Tossing on a pair of sweats, I crept out the door and headed downstairs into the kitchen.

I left all the lights off, using the slice of moonlight streaming through the windows to see my way around the room. Opening the fridge, I grabbed a beer and took it to the table where my laptop was charging. I woke the sleeping machine and popped the top on my drink. As I signed in, I took a sip.

Kenna didn't want to tell me what was wrong or what had roused her, but I had a guess. I went straight to the program monitoring her phone. I didn't have to look far. I wasn't interested in messages from her contacts, only those from numbers she didn't have saved. Her last incoming texts had been from an unknown number.

I slammed half the beer after reading what Sterling sent her. He had another fucking thing coming if he thought I would let Kenna actually show up. The only person he would be meeting on June twenty-fifth was me, and maybe a few of my friends.

I saved the date and time into my calendar.

For the fuck of it, I pulled up the feed to my house, fast-forwarding through the last twenty-four hours. I might not be home, but that didn't mean I still didn't check on my family, especially with my little sister being home for summer vacation. Sterling hadn't involved any of our families so far, but I wasn't taking the chance they could be on his radar.

My head whipped up. Something moved outside. A shadow.

I was out of my chair, racing across the kitchen to the door to fling open the lock and slide the glass open enough for me to slip through. I didn't know if the creep sneaking outside saw me sitting in the dark, but I hoped not.

Slinking along the house, I pressed my back against the siding and peered around the corner. He was cloaked in all back, but despite the dark clothing, I could see his outline as he peeked into a window. With the hood drawn up and his hands on either side of his head, he stared through the glass. I couldn't see his face. Not that it mattered.

I didn't care who he was.

Only why he was glancing into my windows.

Barefoot and shirtless, I snuck up behind the bastard and grabbed him by his shirt, spinning him around. The prick turned swinging, catching the corner of my mouth with his fist. I didn't feel the feeble punch, impulse taking over as I tackled the asshole to the ground.

I landed the first hit into his side and followed with a second to his gut. The air whooshed out of his lungs as he wheezed to draw in air. I didn't let up or climb off him. My fist slammed into the side of his face, and his head snapped to the left. He started to fight back under me, but my hand drew back and collided with his nose. My arm became a machine, delivering blow after blow. I stopped seeing the person on the ground.

If I didn't gain control soon, the ability to question him would be lost, but the rage inside me wouldn't settle or recede. It continued to push me. Hit after hit.

My knuckles were covered in his blood when my senses broke through. "Get the fuck out of here before I call the cops," I growled, shoving his stumbling ass down the driveway. Like a dark figure from hell looming in the shadows, I waited for him to leave. I didn't know what he wanted or what he hoped to accomplish, but it didn't fucking matter now.

He didn't look back but floundered his way into the street, leaving a trail of blood behind. I would have to hose down the driveway or hope it rained.

Satisfied he wouldn't be back tonight, I backpedaled around the house to the deck and cursed when I spotted the open door. I'd left it open in my haste.

So damn stupid.

What if he hadn't been alone? What if he'd been the decoy and someone had snuck in while I'd been beating him to a bloody pulp? What if that person had been Sterling?

"Kenna," I muttered, an icy fear freezing the inferno in my veins.

I took off, rushing inside the house and bolting for the stairs. It would do her no good if I got taken by surprise. *Be smart.* But the panic racing through my blood didn't care about caution or safety. It only wanted to reach Kenna.

Hurtling up the stairs three at a time, my eyes darted from room to room as I ran down the hallway toward my bedroom. The door was partly opened, and I couldn't remember for the life of me if I had left it that way.

Cold sweat beaded between my shoulder blades, but I tried to push aside the fear dominating me for Kenna's sake. I needed to be levelheaded and not lose my shit.

My bare feet pounded into the floor. I reached the door in just a few steps and flung it open, my breathing rapid. My gaze immediately went to the bed. I grabbed the door frame, my heart sprinting a million miles a minute as my fingers dug into the wood.

Dark strands of hair spilled over the white pillows, her figure outlined under the blanket where she lay curled on her side. Her back was toward me.

A long sigh left me, and my hands fell to my sides.

She was safe.

I slumped against the doorway, catching my breath. For a few minutes, all I did was stare at her, letting the relief of her safety wash over me. If anything had happened to her...

I never would have forgiven myself. Kenna was under my protection. Grayson trusted that I would look after her. We had let her down once before.

Never. Fucking. Again.

Climbing into bed beside her, I brushed a kiss over her forehead before lying down. Only a few hours were left until the sun crested over the ocean, but I had no plans to sleep. I would stay alongside her, never taking my eyes off the girl who had my heart.

She drove me absolutely insane most days with her recklessness, stubbornness, and bravery. And yet those were also qualities I loved about her.

Kenna could be fearless when she had to be. Generous. Loyal to a fault. She could also be the most selfish yet selfless person.

Her long lashes fluttered as she opened her eyes, and a soft smile curved her lips. "I could really get used to waking up beside you, gorgeous."

My lips twitched as the tightness in my chest eased at the sound of her voice. "Is that so?"

She blinked a few times, the sleep slowly clearing from her eyes, and the slip of a smile on her lips shifted to a frown. In an instant, she went from half asleep to fully awake. Sitting up in bed, her gaze ran over me. "What the happened to you?" she took my chin into her grasp and angled my face to get a better look at my lip.

*Shit.* I'd forgotten what I must look like. The stinging at the corner of my lip hadn't registered until Kenna's finger swiped over it. "It's nothing."

She surveyed my face, tilting my head to the side. "When I went to bed last night, your lip didn't look like this. Did I do that?"

I couldn't handle the seriousness of her question. Kenna was known to have nightmares, and sometimes she thrashed in her sleep. "No, of course not."

Her hand dropped from my face. "Okay, then if it wasn't me. Did you go out last night?"

Silence.

*Shit.* I didn't want to tell her about the guy peeking in the windows, but how the hell did I explain the split lip? She wouldn't accept bullshit excuses like I ran into a door in the middle of the night. Especially when her eyes moved to my knuckles.

"What the hell, Fynn!" she hissed. "You're bleeding."

"I'm fine." The blood was dried and crusted over my hand, no longer actively oozing, but I had stained the sheets. Splotches of red were splattered on the bed.

"I'm assuming the other guy isn't." She put two and two together.

"If he was smart, he would have skipped the hospital and gone home."

"Fynn," she sighed. "Was it—?"

I shook my head before she could finish. "I wish it had been. I fucking wish it had been."

* * *

I waited. For the rest of the week, I was patient, but Kenna never mentioned her secret scheduled rendezvous with Sterling.

I wanted to confront her, but more than that, I wanted her to trust me. I wanted her to come to me.

But by the end of our time at the beach house, it became clear Kenna had no intentions of telling me she planned to meet up with Sterling.

I was pissed.

I was disappointed.

I was frustrated.

And most of all, I was sad.

Maybe it was my fault that I let my guard down. I allowed myself to get emotionally attached. I let myself believe she was mine.

Perhaps this was nothing more than an experiment for Kenna, but damn was it hard to believe it meant little to her when she moaned my name—when she begged me to go faster—or threatened me not to stop.

Being inside Kenna surpassed any dream I'd had.

We had to talk. I couldn't leave this beach house with so many loose strings between us. She might not like everything I had to say, but she would listen.

Taking the corner, I strolled into the kitchen. My gaze went straight to Kenna at the table.

She stared at my open computer. Her eyes were fixated on the screen until she felt my presence. Those fiery brown eyes lifted. "Are you spying on me?"

*Shit.*

But then I remembered I wasn't the only one concealing a secret.

## 19

## KENNA

I couldn't believe what I was seeing. And yet I wasn't surprised. Not really. The shock only lasted seconds before moving right into pissed the hell off.

Of course, to some extent, I knew the Elite kept tabs on us. Tracking our phones, our cars, our laptops, basically anything electronic, but this went deeper. Much deeper. This was an invasion of my privacy. Every message I'd ever sent. Every phone call I'd made.

I glared at the guy in the doorway, heat burning my cheeks. It didn't matter that he was shirtless, standing there in just a pair of sweatpants. Or that only an hour ago he'd been deep inside me. "This is bullshit, Fynn! How could you do this?"

His shoulder leaned against the frame, a hand rubbing the back of his neck. "I wouldn't have had to if you'd told us what was going on." A flash of ire glowed in his eyes.

"And what exactly do you think is going on?" I snapped, my teeth literally clamping shut, and shoved out of my seat.

"You've been talking to *him*," he hurled, venom in his tone. Not entirely all of it was aimed at me. The bulk of his fury was for Sterling. I knew that, and yet his anger still hurt.

I flinched in surprise before stomping across the kitchen until I stood directly in front of him. "What *I* do and who *I* talk to is not your business." I punctuated my words by poking him in the chest repeatedly. "You can't control me. I'm not a doll for you to manipulate."

"You know damn well that's not what I'm doing. I need to know what he's doing to track down his whereabouts." Fynn made it seem so reasonable, but I was no fool. There was always an underlying agenda.

"You could have asked." My finger was still digging into his chest.

His fingers wrapped around my wrist. "And would you have told me?" he challenged.

Silence.

A darker emotion took over his expression, one I rarely got to see. "Exactly. You're not meeting him, Kenna."

Few might square off with Fynn when his eyes promised violence. I was one of them. He wouldn't hurt me, so I didn't back down. "Try and stop me."

The hand holding my wrist twisted so my forearm pressed against his chest, bringing me almost flush with his body. "If I have to tie you up and lock in you a room, I will," he threatened.

I folded my arms over my chest, standing off against him. "I'd love to see you try." The last thing I wanted to do was argue with Fynn.

He shook his head, taking my chin between his thumb and index finger and tipping it up until my eyes had no choice but to gaze into his. "I'm not playing with you. Not with your safety, not with your emotions, and not with your heart."

"What does any of that have to do with this?"

The intensity in his expression never wavered. "I have feelings for you, brat. I always have, and I'm done waiting for you to catch up."

"Feelings for me. Catch up," I sputtered, unable to believe the audacity of this man. He was the one who pushed me away all those years ago, and since the other night, he hadn't made a single advance toward me.

He held my gaze. His hand dropped to the small of my back. "I'm in love with you, Kenna. And I can't lose you. Deal with that."

I blinked. "You're in love with me?" The reality of his confession didn't really sink in. Not at first. "You can't do this to me. Why would you wait so long to tell me?"

Our hands were trapped between us, but the fingers clasping my wrist loosened. "For you. I didn't want to push you. Not until you were ready."

I swallowed hard. My mind was whirling, thoughts going through my head at a million miles a second. "This wasn't part of the deal. You weren't supposed to fall for me."

"We can't always control our emotions, brat."

"Did you even try?"

His eyes grew serious, the sparks in them cooling. "No. Not with you."

"I need to think." But it was impossible to do that when he was so close.

I thought he might kiss me, but he didn't. The hand at the small of my back fell to his side, and he released my wrist as he leaned back against the wall. "Take as long as you need. I'm not going anywhere. Besides, I've been waiting for years. What's a little longer?"

This was what I had always wanted. Then why was I so upset? Was I scared? Angry? Annoyed?

I couldn't tell what emotions pressed inside me.

"But I need to make it clear that I'm your only option," he added when I stared at him tongue-tied. "I'm not letting you go. I've waited a long time."

*What the actual fuck?*

How the hell was I supposed to process that? To deal with Fynn unloading all these pent-up feelings on me and then telling me no one else can have me? No one else but him?

It was a lot to unpack, but first I had to get over the annoyance. I despised being told what to do or what was best for me. Fynn knew that better than anyone, and yet he plainly informed me that he would scare off any other guy who looked at me.

Shit, he had probably been doing so for years and I just didn't notice.

Not that it mattered. I hadn't been ready.

Fynn wasn't done yet. "And you're not to go anywhere near Sterling. Is that clear? You can be mad at me all you want."

I glared at him, holding his stare in a fucking pissing match before huffing and whirling upstairs to get my shit. I was leaving.

* * *

Fynn was right. I needed space. I needed to think.

Yet each mile I drove away from Oceanbay, my heart ached more.

Anger clashed with a spear of pain within me. I didn't know how to feel. I was furious, but I was also sad, and I couldn't figure out what made me want to cry.

Tears pricked at the backs of my eyes. I wasn't a girl who cried easily. Just the opposite. I was someone who found it difficult to shed tears. It wasn't because I was heartless or didn't have emotions.

Perhaps that was just another thing broken inside me.

Upset at how our trip to the beach ended, I stared out at the road, the ocean rolling by off to the side. I hadn't even bothered to put the top down. As if the weather reflected my mood, the sun hid behind a sky of grim clouds. It had hardly rained at all in June, and the earth was in desperate need of a drink, but like the tears that wouldn't shed, the clouds refused to pour.

My fingers tapped on the steering wheel as the car cruised along. There was hardly any traffic on this Sunday afternoon, giving me too much time to get lost in my head.

I loved Fynn.

Of course, I loved him.

But was I *in love* with him?

There would have been a time when I would have answered that question without hesitating. It would have been a simple response.

But so much happened since then.

I wasn't the same.

And Fynn wasn't the same.

I hadn't been looking for love or to complicate feelings when I'd asked him to be my first real lover. I'd stupidly believed he felt nothing but friendship for me, that he loved me like a sister. Perhaps I'd known and I just didn't want to admit it. I'd seen the way Fynn looked at me. The way he took care of me first above others—above himself. Yet somehow, I'd convinced myself that was his nature.

And to some extent, it was, but only with people he loved.

Fynn Dupree was in love with me.

*Holy shit.*

I think I loved him too.

That was why I was so upset about what I saw on his computer. I felt violated. Nothing like being raped. That was a completely different type of violation. This had been trust.

He hadn't trusted me enough.

Had I given him a reason to doubt me?

Maybe.

I'd been keeping secrets.

But so had he.

When I imagined not having him in my life, a soul-crushing weight descended on my chest as if someone or something was ripping my heart apart into tiny pieces. Fynn had always been a constant in my life just as Micah and Brock had been. I depended on them, but I relied on Fynn more.

He might not have completely trusted me, but I trusted him.

Not just with my life. But with my heart.

And yet, I kept my interactions with Sterling from him.

Did I have a right to be mad?

The whole situation was messed up.

I needed to be honest. Not just with him. But with me. I wouldn't have been able to let Fynn touch me if I didn't love him.

It seemed clear. I loved him, and because I'd fallen for him, everything I felt was so much stronger. The hurt. The anger. The pain. The love.

So what was I going to do with this information?

I had to tell Fynn.

The urge to confess my love, to scream it at the top of my lungs, to throw myself in his arms and tell him over and over how much I loved him consumed me.

If there was one thing I'd learned from tragedy, it was to live without regrets. To take every moment as it came. Some things couldn't wait.

This was one of them.

I didn't want to run away.

The only place I wanted to run was toward Fynn.

Only half paying attention to the traffic on the road, I whipped my car around, doing a U-turn to head back to the beach house. My tires skidded over a rocky patch between the roads but caught a second later as I straightened out the wheel. A horn honked as a car zoomed past.

My foot moved off the brake to the pedal, giving the convertible gas as I came out of the turn. If I hurried, I could catch him before he left after closing up the house.

*Crash.*

I didn't see the car. Not even as it impaled my side of the BMW, but I felt the fucking impact and heard the nasty, ear-piercing shriek of metal on metal.

My head rammed into the window, glass shattering. The car spun, and I lost control, not just of the vehicle but the world.

Oblivion took me under, and I blacked out, not knowing if the car ever stopped.

---

## 20

## FYNN

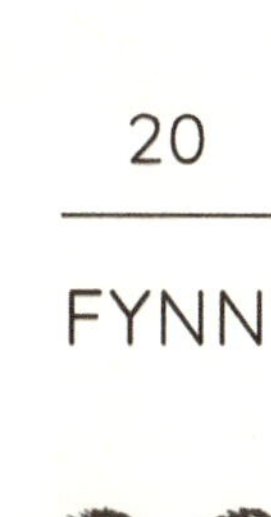

I locked the beach house up and activated the security. Letting Kenna go had been hard, but I knew her well enough to know she needed time to cool off. I got why her temper flared, but I wasn't fucking sorry.

I'd never apologize for keeping her safe.

Even now, I tracked the location of her car. All I had to do was pull the app up on my phone to see the little icon move across the map.

Hopping into my Infiniti, I started the engine and called Grayson. I didn't want to burden him with my problems, but he needed to know Kenna found out because it wouldn't be long until that train trickled down to the other girls.

There would be backlash from all.

Better the guys were prepared for the wrath coming their way.

Grayson didn't pick up, so I left him a voicemail to call me.

With each mile I drove, I came closer to picking up the phone and calling Kenna. I kept having to remind myself I'd told her I'd give her space, but space was the last thing *I* wanted.

Maybe I hadn't handled the situation with finesse, but I'd tried to be honest. That had to count for something.

*Fuck.*

My hands hit the steering wheel.

This was not how I wanted things to end. Not when they were just beginning between us. The idea that I could have messed it up or that she might not need me anymore sent me spiraling. I didn't want to contemplate a world where Kenna wasn't in my life.

I had to trust she would come to her senses—that she would pick me.

And she wouldn't do anything stupid on the way home.

About halfway to Elmwood, traffic started to congest. I swore, glaring at the line of cars in front of me. An accident, no doubt. I thought about having my GPS reroute a different way home, but at this point, I was deep in the thick of it, and turning around wasn't an option. I'd just have to ride through it.

Hopefully, Kenna missed the bumper-to-bumper traffic and made it through before the accident occurred. Again, my first instinct was to reach for the phone and call her. Not only did I want to hear her voice, but the protective streak inside me wouldn't rest until she was safe.

They had traffic merging into one lane. When I finally got a glimpse of the red and blue lights swirling ahead, it was like seeing the light at the end of the tunnel, but the relief was short-fucking-lived.

As I approached the accident, I was confused when I saw only one vehicle involved. There was a lot of fuss for a single car, but then I got a good look at it. A white BMW convertible just like Kenna's.

Not like Kenna's. It was Kenna's.

No one else drove around with license plates that read NVR MYND.

I whipped my car out of the line of traffic, slamming my brakes beside a police car.

*No. No. No.*

This can't be happening.

Not to her.

My heart had never beaten so fast, and as I rushed out of the car, my vision blurred. I ran and scanned the car, seeing not a glimpse of Kenna, and quickly panned the area, desperate to see her face.

*Where the fuck is she?*

I grew closer to the car and saw...

Blood.

It was splattered on the window.

Her fucking blood.

The driver's side door was smashed in like something had rammed it. The window was cracked, shards of glass littering the ground and front seat. It didn't make sense.

For this type of damage, there had to be another car involved. I didn't like what I saw. The convertible's engine still ran. The passenger side door was left wide-open. But where was the other car? More importantly, where was Kenna?

Had the EMTs already taken her away in an ambulance? Should I be speeding to the hospital instead of wasting time here? I needed answers. And I needed them ten minutes ago.

Seconds away from losing my shit, I whirled around, locating the first man in uniform I laid eyes on. I felt sorry for him. He was about to get the brunt of my wrath.

"Where is she? Where the fuck is she?" I demanded, not a single note of friendliness in my features.

"You can't be here—"

I cut him off before he could say more. They would have to physically remove me if they wanted me out of the way. "Just tell me where she is." *You dumbass,* I added in my head when I really wanted to spit it at him.

He put his hands on his belt, puffing out his chest. The twitch near his eye indicated he didn't like my tone, but I didn't give two shits what he liked and didn't like. The longer I went without answers was precious time wasted. "Who, son?" he asked.

Didn't they fucking know? Hadn't they pulled her from the car that looked as if it had been bulldozed? "The girl driving the car."

The officer's brows drew together, his expression sharpening. "The car was abandoned when we arrived. Someone passing by saw the accident and phoned it in. But there was no one here when we arrived. Just the car. No girl."

If someone didn't start giving me some goddamn answers, I was going to fucking go ballistic. "Where's the vehicle that hit her? Her car didn't just get mangled by itself. You need to radio this in. Get every cop in the state looking for the other car." Specifically, the driver.

"It could be that she's wandering around. I'll have someone keep an ear out for any reports of an injured girl and have a few patrol cars scan the area. What did you say her name was?"

"I didn't. It's Kenna Edwards."

"Edwards. Why is that familiar?" He scratched the side of his head.

"Because she is the fucking daughter of Chandler Edwards. You heard of him?" I growled.

It took a moment, but the recognition jostled in his brain. "Yeah. The movie producer."

Rage swelled inside me. "One and the same. If you don't locate his daughter, you can bet your ass he will rain hell down on the department. And if he doesn't, I will."

The officer's expression grew suspicious. "I'm going to need your name."

"Fynn Dupree."

He recognized my name and straightened his shoulders.

"I'm telling you she's missing. Now do your job and find her and the son of a bitch that hit her," I said firmly.

"Do you know anyone who would like to hurt Ms. Edwards?" he interrogated.

"Yeah. Sterling Weston. And my guess is if you find him you'll find her."

It didn't take a genius to figure out this was a hit-and-run. Or more accurately, a hit-and-kidnap.

The radio attached to his shoulder went off. He waited until the static voice stopped before he said, "I'm going to need you to answer some more questions and give a statement. It's probably best you come down to the station."

Fear mixed with frustration put me in a sour mood. The urge to scream rose like a dragon breathing fire inside me. "I don't have time for this."

Another officer called over to him, and he didn't try to stop me as I turned away. I had to make a few calls. I couldn't rely on the police to do their job or work fast enough for me.

Sterling.

It had to be him.

My blood went cold at the thought of him having my girl. Or... what he might do to her.

Storming back to my car, I reached into the back seat for my laptop. The cops could take hours to find her, and I didn't have that kind of time. I needed to know where she was now.

I threw open my laptop and called Brock while I put in my password. It rang and rang, my agitation growing with each passing bell-like chime echoing through my car.

Brock answered on the fifth ring.

"He has Kenna." I bit out each word before he could even say a thing.

A pause bridged from the other line before he processed and said, "You're sure?"

My eyes lifted, and I glanced out the window at the crash. Rage boiled in my blood. "Pretty fucking sure. I'm staring at her demolished car. She could be hurt. There's blood at the scene."

"What have you got?" he asked, all business.

"Not much. The police are dragging their feet. The car that hit her was black." I'd seen the transfer paint on her car's white door.

"That's all you got?"

"At the moment," I replied, my fingers flying over my laptop's keyboard. "I'm working on more as we speak." I opened the program to track her phone. "Fuck," I hissed.

"What is it?" Brock asked icily, his voice cold and hard.

My head sunk back into my seat as I pinched the bridge of my nose. "Her phone's turned off. We have to find him, Brock."

"We will. No matter what it takes. Keep digging. I'm going to make a few calls."

One of those calls would be to the police department, which would put a fire under their asses.

Speaking of which...

Knuckles rapped on my windshield. I glanced up, furious at the interruption.

"Find me something," I told Brock, eyeing the cop through my window. "I can't just sit here." But I also couldn't leave. I felt so fucking stuck and helpless.

I had to make a choice. If I rolled down my window or got out of the car as the officer indicated with his hand, I couldn't do what I needed to do.

I made a split-second decision. I put my Infiniti into Drive and hit the gas, going in the opposite direction from which I'd been driving. When the first exit came up, I got off the highway and sped into a diner parking lot.

Taking thirty seconds to calm my breathing, I reached for my laptop again, staring at the screen. I had to find her. To do that, I had to think like Sterling. Where would he take her?

Somewhere remote.

Somewhere no one would come looking for them.

Somewhere secure.

Everyone left some kind of trail, breadcrumbs, and all I had to do was follow them. First, I had to pick up the trail, and to do that, I needed time I didn't have and better fucking internet access.

I had to get home. As much as I didn't want to leave this area in case she was close by, I had little hope of finding her driving around. He could be miles away for all I knew.

It took me an extra twenty minutes to get to Elmwood, and I went straight to Brock's. The guys were all there. "Anything?" I asked.

Brock shook his head. "Not yet. You?"

Micah handed me a drink. I declined, wanting to keep a clear head, despite craving the buzz. "No. She hasn't tried to call?"

Grayson heaved a deep sigh. "Not that we know of. None of us at least."

I clenched my jaw, the side of my face hurting from the tension I held there. "It's him. The bastard took her."

"We'll get her back, Fynn," Brock assured in a deadly quiet voice.

And what happened between then and now? "Fuck!" I screamed, putting my fist into the drywall.

## 21

## KENNA

Before I opened my eyes—before I fully gained consciousness —agonizing pain sliced through my head. It was what pulled me out of the darkness, but once I was aware, I wished to be back in the place of numbness and oblivion. At least then I wouldn't be suffering.

It was a struggle to open my eyes.

Besides the hammering in my head, a shrieking echo pierced my ears, and I could tell something wasn't right. Not just with my head and my hearing but my entire body. I lifted my arm to rub my eyes, and every muscle and bone I possessed screamed in protest.

I finally peeled my eyes open and stared at the ceiling until it came into focus. It was stained with little splotches of water stains. Just moving my eyes, I glanced around the unfamiliar room, taking in my surroundings. I was in a bed. The walls were covered with peeling floral wallpaper. The furniture was mismatched, and the room was small with only one tiny window. The shades and curtains were drawn shut, blocking out light. I couldn't tell what time of day it was.

Nor did I know where the fuck I was.

I had a lot of questions, but just thinking at all made my brain hurt.

"Oh, good. You're awake. I was starting to worry." The deep voice drew my gaze to the doorway. A guy with hair as dark as midnight and amber eyes looked upon me with specks of worry hidden behind a gentle smile.

His face tugged at my memory, but I couldn't recall his name. Something told me that we knew each other.

"Where am I?" I asked. My voice came out hoarse and croaky, not sounding like me at all.

He moved into the room with cautious steps as if not to frighten me, favoring one of his legs. I shifted my hands to the bed, attempting to push myself up. "Don't try to move," he said, coming to the side of the bed. "You took a nasty hit to the head. Here..." He reached over to the nightstand and grabbed a white bottle and a glass of water. "Take two of these."

I eyed the medicine container, uncertainty I couldn't explain swimming in my belly. "What is it?"

Now that he was closer, I noticed the scars on his face—burn marks. They traveled down one side of his face, from his cheek to his neck, and disappeared into his shirt. Yet they didn't take away from his attractiveness. "Pain relievers. Your body took a beating and will probably ache for a few days still. I'm sure your head is killing you."

I took the pills and the water he held out to me. "That's an understatement." Staring at the tiny white ovals in my palm, I got this sick feeling when I looked at them. Something about the drugs made me leery, but I couldn't figure out why.

The pounding in my head wouldn't be silenced and ultimately won. I just wanted it to stop.

Lifting my head, I popped the pills into my mouth and drank deeply from the glass, washing them down. The happiness my head and neck felt when I sunk back down into the pillow was overwhelming and a sharp reminder my body had been through hell.

"What happened?" I asked after I got settled.

He sat on the edge of the bed, careful not to jostle the mattress too much. "You don't remember the accident?"

I sucked in my lower lip, thinking, but every time I tried to draw out memories, I hit a roadblock. My mind refused to go past right now. "No, not really," I said defeatedly. "I remember driving on the road, but I didn't know where I was going. Or where I'd come from. A car hit me, but all the details after are a blur."

"Not surprising, considering how hard you hit your head. A concussion can scramble your memories."

"Concussion?" I echoed. I had a concussion? Explained the bandage on the side of my head.

He nodded. "According to the doctor, but nothing too serious."

"Shouldn't I be in the hospital?"

Fussing with the blanket draped over me, he replied, "You were released yesterday."

None of this rang a bell. "I was?"

His eyes brimmed with sympathy. "You don't remember? I drove you home and carried you to bed."

I went to twist the ring on my hand, but there was nothing there. "No." But then again, perhaps that shouldn't have shocked me. "What kind of accident?" I asked, but as the question left my mouth, a flash of light flickered behind my eyes, and I saw a car. "It was a car crash," I muttered before he could reply.

"Yes. That's right. What else can you remember?"

"Nothing. I just know I was driving and then nothing." In my head, I could hear the shrilling and crunch of metal. I couldn't visualize or see the events, but I could hear them. It was like being blind, only able to rely on my ears.

I tried again and again, my hands fisting at my sides, but I kept running into a brick wall over and over again.

My breathing quickened while I continued to try to remember anything. Including who I was. The sudden realization that even my name was lost sent me whirling.

"Hey, it's okay." He reached for my hand, lacing our fingers together. "Everything's going to be okay." His tone was smooth and reassuring.

"I-I can't remember my name." Panic made my voice choppy.

His thumb rubbed over my hand. "It's Kenna. Your name is Kenna. And I'll fill in the blanks. As many as I can until they start to come back on their own. Okay?"

I exhaled, my back sinking deeper into the mattress. "I'm sure I know, but who are you?"

A crestfallen expression descended on his features.

"I'm sorry." I winced, my fingers touching the bandage at my temple.

"It's okay. The doctor said this could happen. You just need to take it slow. I'm Sterling, your boyfriend."

"Boyfriend?" I echoed.

He nodded. "We met at college. Kingsley University. You're going to be a junior in the fall."

He seemed so genuine. Despite the pit in my stomach that appeared as he talked, how could it not be true? "What month is it?"

A smile brightened his features. "It's the end of June. Almost the fourth of July."

Summer. I loved summer.

Well, I was pretty sure I did.

The fingers on my hand gave it a squeeze. "You should probably rest and not overwhelm yourself with too much information. Are you hungry?" he asked.

Food hadn't crossed my mind, but at the mention of it, my stomach rumbled. "I think so."

Releasing my hand, Sterling stood from the bed, glancing down at me. "I hope you like ramen."

"I don't know. Do I?" Surely my boyfriend would know what kinds of foods I liked.

He smiled.

* * *

The moment Sterling left the room, I forced myself upright. It wasn't easy. Pain rippled from my neck down my spine to my hips and into my legs. Hell, even my fingers and toes hurt, but the agony splitting my head open was subsiding, thanks to the pills.

Taking a few breaths to work through the pain, I inched to the edge of the bed and swung my legs over the side. My hands balanced on the mattress as I tested out the strength in my legs, putting a bit of weight on them. They were weak but still worked.

I glanced down and noticed my clothes. I hadn't thought much of what I was wearing up until this point, but even without my memory, I knew the oversized graphic tee that came down to mid-thigh didn't belong to me. It was soft and smelled clean with a hint of something masculine like aftershave or deodorant. The print was a throwback to an eighties rock band, Poison.

My arms and legs had a few cuts and scratches that had been cleaned up and attended to, but none of them looked serious, not like the one on my head. Even through the bandage, I could feel the knot.

I used the furniture to help stabilize myself as I moved about the room. A layer of dust covered the furniture, and the air had a stale stench to it like it hadn't been cleaned in a decade.

There was no way this was my house or my room. So whose was it? Did Sterling live here?

I went to the single window and glanced outside. A long winding driveway disappeared around the corner, flanked by field after rolling field. Not far from the house sat a weathered red barn. It was clear I was miles from civilization.

The room began to stifle me, and I couldn't breathe. It was so small, boxing me in like a coffin underground. My lungs greedy for fresh air, I tried to open the window, putting my palms on the glass and pushing up.

But no matter how much I shoved, the frame wouldn't budge. It was stuck. I pressed my nose to the glass. Not stuck. The window was locked. Not from the inside, but the outside.

Why was it locked?

For one reason.

To keep someone in.

I heard his footsteps coming down the hall and rushed back to the bed. A little too fast. My head wailed at me for moving so fast.

I just got myself tucked into bed when the door opened. He didn't knock, and I don't know why I found that strange.

How was it I could remember basic shit like etiquette but couldn't remember I had a boyfriend?

Sterling entered with a steaming bowl of noodles and a lemon-lime soda. I couldn't say how I knew it, but it was my favorite flavor. He set the tray on the dresser before approaching the bed. His limp was a little more prominent than it had been when I first saw him. "Let me help you sit up." He fluffed the pillows behind me, giving me something to prop up on before placing the wooden tray on my lap.

I stared at the food, reaching for the drink first. My dry throat craved something cold, and the sweet drink did not disappoint.

"You need to eat to gain back your strength."

Dutifully, I picked up the fork.

"The bathroom is through that door if you would like to take a bath or get cleaned up. I can help if you need me to." He rambled while I ate, giving me the rundown of the house.

Sterling stayed until every last noodle disappeared into my mouth. He took the empty dishes and shut the door behind him. I swore I heard a click, like the flipping of a lock, before the gentle thud of his footsteps traveled down the hall.

Alone again, I stared at the bathroom door. I was dying for a shower, but I was also a little afraid of the bathroom. My gaze moved to the other door Sterling had left through and closed behind him.

I didn't know what propelled me out of bed to check the door. Perhaps I was curious about the rest of the house, about what lay outside this room. Perhaps I didn't want to be alone and wanted to seek out Sterling's company.

My feet squished into the worn carpet, padding toward the two doors. They sat cornered to each other, one on each wall. The bathroom was on the left and the exit was on the right. I went to the right first.

Chewing on my lip, I grabbed the knob and twisted slowly, but I ran into a problem quickly. The handle didn't budge. I tried again with a bit more force this time.

Nothing.

I took a step back, my brows drawn together. Who locked their girlfriend up in a room? Was it so I didn't accidentally wander off?

He might have his reasons, and I planned to ask, but for now...

I was a prisoner.

And I didn't like it.

## 22

## STERLING

I glanced down the hallway at the closed door, thinking about the girl on the other side. What were the fucking chances that she would lose her memory?

It hadn't been my intention when I rammed my car into hers. I'd only meant to render her stunned or unconscious for a few moments. Just long enough for me to transport her into my car.

I'd taken precautions to make sure I didn't suffer any serious injuries, but even with them, not everything could be accounted for. Like jamming my knee. The limp was a mild inconvenience compared to the other shit I'd suffered in my life.

A banged-up knee was child's play compared to recovering from burns or losing my sister. Some pains couldn't be seen. Especially those of the heart. No pills, no needles, no kisses could fix the ache I still suffered from Sadie's death.

I would gladly have walked through a million burning buildings if it meant she got to live.

Kenna had only been unconscious for about seventy minutes, long enough for me to get her to the farm, attend to her wounds, change her bloody clothes, and tuck her into the room. I'd started to worry she might not ever wake up. My goal hadn't been to kill her.

No. I needed her very much alive.

I sat down at the table, checking the security feed. It had been hours now since I abducted Kenna from the crash and not a sign of the Elite. I half expected them to come crashing through the front door with a SWAT team behind them, but each hour that went by without a peep from anyone, I grew a little bit more relaxed.

Had I really gotten away with it?

Perhaps the bigger question was whether Kenna really didn't recognize me.

I couldn't trust her, no matter how big and captivating her eyes were. She had this face that made me want to believe everything that came out of her mouth. It was hard for me to believe she had lost her memory, but no fear reflected in her eyes when she looked at me. Just confusion.

I also knew she could be conniving. It was why I was drawn to her.

For now, I was content. She was here. Things couldn't have gone better if I had planned it, which I did, but Kenna losing her memories was an added bonus I hadn't calculated.

Leaning over the table, I shoved the curtain aside and glanced out the window at the barn where I'd stashed the smashed truck inside and locked the door.

It had taken me months to find this place. Somewhere far enough away from Elmwood in a town where I could recover from my burns. My father purchased it under one of his shell companies, who bought it under one of their shell entities, making it more difficult to track. Precisely what I needed.

But now that I had something the Elite deemed valuable, it was a ticking bomb until they found me. Then the real fun would start.

Letting the curtain fall back over the window, I checked the live feed cameras I set up around the property. Every entrance and exit was covered from the beginning of the long winding driveway to the front porch. The cameras were the most modern thing here.

The old farmhouse might not be my aesthetic, but I wasn't here to impress anyone. Besides, no one who knew me would believe I'd spend a night in a place like this, let alone months.

I listened to the shower turn on, the old pipes groaning from the water pressure. It had been so long since I had any human companionship. I'd been alone for so long I'd been a little unsure about having her here, but I liked it. Perhaps too much. Caring for her. Talking to her. Seeing her face. It reminded me of everything I'd lost and had to give up.

All because of Micah and his fucking crew.

Disgust and hatred breathed inside me.

If I went into her room, would she welcome me into her bed? She thought I was her boyfriend. Perhaps a picture of us sleeping together tonight would be the gift they didn't know they needed.

I was the one with the power.

I called the shots.

Now that I had her here, I wasn't ready to let her go. My plan could be adjusted. It was even sweeter to let them sweat it for a few days. Hell, a few weeks. They deserved it and so much fucking more. Those bastards.

What they took from me wasn't something that could be forgiven or repaid.

I waited in the dark kitchen until what I thought was a significant amount of time for Kenna to have cleaned up, gotten back into bed, and hopefully fallen asleep. It had been a tiring day for both of us.

I was only going to check on her. That was it.

But when I opened the door and saw her lying on the bed, something in my chest squeezed. A part of me despised this girl and all she represented. And yet, I found myself intrigued by her.

Dark strands of wet hair cascaded over the floral-patterned pillow. She had her back toward me, the outline of her form curved on the bed.

I couldn't see her face, but I didn't need to. The image of her could easily be conjured in my head.

She was gorgeous. I'd give her that.

Curvy yet slender. Tall but not too tall. It wasn't her physical appearance that caught my attention. Her venomous tongue and the way it struck like a viper gave me a fucking hard-on.

She didn't move as I climbed into bed beside her, and her breathing remained calm and even. My hand snaked over her waist as I curled behind her, breathing in the scent of fresh soap and shampoo from her skin and hair.

It had been too long since I touched a girl or had one curved against me. A wave of calmness washed over me that reminded me of my summers growing up by the ocean. But the peace didn't last long.

Kenna moaned in her sleep. And then she said his name. It was the scantest of whispers yet unmistakable. "Fynn," she said breathily.

My body stiffened against hers.

A flash of red flared behind my eyes, and for a moment, I pictured myself grabbing a handful of her dark hair and shoving her face into the mattress until she couldn't say any of their names again.

They would pay. The things I had planned for their beloved Kenna. She was like a sister to them all. But perhaps a different plan might be suitable considering Kenna's unforeseen condition.

My lips curled.

What sweeter revenge than to have one of their precious girls fall in love with me?

# 23

## KENNA

I heard the click of the door unlocking, the handle turn, and the door slowly opening.

My body went still, and I forced my muscles not to move. Hell, I barely breathed as he walked into the room. I couldn't see him. My eyes were closed, and my back was turned away from the door as I lay curled on my side in the bed. But I could sense his presence, looming like a shadow over me. He didn't say a word.

I lay there unsure of myself and of what he would do. For a minute, maybe more, nothing happened. The silence spanning the room seemed to go on endlessly, a torment on its own. When I thought he would leave, I felt the shift of the mattress.

He crawled into bed alongside me. I did nothing and continued to feign sleep. Someone who locked his girlfriend in a room wasn't someone I could trust.

*Stay calm. Just continue to breathe.*

I did just that even when he snuggled up behind me. An ick rose within me, and I banked the urge to move away. We lay there on the small bed, our bodies touching as his breath sent a shiver down my neck, cold and eerie.

How was I possibly going to get any sleep? Exhaustion nagged at every part of my body.

Maybe if he fell asleep, I could sneak out of the room. Then his arm went around my waist like a heavy chain pinning me to the bed. I had no idea if he was a light or heavy sleeper.

Did I want to take the chance of waking him up by trying to slip out of his arms?

But I had so many questions, and the answers could be waiting outside the door. I didn't think he locked it behind him, but that was another risk. What happened if I managed to get out of bed without disturbing him? Would I be able to leave?

Was it better to bear the night and ask him my questions directly? Surely, he didn't plan to keep me locked up in this room forever.

It was the *what if he did* that kept me up.

* * *

I managed to get patches of sleep here and there throughout the night. Sterling was gone when I woke up, the bed beside me cold as I rolled over, and the door...

It was closed, and my guess, if I got up to check, was it would be locked.

I tried to suppress the panic bubble rising in my chest. It wouldn't do me any good. I needed to be clearheaded and figure shit out. Allowing my fears and uncertainties to take over wouldn't help.

He hadn't tried anything with me last night, only lay beside me, holding me, almost comforting, but I got the feeling *he* was the one seeking comfort instead of offering it to me.

When I sat up, the antique bed frame squawked at my movements as I surveyed the room, this time with a more critical eye. I'd never seen so many different floral patterns used in one space. It nearly made me dizzy to look at. If his goal was to make me insane, he was using the right methods.

But I really didn't think that.

Why feed and take care of me?

His actions confused me.

The aroma of freshly brewed coffee teased my senses. I found the source a moment later.

A tray of food sat beside the bed. Nothing fancy. A bagel and a cup of coffee. My stomach growled at the sight.

Crossing my legs, I nibbled on the bagel as I added cream and sugar to my mug. It was basic, but my stomach danced happily at having something in it.

With the bagel nearly gone, I glanced down at my attire. Did he plan to keep me in just a T-shirt? I was dying for some actual clothes. Something that covered my legs and didn't make me feel exposed.

My attention went to the dresser across from the bed. The room was barely big enough for it with only a small space to pass between the foot of the bed and the dresser. I reached for my coffee, taking a careful drink to not burn my tongue, and shimmied my way off the bed. I took my cup over to the dresser and set it on top so I could rummage through the drawers. Perhaps there was something useful inside.

One by one, I opened each one to find them as empty as the one before, deflating the bit of hope inside me.

*Brrrrpp. Brrrrpp.*

The noise vibrated from somewhere in the house, and my head snapped toward the door. I recognized the sound. It was a drill.

My heart dropped.

There could be a million reasons he was using power tools, especially with a house like this that was in desperate need of fixing, but I had this sinking feeling he was making modifications instead. Like adding locks to doors or windows. He could also be securing restraints to walls or building a fucking cage. My mind went there—to dark places.

Forgetting about my coffee, I stared at the door, my thoughts all over the place. I lost track of time, just staring into space, until the door handle jiggled. I lifted my eyes and Sterling appeared on the threshold, half inside and half outside the bedroom.

The ends of his dark hair were damp like he'd recently showered. He smiled at me. Despite the scars along the side of his cheek and neck, he was attractive. "Good morning. I see you had breakfast."

I crossed my legs, my fingers tugging at the hem of my shirt. "Thank you."

"Are you still hungry?" he asked, leaning a shoulder against the door frame. He was tall, or maybe it was because the ceilings were low.

I shook my head, my back pressing into the dresser. "No."

He angled his head to the side, regarding me. "Are you okay? Is your head bothering you?"

"A little," I admitted. "But it's better than yesterday."

"Let me get you some more aspirin," he offered.

"Wait," I called as he turned to leave.

Sterling glanced back at me, an eyebrow lifting.

I swallowed. The last thing I wanted was for him to shut me inside here again. "Why is my door locked?"

His expression didn't change, and I didn't know what to make of his lack of reaction. "I was afraid you might wander off. With your memory being spotty, I didn't want to take any chances you might get lost."

"Oh." It sounded reasonable but didn't make me feel better.

"Did you want to come into the kitchen with me?" he offered.

I nodded. "Yeah." Did he see that frantic tremor in my eyes? The room was so small and the idea of spending another minute locked inside made me feel claustrophobic as fuck.

He held out his hand.

I glanced at his outstretched arm and then back at his face. His lips twisted in a wry grin. I didn't want him to pick up on the turmoil rolling within me, so I took a step forward and another until I reached him and placed my hand in his.

Sterling led me into the narrow hallway. It wasn't big enough for us to walk shoulder to shoulder, so I stayed slightly behind, yet our fingers remained intertwined. He wasn't letting go.

"Do you live here?" I asked, my eyes roaming the small living space as we emerged from the hallway.

It was sparingly furnished with a tattered couch that had a woven blanket tossed over it. A faded brick fireplace, covered in soot and ash with burnt logs inside, took up one wall. Frayed rugs lined the floors under the furniture. A small TV that looked as if it had been bought more than twenty years ago sat in the corner. Some might call the space cozy. It didn't instill those feelings within me. I felt suffocated. Not just by the close four walls, or the lack of legroom, but by the dust circulating in the room.

I was dying to open a window, yet Sterling seemed to be against fresh air. Or perhaps he was unable to open them.

"Only for the summer," he replied, moving around the coffee table to the square doorway of the kitchen.

I followed behind him. "And I came to stay with you?"

He pulled out a wooden chair from the table tucked into the corner. "Yeah, you were on your way here when the accident happened."

Sitting down, I propped my feet on the bar supporting the two front chair legs. The kitchen was in worse shape than the family room if that was even possible. Stained yellow wallpaper that had once been a creamy white lifted at the seams. The ivy and grape patterns were busy despite the colors being muted with age. Walnut cabinets lined the walls, the corners home to many cobwebs. "How did you find me?" I asked.

He moved casually around the kitchen, pouring himself a cup of coffee. "I was following in my car behind you when it happened."

My fingers laced together on the table. I didn't remember seeing another car in the driveway outside my window. "What did happen?" I pressed, needing details.

Holding up the coffee pot, he silently asked if I wanted a mug as well. I shook my head as he said, "I'm not entirely sure. It looked like you drifted off the road and lost control. The next thing I knew you were flying into a tree off the side of the shoulder."

"None of it makes sense," I muttered, brows drawing together.

Sterling turned and leaned his ass against the counter. "Give it time."

I went to toy with the ring on my right hand, but the finger was empty. Where was my ring? I glanced down, seeing the circle indent around the bottom of my middle finger before looking back up. "Sorry, I'm just trying to put together the pieces."

He blew on his coffee before taking a sip. No cream or sugar. Straight bitter and black. "It will come back eventually. Try not to push yourself too hard too fast."

Sterling might be into the slow country life, but I had an urgency howling within me that wouldn't be ignored. "Do I happen to have any clothes here?" I asked. It would be nice to wear something that I didn't have to worry about flashing my underwear when I moved, not that Sterling would have minded.

A flicker of irritation passed in his eyes. "I grabbed your bag from the back seat. It should have what you need. I think I left it by the door."

My shoulders relaxed a fraction. The idea of putting on something belonging to me gave me a sense of comfort.

Silence dangled between us for a few awkward moments as we sat in the kitchen. Avoiding his perceptive gaze, I gave the kitchen a closer examination, and I couldn't help but think it looked as if someone had been living here longer than a few days. "I don't mean to be rude, but why would we stay here for the summer?"

He was quick to answer. "We wanted to get away from the city and the pressures of college."

Leaning toward the window, I parted the curtain to peek outside. "I see. Well, this place is definitely private," I said, glancing at the yard. If I'd been hoping for a different view than the one my bedroom had, I was sorely disappointed. More fields stretched on one side. On the other was a dense forest. Neither gave the prospect of someone being close by. We were really alone out here. Just Sterling and me.

* * *

I found a Louis Vuitton travel bag right where Sterling said it would be by the front door. The weird thing...it was packed with beachwear. Swimsuits, shorts, tanks, sandals, suntan lotion, nothing practical for a summer in the country unless there was a pool somewhere on the land.

Everything in the bag belonged to someone who wouldn't find roughing it in the country enjoyable or relaxing. I'd packed more bathing suits than underwear. What did that say?

It looked like a trip to the beach with sunglasses, tanning lotions, and flip-flops.

There was also a compartment stuffed with expensive skincare and makeup. I was obviously a girl who took her skin seriously.

Hell, the bag itself cost more than anything inside this house.

Sitting on the bed, the contents strewn around me, I held up a short crop top. This was no better than walking around in a T-shirt.

I wanted to cry.

I was alone. If there was ever a perfect opportunity to let the emotional damn burst, it was now, but I stiffened my lip, swallowed down the lump in my throat, and shoved aside the water stinging my eyes.

No.

I would not fall apart.

Not yet.

The zipper compartment inside the bag caught my eye. I slid it open and looked inside. Disappointment clutched my stomach. I'd been certain I would have found a knife in the pocket. I was the kind of girl who liked to be prepared.

## 24

## FYNN

Four hours, thirty-seven minutes, and twenty seconds had passed since I'd last seen Kenna. I'd always thought of myself as a guy who worked well under stress. I kept my cool. I didn't let the pressure get to me. But fuck me, not knowing where she was or if she was okay drove me goddamn insane.

The bitter anger surging through me wouldn't stop until I found her. The alternative wasn't an option. I refused to even entertain the idea.

I would fucking find her even if I had to comb every inch of this world.

My brain churned. It hadn't stopped from the second I saw Kenna's smashed car.

Other than getting to Brock's, I didn't have much of a plan. Nothing concrete, yet the more people we had looking for her, the better our chances were.

Shit wasn't moving fast enough for me. I'd been at Brock's for what felt like hours, and nothing had happened.

I half expected to hear from Sterling, but regardless of how many times I checked my phone, no tormenting texts. It wasn't like him. If he had Kenna, the bastard would want us to know. So why hadn't he reached out? Where was the gloating? The threats?

A deep pain sliced across my chest at the thought of her alone with him.

*God, I miss her.* I might have known Kenna most of my life, but it felt as if I'd barely had any time with her. This last week, when it had just been her and me, was what I'd been waiting years for.

And now she was gone.

Taken from me.

It killed me knowing Sterling had her.

And only when I'd ended his life would the pain inside me depart.

"Why were you and Kenna still at the beach house?" Grayson grilled me.

I'd been expecting the question. "Kenna asked to stay a few extra days." The goal was to be as vague as possible.

Neither Grayson nor I could sit. He paced the room, wearing out the floor in front of the fireplace. "Why?" he asked. "She told me she was staying with a friend."

Not technically a lie. I was a friend.

I stared at Grayson.

He read the answer in my silence. "You motherfucker. You're sleeping with my sister."

Micah watched us from the couch, his eyes bouncing between us. Brock sat in one of the oversized chairs scowling.

I kept my gaze on Grayson who halted and glared at me from where I stood behind the couch. "It's not like that."

The answer didn't satisfy him. Grayson's eyes darkened. "Either you are or you aren't. It's that simple, Fynn."

Tension crackled in the room. We were all fucking frustrated, angry, and scared. Emotions were high. The last thing I wanted to do was get into it with my best friend. The four of us arguing wouldn't save Kenna, but I recognized the look in Grayson's eyes.

My chest rose sharply. "Nothing is simple with Kenna."

"You slept with her." When my denial didn't immediately come, Grayson leaped over the couch, coming straight for me. "You bastard," he growled, slamming me against the wall. His hands were bunched into my shirt.

I didn't stop him. In fact, I wanted him to hit me. It had been my job to see that Kenna got home safely, and I fucking failed. I never should have let her leave before me. I should have followed her home. I made a monumental mistake, and I had to live with the consequences.

My arms hung at my sides. "Do it, Grayson. It's nothing more than I deserve."

His fist cracked into the side of my face, and I fucking welcomed the sting of pain. "This is on you," Grayson seethed.

"Yeah, it is. Hit me again if you want. I won't stop you."

We rarely fought, but when we did, it could be as deep as we loved. "Come on, asshole. Fight me." Grayson shoved me into the wall again.

"Knock it the fuck off," Brock said with deadly calm. He didn't need to raise his voice or yell. It was his tone that got his point across. "This isn't helping. And I seriously don't want to have to wipe your blood off my walls and floors."

Grayson stayed in my face.

I let him see the regret in my features. "I can't even say sorry. There aren't words to express what I feel or the regret living inside me. It's choking me, and I don't want it to stop."

His fingers released the hold on my shirt and shoved my chest, not that I had anywhere to go. My back pressed deeper into the wall. "Fucking hell, Fynn." He backed off, running a hand through his hair. "You know there are girls outside my family."

Micah chuckled. "Good thing you found one."

Grayson turned and whacked Micah on the back of the head.

"Enough," Brock stated. "We need to put our energy into finding Kenna and not bickering among ourselves." Brock had this single-minded determination I admired. He never lost focus on the task.

Even when we thought shit wasn't getting done, we could count on Brock working an angle. He could be like a dog with a bone. Relentless as fuck until the job was done.

Grayson's face crumpled. "Where do we start?"

* * *

It was late. The kind of late that when your phone goes off it's never a good thing. Before I even picked it up off the table beside me, I knew it was Sterling.

The prick finally decided to make his next move.

Taking a deep breath, I tried to brace myself. He could be doing any number of torturous things to Kenna. My mind went to worst-case scenarios. Hands tied or taped up. Her mouth gagged. Feet bound. I imagined the tears I would see swimming through her eyes. I prayed it was a picture and not a video. I wasn't sure I could handle seeing the fear or hearing her whimpers of pain.

Unlocking my phone, I glanced at the message, seeing a video was attached. Dread weighed like a ton of bricks in my gut. I stared at the preview image, attempting to decipher what I was looking at. It was dark and fuzzy.

There was only one way to find out.

I lifted my hand and hit play.

My heart sprinted in my chest as I waited. The longest second of my life.

The dark screen remained for a few moments, a white-noise silence coming from my phone's speakers, and for a heartbeat, I hoped the video had nothing on it, but no sooner had the thought crossed my mind than the angle of the camera moved.

An arm came onto the screen. The video continued to move, panning out until I could see her. My breath caught. She wasn't tied or restrained. Although the lighting was dark, she didn't look hurt. She was...sleeping.

Well, I assumed. She could have very well been unconscious.

I couldn't see much of her face. She was curled on her side, but it was the arm draped over her waist that I couldn't stop glaring at. A gust of heat flooded my veins. I didn't just want to kill him. I wanted to make him suffer. I wanted to tear off his limbs piece by piece, sew him together, and repeat again and again.

Even then, his pain wouldn't be satisfying enough.

The anger smoldering inside me surged so intently I thought I might be consumed by it.

He was sleeping with her, and he wanted me to know it. The caption under the video read: **She's mine now. My darling.**

The fuck she was.

It was difficult to be relieved Kenna appeared unharmed. Not with the amount of violence swimming in my blood. I had to do something. I couldn't sit in front of my computer any longer. Every pore in my body demanded action.

And yet, I didn't know where to steer the scalding energy. I had no location. No destination. No face for my fists to slam into. Nowhere to unleash the rage, so it continued to fester, and it would until I found him.

* * *

I don't know how, but six days passed.

Six fucking long-ass days.

A hundred and sixty-nine hours, eighteen minutes, and too many damn seconds.

And still, we weren't any closer to finding Kenna. It was as if she'd fallen off the planet.

The police had no leads either. Grayson had filed an official missing person report, but he hadn't told his parents. We were all holding out hope that we would find her before it got to that point; however, as the hours turned into days, the colder the trail got. Everyone knew how important the first forty-eight hours were in a disappearance.

We were well past that.

I hadn't slept.

Didn't bother to try.

Every time I closed my eyes, I saw Kenna in those damn cutoff shorts she loved or laying in my bed wearing nothing, her tan legs wrapped around me.

The number of times I'd refreshed my computer screen, hoping against all hope that her phone would ping.

It hadn't.

Not once.

Not for a single fucking second.

If I wasn't checking her phone, I combed through everything I could find on Sterling and his family. Every house they owned, including those belonging to relatives of relatives. I didn't care how far down the family tree I had to go. Diving into his father's business, uncovering those silent partners and shell companies. Monitoring their credit card activity. If one of them sneezed, I wanted to be the first to know.

As an influential family, they had a lot of connections, and it took more fucking time than I alone could handle. But I refused to give up. All I needed was one crumb. From there, it would lead to another and another.

I would find the bastard.

I was leaving no stone unturned.

I just needed Kenna to hang on until I got there.

We all agreed our best bet was to start searching places we thought Sterling could be hiding. He had to keep Kenna somewhere, and knowing her, she wouldn't make it easy. My guess wouldn't be a hotel or anywhere public. If it had been me, I would have gone remote.

That's where we were starting, but so far, every possible place I uncovered turned into a dead end. Eight addresses. We'd checked out eight places in six days. From abandoned buildings to trailers to cabins. Not a single one panned out.

"Anything?" Brock asked, pacing his kitchen. His parents were out of town, so we were using his house as our center of operations.

I rubbed at the back of my neck. "I don't know. Maybe." I'd been working on a location. "It might be a long shot."

He poured a cup of coffee, not that any of us needed more caffeine. "Doesn't matter. We need to check out every lead no matter how far a stretch it might be."

Grayson was going through a rough time. Kenna had been through something traumatic before, and we hadn't been there to protect her. Her being in the enemy's clutches wreaked havoc on Grayson. He'd been the overprotective brother since, vowing to keep both his sisters safe. He took Kenna's kidnapping personally, and I hated seeing my best friend be so damn hard on himself, especially when it was my fault.

We'd already gone through every property Sterling's family owned. Those were easy to check and eliminate. Then we moved to extended family and friends. A few prospects, but again, nothing. Things got a little more complicated when it came to properties owned by a business, particularly if using a shell company, but we had weeded through the last of those yesterday.

Again, not a damn thing.

Today, I expanded that search, furthering the stretch to see if any of those shell companies had businesses with assets. It wasn't unheard of, especially for a corrupt family like the Westons.

"If we don't find her—" I growled, a shred of despair lingering underneath my anger.

"We will," Brock vehemently interrupted.

The thought of Sterling touching her or harming her by any means sucked all the oxygen from the room. "I need her to be okay."

"I know," Brock said, having yet to take a drink of his coffee. I didn't have to tell him I was in love with her. He knew.

Micah moseyed into the kitchen with Grayson behind him, both with bloodshot eyes. "We all love her."

I wished I had told her sooner. I wished I had told her more often.

The burn crawled up my chest. "One of their offshore companies has a shell investment that owns a piece of land not far from here."

Grayson nodded, taking a seat across from me at the table. "That sounds promising and hidden enough for Sterling to bank on it taking us days to uncover."

"My thoughts as well," I agreed. It hadn't been easy to find the offshore company, and it had been more difficult to put the connection to the shell corporation.

Micah skipped the coffee and went right to the fridge, pulling out a bottle of beer. He twisted off the top. "What are we waiting for?"

I rattled off an address, and Micah jotted it down on a used napkin, shoving it into his pocket. He took a drink off the bottle and said, "Let's go."

Since Micah decided to start the morning off with a buzz, I replied, "I'll drive. I need to do something. I can't sit in the car and wait."

"I'm with Fynn," Grayson agreed, tapping the table with his fingers. "If I don't get behind the wheel and burn off some of this tension, I'm likely to kill someone."

Brock met each of our eyes. "Fine, but nobody does anything stupid. We stay together."

If this turned out to be another dead end, I didn't know what I would do. Each failed attempt wore on me. I had to bring her home.

Nothing in the world would stop me.

## 25

## KENNA

The hours in the days were long, and I began to lose track of time. It had been nearly a week since my accident, and the aches and pains my body suffered healed. The cut close to my temple no longer needed to be bandaged, and the headaches subsided, and yet despite all these positives, I didn't feel optimistic.

Just the opposite.

I was sad.

Angry.

Suffocated.

Restless.

Lonely, regardless that I was rarely alone.

It felt as if a dark cloud hung over the house, sucking any joy out of my life. The feeling was familiar, and it scared me.

But I had to push through.

I had to.

The side of my head pressed against the glass window. In the family room, I'd discovered a built-in wooden bench behind a set of thick curtains. It had become my favorite spot in the small farmhouse. I took to sitting here with a few pillows for hours, just staring.

Sterling offered me a few books to read, and try as I might, I couldn't concentrate on the words written over the pages. Sterling, on the other hand, had no problem losing himself for hours at a time in a book.

He would catch me staring at him every so often when he glanced up from the page and smiled. I wondered what went through his mind when he caught me.

There wasn't much to do in the house, and I still wasn't allowed outside, but from my seat at the window, it didn't look as if there was much to do there as well.

No animals to tend to.

If the crops growing were his, he never seemed concerned with their growth.

The only thing that moved outside was the wind, blowing the tops of the fields or the branches on the trees. Occasionally I'd see a pair of squirrels chasing each other. That was the highlight of my day.

Not today though.

Rain pattered against the glass pane. I watched it ping off the ground, splashing in mud puddles formed by the dreary summer storm, taking over the morning and into the afternoon.

My life was wrong.

This was wrong.

Sterling and I were wrong. We didn't fit.

I couldn't tell if Sterling picked up on this as well. At times, he was difficult to read. On numerous occasions I caught him lost in thought. Other times, he was attentive and entertaining. He hadn't snuck into my bed again, not since that first night, but I did hear him crack my door when he thought I was asleep and right before he locked me in.

I believed he thought I didn't know. Come morning, my door would be unlocked when I woke up.

We played games to occupy our time. Board games and cards mostly. I was pretty damn good at Rummy and Hearts, but I could only play so many rounds before I lost interest. It wasn't just boredom that affected me. The claustrophobia never fully went away. It might have moments subdued with distraction, but it was only ever temporary, and when it returned, the stifling feeling seemed magnified.

Sterling cooked all our meals, and surprisingly, he was good at it. They were basic meals. Nothing gourmet or fancy like butter-poached lobster or mint pork chops. We didn't have wine with dinner, and I was really craving a good rosé.

At some point, we would run out of food, and he would have to go to the store. I was eager for that moment. The prospect of leaving the house was all I thought about.

Gaining Sterling's trust was difficult.

A deep throat cleared, drawing my attention away from the gentle storm outside. Sterling watched me, his amber eyes guarded and wary.

He always looked at me with suspicion.

"I need to run into town," he announced.

My mouth opened to ask if I could come.

"I'll only be gone an hour or so. Is there anything you need?" he asked before I could propose my offer of tagging along.

I snapped my mouth closed. *Yes, to get out of this house,* I silently screamed. My shoulders slumped against the window frame supporting me. "No."

He noticed the crestfallen expression descend over my features. "Maybe when I get back, we can go outside for a bit. The rain looks as if it might let up soon. Would you like that?"

"Yes, very much." I wanted to feel the fresh air on my face. The light drops of rain kiss my cheeks. I wanted to dance in the puddles.

He smiled. The scars on his face were less intense and scary when his lips curved.

The door closed behind him, followed by the clicking of a lock. I didn't have to get up and check to know he had locked me inside. I would anyway on the slimmest of chances he'd forgotten.

With my nose pressed to the window, I watched Sterling walk down the rocky driveway and behind a weathered barn that looked like it was one plank short of collapsing. If the wind picked up, I didn't see how it would stay standing.

A minute later, the rumble of an engine started. Sterling backed a truck out and drove down the driveway, disappearing behind a bend in the road covered by trees. Seconds ticked by, and I stared at the spot where he had disappeared, half expecting his truck to turn around and come back into view. I listened over the pitter-patter of raindrops for the rumble of his engine, but only the gentle storm's harmony continued.

I was truly alone.

Just for shits and giggles, I pushed off the window seat and went to the front door, checking the handle. As expected, it didn't budge. The panic living inside me rose like a beast. I wanted out. Even if I had to claw my way through wood and drywall.

Running my hand through my hair, I paced in front of the door, only able to walk four or five steps before having to turn around and go back the other way.

My once beautifully manicured nails were chewed off and chipped. I ripped my nail out of my mouth.

I had to do something.

This was the opportunity I'd been waiting for.

*Pull it together, Kenna.*

Turning my back to the door, I went straight for his bedroom. Big surprise. It was fucking locked.

Not that something like a locked door would stop me.

I dashed into the kitchen, opening every drawer and cabinet searching for something useful. There were no knives lying around.

Smart, but damn inconvenient.

I looked around the kitchen. *Think. Think. Think.* I had to be smart and clever. Then I saw it.

It wasn't precisely what I had in mind, but fuck me if it wasn't better.

Tucked in the corner beside the stone age toaster was a drill. I wasn't what I would call tool inclined, but how hard could it be to take off a door handle?

Snatching the drill off the counter, I held it in my hand and pressed the button. *Bzzzz.* The bit spun as the power kicked on.

*Thank fucking God.*

The tool had weight to it and was heavier than I anticipated. I dashed out of the kitchen into the hallway, heading straight for Sterling's bedroom. I examined what I was working with and noticed two screws on either side of the metal plate flush against the door. Most stuff in this house was antique except for the locks. Those were shining and new, freshly installed by Sterling.

I got to work, fitting the bit into each screw head and letting the drill do the work. Within seconds, I had the handle off on one side. Picking the lock would have probably taken me hours if I'd been able to do it at all.

I finagled the knob, twisting until it came undone from the piece on the other side. It took another minute or so to dismantle the remaining bits, allowing me to push open the door.

The hinges squeaked as it swung, revealing Sterling's room.

I stood in the doorway and stared. My first impression was the space looked far more lived in than the bedroom where I slept as if he'd been here for weeks instead of days. When I crossed over the threshold, his scent lingered in the air. A pristinely made bed, not a single wrinkle in the blanket, took up most of the space.

Shaking my head, I got to work rummaging through his personal belongings. I started with the nightstand and then moved on to the dresser, looking through his shirts, socks, and boxers. All his clothes were so neatly organized. I was afraid he would be able to tell I'd been poking about. Then I remembered the doorknob. The chances of me being able to put that back together were slim.

*Shit.*

This was what happened when I didn't think things through.

What would happen if Sterling came home and caught me?

Would I see a different side of him?

What would he do if he came home to an empty house?

I didn't want to find out the answers, but I also realized I might have little say over the matter. Timing could be everything.

The dresser was a bust, so I moved on to the closet. I had no clue what I was looking for, but when I saw it, I would know. I got down on my hands and knees, rummaging through the boxes stored at the back of the closet behind a row of shoes.

"Fuck." The curse breezed through my lips.

Junk. Junk. And more junk. Stacks of papers, bills, old photos, and a bunch of crap that meant little to me.

Frustrated, I turned back toward the bed, noticing a laptop tucked slightly under a stack of pillows. As far as I knew, this place didn't have internet, and I didn't know if I had time to find out.

Crouching down, I looked under the bed, spotting another box. I shimmied it out and slid off the top.

*Holy. Shit.*

My fingers dipped inside, pulling out a knife that felt cool and familiar in my hands. I ran a nail down the hilt and over the initials carved into the side. KE. My initials.

This was my blade.

What was he doing with my knife tucked under his bed?

Hiding it from me?

I set the weapon on the floor beside me and looked at what else was in the box. My blade hadn't been the only thing that caught my eye.

A sleek, small handgun I was pretty damn sure wasn't mine lay nestled in the box alongside a few cartridges of ammo. I lifted the weapon out of the box, testing the weight of it in my hand. It felt good. Like it wasn't my first time wielding a gun.

I didn't know what scared me more, Sterling having a gun in the house or that I wasn't afraid of the weapon in my hand. I didn't want to think what he had planned to do with the weapon. I couldn't think like that.

Pocketing some ammo, I shoved the top back onto the box and

pushed it under the bed where I'd found it. Before straightening to my feet, I put the knife into my jeans pocket and took the gun.

With my heart thundering in my ears, I rushed out of the bedroom, looking for somewhere to stash it. Under my bed seemed too obvious considering where I'd found the thing.

I had to make a decision fast because I swore my ears picked up something sounding eerily like a car door slamming shut.

*No. No. No.*

Not yet.

I wasn't ready for him to come back.

Racing to the window, I peeked between the curtains. "Shit," I mumbled under my breath, seeing Sterling's truck parked in front of the house.

He was back.

And that meant I was out of time.

I was busted.

He would come inside and see what I'd done to his bedroom. See that I'd been inside.

Would he check under the bed first?

I had an inkling he would. If the roles were reversed, it would have been my move.

But the only person I had to worry about right now was me and how I was going to get out of this situation. I knew one thing for certain.

Today was the last day I was anyone's prisoner.

Checking the gun, I made sure it was loaded before creeping toward my door. It was open, and as I pressed to the side of the wall, Sterling unlocked the front entrance. The wrestling of plastic bags traveled down the hallway, along with the clatter of his shoes. I could tell he moved into the kitchen and set down his bags.

"Kenna darling, where are you?" he called, his voice carrying through the house.

I didn't respond but stayed as still as possible, keeping my breath low and even despite the panic crawling up my chest. Listening to his footsteps, I judged where he was in the house and how long until he came this way looking for me.

"Kenna?" he called again. This time his tone carried an edge.

I tightened my grip on the gun. His bedroom was on the other side of the hallway. The kitchen and family area were at the heart of the house, separating my space from his. His shoes stopped moving.

My brain clicked off as I raised the gun and stepped in front of the open door aiming the barrel into the long hallway stretching the length of the house. Something primitive and instinctual took over. The need to survive.

Sterling stood in front of his bedroom, inspecting the dismantled handle with his back facing me. I knew it was Sterling, yet somehow my eyes and mind blended him with Carter, the guy who raped me all those years ago. They were one enemy.

Just like Carter, I had to destroy Sterling.

No matter the costs.

Even if that cost was me.

Memories of the knife Sterling held at my cousin's throat flashed behind my eyes. The moment he slashed her cheek burned in my mind, an image I'd never been able to forget. He would pay. I'd waited days, weeks, years for this fucking moment. The wait was finally fucking over.

I tiptoed behind the bastard, careful to watch my every step. One wrong move and he would hear me coming thanks to the old house's squeaky floorboards. I held my breath the entire way, afraid to breathe, the gun clutched tight in my slightly sweaty hand. When I raised the weapon, it felt heavier in my grasp, and once I got close enough, I stopped.

"Sterling," I called, every bit of my pent-up anger and hatred packed into his name.

Startled, he jumped before he whirled around, and I pulled the fucking trigger.

## 26

## KENNA

The gun discharged, jerking my hand, but I kept my grip firm, my finger steady on the trigger in case I missed.

I hadn't.

His amber eyes widened in surprise as the bullet entered his arm, and he staggered into the wall. He lifted his other hand, pressing it below his injured shoulder. The scent of gunpowder clung in the air, and my ears rang.

Sterling glanced away from his arm, our eyes connecting. "You found my gun."

Unfortunately, my aim was off, and the bullet hadn't hit him in the chest as I hoped. Blood seeped through his shirt. "I did. And I'll shoot you again. And again. And again. As many times as it takes for you to die."

Those cunning amber eyes were quick to catch on, his mind working through the reality of our situation and what I'd done. It was starting to sink in. His lips carved a deep frown. "You remember," he grunted, the pain in his biceps registering.

A grin tugged at the corners of my mouth. I shouldn't get cocky and smug, but it was hard not to. I'd actually done it. "Try I never forgot, you bastard. You honestly believe I didn't know who you were? That I lost my memory? Who's the mastermind now?"

His chuckle came out a tad manic. "Bravo, Kenna darling. Well done. I'm impressed, but I shouldn't be. I knew you had it in you. I saw your potential. I told you we were alike."

"Maybe," I conceded. "Or maybe I'm better than you."

Pressing a bloody hand on the wall for support, he stumbled toward me. "The pupil surpasses the teacher."

"You were never my teacher." I had only one teacher, and it was Fynn.

He watched me darkly, leaving red handprints behind on the wall. "Regardless, I'm glad it was you."

"Me too." My finger twitched on the trigger as he drew closer.

"I wouldn't do that if I were you." he rasped, glaring at me with annoyance.

I hesitated, and it cost me.

Sterling took advantage of that single moment. His hand lifted, and he backhanded me across my face.

Stunned, I lost control of my body for a few seconds, the hit flinging me against the wall. White-hot pain danced across my cheek. The bastard struck me.

I lifted my face, strands of hair partially curtaining my eyes. "Fuck you," I hurled at Sterling.

"I never wanted to hurt you." The expression on his face almost looked remorseful, but I didn't buy it. Not for a second.

"No, you just wanted to use me," I spat, the pain I felt making my voice poisonous. "I've been used by guys before. Never again. That was where you misjudged me, thinking I would be a pawn."

"Perhaps I did misjudge you. Not that it matters. I still have you. Locked away. Miles from anyone. It's been a week. Where are your saviors? No one is coming to save you." The smugness curling on his lips made me want to punch him. Or shoot him again, which I fully intended to do.

My hand had fallen to my side after being struck. I steadied my finger above the trigger, readying the gun. "I don't need anyone to save me. Have you forgotten I'm the one with the gun, you sadistic prick?"

Sterling lifted a brow as blood continued to ooze from his wound. "You think I'm a monster?"

"Aren't you?" I replied, ignoring the throb at my cheek.

He winced, the pain in his shoulder clearly bothering him. "The things I've done—are they really worse than your Elite?"

"They wouldn't have to do those things if guys like you didn't exist."

"So they're the heroes in your eyes, and I'm the villain. What does that make you, Kenna darling?"

He knew what buttons to push, my insecurities, and it fueled my anger, but I hated to admit that, for a moment, I doubted myself. Doubted what I was doing.

I wasn't God. What right did I have to take a life? Even someone as evil as Sterling. Maybe I should let the law deal with him and dish out his penalty.

Then the faces of Mads, Josie, and Ainsley flashed in my head. Their pain and suffering. The guys who fiercely protected them.

If distracting me was his scheme, it fucking worked. I'd let him get inside my head, and I paid the price.

He caught me off guard in what could be my fatal mistake. Sterling sprang forward, faster than I would have given credit to someone who'd been shot. His hand snatched onto my wrist, the one holding the gun, and twisted. Pain flared up my arm, and I let out a groan.

He slammed my arm into the side of the door frame, and the gun slipped in my hand. The fucker was lucky the gun didn't discharge.

Using the hold on my arm, he spun me around, my back pressing into his chest and trapping me in his arms. Even wounded, the asshole was stronger than me.

He let out a ragged breath. "Did you really believe you could take me? I'll admit you gave it a good go."

"The night's not over yet." I struggled against his hold, testing its strength. I had to figure a way out of this tangled mess before shit went south.

"I like your tenacity. It's one of your admirable qualities," he whispered in my ear.

He was weaker, and I had to use that to my advantage. "Good, then I hope you like my next move," I said at the same time I lifted my arm, stretching it across my body to his biceps, clamping my fingers into his bleeding wound. I couldn't tell exactly where the blood was, but the red stain on his sleeve gave me a general location.

It was enough. Sterling cried out in pain, his grip loosening. "You bitch," he hissed.

I spun, jerking out of his grasp, desiring nothing more than space between us, but the bastard recovered quickly. Just as I took a step away from him, his fingers snaked into my hair, yanking me back.

My shriek was cut off by sharp pain radiating through the right side of my body, and it took me a second to realize what happened. The jerk had slammed me up against the wall, and the torment was only just beginning.

Before I had a chance to catch my bearings, his hand was at my wrist, lifting my arm up, and bringing it down into the wallpapered drywall. My fingers clasping the gun slackened, and I feared I would lose the only advantage I had. He slammed my hand against the wall again and again until I couldn't hold on any longer.

The gun plummeted to the floor, clattering over the warped wooden planks. A defeated cry escaped from my chest. Hot angry tears pricked at my eyes. I couldn't be sure, but it felt like the asshole broke my wrist.

Pressing my face and chest hard into the wall with his body, Sterling's mouth moved close to my ear, his breath sending an icy chill down the side of my neck. "You shouldn't have done that, Kenna darling."

"Go fuck yourself."

"You would like that, wouldn't you?" His hips ground against my ass.

God, he was fucking hard.

This shit turned him on. The fighting. The thrill of danger. The pain. Who the hell could possibly maintain an erection after being shot?

Only someone as twisted and messed up in the head as Sterling.

Horror and fear bled through me. I wanted to believe he wouldn't do the one thing I feared most. I could handle being hit or tossed around. I could take being threatened.

The one thing I didn't think I could deal with was being raped. Not again.

And I was sure Sterling knew this and used it against me to instill the kind of fear that made a person freeze or cower.

I would do neither.

I'd been broken before and locked in the dark, but I'd clawed my way out. If I had to, I would do it all again.

*I am strong enough.*

*I am fearless.*

*I am ruthless.*

*I am cunning.*

*I am not alone.*

Jerking my chin up, I stiffened in his arms. "I'm not afraid of you."

"Then maybe I'm not doing it right."

I was suddenly ripped off the wall. Air punched out of my lungs when I hit the ground, and I lost my shit when Sterling landed on top of me. I panicked at the feel of his weight on me, his leg shoved between mine. "Is this how you like it?"

Frenzy clawed in my chest as I squirmed and fought under him, desperate to get him off me. His weight alone pinned me to the ground, and patchy memories I fought hopelessly to bury surfaced.

He pinched my chin, his fingers digging into my cheeks as he forced me to look at him. Rage churned in his amber eyes. "Stop fighting or you'll hurt yourself. I don't want to hurt you."

"Too late," I seethed, and the tears I tried so hard to keep from falling spilled from my eyes, blurring my vision.

I went feral underneath him, kicking, biting, scratching, punching, but all it did was waste my energy. Nothing got him off me. My hope sapped out of me, bit by bit.

My head turned to the side as I searched for something, anything, to save me. I spotted the gun sitting only a foot away, but it was inches too far from my fingers. No matter how much I stretched my arm, even to the point where my shoulder felt as if it would pop out of the socket, I just couldn't touch it.

Aggravation surged within me, a bubbling scream begging to be released.

The gun was my last hope. Sterling overpowered me in every way. Without an advantage, I had no chance of escaping—no chance at defeating him, which I so very desperately wanted.

So desperately that I went through days of lies and hours of horror for what?

To fail?

No.

I refused to let this be my fate.

Something poked my thigh, and I suddenly remembered the knife I'd stuck into my pocket. If I could wiggle my hand inside...

I continued to fight him as best I could, but this time, it was for distraction as my hand shimmied into my pocket. It had been a task just to find the opening. I nearly whimpered when the tips of my fingers grazed the blade. Just another inch and...

*Got it.*

Clasping my fingers tight around the hilt, I pulled it out of my pocket. Sterling had my other arm pinned to the floor after realizing I'd been going for the gun. I wanted him fixated on that hand versus the one now clutching a knife. I pressed the button freeing the sharp end. My teeth gritted. My heart thundered so loud in my chest I feared he would hear it, but he would have probably mistaken it for fear. Part of it was, but most of it came from adrenaline.

His weight crushed me, and I exhaled, which did nothing for my skyrocketing nerves. A breath of warm air grazed my ear. "What are you up to, Kenna darling?"

"I really fucking hate when you call me that," I spat.

He chuckled, but the mocking rumble in his chest turned into a gasp of agony as my knife sunk into the flesh on his side, right above his hip, close to his stomach.

I had no qualms about stabbing another person, especially when my life was threatened. I'd already shot the bastard, and I meant to do more than harm him. The goal was to watch him take his last breath without remorse.

Plunging my blade into him had been harder than pulling the trigger, and yanking it out wasn't easy, not one-handed, but I got it done with one quick wrench.

Sterling groaned, rolling off me and clutching his side. His features pinched in pain, his breathing growing ragged. As he glanced down to inspect the newly inflicted wound, I scrambled away, going for the gun.

As soon as I picked it up, I surged to my feet and whirled around. "Don't fucking move."

He had his back propped up against the wall, blood staining his shirt and hand. He applied pressure to the knife wound. "I might have underestimated you."

I slipped the knife back into my pocket, ignoring how much my fingers shook, and clasped my hands onto the gun. It was my only hope now. "You think," I snapped. My eyes darted between Sterling and the door to freedom. I fiercely wanted to run like hell and never look back. I wanted out of this damn house. I wanted my freedom, but despite desiring those things down to the pit of my soul, I couldn't leave. Not until Sterling died.

It was like walking a razor's edge between good and evil.

I had to finish what I started.

Finish him.

I couldn't leave knowing he was still alive, still out there.

I affirmed my grip on the gun and turned away from the door, away from any chance at escape. Besides, I didn't have the goddamn key to open the door. I doubted Sterling would hand it over if I politely asked. The only way I would get out of here was if I took it from him.

I knew what I had to do.

Backing up, I pointed the gun at Sterling. "Give me the key, or I shoot you."

"Don't lie to me, Kenna. We both know you're not going to kill me."

My feet spread slightly apart as I centered my legs evenly. "Do you really want to take that chance?"

The wall took the bulk of his weight as he slid down to the floor. "What do I have to lose?"

"You're right. This has gone on long enough." I cocked the gun, my finger hovering over the trigger.

Something rumbled outside as I was about to shoot Sterling again. The noise grew louder and close enough until I could identify the sound.

A car engine.

"Looks like your friends finally arrived. Or perhaps my friends?" He let the question dangle in the air casting doubt and a speck of fear. What if Sterling really did have someone coming over as reinforcements? Would I have to shoot them too? I had no way of knowing if he called someone while he was out. Maybe he sent someone a message.

"Shut up." Like he had any friends.

I glanced at the front window.

*Son of a bitch.*

"Don't fucking move." I backed up, keeping the gun pointed at him. The window wasn't far. My scuffle with him had brought us nearly out of the hallway. I could get to the window and still keep my eye on Sterling.

Taking one hand off the gun, I did my best to keep the other steady as I leaned my back against the wall. It did little to stabilize the shakes quaking through my body. My adrenaline was crashing.

My eyes never left Sterling's as I peeled back a corner of the curtain. The roar of the engine seemed to echo over the field, reminding me of the races my brother participated in. It didn't sound like just one car but a pack.

Sterling hadn't moved from where he huddled on the floor against the wall. His face grew paler.

"If you so much as twitch, you're dead," I warned him.

"Why wait?" he wheezed. "Just kill me now."

Ignoring him, I took my eyes off him for a few seconds to glance out the window. A familiar Infiniti came flying down the driveway, dust kicking up in a storm behind the car.

*Fynn.* My entire body sighed. I couldn't tear my gaze from the sight of him, from knowing that inside that car was the man I loved. I didn't bother to repress the cluster of tears spilling down my cheeks. Happiness burst inside me like a grenade, radiating to every part of my fucking tired and worn-out body.

I wanted nothing more than to collapse to the floor and sob in relief.

A few heart-pounding seconds later, another car came barreling through the smoke. My brother. Then an SUV. And finally, a Hummer.

The Elite had arrived.

And with their arrival, the tears fell thicker and harder, blurring my vision.

My eyes were desperate to get a glimpse of Fynn. I needed to see him. It might have only been a week since I laid eyes on him, but it felt as if had been forever.

I had to get myself together.

As much as I didn't want to rip my eyes away from the window, I had to deal with Sterling, but I wouldn't have to do it alone now.

Swallowing over a lump of emotion, I took a breath, and with my last bit of willpower, I jerked my gaze away from Fynn and my family, letting the curtain fall closed. When I looked back to Sterling, I gasped.

*Motherfucker.*

The bastard was gone. Only his bloodstains remained.

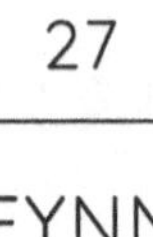

## FYNN

My car skidded to a halt in front of a beatdown farm. It looked like Michael fucking Myers's house. The idea Kenna could be inside with Sterling filled me with cold rage. I wanted to do more than burn it to the ground. But *first* I had to know if Kenna was somewhere on this property.

Hell, she could be caged in a barn or tied up in a bedroom. There was a lot of ground to cover, but the house seemed like an obvious place to start.

If he had hurt her...

I couldn't let myself go there, not without losing my ever-loving shit.

A sense of urgency propelled me out of the car and toward the front door when I should have waited for the guys. We had rules, and one of those was to never walk into a situation alone, not without canvassing the area first. You never knew what waited around the corner.

But the shining new lock on the door grabbed my attention. My eyes narrowed as I grew closer.

*What the fuck is this?*

Behind me, the crunching of tires over gravel grew louder as my friends arrived, but my focus zeroed in on the lock. It was obvious someone recently replaced it.

There could be a dozen rational explanations for installing a new lock on a door. People did it daily, and yet somehow it looked so fucking out of place from the rest of the house.

Why would someone be so worried about security when their roof was one storm short of collapsing?

My instincts told me it was odd, and we were finally onto something.

A cold, distant part of me could think of one important reason Sterling would have for changing out the locks.

She was here. I felt it.

My gaze lifted, and in the corner of the door frame, I spotted a camera. *Bingo. I got you bastard.*

As the car doors opened one by one, I reached for the knob and twisted. The damn thing didn't budge. I hadn't expected it to be unlocked. That would have been too easy, but it was worth a shot.

"It's locked," I said when Brock came to stand beside me. "She's in there."

"You're sure?" Brock insisted, scowling ominously at the door. We'd had so many setbacks that I understood his hesitancy.

Somewhere behind us, a crow cawed. "My gut is telling me she is."

Grayson's lips were turned down, his hands shoved into his pockets, as Micah cracked his knuckles. "What are we waiting for?" Micah asked, eager to do something.

"We'll scope the perimeter, see if we can find another way in, and cover the exits. You got the front door, Fynn," Brock said.

I nodded, glaring at the wooden slab that stood between me and possibly seeing the girl I couldn't live without. The guys were gone only a few seconds when I heard something inside the house.

"Fynn!" My muffled name came from the other side of the door. *Holy shit!*

I'd know that voice anywhere.

My heart jackhammered in my chest, unable to believe we'd found her. Despite my gut's intuition, I'd been so fucking afraid she wasn't here. "Kenna!" I screamed, my fists beating on the door. If I'd felt urgency before, nothing compared to the pressure beating in my chest.

"Fynn, I'm in here." Her frantic response came a moment later.

After days of looking, I'd been so damn scared to admit she might be lost to me. Hearing her voice weakened my knees.

"Open the door," I told her, my hand yanking and shaking the handle as I willed the thing to turn with all my might.

"I can't." Her voice broke, and I felt it in my chest. "I'm locked in."

A dozen f-bombs went off in my head. Come hell or high water, I was getting her out of this damn house.

"Stay back. Can you do that?"

"Yeah. Fynn, hurry!" The edge of hysteria in her tone stabbed my heart. She was scared, and that caused a not so nice reaction within me.

Anger bubbled up.

Good. I needed that mad rage.

Taking a few steps away from the house, I rammed my shoulder into the door, the wood groaning under my weight. I'd hit linebackers that were tougher than this. It would give. It had to give.

Again. And again. I slammed into the door, waiting for the door hinges to snap. It would have been easier with a sledgehammer, crowbar, or axe, but I didn't want to waste any time looking for tools.

I'd break my shoulder before I stopped. Luckily, it didn't get to that point, and the wood holding the mechanics splintered. I gave the door a swift kick and the fucker swung open.

She stood on the other side, her brown eyes wide, blood splattered on her face, hands, and clothes. Not enough to be hers, but the sight was still concerning. If she suffered even a scratch, I'd go ballistic.

My eyes ate her up, devouring every inch of her.

"Fynn," she sobbed. My name broke on her lips, tearing me up inside, and then she was running out the door, straight for me.

My arms went around her, securing Kenna against me. I lifted her off her feet. Her body shook, and I held on. I wasn't letting her go.

She buried her face into my neck. "You're here."

My chest rose as I inhaled, taking a deep breath. She didn't smell altogether like Kenna, her scent tainted by her surroundings. "I'm sorry it took me so long," I murmured.

Plastered against me, she clung to my shirt. "You found me. That's all that matters. I knew you'd find me."

I dropped a kiss on her head, brushing my lips through her hair. "Nothing would stop me from finding you."

Micah and Grayson rounded the corner of the house, faltering a step when they saw the girl in my arms. Micah whacked Grayson in the chest. "I told you he broke in."

Grayson rolled his eyes.

Kenna lifted her head at their voices, and a feeble smile touched her lips. She still trembled in my arms.

I didn't want to let her go, but he was her brother. Of course, he'd been worried.

Grayson rushed forward. "Are you hurt?"

She shook my head, stepping out of my arms and into his. "No. I'm okay."

"Whoa, careful with that thing," Grayson said, noticing the gun in her hand. I hadn't even noticed it in her hands until now.

My heart lurched and with it came a fresh, raw bout of fury. The only reason she had a gun was to defend herself. On one hand, I was proud that she was smart, strong, and cunning enough to fight. But on the other hand, I was sad, pissed, and anguished that she had to protect herself at all.

I should have been there.

I should have gotten here sooner.

She glanced down at her hand as if she was surprised to see the weapon still clutched in her fingers.

Micah held out his hand. "Here, I'll take it before you shoot one of us," he said softly, a partial smile on his lips as if he didn't want to spook her.

Kenna lifted her haunted gaze from the gun to Micah and handed it over to him but not before I caught the moment of hesitancy when she clasped her bottom lip between her teeth.

Grayson fully hugged her, his arms squeezing tighter than usual. "Don't ever fucking scare me like that again."

"Trust me," she muttered against his shoulder. "I don't plan on getting kidnapped again."

Overwhelming emotion gripped my throat seeing her back where she belonged. With us.

Micah stole her from Grayson, tugging her into his chest. "Come here, KK," he said, wrapping her in a Micah-sized bear hug. He lifted her off her feet.

"Where's Brock?" I asked, noticing his absence.

"Sterling." Kenna gasped, a wild look shifting into her eyes as her feet touched the ground. "He's still alive. I lost him, but he's hurt."

"We need to find him," I said. If we located Sterling, we'd find Brock.

Grayson stepped into the house and took a sweeping glance around, analyzing the room. He swallowed hard, the ice in his eyes hardening. "We'll just follow the trail of blood. Shouldn't be hard."

"Be careful," Kenna warned after her brother. "He might be armed. Or dead."

Micah grinned. "Dead wouldn't be fun."

I had to agree. After what he put Kenna through, Sterling deserved to be our prisoner for a week

Staring at Grayson's back, I struggled with the choice to stay behind with Kenna or go in after him. I didn't want to leave her alone, and there was no way I was letting her back into that house.

The choice was taken out of my hands.

A body rolled into view from the side of the house, like they had been shoved, tumbling into the dirt with a clumsy thud. We all turned to see Sterling sprawled out only feet away from us. Grayson stepped back outside, noticing something had grabbed our attention.

Brock loomed over Sterling like the devil about to sentence him to life in Hell. Sterling tried to roll away and drag himself through the grass. Brock stepped on his arm, pinning it to the ground. "Look who I stumbled into trying to weasel his way out a fucking window."

Pride swelled in my chest at the sight of him covered in his blood. Kenna had done that. She had made the bastard bleed.

Shoving Kenna behind me, I squared off toward Brock, Micah and Grayson coming to stand on either side of me. The four of us were itching for the prick to get up. I wanted to do more than just lay into him. I wanted to make him suffer.

Sterling flopped down on his back, the fight leaving his body. He smiled, staring up at the sky, blood staining his teeth. "Took you long enough. Where have you been? I hate waiting, especially when I have shit to do. There's this new movie on Netflix I've been dying to watch. I thought some popcorn and a cold beer would go perfectly. Oh, and a trip to the fucking hospital—"

Micah kicked him in the side, shutting the lunatic up. "Two out of three isn't bad. The hospital is definitely out of the question, but I'm sure I can get Grayson to turn on the TV, and Fynn here can grab that beer for you right before I blow off your fucking head."

He laughed, and it was clear he'd lost too much blood. Sterling was losing his damn wits. "I have to give it to you guys. You did quite the job coaching Kenna all these years. She's impressive. I always thought you, Fynn, would be my match. You were the one with the brains to do it, and that was my fatal flaw it seems. I shouldn't have underestimated her."

I scowled at him, Kenna safely pressed against my back. "No, you shouldn't have," I said, making a fist at my side.

"She was brilliant, making me think she'd lost her memory. I believed her." He laughed again. "I fucking believed her. She had me fooled. That girl has more dedication than all four of you. You don't deserve her."

I didn't understand everything he spewed, but I got the gist of what went down. "And you think you're worthy of her?"

A torn expression was written on his face. "I could have been."

Unbridled rage like I'd never felt tore through me with such force and speed it left me breathless for a heartbeat. This was Micah's gig. I had every intention of letting him blow Sterling's head off or torture him for days if he wanted, but hearing the way he talked about Kenna made me snap.

My gaze flicked to the gun in Micah's hands, and before I knew what I was doing, I snatched the weapon from him, firing two rounds into Sterling. One in the forehead and another at the heart.

The shots echoed over the fields, disappearing with the winds.

Micah whirled away from Sterling's limp body toward me. His brows drew together. "What the hell, Fynn."

I could still feel the vibrations from the discharges in my fingers. "I'm sorry. I couldn't take it. The shit he was saying about Kenna..." I wasn't sorry I shot him. Only remorseful that I'd taken the glory from Micah.

"Fuck," Micah groaned, frustration darkening his blue eyes. A moment later he put his hand on my shoulder. "I get it man."

And he did. They all did.

Brock blew out a breath, his gaze shifting to Sterling's dead eyes. "It's over."

"Almost." Micah grinned, his spirits suddenly lifting, and we all knew that meant he was up to something. "It only seems fitting that he burns."

The four of us shared a look. Kenna wedged her way out from behind me, slipping under my arm. "I want to help."

I pressed a kiss to her temple, not caring that blood streaked her cheek. It wasn't hers. That was what mattered. "You've done enough."

She glanced at the others before looking up at me. "I need to see this through."

Brock nodded. Then one by one so did the others.

Kenna was staying.

Micah went into his Hummer and came back with two cans full of gas. He set one down in front of Grayson, keeping the other one in his grasp.

I lifted a brow. "Do I want to know why you have gallons of gasoline in your car?"

"It's good to be prepared for situations like this."

"You planning on setting fire to a lot of buildings?"

He shrugged as if it was a hobby he partook in during the weekends. "Let's burn this motherfucker to the ground."

I nodded. Hell yes, I wanted to douse this place in flames.

Fuck him.

Micah and Grayson saturated the house with gas, leading a trail straight to Sterling's body and tossing the empty cans onto the porch. Brock struck the match. He looked to his right at the four of us standing beside him in a row. Then he flicked the flaming stick to the ground. We watched it quickly catch, igniting Sterling's clothes. The flames were hungry much like we were for revenge. They licked at him and ate him up before moving onto a trail straight to the rickety wooden porch.

The house was already a fire hazard. It didn't take much for it to catch and inflame. In minutes, the whole structure was immersed in fire. Scorching heat came off the house in waves as the fire engulfed every room. The five of us stood there, my hand laced with Kenna's, as we watched the roof collapse. Smoke, bits of ash, and debris littered the air. The smell wasn't something I'd ever forget.

None of us would.

No one called the fire department.

Eventually, someone would see the billows of smoke clustering the sky, but from a distance, who knew, they might think it was just a bonfire. Unlikely, but it mattered little to me. We'd be long gone from this hellhole by then.

Brock, Micah, Grayson, and I shared one last look, a silent message passing between us.

It was done.

Without saying a word, we got into our cars, the engines ripping to life. Tires peeled over gravel as we left behind our past. I glanced once in the rearview mirror seeing nothing but a thick cloud of smoke with bright flames lashing out.

I drove, needing to get Kenna away from the farm. For ten miles, we sped down the road, the engine purring under the acceleration of my foot. And when I couldn't take it anymore, I pulled the car off onto the shoulder.

Resting my hands over the steering wheel, I stared at the sinking horizon through the windshield. "I've never been so scared," I said softly. "When I couldn't find you..."

"Hey," she replied, twisting in her seat so she partially faced me. "You couldn't have known. This isn't your fault, Fynn. I won't let you take the blame for something none of us could control."

If he'd hurt her in any way... "Did he—?"

"He didn't touch me." She quickly cut me off, shaking her head. "I'm okay. Really."

I turned my head to her then and really looked at her, studying her expression. The side of her cheek was red. I lifted my hand off the steering wheel and lightly skimmed the side of her face.

Kenna leaned into my touch, her eyes closing for a few seconds.

I loosed a long breath, my hand falling away from her, and whispered, "I don't know how to breathe air that you don't exhale."

Her lips curled into a small smirk. "You've always been the romantic one."

"Does that bother you?"

She shook her head. "I was on my way back to the beach house when he ambushed me."

A broken exhale escaped my lungs. "Why? Why did you turn around?"

Tears pricked her eyes. "So I could tell you I love you."

My heart thudded in my chest as I held her gaze. "Define love."

Her lips curved, and I wanted nothing more than to kiss them. "I'm in love with you, gorgeous."

A bloom of warmth beamed inside my chest, spreading through my blood until I was glowing inside. "Do you have any idea how long I've waited to hear you say that?"

"I'm sorry I made you wait so long."

My lips grazed hers, my eyes closing and my tone softening. "Don't ever apologize. Not to me. I love you, brat. You were worth the wait."

I kissed her with every fiber of love radiating within me. My hand curved around the back of her neck, savoring the feel of her lips pressed against mine. Her lips were soft, and she sighed into the kiss. We'd both been waiting too fucking long for this moment.

She was mine.

And I was never letting her go.

I buried my face into the side of her neck, taking in a greedy breath of her hair. "I thought I lost you."

"He couldn't break me. Not when I learned from the best." She gripped the side of my face, pulling my face up so she could look me in the eyes. "Will you tell me again?"

My blood was buzzing. I knew what she wanted to hear. I'd never get tired of telling her. "I love you like fucking crazy, Kenna."

"Like crazy," she repeated, smiling.

What do normal college kids do on one of the last Friday summer nights before school starts?

Go out. Party. Have fun. Hang with friends. Have a bonfire on the beach. Drink until they black out. Make out under the stars with their boyfriend or girlfriend. Hell, both.

What was I doing on one of the last weekends before the start of my junior year?

I was babysitting.

An adult.

A very thirty-nine-weeks pregnant adult.

Okay, babysitting might be a stretch, but it sort of felt like it. Grayson and the crew were busy moving crap into my brother and Ainsley's new place, a three-bedroom cottage Ainsley had fallen in love with. It was a bit bigger than the apartments they had been looking at, but leave it to my brother to surprise the girl he loved with the house she dreamed of. Under all those scowls, he was totally a grand-gesture type of guy.

Since she was so close to her due date and had been riddled with those fake contractions the last few days, no one wanted her to do anything except sit on the couch with her swollen feet elevated and binge-watch her favorite anime, which was torture for me.

At first.

By the fourth hour, I hated to admit I was invested in the series. I might not completely understand it, but when some guy named Ken went full ghoul, I could relate. Somedays, I felt like a ghoul. I imagined Ainsley did too with her sleepless nights as of late. Or maybe she was more zombie. I honestly didn't know the difference, and I wasn't about to ask because it would lead to an hour-long explanation, and I still wouldn't understand.

I saved us both the hassle.

"I think this baby is trying to kick her way out of me," Ainsley grumbled, a hand resting on her swollen belly, which also doubled as a place to rest food. Convenient? Maybe.

Ainsley had been miserable the last few weeks, and I could see why. Her stomach was the size of a beach ball. I didn't know how she carried the extra weight around with her all day every day.

If something could hurt, she complained about it. Feet. Back. Bladder. Ribs. Boobs. The list was endless, and I was pretty damn sure I wasn't having a baby for a least a decade. I could handle a decent amount of pain and agony, but no shit, pregnancy was a different beast.

"You're lucky it's only one baby and not three," I said as she groaned on the couch.

"Fuck, I can't even imagine. How the hell did your mom do that?"

"I'm sure she would love to tell you." I'd heard the story of our birth a million times. It was a memory Mom loved to relive, especially on our birthday. You could be sure she would cry. The first birthday with Josie back in our lives, she'd been an emotional wreck. "They say it usually skips a generation, but damn, if I don't secretly want Josie and Brock to be stuck with three babies at once. God, that would be freaking amusing and a bit cruel."

Ainsley blinked at me. "What's wrong with you?"

I grinned. "How long do you have?"

She shook her head. "I would normally say to spare me the agony, but I think this baby girl likes the sound of your voice."

Scooting over on the couch, I rubbed a hand over Ainsley's belly. "That's because she has taste, and she knows I'm going to be her favorite auntie," I said to the little baby inside.

"Don't tell Josie that," Ainsley muttered.

I plopped back in my spot on the far end of the couch, giving her most of the space to stretch out and elevate her swollen ankles. "Oh, we've already had that fight plenty of times."

"You know, it could be you who has the triplets," she cautioned.

"I'm not having kids," I replied matter-of-factly.

"Since when?"

"Since now." I grinned.

She shifted her weight, adjusting the pillow between her legs. "You'll change your mind. Just wait. Plus, can you imagine how fucking cute your babies would be with Fynn?"

I could and that was a problem. "Just watch your show."

She laughed, her big belly jiggling, but the laugh turned into something like a gasp, her mouth making a funny O shape. A hand flew to the lower part of her stomach right underneath her belly button.

My brows bunched together as I stared at her. "What's wrong? Is it a contraction? What do you need?" The questions rapidly flew out of my mouth, one after the other.

"Fuck," Ainsley hissed, her wide eyes lifting to meet mine. "I think my water broke."

A frown pulled at my lips. I blinked, wanting my ears to believe they'd been mistaken. "This is not the time to mess around." I wasn't prepared to deal with Ainsley in labor. That went beyond my babysitting duties. *And* I wasn't even being fucking paid for this job.

She shook her head, a tinge of fear wavering in her mossy-green eyes. "I'm not kidding."

I heard the seriousness and the fright in her voice accompanying what I saw in her expression. "Oh god. You're not. Fuck. What do we do?" I'd felt a variety of panic in my life but nothing like this. I scrambled off the couch, my knee bumping into the coffee table. Swearing, I hobbled around, my brain trying to figure out what I should be doing and came up blank. I looked desperately at Ainsley, hoping she would have the answers.

She eyed me, her eyes bouncing up and down with my movements. "I don't know. I've never done this before."

"Well, neither have I," I fired back, the pain in my knee subsiding. I raked a hand through my hair. "Have you been having any contractions?"

She nodded. "Yeah. Off and on all day."

My hands fell to my sides, and I glared down at her. "Christ, and you didn't think to tell me?"

Her expression pinched, and a flash of pain went through her eyes. A few moments passed before she exhaled. "I thought they were just Braxton Hicks."

"News flash. They're most definitely not."

"I'm aware of that now," she snapped, meeting my level of sarcasm.

In another situation, I would have been amused, but the stress in the room was going up, and I had no space inside me for amusement. "We need to get you to the hospital or something. I'm not equipped to deliver my niece."

A ghost of a smirk touched her lips. "Can you imagine?"

Nothing about my facial expression said this was funny. "I'd rather not, but I'm glad you can maintain your sense of humor while I'm losing my shit."

"It would be an interesting story to tell during Christmas gatherings."

"Tempting, but no," I replied, reaching for my phone. I needed to be relieved of duty. Immediately.

"Oh, Kenna," she grunted, holding out a hand she expected me to take. "It fucking hurts."

I closed my fingers around hers as she squeezed through the

sudden onslaught of pain. "You're having a contraction again? Okay, we need to go. Get your pregnant ass in my car." I refused to take any chances with my niece or her mother.

"Help me? I don't think I can get up on my own. Oh, and I need my bag. It's in Grayson's room. And a change of clothes. It feels like I fucking peed my pants," she rattled off, sounding as scattered as I felt.

My nose scrunched. "Gross. One thing at a time. My brain can't multitask right now."

"Do you think I have time to shower?" she asked, glancing down at the black biker shorts she wore.

"How am I supposed to know? Do you want me to call the doctor? Or Grayson?" I asked, my phone still clutched in my hand.

Her gaze met mine. "Both."

I started to dial my brother first, but then she was talking again.

"Ask if I can eat. I'm kind of hungry, and I don't want to starve during the hours ahead of me. I have a feeling it's going to be a long night," she said, pressing a hand to the small of her back as she swung her legs off the couch.

Blinking, I stared at her. *She is out of her mind.* "You want to eat right now?"

Unconcerned about the inflection in my tone, she sucked on the corner of her lip. "Hmm. Maybe we can stop at Taco Bell on the way to the hospital."

"Jesus Christ. I can't with you. I'm calling Grayson. He needs to handle this."

Her expression brightened. "Tell him to stop and get food."

I rolled my eyes and frantically called my brother, who had the audacity to not answer my damn call.

"Kenna!" Ainsley half cried, half groaned.

I whirled toward her.

The sudden worry in her green eyes caused my heart to stop. "We need to go. Now. I don't think I can wait."

"Don't move." Like I was being chased by a dozen screaming pregnant zombie Ainsleys, I ran upstairs and busted into Grayson's room. I grabbed an armful of clothes from the closet, picked up the bag sitting in the corner, and hoped it was the right one.

For once, Ainsley listened and hadn't budged. I found her right on the couch where I left her. Dropping the clothes on the couch next to her, I set down the bag. "Pick something to wear and do it quickly. We're not winning any beauty pageants at labor and delivery."

I helped her sit up and swivel her feet to the floor. Not an easy task. It consisted of us laughing and her groaning and then laughing. The stress of the situation was making me loopy.

She shimmied out of her shorts and let them fall to the ground.

"God, you really did pee your pants," I said, staring at the huge wet spot.

Slipping her legs into a fresh pair of leggings, she hiked them up over her waist, wincing and making funny faces the whole time. "Every time I move, a little more leaks out. See what you have to look forward to?"

That was information I could have done without knowing. "Fat chance. I like my skinny body the way it is. Do you need a pad or diaper?"

She shot me a dull look. "I'm pregnant, not ninety. And a pad would be great."

After a quick jog to the bathroom, we were in my Jeep a few minutes later, her overnight bag stashed in the back seat. I didn't know whether to drive like a crazy person or safely. Ainsley held on to the door handle, her fingers clutching it tight through the pain when a contraction hit. "Fuck, this is really starting to hurt."

"That's a good sign, right?" I asked, flipping on my blinker to make a left turn.

Huffing as her hand gripped the door, she replied, "I don't know. I've never done this before."

"I can't believe you're about to have a baby. Shit. My brother's going to be a dad."

"You had nine months, and it's just now hitting you."

"It almost didn't seem real before. And now..."

Her features pinched in pain, and she hissed under her breath. "Oh, this shit is very real. I think I'm starting to feel pressure. You know, down there."

"Fuck," I muttered. "Don't say that. We're not having this baby in my car. Besides, giving birth the first time is supposed to take like hours."

"Tell that to this baby. Hurry, Kenna," she pleaded, a bead of sweat forming on her brow.

I hit the gas, lurching the car forward through traffic. My brother wasn't the only one who could drive like the devil was on his ass.

We made it to the hospital in record time, and I could tell Ainsley's pain was intensifying as were the contractions. They grew longer yet came more frequently.

Parking in front of the building, I ran inside, leaving Ainsley in the car to grab a nurse. A young woman in uniform came out with a wheelchair a few minutes later and helped me put Ainsley into the chair.

"My bag!" she yelled over her shoulder at me as the nurse started to wheel her through the parting double glass doors.

This was turning out to be the most chaotic day, and yet swirling with my anxiety was excitement.

I quickly parked the car and grabbed Ainsley's overnight bag, rushing into the hospital and up to the labor and delivery floor. As I navigated through the hospital halls, I called Grayson again only to get his voicemail. I vowed to wring my brother's neck when I saw him.

When I couldn't reach Grayson, I tried Fynn.

I nearly tossed my phone into the wall when he didn't pick up either. I get they were busy moving furniture and unpacking so they had a place to bring the baby back to, but would it be that damn difficult to turn your ringer on?

I moved down my contact list to Josie. If I had to go through every one of them, so be it, but I was determined that my brother didn't miss the birth of his first child. Hell, I'd drive to the house myself and haul his ass to the hospital, but I wasn't sure I had that kind of time.

At the sound of Josie's voice, I sighed. "Thank fucking God. Tell Grayson I'm going to kill him. Then tell him his girlfriend is at the hospital about to give birth."

"What? Are you joking?" Josie shrieked.

"Do I sound like I'm joking?" I deadpanned.

"Holy shit. I can't believe it. She's going to have a baby." I could relate to the disbelief in her tone. It mimicked pretty much how I felt.

"Yeah, and she'll be having this baby *alone* if he doesn't get his ass here."

From the other end of the phone, I could hear Josie's footsteps. "We're on our way."

"Hurry, she's in a lot of pain," I told her.

"Stay with her," Josie pleaded like I was the type of person who would drop her off and leave.

She couldn't see me, but it didn't stop my eyes from rolling. "Where else would I be?"

A pause came through the other side of the phone before Josie said, "I love you, Kenna."

My heart swelled in my chest. It was rare for Josie and me to share such vulnerable emotions with each other. "I love you too, baby sis."

She snorted and hung up.

By the time I made it up to the fourth floor, they had Ainsley on the bed in a private room. She was draped in a hospital gown, and they were hooking her up to machines and wrapping monitors around her belly when I walked in.

"Where's Grayson?" she gritted between clenched teeth as she spotted me enter the room.

I went to the other side of the bed, opposite the nurse who smiled at me. "He's on his way. I promise he'll make it in time. There's no way my brother's going to miss the birth of his baby."

"I'll kill him if he doesn't." Her voice strained with the dark promise of violence stemming from agonizing pain.

My lips twitched. "You have my permission."

The nurse finished putting in Ainsley's IV. "I need to check you to see how far along you are."

"Do you want me to leave?" I asked, unsure how comfortable Ainsley was with me seeing all of her. Hell, I wasn't sure how comfortable I was.

Her hand reached out to cover mine with a firm grip. "Don't go."

I squeezed her fingers in return. "Okay, I won't."

The nurse chatted while she checked Ainsley's progress. "It's a good thing you came in when you did. This baby is an impatient one."

"Sounds about right," I mumbled, still holding tightly on to Ainsley's hand.

"You're seven centimeters dilated," she informed.

Seven seemed like a lot. I began to get nervous. "What does that mean?" I asked.

The nurse dropped the sheet down over Ainsley's legs and gave us a reassuring smile. "The baby is already crowning. You're going to have this little bundle of joy very soon. Things will progress hard and fast now, and unfortunately, you're too far along for an epidural."

Ainsley's head snapped up. "No drugs?"

The nurse smiled sympathetically. "Sorry, honey. The doctor will be in to see you soon." She patted Ainsley's knee before leaving.

Ainsley whipped toward me seconds after the nurse left. Her expression clouded. "Kenna, did you hear what she said? How the hell am I going to do this with no medication? That wasn't the plan."

It would do neither of us any good if we both freaked out. I had to stay calm...somehow. Keeping my voice level and composed, I sat down on the edge of the bed. "I know, but we're at the mercy of this baby, and she's very eager to come into this world. I can't blame her. She has the most wonderful parents."

Ainsley's eyes were wide, and her lip trembled. "I don't know if I can do this."

My hand squeezed hers. "Yes, you can. You, Ainsley Fisher, are one of the strongest people I know. You can do anything."

Nodding, she inhaled a long breath and let it out a tad steadier. "Is he almost here?"

I checked my phone, skimming through the string of text messages that had come in the last few minutes. "Ten minutes. Probably less the way my brother drives."

Her head sunk into the pillow, but she turned her face toward me. "I'm not going to lie. You're the last person I expected to be here with me."

My chuckle was genuine. "I'm as surprised as you."

We laughed. "But seriously, I'm so glad you are." She paused a moment, breathing and working through a contraction. "You probably don't know this about yourself, but you give off this aura that gives people strength. It's like you lend them some of yours."

I swallowed over a pebble of emotion that rose into my throat at her words. "Stop, or you're going to make me cry."

"I'm scared," she admitted, and I could see the uncertainty of what lay ahead alongside the fear of not just the pain to come but her future as a mother swimming in her eyes.

I didn't bullshit her. "You'd be a fool not to be."

She shot me daggers and looked as if she was regretting asking me to stay.

"But..." I added, "I envy your strength. Giving birth is going to be a piece of cake for you."

"Fuck, I could really go for a piece of cake."

I smiled. "Same. Everything's going to be fine. You got this. I'll get you a whole damn cake when this is over."

Tears misted over her eyes. She closed them as another contraction registered on the monitor, and I watched the recording rise, and rise, and then spike. I could only imagine the pain she felt was like the worst period cramps of her life. The death grip she had on my hand made me wonder if I'd have any circulation left in it by the time this baby arrived.

Since the accident, my mind sometimes went off into this blank spot, and I sort of just stared into space. It was a coping mechanism, apparently to avoid dragging up memories I wanted to forget. My brain just shut down.

"Hey," Ainsley said, pulling me out of my head. She looked suddenly far too calm for a woman about to have a baby. "You okay?"

I forced a smile on my lips. "Yeah, of course. Don't worry about me."

"I do, unfortunately. What happened...it's a lot for anyone to handle. Even a badass like you."

No one pressed me when I came home, and I'd been grateful. I hadn't wanted to talk about it. Not then. And not now. It was in the past. And that was where I wanted it to remain. What happened with Sterling had no place in this delivery room where a miracle was about to take place. "The important thing is he can never hurt you or this little baby about to come into the world. He won't hurt any one of us again."

"Because of you. What you did Kenna..." Her voice trailed off, clogged with emotion. "I'll never understand how you had the strength to do what you did. You sacrificed yourself for us. As much as I wanted to kick your ass for putting yourself in such a dangerous situation, I'm also eternally grateful to you. None of us will ever forget."

"I would do it all again in a heartbeat." I swiped under my eyes, brushing away the tears that broke free.

Grayson burst through the hospital door, paler than I'd ever seen him and out of breath. He glanced between Ainsley and me. "What happened? Is the baby okay?"

Ainsley let out a watery laugh. "She's fine. We're both good."

Grayson scowled as he moved to the other side of the bed. "Then why are you both crying?"

Ainsley and I glanced at each other and laughed. "Talk about cutting it close, dipshit," I said.

Ignoring me, my brother brushed aside a few loose strands of Ainsley's hair from her damp forehead. "Are you okay?"

She nodded. "I am now."

I made a gagging sound in the back of my throat. "If you guys start making out, I'm leaving."

Ainsley hadn't let go of my hand. "You promised."

I held her gaze, letting her know I wouldn't leave.

"Is Josie with you?" Ainsley asked my brother.

Josie was originally supposed to be in the delivery room with her best friend; that had been the plan. "Yeah, she's out in the waiting area with everyone."

"Everyone?" Ainsley echoed.

The corner of his lips tipped. "Everyone." I could picture my crew overtaking the designated maternity waiting area, and it brought a smile to my lips. Knowing Fynn was so close lit a warmth in my chest.

"Did you call Mom and Dad?" I asked, knowing my brother wouldn't remember.

"Josie's handling it for me. She'll be in once she's done," he said.

I nodded. "Good."

The hospital door opened again as Ainsley let the f-bomb fly. Grayson got his first glimpse of how agonizing her contractions were. He paled.

"I swear you better not be one of those guys who pass out," I warned, my eyes lifting to see who was coming in.

It wasn't Josie but the nurse from before. This time, she wasn't alone. A woman in her mid-thirties entered with a gentle smile on her lips.

"Hello, I'm Dr. Ramona," she introduced herself with a serene smile meant to put anxious parents at ease. "I'll be delivering your baby, and from what I hear, that might be very soon. Should we have a check?"

"Already?" Grayson glanced from Ainsley to the doctor and back to his girlfriend.

Things progressed at rapid speeds. One minute the doctor had her head between Ainsley's legs, and the next, she had Ainsley with her knees crunched up to her ears, Grayson holding one foot and me grasping the other. Josie came into the room as the doctor instructed Ainsley to push.

It was an unbelievable thing to witness.

Josie stood beside me, Ainsley reaching for her hand. I smiled at her, feeling giddy and nervous.

Ainsley was determined to have this baby despite the pain her body endured. Every time the doctor told her to bear down and push, she did so without complaint. Her face was strained, sweaty, and red.

"We're never having sex again," she said, looking at Grayson during one of her brief moments of rest before the next contraction barreled into her body and she was pushing again.

I didn't realize how long this phase of labor could last until the doctor informed Ainsley she could be pushing for two hours.

Not Ainsley.

Twenty minutes later, she gave a final push, and the baby's head was out. I choked on emotion at the sight of all the dark hair. The shoulders were next, and then she was here, a beautiful, healthy little...

"It's a girl," the doctor announced a second before tiny wails filled the room. I'd been so enamored by the delivery and coaxing Ainsley through her pushing that I hadn't noticed the baby's gender.

A collective sob of happiness filled the room from all of us, including my brother. I glanced at him on the other side of the bed. Our watery eyes met. I couldn't remember the last time I'd seen him cry. It had been too long.

Ainsley got to hold her daughter immediately after birth for some skin-to-skin contact with the three of us looking on with adoration. I'd never felt instant love before. It was the most overwhelming experience of my life.

The nurse did her routine check on the baby before bringing her back swaddled in a blanket with an adorable pink knitted hat on her small head and handed her off to my brother.

Josie, Ainsley, and I watched the hard-ass completely melt over his six-pound-seven-ounce daughter.

Grayson grinned. It was the brightest and biggest smile I'd ever seen from him. Happiness. That was what I saw when I looked at him. True, dazzling happiness. And it was contagious as fuck.

Everyone in the room was enamored by this tiny little human. No one else in the world existed but her for the time being. "God, she's beautiful," Josie murmured softly.

"What's her name, Momma?" I whispered as the baby's hand wrapped around my finger. She had quite the grip.

Ainsley looked at Grayson, a mischievous smile forming on her lips, and I immediately thought she named her after an anime character like Sailor Moon, which actually wasn't bad. With those sparkling green eyes, she turned back toward Josie and me. "Kensie. After her two aunts."

The clog of emotions in my throat doubled. "Seriously." I sniffed. "Haven't I cried enough today?"

Josie hugged me, the two of us a weeping mess. "It's beautiful, Ains. She's beautiful."

"Do you want to hold her?" Ainsley asked.

I nodded, swiping at the tears.

She was so damn tiny in my arms. A part of me feared I might break her. "Hey there, Kensie. I'm your favorite aunt."

Josie scoffed.

Her arms and feet were bundled up inside her swaddle, so I carefully stroked her cheek. "Her skin is so soft."

And in just a few seconds, the idea of having a baby no longer made my stomach turn but filled me with hope. I was blaming it on the high feeling circulating in the room, but really, after one look at my squishing, wailing little niece, I was fucking in love.

And just like that, everything I'd been through was worth it a million times over.

I didn't think any of us wanted to give up the baby when the nurse announced she needed to take Kensie for her newborn screening tests. Josie and I left the new parents as the nurses prepared to transfer Ainsley to her postpartum recovery room.

In the waiting area, our crew had seemingly taken over. Micah paced. Fynn and Brock were in front of the TV, not seeing anything on the screen. Mads sat scrolling on her phone.

Everyone glanced up as Josie and I came into the room. "We have ourselves a little girl," I said. "Everyone is healthy and fine."

Sighs of relief erupted, quickly followed by grins. "The next generation of Elite has begun." Brock smirked, sliding an arm around Josie's waist.

"You know what that means?" Micah grinned, waiting a beat for dramatic effect. "Time to fucking celebrate." He pulled out a stash of champagne shooters from Mads's bag.

My eyes narrowed at him. "Did you sneak those in?"

"The how doesn't matter, KK." He tossed one to each of us. "To the new parents who made us aunts and uncles for the first time." Unscrewing the cap, he lifted his bottle.

Brock raised his next. "To the next generation of Elite. World, beware."

We all drank.

Fynn folded me into his embrace. "Maybe in the not-too-distant future, it will be you holding our daughter," he murmured into my ear.

My hand landed on his chest, just over his heart. "Don't get ahead of yourself. But...someday, I think I'd really love that. You'd make a hot dad."

"I would," he agreed, smiling. "When did you change your mind about kids?"

Lifting on my tiptoes, I brushed my lips over his. "About five minutes ago."

His eyes sparkled as his hands moved to my waist. "I'm not going to let you forget this moment."

I really hoped he didn't. "I love you."

"Like crazy," he replied, dipping his head to cover my lips with his in a kiss that always left me breathless.

## THE END

## THANK YOU FOR READING!

I hope you enjoyed the conclusion to the Elites of Elmwood. What a ride it's been. When I first came up with the idea to do a Dark High School Romance, it had been all about the four guys and Josie, but as the stories progressed, it became clear to me that the girls were just as badass and deserved their spotlight. They stole the show!

ALSO BY J. L. WEIL

**ELITE OF ELMWOOD ACADEMY**
(New Adult Dark High School Romance)
*Turmoil*
*Disorder*
*Revenge*
*Rival*
*Unchained*
*Broken*

**DIVISA HUNTRESS**
(New Adult Paranormal Romance)
*Crown of Darkness*
*Inferno of Darkness*
*Eternity of Darkness*

**DRAGON DESCENDANTS SERIES**
(Upper Teen Reverse Harem Fantasy)
*Stealing Tranquility*
*Absorbing Poison*

*Taming Fire*
*Thawing Frost*

## THE DIVISA SERIES
(Full series completed – Teen Paranormal Romance)
*Losing Emma: A Divisa novella*
*Saving Angel*
*Hunting Angel*
*Breaking Emma: A Divisa novella*
*Chasing Angel*
*Loving Angel*
*Redeeming Angel*

## LUMINESCENCE TRILOGY
(Full series completed – Teen Paranormal Romance)
*Luminescence*
*Amethyst Tears*
*Moondust*
*Darkmist – A Luminescence novella*

## RAVEN SERIES
(Full series completed – Teen Paranormal Romance)
*White Raven*
*Black Crow*
*Soul Symmetry*

## BEAUTY NEVER DIES CHRONICLES
(Teen Dystopian Romance)
*Slumber*
*Entangled*
*Forsaken*

## NINE TAILS SERIES
(Teen Paranormal Romance)

*First Shift*
*Storm Shift*
*Flame Shift*
*Time Shift*
*Void Shift*
*Spirit Shift*
*Tide Shift*
*Wind Shift*
*Celestial Shift*

## HAVENWOOD FALLS HIGH
(Teen Paranormal Romance)
*Falling Deep*
*Ascending Darkness*

## SINGLE NOVELS
*Starbound*
(Teen Paranormal Romance)
*Casting Dreams*
(New Adult Paranormal Romance)
*Ancient Tides*
(New Adult Paranormal Romance)

For an updated list of my books, please visit my website:
www.jlweil.com

Join my VIP email list and I'll personally send you an email reminder as soon as my next book is out! Click here to sign up: www.jlweil.com

# ABOUT THE AUTHOR

J.L. Weil is a USA TODAY Bestselling author of teen & new adult paranormal romance, fantasy, and urban fantasy books about spunky, smart mouth girls who always wind up in dire situations. For every sassy girl, there is an equally mouthwatering, overprotective guy.

You can visit her online at: www.jlweil.com or come hang out with her at JL Weil's Dark Divas on FB.

*Stalk Me Online*
www.jlweil.com
jenniferlweil@gmail.com